Lovely though Randi was, the *child* claimed Travis's attention

Matt's small body already held evidence of the long-boned height that was as much a McLean trait as the square jaw and blond curls. His legs pumped furiously as he went after the beach ball.

His son. Oh, yeah, most definitely his son. Travis was overcome by an emotion so new he wasn't sure what it was, except that his heart seemed to somersault. Without thinking, he caught the ball. He found himself looking into a small upturned face.

"Sorry, mister," said the boy. "My name's Matt. Wanna play catch with my mom 'n me?" he asked hopefully.

Travis stared into the eager face of his son, swallowed past the lump in his throat and remembered feeling the way Matt looked right now....

Dad, would you play a game of catch with me?

Sorry, Travis, but I'm late for a meeting at the hospital.

"Sure thing, Matt," he said.

ABOUT THE AUTHOR

Born in New Jersey, author Veronica Sattler has had several career interests, ranging from teaching to selling antiques to her ultimate passion, writing. She was inspired by historical writer Kathleen Woodiwiss, and went on to win several awards in the historical genre. *Wild Honey* is her second contemporary novel.

Veronica, who also enjoys gourmet cooking and American folk art, currently resides in rural Pennsylvania with her daughter, Alyssa, and an Irish wolfhound named Brendan.

Books by Veronica Sattler

HARLEQUIN SUPERROMANCE
612—WILD CHERRIES

WILD HONEY
Veronica Sattler

Harlequin Books

TORONTO • NEW YORK • LONDON
AMSTERDAM • PARIS • SYDNEY • HAMBURG
STOCKHOLM • ATHENS • TOKYO • MILAN
MADRID • WARSAW • BUDAPEST • AUCKLAND

ISBN 0-373-70731-2

WILD HONEY

To Peg and Bill Kreitler with love.

CHAPTER ONE

DEAR GOD, it can't be! Please, oh, please, it can't be him! Randi Terhune mouthed the silent plea, her bloodless lips moving almost imperceptibly.

She stared at the big handsome man being transferred from a stretcher to an emergency-room gurney. It *was* him, she realized as she fought to steady her trembling hands. There couldn't be two such perfect male specimens walking the earth, unless they were twins, and Travis McLean's information profile had revealed no such thing. *Dear Lord, what am I going to do?*

Dimly she was aware he was the patient they'd just re-routed from Bethesda Naval Hospital. Brought in by special helicopter, he'd been flown here to Johns Hopkins when fog prevented landing at the original destination.

At the forefront of her mind, however, other things about him loomed much larger. Like the fact that he was the father of her child. A child he knew nothing about. Had never seen.

A child whose mother was still a virgin.

Randi managed to pull herself together enough to issue an order to one of her staff to assist in the admittance procedure. She was buying herself some time, but that was all. As head ER nurse, she'd be the one expected to deal with this VIP patient. The call from Bethesda had been very specific about the man's importance, although they hadn't given any details.

Glancing at the memo she pulled from her clipboard,

Randi frowned. He'd be a doctor, of course. He'd been a fourth-year medical student back then, so he had to be a full-fledged physician by now. But why would the brass at Bethesda be ordering the red-carpet treatment for a doctor—a doctor with a gunshot wound?

Hope flared as she redirected her gaze to the tall blond man now stretched out on the gurney. Maybe there *were* two of them! There were such things as doubles, she'd heard. The Germans even had a word for it—*Doppelgänger,* if she recalled her high-school German correctly.

Carefully, trying to appear casual amid the usual emergency-room chaos, she made her way toward the nurse she'd directed to admit the man on the gurney. She saw John Ames, the second-year resident in surgery on duty tonight, and managed a smile as he approached the gurney from the opposite side.

At least, she hoped what she did passed for a smile. Inwardly she was quaking like a leaf in a storm.

Randi held her breath and prayed as she stole a glance over her assistant's shoulder. At the form on the clipboard that gave the patient's full name.

And felt her heart sink as she read, "Travis Paxton McLean."

"E-excuse me, Pierson," she stammered when her assistant, a big capable black woman, glanced up at her and then offered her the clipboard. "I...there's something I forgot to take care of in my office. Continue until I get back, please. I'll...I'll only be a minute."

How she managed to get to her tiny office at the far end of the corridor, Randi never knew. But somehow, agonizing minutes later, she was shutting the door behind her. She leaned back against it in the unlit room, her heart slamming against her ribs.

She hadn't really expected to learn he was someone else of course. No, reading his name had only compounded the feeling that the floor had just opened under her. The feeling she got when she'd risked a glance at the man's eyes: the exact same eyes as her son's.

Images swirled as the past came up to confront her—the tastefully decorated waiting room of the doctor's office outside Cambridge, the look that might have hinted at embarrassment on the handsome face, the lazy Southern drawl as he asked for an application, and finally the sharp crystalline blue of those eyes.

Matt's eyes.

Matt. Seizing on the image of her son, Randi fought for control; she sucked in a deep calming breath, then another. *Matt,* she repeated silently. Matt had been worth it!

Miranda Terhune was thirty-two years old; because of a rapid shift in personnel that had left several unexpected vacancies, and because of her own professional skill and competence, she'd been promoted to her present position at Johns Hopkins Medical Center in a little more than two years.

But it wasn't the scene of her current job she was remembering now. It was the place where she'd worked five years before. A fertility clinic near Cambridge.

She'd gotten the job because of Connie, her old college roommate. She, Randi, had been working at the time at a hospital in Washington, D.C., and not really enjoying it. But it hadn't been just the work; she'd felt a vague dissatisfaction, an odd restlessness, though she'd been unable to put her finger on the source of these feelings.

Now, with the twenty-twenty vision of hindsight, she knew why she'd felt that way. She'd always thrown herself into her work, but as time wore on, it hadn't been enough. Perhaps earlier than most women who chose career over marriage and family, she'd felt her biological clock ticking. Reminding her that her prime child-bearing years were passing. That one day she could wake up and find it was too late.

Of course, she hadn't had an inkling she might be yearning for a child when Connie had called, asking if she'd like to fill in for her at the clinic while she was on maternity leave. Yet she might have picked up a clue from something Connie had said.

"Never thought I'd be one to opt for the Pablum and Pampers scene, but you know, Randi, there's something about being in a place like this day after day, seeing all these women with big bellies—and grins on their faces, instead of the urgent hungry looks they came in with. Maybe it's catching, y'know?"

Yes, the clue had been there, all right. Because when Connie had said that, Randi had said yes.

But the yearning had been strong and recognizable after only a few months of working in Dr. Philip Burgess's clinic. Randi wanted a child, hungered for one. The trouble was, she was unmarried and determined to remain so.

Because Randi Terhune was afraid of men.

Leaning against her office door now, she felt herself shudder with the silent admission. It was the first time she'd admitted it, to herself or anyone else. She suspected Jill knew, though. Jill and Dr. Carol Martin.

Fighting a wave of nausea, she tried to block the images, but they came at her with the ruthlessness of long-suppressed demons. Demons straight out of hell.

He was stalking her. She knew it as well as she knew her own name. Or that she was twelve years old. Or that her mother had been dead more than six months now, and all she had left was Jill.

But Jill couldn't help her, couldn't protect her. Her sister was only fourteen, and she hadn't been able to protect herself! He'd come to Jill's bedroom at night, when he'd thought both girls were asleep. But Randi hadn't been asleep. She'd gotten up to get a drink of water from the bathroom and glanced into her sister's room. The door was open and the hall light spilled in. And she'd seen.

Just as she'd seen him stalking Jill for days. Touching

her back and shoulders and arms with lingering hands, brushing against her small breasts in passing. Watching her with eyes that burned as they fastened on those breasts, and on Jill's bottom when she bent over, or her bare legs when she wore shorts.

Soon he'd begun stalking Randi, too. Waiting until he thought the time was right to come into her room and make her whimper, just as Jill had whimpered, to push her down on the bed and—

"Oh, God!"

The sound of her cry startled her in the still, dark room. She became aware that tears were streaming down her face.

Impatiently she swiped at them with her fingers. She'd thought all that was behind her. Jill had put it behind *her*, hadn't she? And Randi'd had just as many hours of counseling as her sister. Jill was happily engaged to marry David in the fall, and Dr. Martin was so certain of Jill's recovery she'd delightedly consented to be a bridesmaid.

But the doctor isn't so certain of your recovery, is she? an inner voice taunted.

Carol Martin was the psychiatric counselor they'd both seen following their stepfather's death in a car crash. The car crash that had mercifully ended his months-long sexual abuse of Jill Terhune and prevented him from ever actually laying hands on Randi.

Yet Randi had been the one with the nightmares after they'd gone to live with Aunt Tess. The nightmares that had awakened Jill, if not the kindly old woman who was their dead mother's maiden aunt. And so Randi had finally been forced to tell Jill that she *knew*.

The two of them had always been close, but that night, as they'd wept together, an even closer bond had been forged. A bond that gave them the courage to approach the guidance counselor at school. The woman had broken the news to their elderly guardian, and it was then they'd begun the sessions with Carol Martin.

Sessions that had healed the actual victim of the abuse, but not her younger sister? In the silence of the darkened office now, Randi wanted to deny it, but how could she with the man whose sperm she'd stolen lying on a gurney a room away? Stolen, because she'd longed desperately for a child, but was terrified to conceive in the normal way.

Still, old habits die hard, and so Randi did find herself denying it as she switched on the light and reached for a tissue from the box on her desk. *Nonsense,* she thought as she blotted her face and checked it in the small mirror from her purse. *You aren't afraid of men. You just aren't one of those women who feels she needs a man to make her life complete.*

Feeling more resolute with this assessment, she switched off the light and, straightening her shoulders, headed back to the ER. She scrubbed her hands carefully and nodded to her assistant. Martha Pierson was still beside the gurney across the room, and Randi signaled she'd be right there. But as she approached the figure now sitting up on the gurney, her resolution took a nose dive.

Matt will look like that in thirty years, she found herself thinking as she took in Travis McLean's chiseled features. She'd already noticed several women in the room staring at him with unconcealed admiration, and she didn't have to guess why. She'd looked at him the same way five years ago; he was too beautiful to believe.

Pierson handed her a tray of sterilized instruments. Randi paused, feeling the inner tension mount as she stole glances at Travis McLean's profile while Dr. Ames examined his shoulder. So much like Matt...

Her own hair was a fine and silky honey blond. McLean's was sun-streaked with flaxen. And coarser, thick and springy, with a lot more curl. Like Matt's. The lean planes beneath the prominent cheekbones weren't evident in her son's young face yet, but she suspected they'd appear with time. Just as Matt's perfect little nose would lengthen, grow into the narrow, straight proportions of his father's. And Matt already had ample evidence of the square jaw she saw on McLean. She found herself wondering if it denoted the same stubbornness that— *Don't think about it! Don't think about things you'll never be able to compare because—*

The tray of instruments she was holding crashed to the floor.

"Good grief, Terhune, what's wrong with you? I've never seen you this way!" The resident's uncharacteristic sharpness told her plenty about how distraught she must appear. She'd better get ahold of herself.

"I...I'm sorry, Doctor. Just having a...a bad night, I guess."

Her face flaming, Randi bent to retrieve the instruments, even though it meant she'd have to scrub again. She needed to get away from those crystalline blue eyes that seemed to look right through her. What if he remembered her? What if...

But, no, he had no way of knowing what she'd done. She'd destroyed all records of his donation after she'd inseminated herself. And she'd told no one but Jill and, reluctantly, Carol Martin. Jill and Carol, both sworn to keep her confidence.

She'd been certain she'd never again lay eyes on the perfect specimen of American manhood she'd selected for his health, intelligence, family background and physical assets to be the father of her child. So certain...

She straightened and handed the tray to an orderly. Taking great pains to avoid the sight of McLean's tanned and muscled bare chest, she asked Pierson to cover for her again, murmured an excuse to Ames and went to scrub.

Making her way across the busy room, she tried to regain a sense of normalcy by taking in the scene. It was chaotic, but familiar.

On her far right a uniformed police officer waited, no

expression on his face, to give her other assistant, Nurse Ryan, details about the young punk he'd just brought in; the teenager was comitose from a suspected drug overdose.

Just to her left, an anxious young couple hovered, the woman clutching the man's hand as they watched an intern stitch up a nasty cut on their little girl's leg. The child was trying hard not to cry, but the words, "Mommy...Daddy," kept erupting through her stilted sobs.

Would she ever be able to watch so bravely if it were Matt lying there on the table? *And no husband to share the agony, to support you, as this woman has?* her inner voice taunted.

Where on earth had that come from? She'd never questioned her single parenthood before. Besides, she wasn't alone. She had Jill, didn't she?

Jill—who was getting married in a few months.

Suddenly Randi began to feel as if she'd never again be certain of anything in her life.

CHAPTER TWO

TRAVIS MCLEAN hated hospitals. Emergency rooms in particular. That he sat in one at the moment was not improving his disposition one iota.

Dammit, he'd told Cord he didn't need this! A local ambulance, maybe the attentions of some small-town country doctor near the scene, and he'd have been fine. But would that SOB listen? Hell, no!

But then, Jason Cord never listened much to anyone these days. Something was eating at that guy, and Travis suspected if Cord didn't unload it mighty soon, there'd be hell to pay.

As for Rafe O'Hara, his other so-called buddy of long standing, yeah, okay, maybe O'Hara had owed him one. And he doubted Rafe could have said anything that would have changed Cord's mind, anyhow.

But, Lord, did he hate hospitals!

Scowling at the tired-looking overworked resident who probed the wound in his shoulder, Travis wanted to bolt and run. The shoulder hurt like a sonofabitch, but physical pain was not the reason. No, nothing that simple. Besides, he was more than acquainted with pain. Hell, any five-year CIA veteran was likely to be, and he'd had a four-year hitch in the navy before that. A hitch that had seen action. He'd been shot during that action, and compared to what he'd endured then, this was nothing. A run-of-the-mill flesh wound. He'd live.

But what wasn't so simple was another kind of pain the

ER, for some reason, brought to mind. The pain of remembering. And something that felt suspiciously like guilt....

Travis, I simply do not understand you! The tear-filled voice of his mother floated back to him on the currents of memory, aided perhaps by the shot of Demerol they'd given him. *To take a lifetime of plannin' and just throw it away. It doesn't make any sense!*

But whose plan are we talkin' about, Mother? His own voice echoed through the corridors of five long years, angry, strident. *Y'all were so certain I'd become a doctor— a heart surgeon, to be specific. Just like my father. And my grandfather, of course. But did anyone ever ask me? Did anyone, just once, ask if that was what I wanted?*

But four years at Harvard Medical School, Travis! Four years of straight A's! Why do all that if you didn't want it? His poor mother, sounding so bewildered, helpless, and so very sad. He hadn't meant to hurt her. He loved her, respected her. But his father, ah, now there—

"Nurse, give me a hand here please." The voice of the young resident cut across his thoughts. Then a loud crash had Travis glancing at the floor beneath his gurney; a tray of surgical instruments lay scattered there.

"Good grief, Terhune, what's wrong with you? I've never seen you this way!" The resident, whose name tag said Dr. Ames, looked more puzzled than angry.

"I...I'm sorry, Doctor. Just having a...a bad night, I guess."

Travis's eyes traveled upward from the tray on the floor. When they came to rest on the flushed face of the woman who'd stammered the apology, he sucked in his breath.

"Sorry," Ames said to him. "I know it's painful, but I'm suturing now. It shouldn't take much longer."

Pain, hell! Pain had nothing to do with it. But Nurse Terhune's gorgeous self sure did! What a stunner! Honey blond hair, whiskey-colored eyes and a figure that...

Travis cleared his throat and quickly looked away as

Nurse Terhune's shapely bottom presented itself when she bent to retrieve the instruments. He was actually getting aroused! *Like some horny adolescent, for Pete's sake!*

He couldn't resist slanting another glance at the beautiful blonde as she handed the tray to an orderly and asked another nurse to stand in for her while she went to scrub. He took in the long leggy figure striding away from him, and his lips formed a silent whistle.

Ames grinned at him, finally aware of what was going on with his patient. "Some piece, huh?"

"Dynamite." Travis's soft drawl was slightly husky, his eyes lazily assessing as they followed the retreating figure.

"Yeah, but don't get your hopes up, buddy." Ames gestured in Nurse Terhune's direction. "That little number comes in at about forty below."

"You're kiddin'."

The resident shrugged. "All I can say is, a lot of us have tried, and no one's gotten to first base. Of course, our little ice queen may have a 'significant other' tucked away somewhere, but nobody's been able to— Uh-oh..."

Travis winced as Ames returned his attention to the wound a bit too energetically; Nurse Terhune was headed back in their direction.

"Lord, Lord, what a shame," Travis murmured softly as his eyes approved of what they saw. Dynamite, coming *and* going.

Ames caught this and barely stifled a grin as he told Nurse Terhune to proceed with dressing the wound.

But Travis frowned. Something had begun to niggle at the back of his mind. Through half-shuttered eyes he traced the features of Nurse Terhune's heart-shaped face as she bent over his shoulder. There was a hazy momentary image of a similar face, but younger maybe...and then it was gone. *Damned Demerol!*

"Ouch!" Travis glared at the woman who'd been the object of his most recent—and scandalous—thoughts.

"Oh, I'm so sorry!"

Her embarrassed apology had Travis swallowing the blistering setdown he'd been about to deliver. But she sure had been clumsy in bandaging his shoulder. A glance at her badge had already told him she was the ER's head nurse. Why, he asked himself, was she acting as nervous as a newly capped rookie? And damned if that wasn't a blush under that porcelain skin.

A slow, lazy grin stole across his face as he watched her from beneath half-closed lids. She caught his casual scrutiny, and the blush deepened.

Lord, he did love a blusher! You hardly ever saw one these days. Fact was, he couldn't recall the last time he had. Unless it had been Sarah, and kid sisters didn't count.

The grin faltered as he recalled how long ago that would have been. He hadn't seen Sarah in five years, hadn't seen any of his family. His sister was in her second year of premed at Georgetown now. Hardly a kid anymore.

Maybe he should go there and try to see her. Would she even let him? Would she dare it? Maybe. She'd always been pretty gutsy.

Suddenly the monstrous inadequacy of relying solely on his sources at the Agency to keep informed about his own sister had him wanting to pound something with his fist. His fingers clenched and he ground his teeth.

"If…if the pain's real bad, I think I could get you something more for it."

The softly murmured offer of Nurse M. Terhune pulled him back to the moment. She'd stammered a bit; still jittery, then. Yet somehow, maybe because of its softness, he'd found her voice soothing. His grin reemerged.

"What's the *M* stand for, Nurse M. Terhune?"

"Hold still, please." Suddenly all thumbs, Randi tried to sound professional and concentrate on the bandaging.

Travis wasn't about to let her ignore him. "Melanie,

maybe? Margaret? No, scratch that—you don't look like a Margaret. I've got it! How 'bout Marcie?''

"Mr.—'' Randi made a show of glancing at the name on his admittance form ''—McLean, I don't—''

"Travis, honey. Just Travis.''

Randi found herself unwillingly seduced by the liquid softness of his voice. Lord, the man was every bit as compelling as she remembered. Unable to stop herself, she risked a glance at his face.

A mistake. He was observing her with a casual indolence that reminded her of a well-fed lion basking lazily in the sun. The clear blue eyes, heavy-lidded and sensual, roamed her face, coming to rest on her mouth. As they did, his own curved into a slow, easy smile.

"Uh, Travis, the sooner you allow me to finish here—''

"Uh-uh, honey. Not fair. Now that you know my name, I reckon it's tit for tat for me to know yours.''

The soft Southern accent had a teasing quality, which curled around the edges of her defenses and stole inside. Something began to unravel somewhere deep within, in a place Randi couldn't name, a place she hadn't known was there.

She looked quickly away, reaching for a pair of scissors on the tray.

"C'mon now, darlin','' he cajoled. "Margie? Molly? Hey, how 'bout Millicent? I know it's old-fashioned, but I do believe Millicent's makin' a comeback.''

He was outrageous. And too persistent by far. Yet Randi felt a tug pulling at the corners of her mouth. She faced him squarely, hands on her hips.

"If I tell you, will you let me finish? We need to get you upstairs.''

"Upstairs? Like hell, lady! I'm walkin' out of here!''

"In a few days, you mean.''

"In a pig's eye, I mean!''

Randi remained prudently silent as she reached for her

clipboard, eyeing him covertly as she did so. All evidence of the lazy cat was gone. Travis McLean had a no-nonsense look in his eye that said he meant business. She couldn't imagine anyone daring to cross this man when he looked as he did now.

"Are we having a problem here?" Dr. Ames approached the gurney.

"Damn right there's a problem! There's no way in hell I'm stayin' in this godforsaken place for more than...."

As Travis launched into a recitation of his grievance, Randi headed for the doors where a pair of paramedics were wheeling in the latest emergency. She was only too glad of the opportunity to get away. She caught terms like "scapula" and "clavicle" as McLean marshaled his arguments, and she felt a little sorry for Ames. Members of the medical profession often made the worst patients.

Still, there'd been no mention on the admittance forms of his being a doctor. Randi mused on this as she oversaw the immediate removal of the patient they'd just brought in—a fully dilated woman in premature labor—to the delivery room. There often wasn't such information of course, not in ER. There frequently wasn't time to record it.

She wondered if he was a doctor attached to the military in some way. That would account for his original destination tonight. Huh. Just her rotten luck that the fog had enveloped Bethesda, but not Hopkins!

After a brief exchange with the ob-gyn supervisor in the delivery room, Randi hurried back to her own station, wishing she didn't have to. Not because she was tired from working extra shifts the past two weeks, although she was. Several unexpected absences among her staff, because of an outbreak of summer flu, had left them shorthanded, and she'd filled in. But that was nothing new. They all pitched in at such times; it was part of being professional.

No, Randi knew her reluctance to return had less to do with the ER than who was *in* the ER—a big blond Virginian with scandalous good looks, as Aunt Tess would have put it. Looks that had been part of Randi's decision five years before to select him as the biological father of her child.

But only *part* of her decision, she reminded herself as she headed back the way she'd come. That his family background was solid had been another part. Not that Randi was a social snob, but if you came from a good family, she'd reasoned at the time, you had to come from a good genetic pool. A pool that was more likely to contain solid citizens than ax murderers, right?

And when Travis McLean had listed the occupations of his parents and grandparents on his application form at Dr. Burgess's clinic, they'd read like a roster of the American Medical Association, for heaven's sake! No wonder he'd been at Harvard Med.

What's more, enrollment at such a school meant he had to have the intelligence Randi was looking for, so there was another part. Oh, yes, McLean had fit the bill to a tee.

She paused briefly outside the ER. Not only to drum up courage, but to say a small prayer that he'd already been taken upstairs. It really wasn't like her at all to cave in this way when something went wrong; that was part of what made her a good ER nurse. But coping with medical emergencies was a far cry from having a hidden part of your past come up and hit you in the face!

Taking a slow deep breath, she again tried to make herself relax by thinking of her son. Adorable, wonderful, bright and loving Matt, who'd come into her life like a shining beacon of pure sunlight four years ago and given it meaning. Purpose. A future where there was safety and hope. And dreams that didn't turn into nightmare.

Feeling a little like the young mother who'd just gone into the delivery room, Randi took another deep breath. She stepped toward the door just as it swung open in front of her. It was her assistant. Martha Pierson had had years of

ER experience and hardly ever looked ruffled, no matter how hectic things got. Right now the look on her face hovered somewhere between exasperation and...amusement?

"Better come quick. That hunk's refusin' to cooperate, and the good doctor wants your help. Yours, and *nobody else's*," Pierson emphasized.

Randi didn't need to ask who the "hunk" was. Yet she did take a second to wonder why Ames would specifically ask for her. More than wonder. Worry, to be exact. Had McLean made the connection she'd been dreading? Was he refusing to cooperate until he got some answers she wasn't prepared to give? Her knees suddenly felt like jelly.

Pierson had been right about his refusing to cooperate. She could see that much from the single glance she risked as she made her way across the room.

McLean was still sitting up on the gurney. He was wearing an expression that reminded her inexorably of Matt. His pose said he wasn't budging.

Nearby stood an orderly with a wheelchair. Hospital regulations said wheelchairs must be used to transport even ambulatory patients from one ward to another. Unless they were so incapacitated they had to be taken by gurney.

Travis's pose said he was taking neither. Well, that was what *he* thought!

"What's the problem now, Doctor?" Randi placed her hands on her hips and managed to glare at their patient, figuring the best defense was a good offense. "Don't tell me this one's still giving us a hard time."

Ames's face bore none of the amusement she'd glimpsed in Pierson's. The resident looked at Pierson now as she came up behind Randi. "*You* tell her, Nurse!" And then Ames rushed off toward a stretcher they were just bringing in.

Pierson complied. "Seems Mr. McLean's not willin' to cooperate until you give him some information, Nurse Terhune."

Randi's apprehension must have shown on her face. McLean unfolded his arms and traded the stubbornly locked jaw for a reassuring smile. "Hey, beautiful, nothin' to get all hot 'n' bothered about."

He reached out to give her nose a playful flick with his finger. At the unexpected touch, Randi jumped.

"Whoa, now, honey, settle down." The smile widened, became the lazy grin she remembered all too well. "All I'm askin', before I agree to let these turkeys trot me off upstairs like a good little patient, is what the *M* stands for, remember, sugar? Seems these, uh—" he glanced at Pierson "—co-professionals of yours aren't allowed to tell me. Said you were the only one who could."

Randi glared at him, more annoyed with the man for the scare he'd given her than his outrageous demand. The scare, which she couldn't even admit to. Not to mention that unexpected touch. It had sent an unfamiliar current shooting straight to her toes.

"You're pretty used to getting your way, aren't you, Mr. McLean?"

The teasing light that entered his eyes had her wishing she could recall her words. "When I go after somethin' I really want—" his eyes roamed lazily over her face— "yeah, I reckon you could say that."

Randi drew herself up to make the most of her five feet, seven inches. Despite her height, she knew that if Travis McLean stood up, he'd dwarf her. She fixed him with her most formidable look. Her I'm-the-one-in-charge-here glare. "Mr. Mc—"

"Ah-ah," he warned, wagging his finger teasingly at her. Behind her, Pierson snorted.

"I beg your pardon?" Randi was doing her best to retain a professional demeanor, but it was getting harder by the minute.

The grin was wider than ever. "It's Travis, remember?"

He had to know how his grin did devastating things to any woman foolish enough to be in the vicinity.

A muffled sound had her glancing behind her. Martha Pierson was grinning, too. Foolishly, Randi thought. Solid no-monkey-business Pierson, who was happily married with five kids.

Damn the man! The sooner she got out of the ER, the better.

She faced him squarely, gave a curt nod. "Very well, Travis—"

"Hey, Randi!" A small boy with a baseball cap worn backward waved at her from the doorway to the waiting room. The rest of his attire consisted of a pair of cotton pajamas decorated with Berenstain Bears and severely battered high-tops, unlaced and minus socks.

"Robbie Spencer, what are you doing here in the middle of the night?" Robbie was the son of her next-door neighbor, and Matt's best friend.

Robbie's smile split his freckled face. "Mom's havin' our new baby, an' Daddy couldn't get holda Grandma in a hurry, so I got to come!"

Just then, a slender, pleasant-faced man put a hand on Robbie's shoulder and bent to whisper something in his ear. Bob Spencer, Robbie's father. After the brief exchange Bob glanced up. He saw Randi and waved.

Randi gave him a thumbs-up. Then father and son withdrew and the door closed behind them.

"Randi, huh?" Travis McLean's drawl drew her attention back to him. He eyed her speculatively, but a teasing light still lingered in his eyes.

"Now, I do know Demerol does frightenin' things to a body's wits," he continued, "but I believe I'm still lucid enough to recall that 'Randi' begins with an *R*. 'Course, the boy could be dealin' with a minor speech defect, I suppose, meanin' to say 'Mandy,' when he really—"

"It's *Miranda!* You lunkhead! Miranda, and Randi for short! *Now* are you satisfied?"

The blue eyes remained speculative as the grin she was beginning to detest reappeared. "Satisfied? My, my, sugar, you do ask the most interestin' questions."

Randi went beet red.

The grin broadened, and she took a step backward as he slid off the gurney and towered over her.

Lord, how tall was he? Six-four? Six-five? Too tall for her own comfort, she decided as he leaned over to whisper in her ear, "the thing is, darlin', are *you* ready for the answers?"

Randi felt perspiration dampen her uniform. He was toying with her, she was sure of it. Toying like a cat with a mouse. But why? Had he recognized her, after all? Was he using this ridiculous banter to draw her out in some way?

Steady, she reminded herself as her knees again began to feel as if they wouldn't support her. *He doesn't know anything, remember? Even if he does recognize you, he can't suspect a thing beyond that.*

She stiffened her spine, pointed authoritatively at the wheelchair waiting beside the patient orderly. "In!" she commanded. "Now."

"Yes, ma'am." Travis gave her a cocky salute and sauntered over to it. A stain of fresh blood had penetrated the gauze of his dressing; it would have to be removed and the sutures checked. Demerol or no, it had to be hurting him a great deal, yet he moved and acted as if he were socializing in somebody's living room. She'd seen a lot of patients attempt to act unaffected by their pain, to appear brave in the face of it, but this was different. He'd put himself beyond it. Functioned as if it didn't exist.

What sort of a man was he to be able to ignore pain that way?

The orderly began to wheel him away; when Travis turned and winked at her, Randi decided that maybe she didn't want to know.

CHAPTER THREE

TRAVIS SAT in his hospital bed, grinding his teeth. He was ready to climb the walls. These jokers were set on keeping him here "at least till the end of the week," he'd been told this morning. By Dr. Wallace Reston, the physician in charge, when he'd made his Monday-morning rounds.

Reston knew his father. He'd gone to med school with the great Trent McLean and still played golf with him once a month. This had allowed him to invoke a familiarity with Travis he wasn't entitled to, and ask too damned many personal questions.

Not that Travis had answered them. The people he counted among those entitled to ask those questions, let alone receive answers, could be tallied on the fingers of one hand. The rest could go to hell.

It had been a long time since he'd felt the need to justify his actions to anyone but himself. The chosen few who'd gotten any explanations at all had received them out of love. Not curiosity, not obligation and definitely not the misconstrued familiarity that came of playing golf with his estranged father!

Oh, Reston had been discreetly courteous about it all. Very polite, as a matter of fact. Old school, Southern-style. Probably thought he was being smoothly oblique, too....

"Heard they had to abandon another blast-off at the Kennedy Space Center yesterday," the elderly doctor had mentioned all too casually. "Makes you wonder how all those scientists and technicians feel when that happens. You know, all that time and energy spent gettin' ready. And then— nothin'. I wonder if it ever bothers them…'' He'd looked pointedly at Travis when he said this. "'Course, it isn't as if they won't have another go at it—not like it would've been for me, had I been talked into abandonin' medicine after years of trainin'. Know what I mean, son?''

Despite the old man's prying, Travis remained courteous to him. Not that he hadn't been mighty tempted to tell him he hadn't the right to call him ''son.'' *That no one had that right anymore.* Mighty tempted not to counter with a query of his own: ''Is that the lie the old bastard's put out to all and sundry these days—that I was talked into it?''

But he hadn't of course. He was old school, too. The proper behavior of a Southern gentleman had been ingrained in him and his brother since the earliest days of their childhood. It was the foremost mark of the Tidewater gentry, their mother had always told them, and a true test of Southern manhood.

And because Judith McLean had a way about her and they loved and respected her, her children had never questioned what she said. Southern gentility might be occasionally threatened and a little ragged around the edges since the Civil War, he and Troy used to joke, but it wasn't dead yet.

So Travis had smiled and gently changed the subject. Now he sat here, pampered like a pet poodle, because Wally Reston likely thought he was doing his old friend a service by mollycoddling the son Trent himself never spoke to. Never spoke to, never saw, never acknowledged as being alive.

Dead, that was what he was to Trent Cunningham McLean III. Just as he was supposed to be dead to Judith McLean and Troy McLean and Sarah. Dear feisty little Sarah…

Travis shifted restlessly on the bed. The agony of his separation from the sister he'd always been close to wasn't something he normally allowed to penetrate the wall he'd built around it. Lord, he wanted out of here! He'd even settle for the chance to work off some of the steam that was building inside him like a pressure cooker. What he wouldn't give for his shorts and running shoes right now!

He eyed the armchair near the window. He could get out of bed and use the chair, of course. But he'd been dumped here, out of state, as an emergency patient—minus toothbrush or robe or anything more than the clothes he came in. Which they'd taken away, the cagey bastards. And he'd be damned if he'd lounge around in a chair wearing nothing but a hospital gown and a bandage!

On the other hand, he could always do it *without* the gown. That'd get their attention all right. He doubted such a stunt was in him, though. It had been years since he'd even thought of cutting loose....

There'd been the ultraserious business of pulling A's in prep school and then as an undergraduate in pre-med to assure him entrance into Harvard of course. Because nothing else would do for the son and grandson of two of its most renowned alumni.

And then had come the exhausting discipline of med school itself and—

His mind tripped on the one exception to that tightly reined discipline. The night he'd gone drinking with three classmates who weren't as disciplined. Who'd convinced him he needed to cut loose a little. The night he'd accepted their dare to go to that clinic and—

Now what had brought *that* up? He hadn't thought about that dumb stunt in years. Not since his little four-year excursion in the navy for Uncle Sam. More discipline. And after that, the Agency. The last place he'd have allowed himself to think about something like that. If you weren't all business in the Agency, you weren't *in* the Agency, period.

And now he was thirty-five. A little long in the tooth for the kid stuff, *a time to put away childish things*...

But the familiar passage from Ecclesiastes was erased when Travis found himself thinking, with a grin, that sitting on the chair in nothing but a bandage might almost be worth it. If it was Miranda Terhune who stumbled across him!

Fat chance, though. He'd seen neither pretty hide nor gorgeous hair of Nurse Randi since the ER. And suspected it was likely to remain so. Not just because the ward he was in wasn't her beat. He'd begun to see what that young resident had meant when he'd called her an ice queen.

Except...those blushes had told him that somewhere under the ice, a lovely little fire burned. He'd bet on it. It was why he couldn't resist those teasing probes, gentlemanly or not. That, and because a challenge was a challenge.

Yet his indulgence in that little byplay had likely ensured her giving him a wide berth for the duration of his stay. No, Nurse Randi wanted no part of challenges. She'd keep her distance.

There was something about the woman, though. Something more than her arresting beauty that nagged at him, had his mind returning to her. He wondered if he hadn't seen her somewhere before. He rarely forgot a face. In his business, his life and the lives of others could depend on such recall. And Randi Terhune's wasn't the sort of face he'd be likely to—

The murmur of voices in the corridor intruded, and Travis lost the thought. Visiting hours. Scowling, he picked up the book a candy striper had brought him and found his place. Vonnegut's *Slaughterhouse Five*. Fit reading for a hospital room? he mused darkly. Maybe not, but it sure fit his mood.

Settling in with the book, he ignored the muted sounds outside his door. He hadn't had any visitors yet, and he wasn't expecting any until tonight. Which was just fine with him.

Jason Cord had said he'd drop by, bring his shaving kit and a few other items Travis had told him where to locate in his apartment. And although Jason could be pretty surly these days, he was never boring, especially talking about the doings at the Agency.

Rafe O'Hara had called, of course, to see how he was, the smug bastard. Ol' Rafe was getting married today, though, so maybe Travis had the last laugh. For he firmly believed in one self-evident truth in this life: romantic love was for poets and fools.

Still, Rafe and Francesca looked so happy together that he'd briefly wondered if there might be an exception....

A low rumble of laughter resounded from the corridor just outside the door, and Travis slapped the book shut. Hell, weren't hospitals supposed to be quiet?

Realizing how grouchy he'd become, he made a conscious effort to relax. If he were honest, he'd have to admit that a few noises wouldn't faze him if *he* had visitors. But he didn't right now, so visiting hours just increased his frustration. And boredom. *Hell and damnation!*

Suddenly Travis's head snapped in the direction of his door as it opened. Then he froze.

The slender, elegantly dressed woman had also stopped moving, except for the clear blue eyes that swept over him, drinking in every detail. Eyes so like his own, although the rest of her patrician face had been passed on only to her younger children, missing Travis entirely.

"Hello, son." She spoke quietly, in the soft Tidewater accent that would forever stir nostalgic echoes from his youth. "May I...may I come in?"

Travis found himself swallowing, unable to speak. He managed a nod, gestured to a chair near the bed.

He watched her as she found the chair, lowering herself into it with as much grace and poise as ever. Judith Paxton

McLean was a year short of sixty, but she'd always looked at least a decade younger than her age. An active life that included daily horseback riding and tennis had preserved the girlish figure in the red Chanel suit; the youthful impression was aided by her expertly applied makeup and the smart beveled cut of her silver hair.

Only when she was seated and he saw her close up could Travis believe she would leave her fifties behind next May. The lines around her eyes, which had seemed faint in the dim light of the doorway, were more sharply etched than he remembered. The frown lines on her brow were new, too.

Well, five years was a long time. *Damn the son of a bitch! Damn him to hell and then some!*

"I suppose it was Reston who told you I was here?" he asked tightly.

Judith McLean nodded. "He...he said it was a gunshot wound! Oh, Travis, I—"

"It's nothin' serious, Mother." How strange it felt to be addressing her like that. *Mother.* After all this time, like something alien on his tongue. "Just a simple flesh wound. I'll be fine."

She eyed the bandaged shoulder, the sling they'd used to immobilize his arm. "Are you certain? It looks as if it might be...You're not in pain, Travis?"

"I said it's not serious. Certainly nothin' that'd require bravin' the wrath of your *husband* by traipsin' all the way up here to see the black sheep of the family!"

Her face went pale, and Travis felt instant remorse. Lord, he hadn't meant to snap at her like that. He heaved a sigh. "I'm sorry, Mother. It's just that..."

Travis ran his hand through his hair in frustration, then sighed again. "He doesn't know you're here, does he?"

Judith looked away and her reply was toneless. "No...no, he doesn't."

"So after five years of obeyin' his dictates, of avoidin'

me, of not takin' my phone calls or answerin' my letters—
five years, Mother!—a hospitalization has finally given you
the courage to come see me. But only on the sly. What
would it take, I wonder, to dredge up the courage to see
me openly? My *funeral?*''

He saw her flinch, and remorse nagged at him again, but
he shook it off. He was her *son* damn it! Her firstborn, on
whom, along with his brother and sister, she'd lavished all
the love and affection of a devoted mother. Yet she'd
thrown him away—on the spiteful orders of a man she
didn't even love!

He still remembered the day she'd admitted that to him.
The day he'd stumbled on her crying in the stables, where
he later learned she often went when she was troubled.
Wadded up on the hay-strewn floor was a lace-edged handkerchief. He'd retrieved it and begun to hand to her, thinking it was hers.

But it hadn't been hers. Before she took it from him, he
noticed the unfamiliar initials embroidered on one corner.
And although he'd been only thirteen, he'd known. When
he asked her, she'd told him that, yes, his father had a
mistress.

''What'll you do, Mother?'' he'd asked next.

''Do, darlin'? Why, what *can* I do?''

''You can leave him! He can't possibly love you if—''

''Love has nothin' to do with it, Travis,'' she'd interrupted.

''But he's lied to you!'' Travis had been outraged. ''Lied
to *all* of us! All those excuses 'bout how he's always tied
up in surgery or goin' off to lecture on—''

''Travis McLean, I'll not have you speak of your father
that way! Of course, he hasn't lied to y'all. Your father
does work long hours at the hospital, and his work most
certainly takes him out of town to lecture sometimes. Your
father is a world-famous heart surgeon!''

And then, with the uncanny perception of the young,

he'd said, "That's why you're stayin', isn't it, Mother? It's because of who he is, not because you love him. Isn't that why you said love has nothin' to do with it?"

Fresh tears welling in her eyes, his mother had nodded, then taken him in her arms. "But I was wrong to say it that way, son," she'd murmured. "I may not love him, but I'd do anythin' for you children. Love has *everythin'* to do with that!"

Now, as he sat in this bland, sterile room, Travis wondered about that, too. Did she really love her children as she'd professed? Over the years he'd assumed they were the reason she stayed in a loveless marriage. But when the day had come when he'd dared his autocratic father's wrath by choosing to follow his own path, she'd meekly aligned with her husband against him. Had let him cut Travis out of their lives.

As for their loveless marriage, Travis soon began to suspect it was nothing out of the ordinary. He'd spent a lot of time growing up amidst the privileged children of families where divorce was rampant; his prep school had been full of them. Soon he began to accept the fact that the love he thought was missing in his parents' marriage simply didn't exist.

Still, until five years ago, he'd believed in parental love. Now he wasn't even sure about that.

With an irritated gesture, he steered the conversation to more certain ground. "Tell me about Sarah. Is she well? Happy?"

Obviously relieved by the shift in topic, his mother managed a smile and nodded. "She loves Georgetown. Doin' splendidly there, too. Of course, we all know she would. Her adviser says she's taken to pre-med like a duck to water."

Unlike her long-lost brother. But Travis didn't voice this. The bitterness was fading now. Maybe he'd exorcised it. "And Troy? He holdin' up all right?"

His thirty-three-year-old brother had had to struggle for the grades that would get him into a decent med school. Or a career in medicine, period.

Troy had been the athlete in the family. A natural, who could have gone on to qualify for the Olympics in swimming, they'd been told. Or a career in tennis. He'd once beaten Bjorn Borg in a match at their club, and Borg had offered to sponsor him.

But that had been out of the question. In fact, Travis was the only one his brother had even told about it, and Troy'd insisted he keep it secret.

"Good Lord, Troy, why?" Travis had exclaimed. He could still recall his incredulousness at Troy's request.

The brother he loved hadn't been able to look him in the eye. "You know why," he'd mumbled, staring at his Nikes as they sat on a bench in the club's locker room.

And Travis had. Telling the family, or more specifically, their father, would only result in the same cold dismissal his swimming coach's suggestion had brought the previous year: "You are a McLean, Troy. With a long and illustrious tradition of medicine to follow. Swimmin' is a fine pastime, but it can't be allowed to distract you from your career. From surgery as a profession. You'll thank the coach and tell him no, of course."

So Troy had acquiesced without a whimper, submitting to a regimen of tutors and summer schools to help him attain the grades necessary to enter medicine. And managing to graduate from a med school that, while not Harvard, was respectable enough for the father he tried so hard to please.

His mother's sigh brought Travis back to the present. "Well, your brother does try hard, but sometimes I think he ought to have pursued another specialty. Your aunt Louise did suggest he join her at Stanford and go into research, you'll recall. But as I told her, your father..."

And so it goes...

"Right." Travis's voice was tight with anger. "Nothin'" would do for *his* sons but to follow in his illustrious footsteps. No matter that the shape of those feet, as they tried to follow—tried so hard, Mother!—was so different. No matter that they longed to take another path."

"Now, Travis, your father—"

"Is a cold, selfish bastard who never had time for any of us while we were growin' up! And made it plain only one thing mattered to him—that we live our lives to please him. To be a self-perpetuatin' testament to the great Dr. Trent McLean, heart surgeon nonpareil!"

"Oh, Travis, I know he's hurt you, but try to understand. In his own way, your father loves you. I know you find that hard to believe. I didn't believe it myself at one time. But in the last few years…well, I think he's mellowed. And perhaps…perhaps even begun to realize what his unbendin' ways have cost him."

Travis's smile was bitter. "Like a son, maybe? Well, that shouldn't faze him, Mother. He has one to spare."

"Travis, I don't s'pose I can blame you for feelin' bitter, but—"

"What do you want from me, Mother? Why'd you really come here? It wasn't entirely to see how badly injured I was. Wally Reston could've given you all the particulars—and very likely did."

Travis leaned toward her and didn't let go of her gaze. "So what is it you *really* want from me?"

She made a helpless gesture with her hands. "I—I was hopin' that maybe there was some way to…to put an end to this terrible estrangement. Maybe if you were to go to your father, Travis, and try to—"

"Forget it. He'd never listen, and I…" He sighed, ran a hand through his hair. "Well, let's just say I'm well past tryin', okay? I have my own life now, and while it's—"

"But what *kind* of life, Travis? A life where you're constantly in danger? Where you're shot at and could be gunned down at...at any moment? Dear heaven, sometimes I think I'll go out of my mind, worryin' 'bout you! And missin' you so!''

She'd begun to cry now, and Travis felt like a twenty-four-carat heel. He should've withheld his anger, done his best to soothe her.

And so it goes... Not exactly a banner day for Southern manhood, he thought, again echoing the famous phrase from *Slaughterhouse Five*. Shifting to the side of the bed, Travis put his good arm around his mother's shoulders.

"Shh, don't cry. It's really not as dangerous as all that. A desk job more often than not, honest."

Judith made an effort to pull herself together. Taking care not to jolt his injured side, she embraced him quickly, then groped for a handkerchief in her purse. She nodded gratefully when he handed her a tissue from the bedside box.

"You won't even consider...?" she said tentatively after drying her eyes.

"What? Goin' to see him? D'you recall how many times I tried to—unsuccessfully, I might add—five years ago?" Travis snorted. "I'm not in the habit of knockin' my head against a stone wall, Mother."

Judith bowed her head and sighed. "I s'pose that's what I expected you'd say, but—' she met his eyes again "—I hope you'll understand that...that I had to try?"

He nodded grimly.

"And on the outside chance you'll change your mind, I've taken a room at the inn across the street—just for this evenin', that is. I'll need to leave by—"

"Save your money, Mother. And your hopes. I won't be callin'. I can't."

She nodded, silently rose from the chair and bent to kiss his cheek. "I'll be leavin' now, son. Get yourself well real soon now, hear? And remember, I do love you, no matter what I might've foolishly led you to believe these past five years."

He wanted to ask her about that. About how she could have stayed away all that time, no matter what her husband threatened. But somehow he hadn't the heart for it. What good would it do? Likely just hurt her more than he'd already managed with his less-than-genteel tongue. *And so it goes...*

"I love you, too," he murmured softly, giving her hand a reassuring squeeze. But as he watched her turn to leave, he saw the tears in her eyes, and the remorse was back.

A FEW MINUTES LATER Travis stood at his third-floor window looking down at the street facing the Johns Hopkins Inn. He'd managed, one-handed, to strip off the hospital gown, wrap a towel around his hips and secure it at the waist—all the nod to modesty he was willing to make at the moment; if any more unannounced visitors dropped by, he was more than ready to tell them to go to hell if they complained.

His mood was sour again, and he didn't need to wonder why. A sardonic smile twisted his lips. At one time he'd reckoned a visit from his estranged mother would have made his day. He supposed he'd always been given to optimism in his life, and that had applied even to the one corner of it that rankled. But instead of heartening him, seeing her had only served to make him realize how hopeless it all was.

He caught a flash of red below, and he watched his mother walk toward the street. To a stranger she'd appear utterly poised, her head held gracefully erect, her carriage straight. But he could see things a stranger would miss. The suggestion of a defeated cast to her shoulders, a certain hesitance in her step as she approached the curb, the last lingering look she cast in the direction of his window before she entered the inn.

Sighing heavily, he was about to return to the Vonnegut novel when something else caught his eye. A blonde with a knockout figure emerging from the hospital. She headed toward a dark red Saab that had just pulled up out front.

Nurse Randi Terhune.

"Well, well, well." Travis's first genuine smile of the day accompanied the softly drawled syllables.

Her legs looked longer than ever in a pants uniform with a tunic top that stopped just where they began. Sunlight glinted off her honey-colored hair. Worn loose now and minus her nurse's cap, it hung down her back nearly to her waist. Lord, Lord...

He was able to make out the Saab's driver as she reached across the passenger seat and said something to Terhune. A brunette who bore a strong resemblance to Nurse Randi. He supposed they could be sisters, despite the difference in coloring. Beautiful features like theirs leapt out at you and— *"God almighty!"*

Travis sucked in his breath and closed his eyes, fixing on the image that filled his mind's eye. An image from the past. Now he realized why the dumb stunt he'd pulled in Cambridge had been teasing his brain, just as Randi Terhune's face had been nagging at him. He opened his eyes and gazed into space in stunned awareness. Terhune had been in the clinic that day! She was the nurse who'd admitted him!

His gaze shifted to the scene below. The passenger in the Saab was now opening the door and climbing out. Travis hadn't noticed him at first, and no wonder. This little guy stood only about three feet tall, if that. He was all tousled blond hair and energy about to explode as he gave Terhune a whopping big hug.

It became apparent the boy was giving up the navigator's seat to Terhune, who opened the rear door; there was a car seat in back, and he took a step toward it. Then she said something to him, and he turned toward her, affording Travis his first clear look at the child's face.

Great God in heaven!

Terhune fastened the boy's seat belt, shut the rear door and got in up front, closing her own door. The Saab pulled away from the curb.

Travis was left with his jaw hanging open.

The kid in the car was the spitting image of himself when he was four or five years old!

CHAPTER FOUR

TRAVIS WATCHED the Saab drive away feeling as if he'd been poleaxed. It had been like looking at a mirror into the past. Thirty years past. Even if his memory was playing tricks on him, which he knew it wasn't. He'd seen enough snapshots of himself over the years to know damned well what he looked like as a kid.

Gathering his spinning thoughts, Travis made his way slowly to the bed. He lowered himself to the mattress that barely accommodated his big frame. Tucking his free hand behind his head, he stared pensively at the ceiling.

His thoughts gravitated inexorably to the clinic in Massachusetts. The clinic where he'd first seen Randi Terhune. The fertility clinic where he'd donated his sperm. On a dare. And suddenly he knew: the results of that irresponsible stunt had come home to roost.

"Damn!" The oath exploded in the quiet room as he went over the episode in his mind....

He'd been hitting the books hard, averaging maybe four hours sleep a night. Then exams were over and he'd wanted nothing more than to crash for twenty-four hours. But he hadn't. Jenkins and Henley waylaid him on his way to his apartment and convinced him they all owed themselves a night on the town to celebrate.

So he'd gone with them from one watering hole to the next. Drinking more than he ever had or likely would again. Taking their dare had been the most singularly immature act of his so-called manhood.

Yet he'd done it. Despite the host of misgivings that plagued him when he realized what he'd committed himself to. From the moment he awoke with a king-size hangover the next morning till the instant, two days later, he walked through the clinic's doors, he'd regretted that commitment.

His discomfort level had been acute. He'd always loved kids. The mere thought of a child of his walking around somewhere without him left a bad taste in his mouth.

"Ah, hell!" Travis shifted restlessly on the bed, his mind swinging mercilessly back to that time.

All the regret in the world hadn't swayed him. He'd honored that commitment, no matter how stupid it seemed in the harsh light of day. Because honor was the operative term here. A McLean didn't welsh on a dare.

Another fact of the immaturity that characterized the whole mess, he told himself grimly. A mature man would have gone to Jenkins and Henley and told them flat out that it was a dumb idea. That it violated an underlying code of ethics he intended to live by, and that was that.

But he hadn't. Instead, he'd rationalized, telling himself his donation was a selfless act; he hadn't sold the specimen, after all, as some impecunious med students were rumored to do. What's more, he'd told himself, he would probably be making some childless couple very happy.

That was what he told himself whenever a twinge of conscience nagged him over the years. And eventually the twinges grew fewer and farther between. Hell, he couldn't remember the last time he'd even thought about it.

But he *did* remember. He'd thought about it not an hour ago. Very likely spurred by a subliminal recognition of a face he'd seen before, even if it took a while for his conscious mind to make the connection. And now that kid...

Closing his eyes, he pictured the child—all big blue eyes and engaging grin under a cap of unruly blond curls. Curls exactly like his. And he'd hugged Terhune.

Dammit, there was no getting away from facts. In his

line of work, lives often depended on the ability to quickly assess the facts at hand, no matter how meager, and draw conclusions from them. And right now, the few facts he had were leading him to one earthshaking conclusion: that kid could very likely be his son!

JILL TERHUNE eyed her sister with concern as she handed Randi a mug of decaf. They were in the kitchen of the house they shared, inherited from the great-aunt who'd raised them after their stepfather's death. Matt had gone next door to play with Robbie Spencer the minute they got home, so it was just the two of them. Jill could finally pursue what had been on her mind since picking Randi up.

"Wanna tell me about it?" The older sister kept her voice casual, pouring herself a coffee and taking a seat across the table from Randi.

Randi glanced up from her mug with a look of surprise. "Tell you about what?"

"Whatever it is that's got you so on edge." Jill smiled to soften her words. "You've been strung tighter than a guitar string ever since I picked you up from work."

Randi grinned sheepishly. "That obvious, huh?"

Jill grinned back. "It's me, pipsqueak—ol' eagle eye, Jill the pill, remember?"

Randi laughed, relaxing for the first time since the upsetting encounter in the ER. Jill's use of their childhood names for each other could do that. It could also evoke a host of memories. Memories that bound them, reminding them of what they were to each other. Of the love between them, shared gladly these four years with the small boy they both adored.

Suddenly Randi frowned. Was her sister the only one who'd noted her unease? Besides half the ER staff? "Jill, do you think Matt noticed..."

Jill laughed and shook her head. "Fortunately he was too wrapped up in the news about the Spencers' new baby—even if she isn't the brother Robbie'd been hoping for.''

"True," Randi said with a chuckle. "Remember when he told us Robbie had put in an order for a boy?''

Jill chuckled, too. "And if it turned out to be a girl, he was going to tell his mother to send her back?''

"Uh-huh. And then he asked if *we* could... Oh, God!'' Randi dropped her face into her hands. Matt had asked if they could order a baby brother for *him*.

Jill reached across the table and gently touched her sister's shoulder. "Randi, what is it?''

Randi collected herself, lowering her hands and reaching for her coffee. She took a sip and heaved a sigh. "I'd love to be able to give Matt a baby brother or sister, but...I can't.''

"Not by going the route you used to conceive Matt, I agree.'' Jill knew her conservative sister was troubled by misgivings over the ethics of what she'd done in that clinic, despite her reluctance to voice them. But they were close; she needn't be a mind reader to tune in to Randi's feelings.

"But last I heard,'' Jill went on, "the more conventional means of having kids hasn't gone out of style. Randi, you're only thirty-two. That's hardly over the hill. I mean, look at *me*. I'll be marrying at thirty-four. You could still meet someone special, if only you'd—''

"Jill.'' Randi said her name softly, but to Jill it had the impact of a shout. The topic was not to be pursued. They'd been over this before, always with the same result: Randi wanted no part of dating. No part of men and marriage. Of sex. Although she'd never put it to Jill in those terms.

The problem was that Jill was certain she knew why but could say nothing to Randi about it. *Your sister's not yet ready to deal with the deepest roots of her emotional distress, Jill.* Dr. Carol Martin's words threaded through her mind as she and Randi quietly sipped their coffees. *Beyond that, I can tell you nothing. Her sessions with me—like yours—are entirely confidential....*

Jill could still see the counselor's face on the day she'd told her this. It had been calm, relaxed. But by then Jill and Carol had known each other several years and become friends. So Jill had been able to see that, while her face was professionally neutral, Carol's eyes were troubled. Because on that day, Randi had elected to end her counseling.

Carol had urged Randi to continue, but to no avail. Basing her decision solely on the fact that Carol had declared her sister healed of the emotional wounds of sexual abuse, Randi had reasoned she must be healed, as well.

If Carol says you're okay and ready to get on with your life, I should be, too. Now it was Randi's words that drifted through Jill's mind, spoken in reply to Jill's asking her why she wasn't returning to Martin's office. *After all, Jill, darling, you were the one— I mean, I was only a frightened witness, wasn't I?*

But Jill knew otherwise. She'd seen their stepfather coming out of Randi's room, too, during that terrible time after their mother died. More than once. He'd been abusing Randi, too.

But Randi apparently had no memory of it. "Blocking" was the psychological term for what she was doing, according to the books Jill had read on the subject. Not that Carol Martin would confirm or deny this to Jill—that professional confidentiality again. But Jill had certainly told Carol what she'd seen, so Carol knew the score. She just couldn't discuss it with Jill, although she'd warned the older sister not to broach it with Randi on her own.

She'd likely deny it, Jill, the doctor had said. *And you might even find it causes an estrangement between you. Worse, hearing you recount what you saw might cause a traumatic reaction in Randi—especially if she's not emotionally prepared to deal with it. I caution you to leave it alone.*

And so Jill had. But on the day Randi decided to leave counseling, she'd been sorely tempted to speak. Only her fear of making matters worse had kept her silent. The best she'd been able to manage had been a faint argument that implied she accepted Randi's version of what happened...

But being a witness is still traumatic, Randi. Remember? Remember how we both broke down and cried at school? Jill still thanked God they'd somehow found the courage to approach someone with their tale after their stepfather was killed in that car crash. Their guidance counselor had told Aunt Tess and recommended the sessions with Carol Martin. The sessions that had healed Jill, but not her sister.

Jill barely suppressed a sigh. No matter how hard she'd argued, she hadn't been able to persuade Randi to go back to Martin. *It's time we both put the whole ugly business behind us, Jill,* she'd replied, and had never gone to Carol's office again.

The whole ugly business. Yes, it was ugly, and yes, Jill was able to put it behind her. Carol Martin's work had gently led her to a point where she could. By focusing on her strength as a survivor and helping her to feel empowered. And accentuating the positive in her experience with men. Especially her healthy relationship with the biological father they'd lost. Carol had been able to help Jill reconstruct the positive self-image that was badly threatened by her stepfather's abuse. Threatened, but not shattered, thanks largely to Daddy and the caring relationship the girls had had with both their parents while they were alive.

Jill had come out of counseling a whole woman. Her relationship with David was proof of it. David, a decent, stable man she trusted completely—and loved to distraction! She could barely wait for the wedding. Yes, she was ready to get on with her life.

Just as she knew Randi wasn't. If only she'd go back to see Carol. Something had to give. Her sister was a warm, loving woman. Jill didn't believe a career, even combined with mothering, would be enough to fulfill Randi's deepest needs. Not for the long haul. Besides, kids had a way of growing up and—

"So I seem on edge, huh?" Randi's question pulled her back.

"Oh, I don't know…" Jill shrugged. "You could, of course, have taken up shredding Kleenex as a hobby, I guess."

Randi grimaced, recalling the tissues she'd absently torn to shreds in the car. She took a sip of coffee, setting the mug down with a sigh. "Something, uh, unexpected happened in the ER last night—and I don't mean the emergencies. Except that the man happened to be a patient, that is."

"The man?"

Randi's face tightened with strain. "His name is Travis McLean. I know it means nothing to you, Jill, because I never mentioned it to you. But he's—" she paused for a deep breath "—Matt's father."

Jill stopped in the act of raising her mug and stared at her. "Dear Lord!" she murmured at last. "Are you cer—"

"Dead certain." Randi's eyes closed, then opened again. "I recognized him, but I also confirmed the name—Travis Paxton McLean. It was on the admittance form."

Jill nodded slowly, her eyes on Randi's face. "I can see why that would have been unnerving." Unnerving, yes, but why did her sister look so haunted? "Did he, uh, recognize you?"

"I don't think so, but…" Randi hesitated, reluctant to say anything about the guilt the incident had dredged up. Hadn't she worked all that out years ago? Matt had been worth the unorthodox means she'd used to have him. Dear Lord, if she didn't have Matt in her life, she'd—

Abruptly she shook her head. "No, as far as I could tell, he didn't remember me."

"Well, then—" Jill smiled and patted her hand "—if he

didn't recognize you, there's nothing to worry about." She threw her sister a shrewdly assessing glance. "Is there?"

Randi shrugged and took a sip from her mug. "No, I suppose not, but..." *But then, why can't you stop thinking about the man? Why do you keep seeing his face every time you look at your son? And why do you keep remembering those odd currents that ran right through you when he grinned at you, teased you and bantered with you?*

Jill looked at her expectantly, but Randi had no intention of voicing such things. Big sister would only start in again about her needing to date, and there was *no* way. Especially when the man under discussion was Travis McLean.

"Come on, sis, talk to me," Jill urged, her voice gentle. "But...?"

"Oh, I don't know..." Randi avoided her sister's eyes. "I guess I'm just blowing the whole thing out of proportion because I'm tired. I've been putting in some long hours at the hospital."

"True," Jill said, suspecting there was more to it than that but reluctant to say so. On the other hand, if seeing Matt's biological father had triggered the old guilt in Randi, this might be the perfect opportunity to suggest she do something about it. Obliquely of course.

"I spoke to Carol Martin on the phone this morning, Randi," she said casually, eyeing her sister as she reached for the coffeepot and refilled her mug.

"Oh?"

"She'll be able to be a bridesmaid for sure. Her family reunion's been postponed till December."

"Oh, Jill, I'm glad. I know how much you wanted her in the wedding party."

Jill nodded, sliding a careful glance at her. "She asked about you...how you are."

"Mmm," Randi murmured noncommittally. She knew what was coming.

"You know," Jill said all too cheerfully, "you ought to drop in on her one of these days."

"Drop in on her...at her office, you mean?"

Jill had the grace to blush, then laughed. "Okay, okay, but it was worth a try."

Randi laughed, too, then grew serious. "We've been over this ground before, Jill, and, no, I don't feel I need to see Carol professionally. There's nothing wrong with me that a little R and R wouldn't cure. So, sister mine, bug off!"

With a sigh, Jill used her index fingers to mimic the antennae of a bug and waggled her head—an old joke between them—and they both laughed.

Then Jill said, "Okay, what about the R and R? Is your vacation still on for next week, or is that summer flu gonna put a cramp in your plans?"

"It had better not. I'll lose my five-hundred-dollar deposit on the cottage if I cancel."

Randi had engaged a beach cottage on Maryland's Eastern Shore for three weeks, and she was looking forward to spending some quality time there with Matt. She'd sent in her deposit months ago.

"The hospital wouldn't force you to cancel if they were short-staffed, would they?" Jill asked worriedly.

"Relax. I reminded Dr. Harper of it just yesterday, and all signals are go."

"Good," Jill said, "because I've got something to tell you with regard to those three weeks."

"Shoot."

"Well, David and I were discussing it, and we think it's super that you're doing this with Matt." Jill paused, wanting to phrase this exactly right. Randi was an excellent mother, despite being a single parent with a career. She'd taken great pains, since Matt's birth, to arrange her life to accommodate a child. No, not just accommodate. Matt was a priority in everything she did.

She hadn't gone to work at all for the first year of her son's life, dipping into her savings to support them. And when she went back to nursing, she frequently took night duty to allow her time with Matt during the day. Jill had helped, too.

As an interior decorator working out of her office at home, she'd been able to juggle her schedule; between the two sisters, they'd managed to raise Matt with very little outside assistance.

But as Jill saw it, there were problems lurking on the horizon. She worried about how Randi would manage after the wedding, when Jill left to make her home with David. She also worried her sister might actually be spending too much time with Matt, for every free moment revolved around the child. This hadn't been a bad thing when Matt was an infant, but as he grew older, Jill feared Randi was in danger of overdoing it. A child needed love and affection as much as food to grow up whole and healthy; but just as too much food was a bad idea, so was too much affection; it could be smothering.

And the signs were already there. Randi's concern for Matt bordered on the overprotective. She hired a sitter—even the older woman who lived up the block and whom they'd known for years—only as a last resort; when Jill couldn't stay with Matt, Randi frequently canceled an engagement rather than leave him with someone else.

And Randi never spent recreational time alone; her vacations always included Matt. She didn't seem to think she sometimes needed time for herself, to recharge her batteries.

So when Randi had mentioned this vacation on the Eastern Shore, Jill had discussed her concerns with David, and they'd come up with a plan.

"Listen, Randi," she said, "Matt's a great kid, and I know how much you wanna be with him. Still, wouldn't you enjoy at least part of those three weeks by yourself?"

Randi blinked, looking bemused. "By myself? Whatever for? You know how much I—"

"—love Matt and adore spending quality time with him—I know, I know. But what about *you?* Didn't you just admit to needing some R and R?"

"Sure, I did, and I intend to get it—with Matt."

Jill sighed. "Come on, sis, get real. Matt's a super kid, and we all love him to bits. But you know as well as I do he's a real live wire. A *weekend* with him can wear you out. Where's the rest in that, huh?"

"Jill, I just couldn't leave him while I—"

"Not even for a trip to Disney World with me and David?"

There was a moment of silence as Randi took in Jill's grinning face. "You're kidding, right?"

"Never been more serious in my life. David and I are going there the week after next, and we'd like to take Matt."

"But why? Aren't engaged couples supposed to want, uh, time with each other?"

Jill shrugged. "We already have a lot of that, with both of us living in the same town and the ability to set our own work hours." An architect who owned his own firm, David could arrange his schedule to suit Jill's, so the two shared lots of their own quality time.

"And besides," she added, "we *need* Matt."

"Huh?"

Jill's grin was ear to ear now. "What good is a trip to Disney World without a little kid along to help you enjoy it? It'd be almost as bad as Christmas without children. We need kids for these things—to keep the magic in them."

Randi shook her head and smiled, despite her reluctance to accept the proposal. Vacation without Matt? She'd feel...naked somehow. Hadn't she rearranged her life to include her son wherever she could?

"Aw, come on, sis," Jill pressed. "This would be a terrific opportunity for the kid, and you know it!"

Chuckling, Randi addressed an invisible witness. "Now she appeals to my conscience. You're a rat, Jill the pill."

Jill laughed unabashedly. Randi was weakening and she knew it. "Furthermore," she added, "it isn't as if you'd be missing beach time with Matt entirely. He'd go with you for the first week. Then we'd pick him up at the cottage and drive to Florida with him, while you get the rest you need."

Randi sighed. It made perfect sense. Which, of course, coming from Jill, was to be expected. Jill had always been the sensible one, even as a child, whereas Randi had been the dreamer. As a child. When had she stopped? Somewhere on the road to adulthood, she supposed. Dreams were all well and good, but they didn't put food on the table or clothes on your child. And they didn't protect you from—

"Randi?" Jill's concerned voice cut across Randi's thoughts. "What's the matter, sis? You looked awfully worried there for a moment. Did I say something?"

"You sure did, you sneak. Everything needed to convince me I'd be a selfish meanie not to agree to your plan."

"Does that mean…"

"You win! Matt goes to Disney World—and I go crazy for two weeks, trying to occupy myself without him."

'Oh, I don't know," Jill said as she jumped up to hug her. "A little crazy might be just what the doctor ordered."

But as Randi hugged her back, Jill's words triggered an image. *Doctor*… Travis McLean, former med student, was now certainly a doctor, though in what capacity she hadn't found out. Travis McLean…Matt's father. What would it have been like for Matt to have known him? she wondered. To have his mother and father show him Disney World, instead of an aunt and her fiancé?

With an inward sigh, she swept these questions from her

mind. It was too late to worry about such things. But as she and Jill began to discuss the forthcoming vacation, a remnant of unease remained....

CHAPTER FIVE

TRAVIS GUIDED his rental car along the narrow shaded streets of Georgetown's Heights section. He ignored the stately homes with their manicured lawns and picturesque gardens that made up the posh residential neighborhood. He'd seen it before. One of those homes belonged to his family. But no McLean was in residence now. They always went to their Virginia estate in June, staying through September to escape Washington's notorious summer heat.

Not that he'd drop by if they were here. He was persona non grata with the lofty McLean clan, thanks to his spiteful tyrant of a father, and there was nothing to be done about it. *In his own way, your father loves you...* Travis's mouth twisted angrily as Judith McLean's words echoed through his mind. If that was love, he was damned lucky to have escaped it.

His features steadied with resolve when he spied the entrance to Georgetown University up ahead. His mother had mentioned that Sarah was taking summer courses. With the aim, he supposed, of finishing in three years. He found himself grinning. His sister was a straight-A student with energy to burn. Just like her to be in a hurry!

The grin faded as he slowed for the entrance to the university. By the time he was discharged from the hospital, he'd made up his mind to visit her. If she'd see him. At one time he'd never have questioned this; Sarah was a gutsy little thing and had always had a mind of her own. But five years could change a person, especially one as young as his baby sister. No telling how well the old bastard had succeeded in intimidating her.

Well, he thought as he swung into the entrance drive, he'd soon find out.

"TRAVIS! OH, LORD, is it really you?" Sarah McLean's voice rose with excitement as she flew down the stairs of the old mansion that housed her sorority. Breathless, caught between laughter and tears, she reached the landing and flung herself at her brother. "Oh, Travis, I can't *believe* it. You're *here!*"

"In the flesh, pumpkin," Travis managed past the lump in his throat, "in the everlovin' flesh." His left arm was still in a sling, yet he caught the slender brunette to him with his right, lifting her off the floor with ease.

Both laughing and crying, Sarah wound her arms around his neck, clinging as if she'd never let go. "Travis McLean," she said, "I'd kill you if I didn't love you so much! How come you never wrote? Never answered my letters?"

She found herself swiftly lowered to the floor, her brother's eyes leveled intently on hers. "I never received any letters, Sarah," he said quietly. "And I wrote over two dozen before I finally gave up."

"But...but..."

"It's easy to guess what happened," he said, taking in her bewildered face. "You wrote from Sunnyfields?"

"Well, yes, since it was summer. But I always put the letters in the mailbox myself or gave them to Higgins to..."

"Yeah, well, rural mailboxes have a way of bein' accessible to others besides the postman," Travis said grimly. "And Higgins's salary, of course, is paid by—"

"Daddy." Sarah shook her head and heaved a sigh. "I s'pose I was pretty naive, but I never dreamed a servant who's known me all my life would—"

"How 'bout the father who's known you all your life?" Travis asked bitterly.

Before she could respond, a pair of sorority sisters banged through the front door, calling out greetings to Sarah. She waved to them, then looked at her brother. "We can't stay here and talk decently," she murmured sotto voce, "so let's find— God in heaven! What happened to your arm?"

"Nothin' mortal, darlin', and it hardly even hurt, I swear." Travis put his free arm around her shoulders and ushered her toward the door. "I'll tell you 'bout it when we get some privacy if you want."

"I want," she said firmly. Just like Travis to make light of an injury. Her tone told him she wouldn't be put off by some fairy tale.

The sorority sisters, dressed in cutoffs and T-shirts boasting Greek letters, had paused in the vestibule. They eyed Travis with interest. Not surprised—her brother definitely qualified as a hunk—Sarah took pity on them and performed introductions. Then she and Travis headed outside.

The sultry weather made it impossible to remain outdoors for long. They drove to an air-conditioned coffee shop Sarah knew would be deserted at that hour. Left alone after the waitress had served them a pair of iced coffees, brother and sister both spoke at once.

"Tell me about that…"

"Tell me all about…"

They laughed in unison, their eyes meeting with a shared humor that said the past five years might never have been. They'd always been close, despite the fourteen-year difference in their ages. Realizing how deeply he'd missed that closeness, Travis silently cursed himself for not engineering a reunion sooner. "You first, pumpkin," he said with a hint of chagrin.

"The arm," she replied with a gesture at his sling. "All you told me in the car was that it was just a flesh wound."

He gave her a lopsided grin. "Not good enough, huh?"

"Better believe it," she said as she reached for her coffee.

He sighed, then gave an edited version of the shoot-out that had resulted in the deaths of several members of an international drug cartel. For security reasons, he didn't name names; he suggested she go to the library and view microfiches of the *Miami Herald* for the date in question if she really wanted to know more.

"No thanks," said Sarah with a wave of her hand. She leaned back in her chair and studied him. A look of awe dawned on her pretty face. It reminded him of the way she'd looked at him once when he'd scored a winning touchdown for the Harvard football team.

"So you're truly in the thick of it." She shook her head slowly. "Spyin', runnin' around the globe, chasin' after—"

"Not all that much anymore," he interrupted with a shrug. "The world's changed in the past few years. Our focus has had to change with it. It's true CIA officers have mostly operated overseas, largely as diplomats, but—"

"Diplomats?" she asked archly.

Travis smiled. "Officially, anyway. But nowadays there's an increasin' emphasis on NOCs."

"Knocks?"

"N-O-C-S," he said, spelling out the acronym; he was aware this information was public knowledge and didn't compromise security. "Stands for 'nonofficial covers'. What it usually means is that the agent is quietly placed in an American business that operates overseas, rather than in some war-torn country. Or, as was more often the case, in an embassy, through the diplomatic corps."

"But why?" Sarah had done some reading on the CIA since learning her brother worked for it. She knew about the dangers for men who did "field work." And about case officers who'd operated during the Cold War. Under embassy cover, they'd cruise foreign ministries and cocktail

parties, collecting intelligence on the former Soviet Union
and its satellites.

"Well," Travis said, "more and more, we find ourselves
dealin' with individuals who aren't fightin' guerrilla wars
and aren't on the diplomatic circuit. Nuclear smugglers,
terrorists, drug traffi—"

"Please! I don't think I want to know that much, after
all." She shuddered. "But it's clear you're still brushin' up
against some dangerous characters, Trav. Seein' you in
that—" she gestured at the sling "—well, it wouldn't be
normal if I didn't worry, would it?"

"No, I reckon it wouldn't," he said with a tender smile.

She took a sip of coffee, then stared pensively into the
glass. "Mother worries too, Trav," she said quietly. "She
never talks much about it." She met his gaze. "But she's
taken to readin' the *Post* more than she ever did before you
left. And when she's done, I see the worry in her eyes."

He nodded and told her about their mother's visit to the
hospital.

"Trav, that's wonderful! She finally mustered the courage to see you."

He stifled an obscenity and glared at her. "Come off it,
Sarah! Wonderful? What's so wonderful about a fifty-nine-
year-old woman needin' *courage* to see her own son?"

Sarah winced at the bitterness in his voice. With a deep
sigh, she reached for his hand on the table and gave it a
squeeze; the squeeze was returned, and she smiled sadly.
"It's been awful for everyone, havin' the family ripped
apart like this. Mother's suffered the most, I think. You
must know how difficult Daddy made it for—"

"What, exactly, did Daddy do, Sarah?" He'd wanted to
ask their mother, but somehow hadn't been able to; the
encounter had been awkward enough as it was. "What'd
the SOB threaten? To disinherit you 'n' Troy, maybe?
That'd make sense, I s'pose. Unlike me, y'all had your
schoolin' to complete. But Mother has her own money,

from her trust. Y'all would hardly've gone penniless if she'd stood her ground.''

Sarah heaved a sigh and shook her head. "Unfortunately Daddy knew exactly where we were vulnerable. You see—'' pain and anger flashed in her eyes ''—he threatened to refuse to help Troy pass his surgeon's boards.''

Travis swore vehemently under his breath. Pushed into medicine despite having no aptitude for it, Troy had had a difficult time of it. Quiet gentle Troy, who'd gone dutifully to med school, remaining there only through vast amounts of time and money spent on tutors. They'd all known that passing his surgery boards would be the biggest hurdle. That Trent McLean himself, brilliant surgeon that he was, had been the one who was supposed to see Troy through them.

"Maybe not passin' them would have been the best thing that could've happened to Troy,'' he said angrily. "Maybe then he could've joined Aunt Louise at Stanford.'' If Troy had to be in medicine, they both believed he'd have been happier in research. As his mother had reminded him, an aunt in research at the West Coast institution had offered to sponsor him. But their father had insisted on surgery. Just as he had with Travis.

"Maybe,'' Sarah replied, "but I don't think Mother was willin' to take the chance with Troy's future. And you were right about the will, incidentally. That was the first thing Daddy threatened, along with forbiddin' Mother to help *you*.''

Travis snorted. He'd had no doubt he'd been cut off, but money was never that important to him; lean years in the military had told him he could live without luxuries. No, losing his inheritance was the least of his regrets.

"What about you, Sarah?'' he asked, studying her face. "Happy in the family career plan?''

She eyed him carefully, aware she was about to drop a

bombshell. "I'm not in the family career plan any longer, Travis. As of last semester, I'm not pre-med, but pre-law."

"Huh?" His bemused look was almost comical, and she grinned at him.

"I said I'm—"

"I heard you," he cut in dazedly, "but I still don't believe it. What *happened?*"

She smothered a giggle. "Steve Townsend happened, for one thing, although that only started the process."

"Who the hell is Steve Townsend?"

She was smiling, and he thought he detected a blush under her tan. "He's...well, let's just say he's my new 'significant other.' He also happens to be a top-performin' second-year law student at Georgetown."

Travis groaned. "I think I'm beginnin' to get the picture." *Holy Hannah! She imagines she's in love, and now—*

"No," Sarah said, "I don't think you do. I may or may not be in love with Steve. I haven't decided yet—too soon to tell, I expect. But my feelin's for the man had nothin' to do with my decision, Trav. What happened was, after we began seein' each other, I helped Steve with some research..." She paused as if to gather her thoughts and took a sip of coffee.

"And—?" he prompted irritably. He wasn't certain why he felt irritated, but he felt a vague stirring of guilt. A voice niggled at the back of his mind, saying she was following in his footsteps and no good could come of it. It was one thing to be the rebel himself, but another matter entirely for his kid sister to be influenced enough to take the same route.

"And," she said, "in helpin' with that research, I stumbled across a discipline that fascinated me. I mean *fascinated*, in a way medicine never could. It's a whole new world, Trav, and I can't get into it fast enough."

He stared at her, hearing the conviction in her voice. It

wasn't the boyfriend, then; he'd only been a catalyst. That was a relief, but his stirring of guilt only grew; he realized just how gutsy his little sister was—and perhaps just how like himself she was.

"Does Father know about this?" he asked tightly.

"About Steve?" she asked, deliberately misinterpreting.

"You know what I mean," he growled, then offered a sheepish smile. "Sorry, pumpkin. Guess I'm still havin' a hard time digestin' this. But since you brought him up..."

"Not to worry on that score," she assured him. "Steve's been out to the farm a few times, and they like him. 'Course, I haven't mentioned that we'll be sharin' an apartment in the fall, but I'm workin' on it." She grinned. "By the time it happens...well, they'll adjust to the idea."

Little Sarah, all grown up. Travis wondered if *he* could adjust to the idea. He shook his head, as if to clear it of outgrown notions.

"Back to the big one," he reminded her. "You haven't told them 'bout your new career, have you?" He knew that his mother would've said something if she had.

"Not yet. They all think my takin' summer courses is to finish early. I'm actually pickin' up credits for pre-law."

He stifled a groan, but Sarah caught the hint of regret in his eyes. "Don't you dare go blamin' yourself for my decision, Travis McLean! Or gettin' involved, either. It's about time the men in this family realize a woman—especially *this* woman—is capable of makin' her own choices."

He seemed to chew on this, silent as he sipped his iced coffee. She watched him, wondering what he was thinking. Not too long ago she'd come across material about controlling parents in some of her course work. One of the things that had made an impression on her was that controlling parents—like her father—often spawned controlling offspring. And Travis had always, though in a far gentler manner than their father, been a little too ready to take over the lives of those he cared about.

Sarah wasn't worried about herself. She was strong enough to resist his well-meaning impulses. But she worried about *him*. Would this blind spot in her otherwise sensitive brother cause him problems someday?

"Sarah—" Travis's voice was concerned when he finally spoke "—are you sure, absolutely sure, about this thing?"

"I've never been more sure of anythin' in my life."

He nodded. He believed her. But sweet God almighty, did she realize what a bomb she'd be dropping? Smack in the middle of their already fragmented family? Did she see the enormity of this? Was she prepared to be cut off—like him?

"Look, Sarah," he began carefully, "you know what'll be runnin' through his mind when he hears. Maybe I can—"

"Hold it right there, big brother! I meant what I said. I'm a big girl now, and I don't need you runnin' interference for me. I want your promise—right now—that you'll stay out of it. It was my decision, no matter what you think, and *I'll handle it*. Promise me you'll respect that."

He expelled a long breath, then regarded her adamant face. "You've got it," he said. Baby sister really *had* grown up. Grown up smarter and gutsier than he'd ever suspected. He'd loved her from the first, but now he really admired her, too.

Yet as he escorted her out, Travis couldn't help worrying that Sarah's decision would wrench the family further apart. One thing hadn't changed: the old man was still a heartless bastard who'd never tolerated being crossed.

CHAPTER SIX

TRAVIS RELAXED behind the wheel as he cruised south on I-95. He was headed for Langley, although he knew Jason Cord wouldn't be happy to see him. Jason might be his friend, but he was also Travis's immediate superior, and he'd ordered him to take a month's leave. Travis viewed the shoulder wound as no big deal, but he intended to take that leave; he simply needed a stop at headquarters first.

He left Georgetown feeling more upbeat than he'd felt in a long time. Not that he'd been depressed or anything, far from it. But he realized his life had lacked...balance. The past few years had been entirely devoted to work. Which was ridiculous, because while he liked his job, he wasn't passionate about it. Reestablishing ties with his sister had added a dimension he'd badly needed. After all, Sarah was the only family left to him now that—

His mind tripped on an image of a small boy with blond curls. His son, unless he was imagining things, and he didn't think so. Especially after the discreet inquiries he'd made at Hopkins before he left.

His name was Matthew—Matt, according to a night nurse he'd charmed into sharing what she knew. Matt. He liked the sound of it. A solid masculine name. Which the kid would need, considering who was raising him: a pair of females, with not a male in sight. Or at least, none anyone at the hospital could tell him about.

He'd learned that Nurse Miranda Terhune was unmarried and to anyone's knowledge, had never been married. She was a single parent to four-year-old Matthew, and they both lived with her sister, who was helping her raise the kid. Two women, both of them single.

The thought of a child, especially a boy, being raised without a father, or at least a father figure, didn't sit well with him. Why hadn't a beautiful woman like Randi Terhune ever married? Why did she want to raise a kid by herself? More importantly, why had she used a sperm-bank doner to have one? Was she involved with a guy who was infertile, maybe planning marriage at the time she'd made use of the clinic's resources? But if that was the case, where was the guy now?

These were the kinds of questions he couldn't ask of the people she worked with. As it was, he'd treaded on dangerous turf in seeking the answers he had. Hospital personnel, like personnel everywhere, were hardly obliged to divulge personal information about coworkers. Only by spreading his inquiries among a number of nurses and using that old standby—charm—had he managed to get the information he had. That, and the fact that Terhune was so well liked, people were happy to talk about her.

To give Nurse Randi her due, everyone he'd spoken to regarded her as an excellent mother. But what did they know? Coworkers saw only certain facts of a person's life. Maybe only the facets the person wanted them to see. So how much insight did anyone have into her home life? Into how she handled her son?

His son. Almost certain the child was his, he wasn't content to leave it alone. Which was why he was heading for Langley. He needed to know more. And headquarters, with its vast data base, was a good place to get information on people.

He came upon a slow-moving van in the right lane and swung out to pass. As he did so, he felt a twinge of conscience regarding the ethics—or lack thereof—in using the

CIA's data base to serve his own personal ends. He decided to ignore it.

A state-police car appeared in his rearview mirror, and Travis checked his speed. He wasn't over the limit. He rarely broke any laws, traffic or otherwise—a legacy of Judith McLean's rearing. Even as a youth, he'd never experimented with drugs, never raced the little MG they'd given him for graduating prep school with the highest honors. He'd been a super straight arrow, all right. Except for one fine summer night in Cambridge, when he'd gone out on the town and...

Muttering an expletive, Travis focused on his immediate objective: the life and habits of one Miranda Terhune. The final tidbit he'd learned about the lovely nurse was that she was shortly leaving on a "much deserved" three-week vacation. He hadn't been able to ascertain where, but that shouldn't present a problem. Airline tickets and hotel reservations were usually secured with credit cards. And credit-card use was traceable.

He frowned. The problem was getting past Jason Cord.

"YOU NEED TO WHAT?" Jason Cord thundered, his straight black brows meeting in the middle.

"I said, I need to use the main computer for a bit." Travis ignored the scowl that rearranged Cord's features—his aunt Louise would have called them disgracefully handsome features—and kept his voice casual. "It's nothin' that'll compromise security, Jace, ol' boy. I'll only be a few minutes, 'n' then—"

"In a pig's eye, you will!" Cord rose from behind his desk and thrust out his arm, pointing to the door. "Get your injured hide out of here, McLean, *now,* and I'll forget what you just asked."

Travis stood his ground. Cord intimidated a lot of people with that scowl. But not Travis. For one thing, he was taller than his superior, although Cord came in over six feet. For another, they'd been through hell and back together. In the old days, when they'd been field operatives, along with Rafe O'Hara and Brad Holman. Hell, when they'd lost Brad, Travis and Jason had wept in each other's arms.

Not that he was about to mention Brad. His death was still a raw wound to the three men who'd regarded him as a good friend. Brad had been tortured and killed by a Mexican drug lord; Rafe, despite orders to take the man alive, had recently gunned the bastard down. While Travis sympathized totally with Rafe's action, he doubted Jason felt the same.

Travis wished he'd confide in him, but fat chance of that. Jason was a closemouthed bastard when he wanted to be; the best thing, when he was in one of his moods, was to avoid him entirely. If he hadn't needed the info on Terhune, Travis would have already been out the door.

"Look, Jason," he said calmly, "you know me. Would I ask for somethin' like this if it wasn't important? In fact, when before have I ever—"

"Stuff it, McLean! You're asking now, and it's one time too many. Get the hell out of here."

Travis heaved a sigh. He'd known it wouldn't be easy, yet he'd been hoping… Ah, hell. He hadn't wanted to tell Cord what this was all about, but it looked like that was the only way.

"Jace…this really is important," he said quietly.

Jason had his mouth set to blister his friend's ears, but the look on Travis's face stopped him. McLean was a rogue sometimes, using that Southern charm to get his way. Sometimes, when he had to, he trod the gray areas—they all did—but he wasn't dishonest and he wasn't devious.

In fact, the worst that might be said of him was that he never took life too seriously. Not his personal life, anyway. That break with his family—it could have gotten to some men, but not McLean. "Life's too short to sweat what you can't change," he'd once said when someone asked him about it. And then there was his famous pronouncement on love—that if it existed, it was for poets and fools.

No, Travis McLean wasn't known for getting "deep-down" about things. Not that he didn't have depths; if McLean were shallow, he'd never have had the bond they shared. It was just that Travis rarely tapped into those depths in the day-to-day. Which was why the look in his eyes now stopped Jason short.

"How important?" he found himself asking.

Travis sighed. Hooking the chair across from Jason's desk with his foot, he swung it out and dropped into it. "This'll take a bit," he said. He motioned for Jason to sit, much as if their roles were reversed and it was Travis's office.

Jason snorted, but sat.

"What I'm about to tell, ol' buddy, stops here, okay?" Travis indicated the confines of Jason's office. "I mean, I want it treated like it's classified."

"You've got it," Jason said.

And then Travis told him—about the night in Cambridge, about a nurse at Johns Hopkins who'd looked familiar, and finally about a little boy with blond curls.

"And I need to find out about them, Jace," he finished with an intensity few ever saw. "I *can't* just ignore it. The kid's almost assuredly my own flesh and blood. *My son.*"

Jason pursed his lips and whistled softly. When Travis decided to get deep-down, he didn't mess around.

"Travis..." Jason began slowly, focusing on a paper-weight he toyed with on his desk as he gathered his thoughts. He tried to put himself in Travis's shoes: what would *he* do, faced with such a thing? And what a thing! What an incredible helluva thing! "Let's say I...I look the other way while you do this." He met Travis's eyes. "What then? Where do you go from there?"

"I'm not sure. I s'pose that depends on what I find out. And I'm gonna find out, Jace, make no mistake about that."

Travis's gaze was resolute. "If not through our files here, I'll do it the hard way." He shrugged. "It'll just take me longer, that's all."

Jason shook his head and gave a sardonic half smile. "And I just gave you a month's leave," he said disgustedly.

"Uh-huh." Travis flashed the familiar roguish grin and stood, the movement all catlike grace, despite his size. "Wish me luck, ol' buddy," he drawled. He gave Jason a flippant two-fingered salute and headed for the door.

"Now, wait a minute, McLean!" his superior growled. "Did I say…"

But Travis was already out the door. Muttering something about cocky Southern bastards, Jason sighed and returned to his paperwork.

FROM THE BACK of her Jeep Cherokee, Randi hauled out the last of the bags she'd packed. Matt was in the open doorway of their rental cottage dancing with excitement. He'd already changed into the new swim trunks she'd bought him. Since Matt's suitcase had been the first she'd unloaded, he was way ahead of her. Randi grinned as she approached him. "Ready for the beach, huh?"

"Yeah! Can we go now, Mom? Can we?" Matt looked at the dunes visible beyond the Jeep, then back at his mother. "It's awful sweaty here, y'know!"

Randi chuckled as he followed her inside. "That's because this place was all closed up, sweetheart." The air in the five rooms had been stifling, and opening windows had been the first thing she'd done; already she could feel the fresh ocean breeze sweeping through the cottage.

"Besides," she added as she headed for the bedroom that Matt would occupy, "you might want to check out a couple of the things in this bag." She set the bag down beside one of a pair of twin beds, and Matt tore into it.

"*Barney!* Yippee!" The four-year-old pulled out a pillow case decorated with a magenta dinosaur and waved it at her. "Thanks, Mom!" He began singing the Barney song as he dug through the rest of the bag.

It contained beach towels and Matt's sheets and pillow-cases from home. The cottage came furnished with linens and towels, but she knew Matt preferred sleeping between sheets decorated with Barney, his favorite TV personality.

"You bet, son," she murmured, then went to her own room to change into her swimsuit.

The sweetly sung lyrics followed her out the door, and when she reached the other bedroom, she paused and re-flected on the Barney phenomenon. Why did kids love it so? The answer came at once. Barney's message was sim-ple and clear: love. The eternally smiling dinosaur embod-ied the very bedrock of the only thing children really needed. Love, especially within a happy family.

A tiny frown knitted Randi's brow as she absently reached for the bikini Jill had talked her into. Matt was still singing. About a happy family. *Are we a happy family?* a voice in Randi's head asked. *Of course we are!* her rational self countered. *Matt and Jill and I, we're exactly that.*

But Jill will be leaving to make a home of her own in a few months, the voice whispered. *A family of her own. And then where will you be?*

"Right where I've always been—beside my son," she found herself saying aloud. "We'll *still* be a family, and a darned happy one!" To emphasize her certainty of this, she pulled off her T-shirt with gusto and flung it on the bed. "Who says what size families have to be?"

She could still hear Matt singing about love. Right, she thought, as she peeled off her jeans. Matt loved her and she loved him—unconditionally. It was all they needed.

But as she continued to get ready for the beach, the ques-tions wouldn't go away. *All you need?* the silent voice nagged. *Is it really?*

THE WEATHER was perfect for the beach. With temperatures in the eighties and a good breeze off the ocean, they couldn't have asked for better.

Randi slathered Matt's back and shoulders with sunscreen. "There, that ought to do it, honey," she said at last, recapping the bottle of lotion. "Wanna get wet?"

Matt didn't answer. She was about to repeat the question when she saw where his attention was focused. A pair of boys not much bigger than Matt were tossing a beach ball. With them was a man whose matching red hair and freckles plainly marked him as their father.

Randi flicked a glance at Matt's beach ball, a red-and-yellow affair lying next to their blanket beside a plastic pail and shovel. She touched her son on the shoulder. "Want to toss your ball?" she asked.

Tearing his gaze away from the redheads, Matt glanced at the ball. "Nah," he said with a hint of diffidence. "It's still sweaty out here."

"Well, what are we waiting for?" Randi grinned. "Race you to the water!"

Matt's answering grin was instantaneous. With a whoop, he took off running, the trio with the ball forgotten. Randi laughed as she followed suit. She'd make it a close race but let her four-year-old win.

They shrieked happily as they splashed into the water, Matt a step ahead of her. "It's cold!" Randi shouted with an exaggerated shiver.

"Oh, Mom, girls always say that!"

"Oh, yeah?" A handful of other bathers frolicked in the waves nearby, and she had to raise her voice above their excited shrieks and yells. "Says who?"

"David 'n' me! You 'n' Aunt Jill both said it when we went swimmin' in David's pool, 'member?"

He chortled as she made a face at him. Randi was secretly pleased, however, that Matt remembered this so clearly; it had occurred when he was only three. He was bright and observant, not to mention remarkably coordinated for his age, she thought as he dodged a wave and swam a few yards. The mother-and-child swim classes they'd attended at the local Y had paid off.

They spent a good hour in the water before Matt opted for building a sand castle. Stopping to give him another application of sunscreen first, Randi was surprised to hear him offer to coat her back with the lotion.

"Sure," she answered. She handed him the sunscreen and plopped down on her stomach. As he went diligently to work applying the lotion, however, she saw what had likely prompted this: the red-haired father was in the process of applying lotion to the back of a woman who shared a blanket with him and his boys. Aware his own mother had no husband to help with the task, Matt had assumed the role.

Randi's reaction was ambivalent. On the one hand, she was warmed that her son would be so solicitous of her; on the other, she wondered if Matt was beginning to think of himself as the "man of the family." Had the lack of an adult to fill that role settled more firmly into his consciousness? Was this a fair burden to place on a four-year-old? She frowned.

Without warning, an image came to mind. Of a big blond man who resembled her son. Travis McLean. Randi stiffened. She'd actually pictured him sitting on the blanket with them!

"That's great, son," she said hastily, banishing the image as she rose to her feet. She reached for the pail and shovel. "Let's see about that sand castle, okay?"

But as Matt followed her cheerfully to the wet sand near the water's edge, McLean's lean handsome face hovered at the fringes of her mind. Kneeling in the sand beside her son, she began digging with a spurt of energy meant to drive the image away. That, and something else. Something that felt suspiciously like guilt.

Don't be silly, she told herself as she molded the damp sand. *Matt can't miss what he's never had. As for McLean, what he doesn't know isn't hurting him, either.*

Yet the argument in her head persisted. She told herself McLean's actions precluded his right to know of the son he'd fathered. He'd *chosen* to donate his sperm, *chosen* to be an anonymous father, hadn't he?

But far more disturbing was the question of whether it was right for *her* to choose to bring a fatherless child into the world. Unbidden, more questions came, try as she might to ignore them. Had she robbed her son of one of life's inalienable rights? The right to have and know a father? Had she been selfish in doing what she'd done? Had she stolen from her own child's future?

The sand castle was the largest, most elaborate structure built on the beach that day. Other children and their parents came to admire it, including the trio of redheads. Matt grinned at all the praise, even boasting to a man and his young daughter, "Me 'n' my mom's the bestest team in the world for makin' sand castles!"

And through it all Randi laughed and smiled, determined to shut out the doubts. Doubts that made her wonder if the happiness of one-parent families and sand castles didn't have something in common.

Perhaps neither was built to last.

CHAPTER SEVEN

"HERE YOU ARE, Mr. McLean." The owner of the bed-and-breakfast handed Travis a beach badge. "Go around the side porch and you'll find a path leading straight to the beach."

"Thank you, Mrs. Muncie," Travis said with a smile for the elderly widow. He fastened the badge to his trunks, relishing the simple pleasure of having both hands free; the bullet wound was healing rapidly, and he'd discarded the sling. Waving to Mrs. Muncie, he slung a towel over his shoulder and headed for the beach.

With any luck, he'd find Randi and Matt Terhune on that beach. One of the things the Agency's computer had turned up was the location of Ms. Terhune's vacation spot. She'd rented a cottage on Maryland's Eastern Shore, just a stone's throw from Mrs. Muncie's bed-and-breakfast. Through sheer luck, he'd called Mrs. Muncie just after she'd received a cancelation; he was now booked for the weekend and two weeks following. A stay that just happened to coincide with the remainder of Randi Terhune's vacation.

The computer had turned up other information, too. Terhune and the kid lived in a quiet suburb near D.C., sharing a home—as he'd already learned—with her older sister. Their modest house was in a good neighborhood, served by a decent public-school system. It had been left to the sisters by the aunt who'd raised them; they were orphaned in their early teens.

Randi had a bachelor's and a master's degree in nursing,

and had twice graduated in the top ten percent of her class. She had an excellent work record, had advanced rapidly in her career.

So far, so good.

Then there was the fertility clinic in Cambridge, where she'd worked before having the kid. He'd learned it was still being operated by Dr. Philip Burgess, its founder. Posing as a journalist doing an article on such clinics, Travis had learned a few interesting facts. Facts that convinced him Randi Terhune had acted on her own unethical initiative if she'd availed herself of the clinic's services.

Make that *when,* not *if,* he amended. Any uncertainties he'd had about whether she'd done so had all but vanished. The facts he'd assembled were just too overwhelming to amount to a coincidence. Yeah, she'd acted unethically, all right. According to Burgess, a stern no-nonsense New Englander, employees had always been barred from using the clinic themselves.

But Travis was deeply concerned about the final piece of info that had turned up about Matt's mother: both she and her sister, Jill Terhune, had undergone years of psychological counseling when they were younger. He'd been unable to find out why, but the discovery jarred him. Just the thought of Matt being raised by two women who'd required extensive therapeutic counseling raised his hackles.

Cresting the dunes, Travis halted, his concerns thrust aside for the moment. The salty tang of the sea filled his lungs. Gulls screeched overhead, their cries vying with the rhythmic susurration of the waves. For several minutes he didn't move. He simply drank in the panorama of sand and sea, of sunlight glinting on blue water.

Located north of Ocean City, the bed-and-breakfast and a handful of cottages enjoyed a stretch of shorefront relatively free of the crowds that packed the busier tourist spots. He noted a sprinkling of people in the water and knots of sunbathers here and there. In between were mercifully vacant stretches of clean white sand.

He grinned, his mission forgotten for now. Dropping his towel, he flexed his arms, barely aware of the protest of unused muscles from his injured side. A black T-shirt with the sleeves torn off hid the waterproof bandage on his shoulder. Of course, water would likely find its way to the wound, anyway. And ol' Doc Reston would howl if he could see him. But Travis didn't give a damn. He was going for a swim!

TRAVIS WALKED along the beach at an easy pace, enjoying the sun on his body. The swim had felt good, but he'd kept it brief; he was well enough versed in medicine to know how far he should push his body in its present state. He'd take it slow, increasing the exercise by increments. By the time his leave was up, the gunshot wound would be history.

He was several hundred yards down the beach when he spotted the top of a flagpole just beyond the dunes. He'd seen the pole from the road and had carefully noted its location with regard to Mrs. Muncie's. It belonged to Randi Terhune's rental cottage.

Glancing around, he noted even fewer people on this section of beach. Maybe a dozen in all. A pair of family groups with young kids, a couple strolling at the water's edge, holding hands...

Travis went absolutely still. His eyes fastened on a woman in a yellow bikini tossing a beach ball to a small boy in navy trunks: Randi Terhune...and Matt.

They were about twenty-five yards away. Intent on the ball, they hadn't seen him. Travis couldn't take his eyes off them, his gaze moving from mother to son, then back again.

Randi Terhune's lithe sun-kissed body was as elegant as he remembered, and her honey blond hair was already streaked from the sun. Its shining length swung around her lightly tanned shoulders as she moved; now and then the breeze lifted a yard-long tendril that rippled like silk.

Yet lovely though she was, it was the child that claimed Travis's attention in the end. Matt's sturdy body already held evidence of the long-boned height that was as much a McLean trait as the square jaw and springy blond curls. His legs pumped furiously as he went after the ball when a gust of wind carried it away.

"Got it!" the kid crowed as he pounced on the red-and-yellow sphere. He cocked his head to one side and grinned at his mother.

Travis wanted to crow with him. His son. Oh, yeah, most definitely his son. Even the gestures mimicked his own. He had a snapshot of himself at that age, grinning, his head cocked in precisely that manner. His son. A walking talking image of himself in miniature. He swallowed thickly, overcome by an emotion so new he wasn't certain, exactly, what it was, except that his heart seemed to somersault.

"Here y'go, Mom!" Matt's clear soprano carried over the sound of the ocean as he threw the ball to his mother.

Randi made a dash for it as another gust of wind sent it toward the water. She reached the waterline and bent low to scoop it up just as a wave broke. This succeeded in thoroughly drenching her, and Matt laughed at the face she made.

"Good catch, Mom!" Matt was still laughing as he skirted a family group on a blanket and held out his arms. "Okay, put 'er here!"

Travis watched the ball as it was lifted by the wind; it soared high over Matt's head, eluding his outstretched arms by several feet and heading toward Travis's right. Without thinking, Travis twisted, lunged and caught it. When he turned, he found himself looking into a small upturned face.

"Sorry, mister," said the boy.

"No problem, son," Travis returned with a grin.

Belatedly he realized how he'd addressed the child. Recovering quickly, he glanced in Randi's direction and saw her stooping by a colorful beach blanket to get a towel. He chivied backward in the sand. "Here," he said, gaining what he judged to be the right distance. He threw the ball and, sure enough, Matt caught it with ease. Travis watched the boy in proud wonder.

Matt quietly eyed the huge stranger with the friendly face. "My name's Matt," he said shyly.

Travis smiled and stuck out his hand. "Glad to meet you, Matt. Mine's Travis."

Matt stood still for a moment, then shifted the beach ball to one arm and slipped his small hand into his. That hesitant reaction to his outstretched hand made Travis wonder if the kid had ever been shown how to shake hands. Of course, it could just be he was shy, but that sure had looked like astonishment on his face. As if he'd never shaken hands before. Travis felt a ripple of annoyance. Didn't his mother know a boy had to be taught these things?

"Wanna play catch with my mom 'n' me?" Matt asked.

Debating how to answer, Travis stared into the eager face of his son and swallowed around the lump in his throat. He felt that same nameless emotion he'd experienced when he'd heard Matt exclaim triumphantly about capturing the ball.

And he remembered feeling the way Matt looked right now...

Dad, would you play catch with me?

Sorry, Travis, but I'm late for a meeting at the hospital.

But you just got home, Dad!

I know, son, but these things can't be helped. Some other time, okay?

Sure, Dad...

The long-ago conversation faded, and he found himself staring into the poignantly hopeful eyes of Matt Terhune. "Sure thing, Matt," he said, and positioned his hands to receive the ball.

"I can throw far-er than *that*," Matt said scornfully.

"Uh, sorry," Travis said, hiding a grin as he turned and increased the distance between them. "How's this?" he asked as he spun back to the boy—and heard a gasp.

Randi Terhune was standing behind her son now and staring incredulously at Travis. Their eyes locked. A wealth of conflicting emotions passed between them as the parents of Matt Terhune took each other's measure.

Travis was keenly aware of little things as he stood there, caught in the silent tableau: the feel of the sun-warmed ball in his hands, the sound of gulls in the distance, the hue of a woman's eyes echoed in the wild-honey shades of her hair and skin, the scent of clean sweat and sunscreen lotion carried by the breeze.

And the wistful echo of a small boy's voice as the child gazed at him with hopeful eyes. *Wanna play catch with my mom 'n' me?*

God, yes, he wanted to! Wanted to with all the pent-up longing he remembered from his own childhood. A childhood that had left him perpetually hungry for a father's love. For the father who was there, but not there. Who was too busy being a famous surgeon to remember he had a son who needed him.

Yes, he wanted to, but the unreadable look in Randi Terhune's eyes stopped him. What was she thinking? he wondered. What should he say to her? That is, if he ought to say anything at all. The eyes she speared him with seemed as hard and brittle as the amber they resembled.

Randi made her face into a mask, hoping he couldn't read the fear in her eyes. She was scared to death. Why had Travis McLean suddenly turned up here? There was no way it was a coincidence, so what did he want? Had he recognized her, after all? Put two and two together and come to stake a claim on Matt? *God, please, no...*

Matt suddenly noticed her behind him. "Hey, Mom!" He turned and grinned at her, then indicated the man across from them. "This is my friend Travis." There was a note of proud ownership in his voice. "He's gonna play catch with us." He glanced at Travis, again with that hopeful look that turned Travis's insides to mush. "Uh, y'will, won'tcha Travis?"

"I'm sorry, honey," Randi said hurriedly, "but there's no time. We need to go in and change for supper."

"But, Mom, it's still sunshiny out!"

Randi hunkered down, meeting him at eye level. "I know, sweetheart," she said gently, brushing a lock of hair out of his eyes. "That's because it doesn't get dark until late now. But you'll need a bath and time to change. We're going to a restaurant to eat tonight, remember?"

"Yeah," Matt mumbled, staring at his toes. The reply was as downhearted and reluctant a sound as Travis had ever heard.

"Now, thank the man for catching your ball and say goodbye," Randi prompted.

"He's not 'the man,'" Matt muttered. "He's my friend Travis."

Randi gritted her teeth and sent McLean a fulminating look. "Travis, then," she said as she stood and urged Matt in the direction of the beach ball Travis proffered.

"Thanks, Travis," Matt murmured unhappily. "I gotta go," he added as if the blond giant hadn't heard every word of the exchange with his mother.

"Maybe another time, Matt," Travis returned with a smile he wasn't feeling. The kid's disappointment was almost palpable.

A flare of hope entered the child's eyes. "Are you stayin' here, too?" he asked, gesturing up the beach.

"Matthew..." Randi said warningly, effectively cutting off Travis's reply.

"Bye, Travis," Matt said with a forlorn sigh.

"Bye," Travis said with a regretful smile.

The boy turned reluctantly and trudged toward the cottage.

Randi called to him to say she'd be along in a minute. Both adults were silent until Matt was beyond hearing, then Randi turned to Travis, eyes snapping. "Matt isn't allowed to talk to strangers, mister—and you're a stranger!"

"The hell I am!" Travis countered hotly. "You and I have met more than once, *Miz* Terhune—and that's my *son!*"

Randi blanched, too stricken to deny it; taking her reaction as the ultimate confirmation, Travis felt a surge of satisfaction.

"Mr. McLean," she asked in a almost desperate whisper, "why are you here?"

Seeing the trapped look in her eyes, Travis immediately softened. "I don't mean you or Matt any harm, if that's what you're thinkin'."

Skepticism was written all over her. There was simply no way she could put a benign face on McLean's appearance. Especially since he seemed well armed with the knowledge that Matt was his biological offspring.

"No?" she challenged, resisting the urge to bolt and run. To grab Matt and run with him, run so far McLean would never find them.

Travis heaved a sigh, aware that this was a poor time to discuss it; Matt was halfway to their cottage by now, and he didn't like to think of the kid there alone, even for a few minutes. "Look," he said, "this isn't the time or place. But I'm stayin' nearby. If you'll agree to meet with me— without Matt in tow, naturally—I'll tell you what this is all about. Would that be agreeable?"

Randi was silent while she pondered this. She found herself staring at his black T-shirt; with the sleeves ripped off, it revealed powerful biceps. In fact, everything about him was powerful; she resisted the urge to step back a pace. Travis McLean was accustomed to getting what he wanted.

Their encounter at the hospital had told her that much. He was as relentless as a jungle cat stalking its prey.

And she was the prey.

Quelling a shudder, she tried to think rationally. She needed to learn what he wanted. The sooner she knew, the sooner she could muster her defenses. You were only a victim if you allowed it, she told herself, and she'd be damned if she'd ever let it happen—she nearly added *again*, but cut off the thought. The past was dead, damn it!

Though she wasn't thrilled to make use of the bonded sitter the rental agency had recommended, she had a feeling they'd better have this talk. "Okay, McLean, when and where?"

Travis grinned at her. "It's Travis, remember?"

Randi ignored him—or tried to; when he grinned like that, those deep grooves in his cheeks did something strange to her insides.

"There's an out-of-the-way oyster bar off Route 13, not too far from here," she said, feeling better by taking the initiative. "It's called Ollie's. The setup's conducive to talking privately. I suppose we could meet there."

"Done," Travis said, "and I'll buy you lunch. One o'clock okay?"

Randi hesitated, then nodded. "I'll see you there, then." She turned to go.

"Oh, Randi?" he called after her. He saw her freeze, as if the sound of her nickname had been unexpected. She turned toward him.

"Just wanted you to know," he told her, "my aim isn't to threaten you, honey. Don't lose any sleep over it, huh?"

Looking vexed—he couldn't decide if it was because of his "honey" or her sheer disbelief—she uttered an irritated huff and stalked off.

Probably both, he decided as he watched her go. Not that he blamed her. But he really did have nonthreatening motives, he told himself, and he had every confidence he'd make them clear to her tomorrow.

Of course, he mused as he went to retrieve his towel, first he had to figure out what they were.

CHAPTER EIGHT

"WHY, *WHY* DID I AGREE to this?" Randi muttered as she drove along Route 13 toward Ollie's. It wasn't the first time she'd asked herself the question. She'd tossed and turned half the night with it. In fact, she'd regretted the lunch date with McLean minutes after she'd made it.

"Hah!" she groused in self-disgust. "The minute you escaped his indecently handsome presence, you mean!"

Yet she knew her reasons for accepting were far more complex. His reassuring words aside, she could think of nothing about Travis McLean's sudden appearance that boded well for her and Matt. As far as she was concerned, he was the enemy, and enemies had to be faced and fought, or...

Unable to complete the thought, Randi quelled a shiver that had nothing to do with the Cherokee's air-conditioning.

Minutes later she pulled into the oyster bar's parking lot. A glance at the dashboard clock told her it was several minutes to one. Good. Maybe he hadn't arrived yet; she'd have the advantage of being calmly in place before he did. She needed every advantage she could get.

The day was slightly overcast, hot and humid. She nearly gasped when she climbed out of the Jeep and the thick air hit her like a wall. The tables on the deck were empty, yet the number of cars in the lot indicated a good lunchtime crowd; obviously everybody was inside. At least she'd chosen a place with air-conditioning.

The thought made her grab the gauze shirt-jacket that

matched her khakis. She locked the Cherokee and made for the entrance. She already felt moisture gathering at the waist of the melon knit shell she'd tucked into the khakis, and at the nape of her neck her long French braid felt damp and heavy. She hurried toward the tinted glass doors; as she approached, one swung wide.

"You're early I see." Travis's smile as he held the door for her was exactly like Matt's.

She swallowed nervously and mustered a return smile. "Is that a problem?"

"Hell, no, sugar." He caught the hostess's eye and waited for Randi to precede him as they followed the woman. "I made the reservation for twelve-thirty," he added from somewhere just over her right shoulder.

She halted and turned toward him, taken aback; she quickly raised the shirt-jacket to her shoulders to cover her reaction. Damn him. He already had her off balance. "But why? Didn't we agree on one o'clock?"

In a movement smooth as silk, he assisted her, settling the khaki gauze carefully on her shoulders. She tried to ignore the tingle where his fingers grazed bare skin. Touching a hand lightly to her back, he guided her forward, grinning down at her. "Rule number sixteen," he said.

"Rule number..." she murmured. "Of what?"

He chuckled as they reached a quiet corner table where a half-full glass of white wine indicated he'd been served while waiting. "Of the Southern Gentleman's Rules to Live By," he drawled as he seated her.

"I see," Randi said as he took his seat across from her. "And what does rule number sixteen say?"

Travis gave the hostess a dazzling smile of thanks as she handed them menus. Then he turned the full power of his vivid blue gaze on Randi and grinned mischievously; both the eyes and the grin reminded her of Matt.

"Rule number sixteen? Well, accordin' to my mama, a gentleman not only never keeps a lady waitin', he tries to

see no one else does, either. So while they kept *me* waitin'
twenty minutes for this table, you, ma'am, haven't had to
wait at all.'' He winked at her. "Smart woman, my mama."

Not half as smart as her son, I'll bet. Burying her nose
in the menu, Randi decided to stop wondering how he'd
known just when to leave his glass of wine and be waiting
at the door at precisely the moment she arrived. He had her
utterly discomposed as it was.

A waitress who announced her name was Sally Ann,
took their orders, including a white-wine spritzer for Randi.
Travis declined a second drink, raising what remained of
his wine to propose a toast when Randi's arrived.

"To you, pretty lady, and that fine boy you've raised.
May this vacation be all you've wanted it to be—and
more."

Randi eyed him steadily, despite her irritation. The vacation was already far more than she wanted it to be! "May
it be all we wanted it to be," she echoed. *And the "more"
can go to hell.* She smiled smugly at him and took a sip.

"So, where's the little tiger now?" he asked casually.

"I left him at the cottage with a sitter. But I imagine
she's taken him to the beach, even though it's overcast.
Matt loves the water."

"A sitter, huh?" He realized he'd been the one to suggest meeting without Matt in attendance, but he suddenly
found himself worrying; from what he'd read, you couldn't
be too careful about sitters these days. "Someone you've
used before?"

"No, but I did speak at length with Mrs. Lake after I
contacted the agency. She's an old sweetie."

Travis lowered his wineglass and eyed her sharply. "An
old sweetie? Just how old?" He had disturbing images of
a tottering senior citizen, too decrepit to monitor his son,
especially near water.

Randi set her glass down abruptly and met his gaze. "I
have no idea how old she is. I do know, however, that she

comes highly recommended by the agency and has excellent references.''

She felt her irritation rising. It had been difficult enough for her to use an unknown sitter, but Mrs. Lake's references were impeccable, Matt had taken to her right away, and Randi had felt the situation warranted using a sitter; she certainly hadn't been about to involve Matt in this meeting. And besides, what business was it of McLean's anyway?

''You checked the references?'' Travis questioned, then noted the warning glitter in Randi's eyes and sought to soften his query. ''I mean, you can't be too careful with kids around water. I s'pose you asked if the old sweetie can swim?''

''As a matter of fact, Mr. McLean, she happens to have a certificate in life-saving from the Red Cross.'' She ground this out between clenched teeth.

''Whoa, there, sugar!'' He held up his hands as if to ward her off. ''I was just wonderin' how one goes about these things. Findin' a reliable sitter, I mean.''

He gave his head a doubtful shake. ''I reckon it can't be easy. You don't have a problem with hirin' unknown help?''

''No,'' Randi said, throwing down her napkin, ''but I do have a problem with *you*.'' Rising swiftly, she grabbed her purse and narrowed her eyes at him. ''Mr. McLean, I agreed to meet with you today as a courtesy. *Not* as a candidate for the third degree! Thank you for the drink,'' she added in clipped syllables, and turned to leave.

''Randi, wait.'' Travis cursed himself for his clumsy handling of the situation as he rose to stay her with a hand on her arm. What the hell was wrong with him? ''I apologize...truly,'' he added when she didn't budge an inch.

A rueful boyish smile accompanied the gaze that zeroed in on hers. ''Please don't leave. I was bein' ungracious in the extreme, and I'm sorry. If I promise to explain——uh, not excuse myself, mind, but just explain where I was comin' from—will you stay 'n' hear me out?''

She heaved a sigh. When he looked at her like that, she suspected there wasn't a woman alive who'd deny him anything. Herself included, she thought with annoyance. With a stiff nod, she sank back onto the chair he adroitly held for her.

''It'd better be good,'' she warned as he resumed sitting with that same boyish smile in place.

Good? he thought. There was little that was good, exactly, or that he was proud of, in what he was about to tell her. Still, he'd determined it was necessary if he was ever going to get her to trust him. He'd made up his mind to it last night, as he'd tried to sort out what it was he wanted in this bizarre situation involving the child they'd brought into the world.

Having discovered Matt's existence, he knew it was impossible to go back. No way could he imagine his life now without the kid's presence. He wasn't sure yet what form that presence would take, but he desperately wanted to forge some kind of a link between himself and his son. But to do that, he needed Randi's cooperation. And trust. It all came down to trust.

And so, without stopping to second-guess his decision, Travis found himself revealing more about himself than he'd ever told anyone. He told her first about the night he'd foolishly accepted the dare. And then about the doubt. The stabs of guilt over helping to bring into the world a child he wouldn't be around to parent. And finally, in halting tones, of the less-than-satisfactory relationship with his own father. The father who was never there for him as a child, not physically, not emotionally.

Randi was silent as she heard him out, but she found herself caught in a range of emotions she hadn't been prepared to feel: surprise, at his candor over the incident that prompted his sperm donation; amazement tinged with chagrin, at his decision to leave medicine after most of the grueling preparation was behind him; and sympathy, for the child he'd been, whose father had never participated in his life.

This last, especially, pulled at her. Her own father had been a warm, loving presence in his daughters' lives before he died. How many times had she heard Jill say it was her memory of Daddy, more than any other single force, that had helped her past the abuse she'd suffered? Past what could have been a terror of all men.

Daddy, with his strong arms and ready laughter. She could still see him, reading bedtime stories to Jill and her on the nights Mom was too tired, hugging her seven-year-old self after a spill from her bike—and patiently mending the gash in the tire that had caused it. Daddy, who had always been there, cheering his daughters on at girls' midget softball, taking them to the movies on rainy Saturday afternoons, teasing Randi out of "the grumps," as he'd called them, when she'd had the measles and couldn't go on a class trip....

Lord in heaven, what would her childhood have been like without him? But she had her answer: like what Travis was describing now.

"'Course Mother was properly thrilled for me when we won that squash trophy," Travis was saying. "But it wasn't the same. Not as it would've been if *he'd* been there. Squash was my father's game. Mother, bless her, didn't understand the rules. But her husband wasn't even in the country when I helped the team come from behind and win that tournament. He was in France deliverin' a speech I later learned he could've arranged to deliver earlier in that week-long conference. But instead, he'd— Ah, hell."

He looked up from the coffee he hadn't touched and met Randi's eyes. "Sorry. Guess I've been ramblin'. You're likely bored to tears," he added with a wry grin.

Randi's face was solemn. "No," she said softly. "No, I'm not. Please...go on."

Travis shrugged. "There really isn't much more to tell." He paused reflectively, then leaned forward, holding her gaze. "'Cept this. I haven't told you these things to win your sympathy or, God forbid, your pity. I quit feelin' sorry for myself long before I learned how to shave, Randi. And I won't countenance that feelin' in others.

"But I do know this," he went on. "My childhood is one reason I made up my mind to be actively involved in the parentin' of my own children someday. Actively involved, Randi, in the life of *any* child I might have..."

Randi gasped as the implication hit. Before she could speak, Travis grasped the hand she rested on the table and rushed on.

"Randi, try to understand. The shock and confusion I felt on seein' Matt and then realizin' who he is..." He met her gaze squarely, adding in a soft voice, "And he *is* my son, isn't he? You haven't denied it, but I'd sure appreciate it if we could be honest with each other—please? I swear, I mean y'all no harm. God as my witness, I'd cut off my arm before I allowed anythin' to harm either of you."

Maybe it was the sincerity in his voice. Or the way he squeezed her hand and looked at her with that unselfconscious plea that was so like Matt's. Or maybe it was just that she was tired of avoiding the truth with him, tired of trying to pretend. With a soft sigh, she closed her eyes and nodded.

Travis released her hand along with the breath he'd been holding. "Thanks for that. I 'spect it couldn't've been easy."

She tried to smile, but couldn't quite bring it off; for all she knew, that admission might have been the greatest mistake of her life. "Uh, you were saying?" she prompted.

"Yeah—'bout the way it was when I first laid eyes on the kid." He plowed a hand through his hair. "Well, shock and confusion don't half describe it. It was disturbin' enough to *imagine* a child I'd fathered out there in the world somewhere and me not around to nurture and…and love him. But think, Randi, how much more difficult it was to suddenly come across him in the flesh.''

Randi swallowed and nodded. She *did* see. For the first time since this entire frightening episode had begun. For the first time she was able to place herself in Travis McLean's shoes. And in a way she wished this weren't so. Suddenly a situation that had been alarming, but clear-cut where she was concerned, had taken on a complexity she wasn't certain she could deal with.

''One minute I was gazin' out my hospital window,'' Travis was saying, ''and the next—there he was! The spittin' image of me as a kid! I tell you, lady, it was unnervin'. But after I picked myself up off the floor—''

''You started putting a few things together,'' Randi interjected, knowing that was what she'd have done.

Travis grinned. ''Yeah. First, there was this feelin' I'd had, way back in the emergency room, that I'd met you before.'' His eyes ran over her, the gleam in them appreciative. ''Your hair was shorter then, but I'm unlikely to forget a pretty face, much less a beautiful one— Don't you dare duck your head! You're a beautiful woman, Randi Terhune, and I call 'em like I see 'em.''

After a moment he went on, ''Anyhow, it'd already dawned on me where I'd seen you before. Took me a while, but the image finally fell into place—just before I saw you 'n' Matt together, by the way. After that, I asked a few questions here 'n' there…''

''At the hospital, you mean,'' she said with a note of disapproval.

Travis's sheepish grin was disarming. ''Yeah,'' he said, ''but don't go gettin' all huffy on me, huh? C'mon, admit it. You'd've done the same.''

She gave a noncommittal shrug, then a thought struck.

"But the staff at Johns Hopkins wouldn't have been able to tell you where I'd gone on vacation. How'd you learn that?"

Travis heaved a sigh. He leaned back in his chair, folded his arms across his chest and studied her. He had a strong feeling she wasn't going to like this. Still, in for a dime, in for a dollar. He'd determined to be honest with her; he might as well be completely honest.

Still, it was easier said than done. Despite her calm of the moment, Randi reminded him of a skittish filly. As if, with one wrong word from him, she'd bolt and run—as, in fact, she almost had. He'd sensed an odd sort of vulnerability in her from the beginning. He'd felt it, lying just beneath the surface of that professional facade, and wondered what was behind it. There were those years of therapeutic counseling she'd had....

Well, he'd make it his business to find out more about that. Meanwhile he had some owning up to do. "You'll recall my mentionin' I went into government service when I left medicine?"

She nodded warily.

"Well, in my line of work, I have, uh, access, shall we say, to some computer data banks, and—"

"Data banks? You mean computerized files like— Are you with the IRS or something?" She was familiar with the Internal Revenue Service's use of such files. What taxpayer wasn't? Just the thought of his having access to everything from her social security number to the amount of her net earnings got her dander up. Weren't they supposed to be confidential? Limited to use in tax matters?

Travis was looking more sheepish than ever. "Uh, not the IRS..."

"Well, what exactly?"

"Uh, the CIA."

"The...the Central Intelligence Agency?" She looked incredulous.

He shrugged. "'Fraid so, sugar."

"Oh...my...God," she breathed as several things fell into place. The gunshot wound, the VIP treatment from Bethesda and Johns Hopkins, helicopter and all. Even his cavalier attitude toward the wound. As if such things were commonplace with him—which they probably were! "Y-you mean spying and...and all that?" she asked in an unsteady voice.

Another shrug. "These days, not so much. Matter of fact, it's mostly a desk job."

"Desk job! No desk job got you your shoulder shot up!" She eyed the injured shoulder, now covered by a blue knit sport shirt, and there was no indication that anything was amiss. She felt embarrassed; as a professional, she should have at least asked how it was. But she'd been too shocked when she first saw him on the beach yesterday, and—good God!—he'd been swimming! And tossing a ball! What was he, some kind of superhero or something? *No,* a small inner voice reminded. *Just your routine, average, superspy tough guy. God in heaven—the CIA!*

"Um...how's your shoulder?" she managed, despite the unnerving thoughts swirling in her head. It was too much to think about right now. Maybe later.

"You should have that arm immobilized," she added in her best professional voice. "Where's your sling?"

His slow grin was pure devilry. "Is that concern I hear, sugar?"

"This 'sugar' is a nurse, McLean," she managed over the ragged rhythm of her pulse. Lord, how was she supposed to sound professionally detached when he grinned like that?

He chuckled softly. He loved to watch the color of those eyes deepen, when he teased her, to that unique shade that reminded him of wild honey. "The shoulder's fine," he told her. "Relax, sugar. I have a degree from Harvard says I oughtta know what I'm talkin' 'bout."

Sally Ann arrived, asking if they'd care to order anything else. Randi shook her head, and Travis asked for the check. Minutes later they were out the door.

"Looks like it's coolin' off some," Travis observed as he escorted her to the Jeep. An offshore breeze had swept away the humidity, and patches of blue sky were visible in the east.

His comment was just small talk while he tried to think of a way to steer their conversation back to meaningful ground. She seemed more comfortable with him, but she was still wary. He needed to get beyond that. More importantly, he needed to engineer some time with his son.

"Look, Randi," he said as she took her keys from her purse, "I sure do 'preciate the time you've given me." He took the keys from her and unlocked the car door, then caught her hand; placing the keys in her palm, he sandwiched it between his. "But I think you know we haven't half covered everythin'. How 'bout a repeat, say, dinner tomorrow night?"

She tried to ignore the way she felt as her hand was enveloped by his. The way her heart beat an irregular tattoo with the sense this imparted of his masculine strength—a strength that was somehow gentle. Utterly nonthreatening, despite his size. He had long graceful fingers, she noted, their backs dusted with tiny hairs bleached white against the tan of his skin.

"Haven't—" She had to clear her throat, start again. "Haven't covered everything?" she asked, withdrawing her hand and the keys. She already regretted her admission of Matt's parentage. Travis had sworn he meant no harm, but his idea of harm and hers might be two entirely different things. "What, for instance?"

"Have dinner with me tomorrow night 'n' I'll tell you."

"I—I'm sorry, but I have plans." Jill and David were coming tomorrow night to fetch Matt and take him to Disney World. She was suddenly glad she'd let Jill talk her into it. Matt would soon be hundreds of miles away from Travis—and whatever he had in mind.

She explained about the visit to Disney World, hoping he'd see the futility of hanging around. Hoping he'd give up.

If he was disconcerted, he didn't show it. "Okay, then how 'bout a picnic on the beach tomorrow?"

Tomorrow? On the beach? But that would mean Matt...

As if he'd read her thoughts, he said, "I know—Matt'll be there. Look, Randi." His voice gentled, becoming a softspoken plea. "I'm not an ogre. I'm just a man. A man who's hopin' to be allowed some time to observe, close up, the child he didn't even know he had till just days ago. And that's all I'm askin' for—a chance to spend some harmless time with the boy. Please?"

It sounded so simple, yet she knew it had to involve more than that. "What else, Travis?" she asked carefully. "What about those 'things we haven't half covered'?"

He sighed, wanting to save it for a place better suited to serious talk than a parking lot. But there was one burning question that had been plaguing him. Not only through lunch, but since the beginning. Before he had time to think better of it, he found himself blurting it out.

"Well, for starters, there's the fact that Matt doesn't have a— Forgive me, Randi, but I've gotta ask. Why would an attractive woman like you choose single parenthood? Why decide to bring a kid into the world with no man—no husband, hell, *no father*—to help raise him?"

He knew it was a mistake the moment the question was out. He sensed her withdrawal. A yawning chasm suddenly grew between them, far greater than the small backward step she took.

"Mr. McLean," she said icily, "there are some questions I may be willing to answer, given your honesty so far and your need for certain…reassurances. But there is one question I won't allow. Never, *never* ask me about my decision to do it alone. I absolutely won't discuss it.''

CHAPTER NINE

RESISTING AN URGE to slam the refrigerator door, Randi carried a jug of lemonade to the table. With a glance at Matt, she also refrained from banging the jug down, instead setting it quietly beside the pile of fried chicken she'd made last night. Banging it, she told herself, probably wouldn't vent enough steam, anyway.

Already dressed for the beach and oblivious to his mother's pique, Matt was busily pushing his last Cheerio across the milk in his bowl with a spoon. Thoroughly engrossed, he made serious motorboat noises in his throat as the lone Cheerio sped around a curve. Randi smiled, momentarily forgetting her annoyance with herself.

And with Travis McLean.

Telling Matt he could finish packing the cooler if he was careful, Randi stalked to her bedroom, her thoughts of McLean no less charitable than when she'd risen—early—to make the miserable lemonade. From scratch, no less!

"Face it, Terhune," she muttered as she removed her robe and flung it on the bed. "Where that man is concerned, you're a spineless jellyfish!"

The bald fact was, Travis had somehow managed to talk her into that picnic on the beach today. She still wasn't sure how it happened. But the man had a way about him, and he'd used it to get past her defenses. By the time she left Ollie's yesterday, she'd even offered to bring the picnic lunch. *Offered!* She must be losing her mind. But it had seemed reasonable at the time, what with him treating at Ollie's.

That was just the trouble, she thought as she discarded her pajamas and stepped into the shower. He made everything seem so reasonable. Had she really accepted his revelations about working for the CIA so readily? A desk job, he'd called it. Hah!

And yet she'd meekly decided to shelve her questions until later. Of course, as she'd reviewed everything while lying—sleepless for a good two hours—in bed last night, she'd determined such inquiries moot. After today she'd be rid of Travis McLean, so what he did for a living was immaterial.

But then there was that promise he'd made. That he wouldn't let a hint of his connection to Matt touch her son when he saw him today. That had seemed reasonable, too. At the time.

Only, as she'd lain awake last night, the doubts had crept in. What if Matt picked up vibes, as children often do, of something more than casual in their meeting? Travis had suggested he'd simply "bump into" Matt and her again, as he'd done the other day. But Matt was an observant child. So even if McLean pulled it off—which he might; weren't intelligence men trained in subterfuge?—*she* might not. Matt knew her far better than McLean, after all.

She heaved a sigh as she stepped from the shower and reached for a towel. Wrapping it about her hair like a turban, she grabbed another and absently dried herself as more doubts crowded her mind.

Her worst fear was that Travis wouldn't be content with this single day with Matt. What if he began to demand more time with him? Didn't he say he wanted to be actively involved in the parenting of *any* children he had?

His description of his relationship with his own father, she had to admit, was a persuasive argument for Travis's point of view. His story had moved her, and she appreciated

his honesty and his openness in sharing it with her. But
that didn't mean she was responsible for accommodating
him. She had Matt to think about.

But Matt's begun to notice families with fathers, a small
voice niggled, *and you can't deny the looks of longing
you've seen on your son's face when he does. Not to mention his fascination with McLean during that brief encounter on the beach. Remember? He talked about his "friend
Travis" all through supper!*

With a huff of exasperation, Randi flung her towel over
the bar, refusing to give ear to her traitorous thoughts for
one more second. Travis had elected to be a *biological*
parent, nothing more. So he'd just have to live with the
consequences. Huh, ten days ago, he didn't even know Matt
existed! Why should she let him upset their well-ordered
lives because of a chance encounter? He had no right!

Ripping the towel off her head, she grabbed her comb
and turned to the mirror. It was fogged, so she wrapped the
towel around her like a sarong and opened the door a crack
to let the steam out. She could hear Matt's sweet boyish
soprano from the kitchen. He was again singing the Barney
song...about love and a happy family.

Closing her eyes, she swallowed around the lump that
had formed in her throat. *Dear God, I love him so! Please
help me do what's right by him. If I ever let him down,
even unintentionally, I couldn't bear—*

"Hey, Mom," Matt called from the kitchen, "the cooler's all packed! Can we go now?"

"In a few minutes, honey. Why don't you collect your
beach toys from your room while I finish up, okay?"

Hearing her son's cheerful affirmative, Randi made a
special effort to dispel her doubtful musings. Matt was such
a positive upbeat child. The least she could do today was
dredge up some cheer on her part. This was their vacation,
after all. Their long-awaited hunk of quality time together.
And tonight Jill and David would be coming to pick Matt

up for the Disney World trip. She owed it to her son to make this last day special, McLean or no McLean!

She quickly blew her hair dry, then reached for the yellow bikini hanging on a peg behind the door—and stopped. Did she really want to wear Jill's skimpy selection from Victoria's Secret today? With Travis McLean and his thousand-megawatt masculinity within sizzling distance?

She was all too keenly aware she wasn't blind to the man's devastating looks or the sexuality he exuded. For the first time in her life, she knew what people meant when they spoke of chemistry between male and female. Yet that kind of attraction to a male was the last thing she wanted in her life. She had no intention of disturbing the carefully wrought peace she'd fashioned for herself.

With a decisive nod, she headed for the chest of drawers in the bedroom. Good thing she'd packed that modest one-piece, despite Jill's objections!

"MOM, LOOK—it's Travis!" Matt dropped his pail and shovel beside the blanket and waved at the figure who'd just appeared on the beach. Grinning, he started off in Travis's direction. Suddenly he halted, pivoting toward his mother, who'd made a quiet but firm point about not talking to strangers when they'd come in from the beach two days before. "Can I go talk to him, Mom?" he asked anxiously. "He's not a stranger anymore, is he?"

"No, honey, I guess he's not, but—"

"Thanks, Mom!" With a whoop, Matt bounded off, making a beeline for the man, who'd paused to watch the boy, a broad smile on his face.

Randi chuckled, although she still had reservations about the wisdom of this "chance" encounter. Matt was full of energy as usual, but fairly jumping with excitement today. Despite the fact that Jill had called to say, just as she and Matt were about to head out the door for the picnic, that she and David would be delayed a day and would come for Matt late the next afternoon. Something about a last-minute snafu with a worried client at David's firm.

But it didn't matter because neither sister had told Matt about the Disney World trip yet. It had long been a policy between the sisters not to raise the child's expectations too far in advance of a treat—just in case something happened and plans had to be abandoned. But on the phone they'd decided it was now safe to tell him. As Jill had put it, "Come hell or high water, that nephew of mine's gonna meet the big mouse this weekend, no matter what!"

Matt had gone wide-eyed with astonishment at the news. He'd danced around the kitchen table, singing the Mickey Mouse song Randi and he had learned from television reruns of the "Mickey Mouse Club" recently. Randi had promptly decided "M-I-C...K-E-Y" was a welcome change from the Barney song.

"Mom, here's Travis," Matt announced importantly as the pair approached the blanket. "An' look—his swimsuit's just like mine!"

Randi did look—and had to swallow as some nameless emotion threatened. It wasn't just that they were wearing similar navy trunks, although that added to the impact. Standing side by side, her son and his father were so clearly father and son a person would have to be blind not to see it.

The sun had lightened their blond hair in precisely the same fashion. Identically thick unruly locks shot with flaxen strands, she thought with a painful tightening of her throat. And twin pairs of blue eyes crinkled at the corners in just the same way as they both grinned at her, revealing identical sets of dimples. *Oh, God, this was a mistake. I never should have agreed. Never!*

"Hi, Ms. Terhune. Pleasure meetin' y'all here again." Travis's voice cut across her regret with resonant charm. Her own voice held only the slight Southern inflection common to the D.C. area; his suggested lazy afternoons on shady verandas, indolent strolls along sun-dappled paths lined with live oaks dripping Spanish moss.

Randi could only nod, not trusting her voice as she stared up at him. She had to bend her head back to do so, and that big muscular body seemed to go on forever, towering against the sky. Perhaps, she thought, it was simply her disadvantage of being seated while he stood. Unfortunately this did nothing to calm her hammering pulse.

Matt giggled. "You called her Miz Terhune." He turned to his mother. "But she's Randi most all the time, aren't you, Mom?"

"Well," she began, grateful for the distraction as her gaze swung to her son, "I think—"

"Aunt Jill always calls you Randi, right, Mom?" Matt grinned at her, crinkling blue eyes swinging merrily to Travis, then back again.

The imp! she thought. *He's making sure we're on a first-name basis. Travis and I. That we're not…strangers.*

She chuckled as she met her son's not-quite-guileless gaze, feeling her tension melt away. "Randi, it is," she agreed. She gestured at Travis and the thick rolled-up towel he carried, then at their blanket. "Won't you join us, uh, Travis?"

"Thought you'd never ask," Travis murmured just for Randi's ears as Matt let out a whoop of approval. His wink was also for her alone as he hunkered down beside her to spread out his towel; Matt was busy exclaiming over the football that had dropped on the sand when the towel was unrolled.

"Wanna throw some passes, Travis?" Matt chirped eagerly. He was trying to position the ball high above his shoulder, just as he'd seen on television. "Can we? You 'n' me?"

"Sure can, Tiger." Travis adjusted the four-year-old's small fingers for a better grip on the pigskin, helping him mime a pass. "That's the stuff," he said approvingly, then ruffled his son's curls, grinning down at him. "But how 'bout we get wet first? That water looks mighty invitin'."

"Yeah!' Matt exclaimed. The football fell to the sand, forgotten, and he seized Travis's hand. Without a trace of self-consciousness, Randi noted, as if he'd been doing it all his life. "C'mon!" he said with a tug.

"Whoa, there, Tiger," Travis said with a chuckle. He glanced at Randi. "Could be your mom wants to join us."

"Yeah, Mom! You said you'd go in when the sun got all hotted up." Matt squinted at the sky. "Sure is hotted up now—" his glance fell on the man beside him "—right, Travis?"

Randi laughed, trying not to mind the way her son turned to Travis for approval. "Okay," she managed cheerfully, and McLean extended his free hand, pulling her to her feet. As if she weighed nothing at all, she couldn't help noticing.

Just as she couldn't help noticing the way his eyes moved admiringly over her long-limbed figure in the pale green swimsuit. Her gaze skittering away from his, she quickly released his hand and shouted, "Let's go!"

The three of them ran toward the water, Matt's joyous laughter bringing smiles to the faces of the dozen or so others on the beach.

"MOM MAKES the bestest picnic in the whole world!" Matt exclaimed a few hours later. He was opening the cooler as he sat on the blanket between the two adults. Two adults who, if not utterly exhausted, were giving a pretty good imitation of it.

"I bet she does." Travis slanted a glance at Randi. Flopped on her back, she had her eyes closed and was panting as hard as he was. "Y'know," he told her as Matt began to pull things from the cooler, "I read somewhere that little kids can run circles around adults."

"Huh, tell me about it," she replied, remembering the three hours of wave hopping, serious swimming and touch football they'd just shared with a four-year-old who wasn't even out of breath.

"The article said—" Travis paused as Matt handed him a flattened foil-wrapped parcel "—that some folks once ran a study to prove it."

"Do tell," Randi put in with as much enthusiasm as she could muster. Which wasn't much, given the urge she felt to sleep for ten hours right there on the beach.

"Yup," he went on as Matt handed a similar squashed parcel to his mother. "They asked Jim Thorpe, regarded by many as the greatest athlete of all time, to match the actions of a baby, move for move, to see how they compared."

"What happened?" Matt asked, suddenly interested.

Travis chuckled. "Believe it was only a couple hours till ol' Jim gave up—worn to a frazzle."

"Yeah?" Matt asked. "An' what about the baby?"

Travis chuckled again and affectionately ruffled his son's hair. "The baby, Tiger, was still goin' strong."

"I believe it," Randi muttered as she pushed herself to a sitting position to help Matt pour lemonade into a paper cup.

"Here, let me do that." Travis took the heavy jug from her. "It's the least I can do after y'all went to so much trouble."

"Mom got up *real* early to make this," Matt said as he accepted his lemonade.

"Did she now?" Travis noted the sudden blush beneath Randi's tan.

"Yep," Matt said, "but she made the chicken 'n' stuff last night." He began unwrapping one of the flattened pieces he'd buried under the jug of lemonade when he'd packed the cooler. "I helped, too." He glanced at his mother. "Um, a little bit."

"Let me guess." Travis grinned as he eyed his squashed chicken breast. "You packed the cooler, right?"

"Wow!" Matt exclaimed, regarding him with wonder. He waved a mangled drumstick toward their guest, not noticing Randi's smothered giggle. "You're a awful good guesser!"

"Nah," Travis said with a shrug, "just lucky."

"I'm lucky, too," Matt mumbled around a mouthful of chicken.

"Mind what I said about not talking with your mouth full, young man," Randi admonished.

"Lucky, huh?" Travis prompted as if she hadn't spoken, then caught the reproving glance she darted at him. "Uh, you can tell me 'bout it soon's you finish swallowin', okay?"

Father and son threw identical sheepish grins at her. Sheepish, yet boyishly charming, and Randi felt something twist and curl around the defenses she'd erected. She forced herself to look away. *I won't be drawn into this. I won't! Just a few more hours, and he'll be gone. A few short hours, and things can go back to—*

"I'm lucky," Matt announced excitedly, his mouthful of chicken dutifully swallowed, "'cause Aunt Jill 'n' Uncle David're gonna take me to Disney World!"

"All right!" Travis exclaimed as if learning this for the first time. "You sure *are* lucky, Tiger. When are you goin'?"

"Tomorrow, right, Mom?" Matt said, as Travis cast her a questioning look.

Randi damned her luck. She'd hoped the subject of the Disney trip wouldn't come up. Or at least the specifics of when Jill and David were arriving. Now McLean would learn of the postponement, and she had a hunch he wouldn't hesitate to take advantage of it. Well, she'd just have to stand firm and not let him.

"Mom?" Matt prompted.

"Yes, sweetheart," she made herself say with a smile. "Tomorrow."

Travis still looked questioningly at her while Matt nodded happily and rummaged for more chicken. She murmured quietly to McLean, "Last-minute change of plans."

"No kiddin'," he murmured back, a light slowly dawning in his eyes. His conclusion was all too evident in the satisfied smile he gave her: the change of plans afforded him another day with Matt. "Well, fancy that. Reckon Matt's not the only lucky—"

"Now, wait a minute..." she began warningly.

Ignoring her, he turned to Matt. "Ever gone crabin', Tiger?"

"Crabbin'?" Matt was clearly intrigued, and neither he nor his father caught Randi's frown. Not only had McLean bulldozed right past her intent with regard to tomorrow, but Matt's inflection had assumed the lazy sound of Travis's Tidewater drawl. *Damn the man!*

"Is crabbin' like fishin', but with crabs?" Matt went on excitedly.

Travis's laugh rang with delight. The kid was not only normal, he was sharp as the proverbial tack. "Sure is," he told the boy, "and it so happens, I was plannin' to try my hand at it tomorrow. 'Course, I might need some help..."

As he let his words trail off seductively, he grinned into the widening eyes of his son. *His son!* Lord, it just didn't get any better than this!

"From *me?*" Matt's face was full of wonder as Travis ignored Randi's glare and nodded.

"Hey, Mom, didya hear?" The child's gaze swung to his mother, who quickly pasted a smile on her face while she silently cursed Travis McLean to hell and back. It was happening, just as she'd feared: McLean was moving in with all the subtlety of a locomotive charging downhill. Dear heaven, what could she do to stop him?

There was certainly no stopping Matt's enthusiasm. "Travis needs me!" he caroled as if it was the proudest moment of his young life. "We're gonna catch crabs!

Wow! Wait'll I tell Robbie! Crabbin' 'n' Disney World 'n' all!''

He grinned at the adults, his small face a picture of un- mitigated joy; Randi felt her heart wobble, even as her spir- its took a nosedive. "Wow!" her son said again. "This is my bestest summer ever!"

CHAPTER TEN

"HAVE FUN, you guys!" Randi waved and blew a kiss as David's Volvo wagon backed around the cottage's flagpole. "Bye! Don't forget to call!" Matt and Jill grinned and waved back while David changed gears and gave her a jaunty salute.

"Bye!" she called one more time as the car moved away. She was still waving furiously, despite an arm that was beginning to ache, as David tooted the horn and the Volvo disappeared around the bend.

Randi lowered her arm, relieving the ache in it, but not the one in her throat. It felt clogged with the emotion she'd been holding in ever since Matt had hugged her goodbye and climbed into the Volvo.

This was silly, she thought as she blinked back tears. He was with Jill and David, for heaven's sake! And they'd only be gone ten days.

Still, this would be the longest she and Matt had ever been separated. He was her only child, her baby...

But he's not a baby anymore, her inner voice admonished. *He's growing up. Get with it, Terhune! You can't keep him tied to you forever, even if the ties are made of love.*

Swiping at the tears with the flat of her hand, she turned toward the cottage. She ought to look on the bright side. Matt was in for a wonderful time. Moreover, the trip put him safely out of Travis McLean's reach.

With this last thought, she heaved a sigh and collapsed

into a comfortable overstuffed chair in the living room. She'd done it. Matt was happily on his way to the land of the big mouse, and they'd finally seen the last of McLean.

"You hope," she said to the empty cottage, then gave her head a shake as if to clear it of worry. Of course McLean was out of the picture now. He'd said goodbye to her and Matt that afternoon after their late lunch of crabs, hadn't he? And without a word about seeing either of them again. She'd worried needlessly about that, too.

Or had she? For a man who'd said he'd be seeking involvement in his son's life, Travis had seemed all too laid back when they parted. Cheerful, even.

What was he up to?

An hour later she was still sitting in the living room, her mind going over the day for clues. The morning had dawned bright and sunny and stayed that way, despite her secret hopes for a downpour, she was ashamed to admit. Travis arrived midmorning, well supplied with crabbing paraphernalia. This included several fish heads, which he'd pronounced excellent bait.

Matt had been beside himself with excitement, generously offering to handle the bait for his mother if she found it "too icky."

"Oh?" she'd said, taking mock umbrage. "And just what makes you think I'd find them icky, young man?"

"Robbie's mom thinks worms are icky," he'd replied reasonably, "an' fish heads are way bigger baits. Robbie says his mom thinks baits are icky—" he'd looked at Randi consideringly "—'cause she's a girl."

Randi made a mental note to talk to Robbie Spencer's mother about the male-chauvinist views her son was espousing. "Oh, he does, does he?" she'd said.

Matt had nodded, his manner confiding as he informed her, "Robbie's dad always has to put the baits on her hooks for her, y'know."

She'd sputtered and searched for a suitable reply, but it

was Travis who'd supplied one for her. "Could be Robbie's dad's just bein' helpful, Tiger. I mean, it's the sorta thing a guy does for someone he cares about. Ever think of that?"

He'd glanced at Randi while Matt pondered this. Without thinking about it, she'd thrown him a grateful smile. It had earned her a wink that left her slightly breathless.

"Well, yeah..." Matt had seemed to consider this new slant. Then his eyes had widened and he'd thrown the two of them a dazzling smile. "I guess dads care 'bout moms just like they care 'bout their kids, huh?"

Travis had chuckled affectionately ruffling the boy's hair. "Uh, somethin' like that, Tiger," he'd said, meeting Randi's eyes over Matt's head.

She remembered swallowing and looking away, something she'd found herself doing a lot in McLean's company.

The phone rang, jarring her out of her musings. Glad of the distraction, she headed for the wall phone in the kitchen, wondering who it could be. Jill and David had the number, but it hadn't been all that long since they'd left.

"Hello?" she said catching it midring.

It *was* Jill. "The guys opted for a pit stop at the Dairy Queen," she said, "so I grabbed the car phone. This just couldn't wait."

Randi felt a moment of alarm. "What is it?"

"'It' is someone named Travis, whose name drops from your son's lips about once a minute. Randi, is this the Travis I think it is?"

Randi paused to clear her throat and gather her thoughts. In the rush surrounding their visit, the sisters hadn't had a moment alone. Jill knew nothing about the latest with Travis McLean.

"Randi?" Jill prompted. "What's going on?"

With a sigh, Randi told her most of it, apologizing for not having had the chance to explain earlier.

"Forget the apologies," Jill said, obviously concerned.

"Good grief, Randi, what if he challenges you on Matt's parentage, demands blood tests, demands parental rights?"

Randi sighed again, then told Jill the one item she'd neglected to reveal: that she'd admitted to McLean that he was Matt's biological father.

"Oh, no-o-o," Jill groaned.

Randi felt close to tears. "Yeah, a stupid move, but you had to be there, sis. He'd done some poking around and...and he already seemed so darned sure..."

"Don't beat on yourself, sweetheart. From the way you've described him, it was probably only a matter of time till he went after conclusive proof, anyway. The problem is, what are you gonna do now?"

"Do? What *can* I do? Besides hoping we've seen the last of him."

"I don't know, sis. He sounds mighty determined, if you ask me. And Matt's talking him up as if he's the greatest thing since— Uh-oh, speak of the little devil. Look, let me think about this and we'll talk later, okay?"

They said goodbye, leaving Randi alone with her troubling thoughts. But confiding in her sister had made her feel better. Jill had always been her best sounding board. What would she ever have done over the years without her?

Unbidden, the silent voice she was beginning to hate intruded. *And what will your son do without brothers or sisters at all? Who'll be his* sounding board in the years to come?

"It's not the same thing," she said aloud. "Jill and I *had* to lean on each other. We were orphans. But Matt isn't! He has a mother. And Jill and David, who are crazy about him, plan on having a family—kids who'll be his cousins. He'll have loads of people to confide in."

Yet even as she said the words, she wondered why they didn't reassure her.

TAKING JILL'S ADVICE, Randi decided to make the most of the rare chunk of time to herself. She took a long relaxing bath—a luxury, since her busy routine rarely allowed for anything more than a quick shower. She felt almost wicked lounging in water liberally laced with her favorite scent.

Afterward she pulled on an oversize T-shirt and cutoffs, then grabbed the novel Jill had left her. It had been ages since she'd curled up with a book that wasn't related to her profession. This would be fun!

Humming to herself, she poured a glass of iced tea and padded toward the living-room couch with the book. Maybe she'd read into the wee hours, especially if the book was as good as Jill had promised. Then she'd sleep till noon if she felt like it!

The couch was squishy and soft, perfect for being lazy. She'd left the windows open, and now she took a deep breath, savoring the sea-scented air. Sipping her tea, she opened the book—and heard a knock at the door.

"Who on earth...?" she muttered. Though dark out, it was still early; even so...

"Who is it?" she asked uneasily. She peered cautiously through the peephole, glad she'd locked the door. All she could see was a wrinkled white shirt.

"Just a friendly neighbor come to call, sugar," said a familiar male voice. Travis. She should have guessed.

With a sigh that didn't begin to express a host of conflicting feelings, she fumbled with the latch. One part of her acknowledged dismally that she'd been expecting him. Another told her to get rid of him in no uncertain terms. He didn't belong here, period. But there was yet another part of her that experienced a tiny shiver of anticipation.

She ignored it.

Annoyance stamped her features when she flung open the door. "What do you want, McLean?"

"Tsk-tsk, don't frown so, sugar," he said, touching a finger to her brow. "My mama always told my sister she'd regret it when she reached, uh, a certain age. And Mama's usually right about these things—wrinkles, y'know.''

Batting his hand away, Randi eyed him warily. Casually dressed, he reminded her of a male model in an ad for beachwear. In faded cutoffs and a shirt of crinkled gauze so thin you could see his tan through it. Sun-bleached hair and a pair of Docksiders without socks completed the look. He oozed potent charm, with a masculinity so blatant it was positively sinful.

Despite the urge to retreat from the sheer physical force of him, Randi held her ground. ''You haven't answered my question, McLean. What do you want?''

He heaved a sigh. What he wanted was a future that included his son. But now wasn't the time to tell her that. And, in fact, it wasn't his immediate objective. The kid was on his way to Orlando. Time to concentrate on the other essential part of his plan: Matt's lovely mother.

Nothing could happen between him and the boy without her. But who was Randi Terhune, really? What, besides love for her kid, made this woman tick?

She was clearly being protective of her son, and no fault in that. But there'd been times, in the past couple of days, when he'd glimpsed something else. Something that went beyond suspicion of his motives regarding Matt. He couldn't put his finger on it, but he sensed it. A kind of wariness that wasn't hooked to her role as a mother. She appeared at times almost fearful. She'd begin to loosen up, then suddenly close and back away. Like a doe unsure of herself in a forest that ought to be familiar. What was behind it?

Travis smiled. He was here to find out.

''Oh, nothin' much,'' he drawled, his voice so lazy and offhand she suspected it was deliberate. ''I merely got to thinkin', sugar. Y'know, 'bout how you were all by your lonesome over here, what with the little guy gone 'n' all. So I said to myself maybe you could use a little company.''

He grinned at her, affecting a boyish shrug. "And here I am—your personal anti-lonesome committee of one."

"McLean, I don't need a—"

"Oops!" he cut in, reaching down for something beside the door. "Almost forgot these."

The protest died on her lips as she took in the enormous bouquet of flowers. Not hothouse flowers from some florist's refrigerator. These were wildflowers, picked at the height of their midsummer glory. Daisies and field poppies and black-eyed Susans and cornflowers.

Wildflowers. Her favorite.

"They're...they're beautiful," she stammered. "I...uh, thank you, Travis."

"My pleasure, ma'am." And before she knew it, he'd closed the door and was moving past her into the hallway. "Kinda like 'em myself. Used to pick 'em for my mama when I was a kid. Must be thirty years since I last did it, though."

"Look, Travis, I—"

"Now, we'll need to put 'em in water before they wilt. Uh, kitchen in here?"

"Yes, but—"

"Thought so." He flicked on the light as Randi followed him helplessly into the kitchen, feeling like Dorothy caught in a tornado bound for Oz.

He headed for the sink. "This place come with any vases, sugar? 'Course, an ol' jar'll do." He began opening cabinets, rummaging. "Might even be better. Wildflowers look silly all gussied up in a... Ah, here we go." He held up a mason jar. "What do you think?"

She was thinking she'd been run over by a blond six-foot-five bulldozer, but the boyish query on the bulldozer's face kept her from saying so. God, he looked so much like Matt when his brows lifted that way! With a helpless shrug, she nodded, not trusting herself to speak.

Minutes later the bouquet was resting in water and set

in the middle of the kitchen table. Fortunately the time it took to accomplish this had allowed Randi to sort out her thoughts. "They're lovely, Travis, and I do thank you, but now I really have to ask you to…"

Her words died on her tongue. He was looking at her in a way she recognized all too well. Too late, she remembered how she was dressed. In skimpy cutoffs and a T-shirt with nothing underneath.

She froze, all too aware of the cool breeze that ruffled the kitchen curtains, that made her nipples tighten and thrust against the soft fabric.

Travis caught her stiffened posture and dragged his eyes away, quickly focusing on a point above her head. The display had made his mouth go dry. Lord, she was something! High full breasts and legs that didn't quit. Did she have any idea how she…

But of course she did. And for some crazy reason, she was suddenly strung tighter than a kite. She wasn't merely uncomfortable, either. Dammit, she was terrified!

Deeply puzzled, he nonetheless sensed this was no time to ponder her reaction. *So switch gears, McLean!*

"I swear I'm as thirsty as those flowers," he managed in a casual tone. "Okay if I have a glass of water?"

Without waiting for a reply, he moved to the sink, opening a cabinet beside it to grab a glass. "Tell you what, darlin'," he went on, not looking at her as he turned on the faucet and filled a tumbler. "It's a perfect evenin' for a stroll on the beach. A might chilly, though. Why don't you go put on somethin' warm 'n' help me sample some of that salty air?"

Randi leapt at the chance to escape. Without thinking, she murmured something about a pair of sweats and hurried from the kitchen. In the bedroom, she was pulling a baggy sweatshirt and pants out of a drawer when the realization hit: she'd accepted an invitation she ought to have rejected.

She'd give a lot to know how he'd managed it. She'd

been set on saying no, and before she knew it, he had her saying yes. With a sigh, she pulled on the sweats and made a mental note to be more on her guard.

As for tonight, she supposed there was no harm in a walk on the beach. Maybe it was the least she could do, what with that lovely bouquet. Wildflowers. Who'd have thought it? From a man who dodged bullets for a living. As surprising as snow in August.

"DO YOU EVER HAVE second thoughts about giving up medicine?" Randi asked as she and Travis strolled along the water's edge.

Silvery light from the half-moon that had risen limned his features as he glanced down at her, and she saw him smile. Sadly? she wondered. Moonlight was tricky, and she couldn't be sure.

"I'd be lyin' if I said no regrets," he told her. "A man doesn't spend years of his life preparin' for somethin', then abandon it without payin' a price. Sure, I've had regrets. But I've never let myself dwell on 'em. There's a lot in the practice of medicine that's rewardin', but so's the alternative I chose."

"The CIA?" she said skeptically. "But medicine's about *saving* lives." She shook her head. "From all I've heard and read, the CIA—"

"—has saved countless lives, or I wouldn't be there. Whatever its reputation with the general public—and the press—make no mistake about it, Randi, the Agency's crucial to the national welfare. Workin' there's all about service to one's country. It's been vastly satisfyin'."

"If you say so." She still sounded skeptical.

He glanced at her with amusement. "Lord, woman, you are one hard sell!"

She laughed. "Well, you can't blame me for—"

"Look out!" he yelled, and caught her hand as the tide sent a breaker rolling up the beach.

She yelped and gripped his hand as he pulled her away. Foaming salt water soaked her sneakers and kept on coming as they raced for safer ground.

"Damn, that's cold!" Travis exclaimed, but he was laughing, and so was she.

"Can't...can't imagine...what makes...makes you say that!" she got out between gasps of laughter.

He gave a whoop. "Whoo—ee, lady, you sure are..."

The words faded as he saw her shiver. "Here," he said, removing the windbreaker he'd retrieved from his car before they left. Wrapping it around her, he pulled her against him with one arm, using his free hand to rub her back.

"Better?" he murmured against the crown of her head. Her hair was incredibly soft and silky, and he caught a subtle scent of flowers.

She nodded, despite another shiver. But she wasn't cold. His body heat enveloped her like a warm glove. Her senses swam as she leaned against the solid wall of his chest. "I—I'm fine," she murmured unsteadily.

"You sure?" His voice had a faint huskiness. He could feel her curves through the sweats, was instantly reminded of the way she'd looked in the kitchen. Hell, he was getting hard.

Alerted by the change in his voice, Randi felt reality intrude. And then she felt it: an unmistakable pressure against her belly. *Oh, God...*

Clearing a throat that suddenly felt constricted, she pulled away. "I think we'd better be getting back."

But she couldn't move. He was looking down at her with a question in his eyes, and she knew he wanted to kiss her. What would it feel like? she wondered. His chiseled features washed by moonlight, he reminded her of some ancient pagan god, risen from the sea. Beautiful and terrible at the same time. She quelled another shiver.

Travis had every intention of kissing her. Hell, he wanted to do a lot more than kiss her, though it'd do for starters.

He hadn't been this turned on by a woman in a long time. Maybe never.

But something held him back. There was a wall here. He saw it in her eyes, her body language. For a simple kiss? At her age? What was with her?

Whatever it was, he wasn't going to push the envelope. He was extremely attracted to Randi as a woman, but his main objective was forming a relationship with Matt. A lot was riding on this, and he had time on his side. He could wait.

"Okay, sugar," he said with a gentle smile, and pressed a brotherly kiss to her forehead. "Let's go."

He was aware of a release of some of her tension as he draped an arm casually over her shoulders and turned her toward the cottage. He'd made the right decision.

As they headed back, Randi congratulated herself for keeping him at a distance. And wondered at the stab of disappointment she felt.

CHAPTER ELEVEN

TRAVIS LEFT RANDI at her door with nothing more intimate than another light kiss on the forehead. Which, of course, was a relief. She hadn't known what to expect as they'd come up the walk, but she'd been apprehensive. He could make her feel like a moonstruck teenager. Not that she'd ever been such a teenager, which perhaps explained it.

She realized the night was still young as she let herself inside, but went straight to bed. Somehow the idea of reading into the wee hours had lost its allure. Sleeping till noon, moreover, seemed like a dumb idea. Why waste the beautiful weather holing up in bed?

Especially, she thought as she lay tossing and turning a couple of hours later, when she couldn't sleep anyway.

JILL CALLED the next day from Atlanta. She reported that Matt was excited and happy, getting a huge kick out of waving at the truck drivers they passed and the Dr. Seuss stories Jill played on the car's tape deck.

And he still talked constantly about Travis.

"So here's my advice," Jill said, "though I'm afraid you're not gonna like it. But I talked it over with David last night, and we agree it's your best bet."

"Wonderful," Randi muttered. "I've got a situation I already don't like, and my beloved sister tells me I'm not gonna like the solution."

Jill laughed, and then Randi mentioned Travis's visit the night before.

"Well, that's perfect, then," Jill declared.

"Whaddaya mean, perfect?"

"I'm about to explain, love. Now, listen up…"

Jill had been right, Randi thought as she hung up a few minutes later; she didn't like it. Her sister's advice, seconded by David, was that Randi spend even more time in McLean's company. "It's your best hope of finding out what he wants," she'd argued. "And the fact that Travis is still around makes it perfect. You'll never have a better chance, Randi, what with Matt away."

Randi had done her best to resist, but in the end, Jill's logic won out. It was her own fault. She'd given Jill only a sketchy rundown of Travis's visit. She'd said nothing about her unwilling attention to the man, about the unnerving effect he had on her. Her sister was always going on about how she should be seeing men, dating. She'd probably jump on Randi's attraction to McLean and urge her to pursue it!

No way, she thought as she finished her morning coffee, then dressed for the beach. Still, she found herself taking extra pains with her hair. And the lunch she fixed and took in the cooler had more food than she, herself, could consume in a week.

Yet she wound up toting copious leftovers back to the cottage that afternoon. Travis hadn't appeared at the beach. Nor did he call or show up unannounced at her door, as she'd half anticipated on the walk back.

Evening found her ensconced on the couch, regarding the unread novel with a baleful eye. How was she supposed to follow Jill's plan if Travis wasn't in evidence? Not that she really wanted him to be, she told herself.

She tapped the book against a knee clad in white designer jeans. No skimpy attire for her tonight. She'd dressed modestly, yet not without an eye to style. The handkerchief-linen sleeveless tunic she wore over the jeans was a color called persimmon. Strappy white sandals completed an ensemble that showed off her tan and looked smart. But it appeared all this had been a wasted effort.

Curse the man! Her life, since his recent entrance into it, had become more complicated than—

A knock at the door had her slamming the book down and leaping to her feet. She hurried to answer it, checking herself in the hallway mirror as she passed.

"That you, McLean?" she called through the door.

"In the flesh, sugar. Open up."

She did, then took a small step backward, feeling her pulse race. There was no mistaking the naked appreciation in the eyes he ran over her.

She quickly shifted her gaze, concentrating on what he held in his arms. "What on earth?"

Travis's grin was a bit sheepish as she gestured at the cardboard carton he held. And the shaggy lop-eared puppy inside it.

"Meet Ulysses," Travis said as he sauntered in.

"Ulysses," Randi echoed. She noted a heavily padded bandage on the pup's foreleg and wondered why he'd brought the creature here. "Is he yours? And what's wrong with his leg?"

"He's mine if someone doesn't claim him, but I don't think that'll happen. The consensus of me 'n' my landlady is that his owner doesn't want him. He and a littermate were just dumped, we suspect, on the road."

"The poor thing," she murmured sympathetically. How could people treat helpless animals so cruelly?

"Mrs. Muncie's already decided to keep his brother," Travis went on as he headed for the kitchen. "And because of my, uh, medical background, I was nominated to look out for Ulysses here. His leg's broken—"

"Broken!"

Travis's eyes were angry as he glanced at her before setting the carton carefully on the floor. "A car hit him. It was how we came across the pups. There was a squeal of tires outside the bed-and-breakfast this morning. And then we heard some godawful yelping from this little guy.''

"Dear Lord..." Randi murmured, bending down to stroke Ulysses' head.

"The driver stopped and offered to take him to a vet before he went to work," Travis went on, "but I told him I'd take care of it." He shrugged. "I had the time, and it kept me from thinkin' 'bout the creep that dumped 'em.''

Ulysses gave Randi's hand a gentle lick that made her heart turn over. Then he curled up on the folds of beach towel at the bottom of the carton, put his head on his paws and closed his eyes.

"He's sleepy from the sedative the vet gave him," Travis explained, "and I was told to keep an eye on him, so..." He leaned against the refrigerator and gave her that boyish grin again. "Uh, d'you mind?"

"That you brought him here?" She smiled at the sleeping pup. He was adorable, really, with a shaggy salt-and-pepper coat, feathered whiskers that extended below his chin like a beard, and a snub nose. "Well, no, of course not, but what did you, uh..."

"Have in mind?" Travis's grin became a lazy tantalizing curve of those chiseled lips with nothing of the boy in it. "Oh, I thought we'd just hang out a spell. Y'know, maybe get around to some things we, uh, didn't have a chance to pursue last night."

He was looking directly at her mouth as he said this, and Randi felt her breath catch and a queer little lurch in the pit of her stomach.

She swallowed thickly and lowered her gaze, then swallowed again, an ambivalent mix of emotions confusing her as nothing ever had. His white canvas shorts revealed long powerful bronzed thighs, glinting with blond hairs. Suddenly she didn't know where to look.

"Uh, there's a screened porch out back," she murmured, seizing on the first thing that came to mind. "Why don't you take Ulysses out there, and…and I'll fix us some lemonade?''

"Sounds good, sugar." In a single graceful movement, Travis launched his tall frame from the refrigerator and gently scooped up Ulysses, carton and all. "And while you're fixin' the drinks, I'll run to the car 'n' fetch the clams."

"Clams?"

"Steamers," he clarified on his way out. "They gave Ulysses a painkiller right away, but the vet's office was jammed. Had to spend most of the day waitin' for the leg to be set. Never had supper—lunch, either, come to think of it," he called over his shoulder. "Be right back."

She thought about what he'd said as she made a jug of lemonade. More specifically she thought about him. About the kind of man he was to forgo lunch and dinner to help a wounded animal that wasn't his responsibility in the first place. Her estimation of Travis McLean inched up several notches.

The steamers turned out to be a movable feast. There were two large buckets of them, along with enough broth to float a battleship and the drawn butter to grease it. A loaf of crusty French bread and fresh tomatoes from a roadside stand had Randi wishing she hadn't wasted her appetite on the can of soup she'd heated for supper.

"So, what happens to Ulysses now?" she asked, wiping her fingers on a napkin he'd brought with the food. They'd talked in a desultory fashion during the meal about nothing much in particular. Now, sated and relaxed, they faced each other across a low wicker table over the remains of the feast; she lounged in a cushioned wicker armchair while Travis sprawled lazily on the matching settee.

"And why the name Ulysees, by the way?" she added, pitching her napkin onto the tray of remains on the table.

"Well, the original Ulysses was a wanderer, too.

Through no fault of his own, I might add, other than bein'
in the wrong place at the wrong time.''

Travis leaned down and stroked the pup's fur, then
smiled at her. ''He eventually reached his home, though. I
figured this little fella deserves the same fate. A good home,
that is.''

''So you're going to keep him?''

''Depends,'' Travis said. ''I will if I can't find him somethin' better.'' He rubbed his chin contemplatively. ''Trouble is, I'm not really set up for a dog, much as I love 'em.
I live in an apartment, and I'm away at work most of the
time. It really wouldn't be fair to an animal.''

He eyed her speculatively. ''You 'n' Matt have a dog?''

''No, we—'' She halted abruptly, noting the alert look
in his eyes. ''Now, wait a minute, McLean! If you think—''

''Kids 'n' dogs sorta go together, don't they? I mean,
unless there's a problem. Uh, Matt's not allergic or anythin', is he? Or...he's not afraid of dogs?''

''Of course not! Matt loves animals. I've thought of getting him a pet, but only when he's older. A four-year-old
isn't—''

''I got my first dog when I was four. A chocolate Lab I
named Hershey. Hershey and I were inseparable. He slept
at the foot of my bed, woke me in the mornin' with his big
foolish tongue 'n' went everywhere with me. Heck, ol'
Hersh was the best friend I ever had as a kid.''

''Oh? And I suppose you took him to school with you
when you reached school age? And of course you were the
one who housebroke him?''

For the second time that evening, Travis looked sheepish.
It had been the butler who'd housebroken Hershey, and
there'd been a bevy of servants to see to the dog's needs
when he couldn't. Yet Travis remembered doing his part,
even cleaning up the occasional ''accident.'' It taught him
something about responsibility. *A boy ought to have a dog,
for Pete's sake!*

"What if I were to housebreak him for you?" he suggested. "I could train him some, too. Y'know, give him the basics—sit, lie down, stay."

The more he thought about it, the more he liked the idea. The pup would be a tie between him and his son. God, he'd love to see Matt's face light up when he found out he'd have his very own dog!

Of course, he had to get past Matt's mother first. And she wasn't looking too enthusiastic right now. "What do you say, Randi?" he asked carefully. "Will you at least think about it?"

She had every intention of saying no, but the look of boyish anticipation on his face had her wavering. Again. Her glance fell on the sleeping puppy. Matt would love it of course. But there was Jill to consider. Her sister would still be in charge of Matt during Randi's working hours, but at her new home with David—at least until Matt started school. And Randi had a suspicion Matt would insist on bringing any dog he owned with him.

Still, she supposed she could at least air the idea with Jill and David. "I'll think about it," she told Travis, and rose to clear away the remains of their meal.

"Good." He rose, too, brushing her hands away from the tray. "Here, I'll do that."

"No, I..." She stepped back a pace as a giddy shiver ran through her. That slight brush of his hands on hers had sent the equivalent of an electric current through her.

She couldn't explain it. One moment she'd been relaxing with him over a meal; yet in the space of a heartbeat, she stood here, tingling and tongue-tied. She stared helplessly, utterly drawn by that masculinity he wore with confidence and grace. Like it or not, she knew she'd never been more aware of anyone as a man.

Had he noticed? She glanced at his face and swallowed. From the way he was looking at her, he had.

"Hey, darlin', what's wrong?" Travis quickly set the

tray aside and came around the table. "You okay?" He tilted her face up with a touch of his knuckles under her chin.

A light breeze was building, lifting the napkins on the tray; it provided the excuse she needed. "I'm okay," she told him, rubbing her arms with her hands. "It's just a bit chilly."

"Here," he murmured, taking over for her and running his hands up and down her arms. This only brought another giddy quiver, and he drew her close, wrapping his arms around her like a warm cocoon.

Randi's heart was thudding like a drum, and she told herself to pull away. But there was something oddly non-threatening about the embrace, despite the storm clamoring inside her. These were a man's arms, yes. But they were also arms that had cradled a puppy with tender care. They belonged to a man who'd recently stood beside a tidal creek for hours, and with patience and forbearing, taught a small boy how to catch crabs.

Quit fighting it, Terhune, the familiar inner voice chided. *Just this once. Haven't you wanted to know what it would be like? To let a man hold you? To relax in a man's arms and see where it leads?*

There was a moment's hesitation. Then, with a soft sigh, she leaned her head against his chest.

Travis smiled as he rested his chin on the top of her head. She felt so damned good in his arms he wanted to hold her all night. Not that he'd tell her that. Although he'd made some inroads, she was still skittish. Too bad he didn't know what was behind it. But he still had plenty of time to find out. *Easy does it, McLean. One step at a time.*

"Guess I was right, after all," he murmured, his hand making lazy circles over her shoulders and back.

"Hmm?" she heard her own voice as if it came from a distance. Had anything in the world felt this good? Ever?

He chuckled, the vibration sending tiny pulses through

her nerve endings. "Appears there *was* a thing or two needed pursuin' after last night."

"Mmm," she responded, lulled by his lazy drawl, by the cadence of crickets, the soft night and the faint murmur of the sea in the distance.

"Miz Terhune," he went on, his voice a husky whisper, "I do believe it's time, don't you?"

"Hmm?" She only half heard his words. Eyes closed, her body limp and boneless, she gave herself up to the sensation of those big soothing hands caressing her back and shoulders.

"For this, darlin'," he breathed, pulling slightly away to cup her head between his hands. His gaze roamed over her features as he gently threaded his fingers through her hair, tilting her face upward.

Her eyes felt heavy-lidded as she forced them open and met his gaze. She watched it search hers for several seconds, then drop to her mouth.

"For this," he repeated in a smoky whisper, and his mouth lowered and claimed hers.

The kiss was as lazy and unhurried as his voice. His lips were warm and unbelievably soft as they closed over her own. By tiny increments, they grew firmer, and soon he was shaping her mouth, molding it. Pulling her along in a tide of sensual pleasure as unsuspected as it was delicious.

Caught in a sensual haze, she slid her hands upward without thinking, savoring the feel of the rock-hard wall of his chest and its solid masculine strength. Higher now, over the granite curve of pectorals, their smooth surface broken by the flat male nipples that contracted as her fingers passed. Then on to the corded muscles of his neck and shoulders. Here she clung with unsteady hands and heard the approving murmur deep in his throat as he widened his stance and tightened the embrace.

Randi's awareness focused on the joining of their mouths. His lips continued to shape hers with expert care, moving, moving, sending her into a long sensual glide toward pleasure she'd never dreamed of. Not from a simple kiss, maybe not from anything.

She felt the first touch of his tongue when it slid along the seam of her lips, and a jolt of pleasure sluiced through her belly and thighs. Something deep inside her tightened, became a yearning need as, with his tongue, he gently traced the shape of her mouth.

She heard herself moan as he nipped at her lower lip with his teeth, then soothed the sensitized flesh with lips and tongue. Deftly he sucked and teased until her own lips parted. Then, ever so lightly, he probed the velvet cave of her mouth with his tongue until she couldn't help herself and shyly touched the tip of hers to his.

Travis shuddered, surprised by the jolt of hunger this sent to his groin. Hell, what was happening here? It was just a kiss. And he'd kissed dozens of women, most of them a lot more expert than Randi, from what he could tell. He was reacting like a kid on his first date. Was it her inexperience that intrigued him? Maybe, but it didn't account for the wave of pure lust he was feeling over an uncomplicated kiss. He was hot enough to—'

Whoa, McLean! Chill out. Give yourself time to think, ol' buddy. Lovely though she be, this isn't just any woman. This is Matt's mama, with a world riding on what happens. One wrong step, and you may not get another chance.

Drawing in a breath, he released it slowly, gently disengaged himself and stepped back. But the look on Randi's face didn't help. Her features had softened, and as she looked up at him in mild confusion, he could see that her pupils were dilated. And then there was her mouth. God, in some countries he'd been in, a man could go to jail for what he thought of teaching that mouth to do!

Unaware of his thoughts, she chose that moment to run her tongue over her lips. Shutting his eyes to close out the sensual image, he gave a half-audible groan. Damn, but he wanted her! She was all woman under that icy reserve, though he had a sneaky hunch she didn't realize it.

"Travis?" The sensual haze was starting to fade, but very slowly; yet Randi knew enough to sense something was bothering him. Doubt nibbled at the edges of her mind. Perhaps it was a mistake to—

A whimper issued from the carton on the floor. They both glanced at Ulysses, who was rising awkwardly from the bedding.

"Uh-oh," Travis said, seeing the pup begin to sniff. He moved quickly to the box and scooped it up, then grinned at Randi. "Time to start the housebreakin'."

Laughing, she led the way to the front door. Ulysses wasted no time in relieving himself, and they both praised him. Travis picked him up and was holding him against his chest while his eyes went to Randi. "I'll put him in the car, then come 'n' help you clean up."

"Don't worry about it," she told him. "And thanks for the feast."

"My pleasure, ma'am," he said softly, and from the way his eyes moved to her mouth, she knew he wasn't thinking of the clams.

She felt her breathing go shallow. Tried to gather her wits and decide how to answer. Before she could say a word, he leaned down and pressed a soft kiss to her cheek.

"Tomorrow night 'bout eight," he whispered, his warm breath stirring the hair just above her ear. "Wear somethin' comfortable."

Comfortable? she thought as she watched him head for his car. She doubted if she'd ever use "comfortable" and "Travis" in the same breath.

CHAPTER TWELVE

WHEN SHE AWOKE the next morning, Randi's first thought was to wonder what Travis had planned for that evening. Would it allow her the chance to learn his long-range plans? After all, that was the only reason she was seeing him, wasn't it?

In the next instant she decided the worst thing she could do was sit around all day waiting for eight o'clock to arrive. Bad enough that McLean invaded her dreams—he'd made a crazy appearance in them last night. She wasn't about to let him mess up her daytime hours, too.

Using a chamber-of-commerce guide the rental office had provided, she went antiquing. The home she shared with Jill contained many lovely old treasures they'd inherited from their aunt Tess. The sisters were always hunting for interesting pieces to enhance these furnishings. Jill even had a bumper sticker that read, "This Vehicle Stops for Antique Shops."

The morning passed quickly as Randi wandered through more than a dozen shops. She came across many fine antiques she couldn't afford, but that was par for the course. Among these was a wonderful mermaid weathervane she'd have loved to buy for Jill and David as a wedding gift. She sighed, regretting just this once the need to shop within her modest budget. Giving the weathervane a last lingering look, she told herself she'd find something affordable back home. Meanwhile, the browsing was fun.

Then, just as she was leaving the last shop before pre-

paring to head back, she spied a red-and-white quilt in the
schoolhouse pattern. About a hundred years old and in good
condition, it was pricey, but not exorbitant. Deciding it
would be perfect on a wall in Matt's room, she bought it.

On the way back she stopped at a small roadside eatery
and treated herself to a lunch of crabcakes, an Eastern
Shore specialty. They were delicious, yet she found herself
thinking she preferred her crabs prepared like those they'd
caught with Travis. They'd eaten them steamed, with lemon
and drawn butter. She recalled how Matt had gone on and
on about the crabbing expedition as she'd gotten him ready
for his trip to Disney World.

She frowned. *Admit it, Terhune,* she told herself irritably.
*It wasn't just the crabbing he enthused about. It was the
man who organized it!*

That she currently found herself succumbing to a similar
phenomenon—she wryly dubbed it ''Travis on the
Brain''—didn't sit well with her. She'd been hoping Matt
would get over his fascination with McLean by the time he
returned; but what use was that if *she* was preoccupied with
the man?

Determined to concentrate on her R and R, she returned
to the cottage and went for a swim. After an hour or so in
the water, she decided to remain on the beach until sup-
pertime. Slathering on sunscreen, she stretched out on her
towel and took in the scene around her.

Sunlight glinted off the water under a cloudless sky so
blue it almost hurt the eyes to look at it. At the water's
edge, several children shrieked and romped in the surf.
About a dozen people lounged nearby, and all were families
she recognized by now, with young children.

Two-parent families, every one of them.

She heaved a sigh. It wasn't as if single-parent families
weren't common in today's world. The media were full of
stories about single mothers. Fathers, too. Just her luck the

particular vacation spot she'd chosen didn't have any in evidence. Besides her, of course.

Her interest in the beach gone, she trudged back to the cottage. Next year, she promised herself, she'd do a little more research when planning a getaway; maybe there was a resort that catered to single parents with kids.

Back at the cottage she realized she felt drowsy. All that sun and surf, she thought, frowning when a tenderness on her shoulders told her she'd gotten a slight burn. Grinning to herself between yawns as she showered, she decided to take a nap. A nap, right in the middle of the afternoon! She hadn't considered such an idea in years.

There were definite advantages to having some time to yourself, she decided. And when that nagging inner voice suggested that mothers in two-parent families probably had a lot more, she ignored it.

As she stepped from the shower, Jill called, sounding excited. "Randi, are you sitting down? I just came across a piece of information that knocked my socks off."

"What?" Randi asked, reaching for her robe and stifling a yawn.

"Not what, *who!*"

Randi was too sleepy to manage much enthusiasm. She barely squelched another yawn as she tied the thin cotton robe in place. "Who, then?"

"Your son's granddad, that's who!"

Randi came wide awake. "How do you know—"

"Just listen," Jill broke in. "David picked up some of the local papers this morning, and the features section of the *Miami Herald* just happened to be running a story on a medical convention in Miami this week. There was an article on the keynote speaker. Seems he's a world-renowned heart surgeon from Virginia."

"Go on." Randi was fully alert now. She remembered what Travis had told her about the surgeon father who'd had no time for his children. Was this the man?

"Well," Jill said, "the article included the guy's professional background, highlights from an illustrious career in medicine, that sort of thing. It also gave some family background. His name's Dr. Trent *McLean*, Randi. He's gotta be Matt's granddad because the article mentioned a wife and three children—one, a son named Travis. A world-famous heart surgeon, and he's Matt's granddad!"

"Let's skip the 'granddad' bit, okay?" Randi said. "'Biological grandfather' will do if we must discuss it at all, but that's as far as I go."

"Picky, picky," Jill teased, to which Randi gave a noncommittal grunt. Granddads, in her mind, were pleasant white-haired old gentlemen who, if you were lucky enough to have one, occupied a warm comforting place in a kid's life. She'd never known her own grandparents, who died before she and Jill were born, but she knew how it was supposed to work.

Granddads were backups for dads. They did stuff like helping kids build model airplanes and taking them fishing, or told wonderful stories about what it was like in the old days. They were *not* doctor celebrities who'd probably never built a model airplane in their lives. And they most definitely were not old-money aristocrats who'd never had time for their own sons, let alone grandsons.

The noncommittal grunt was followed by a guttural sound of disgust.

"Hmm," Jill mused, "sounds as if I got you at a bad time. It isn't like you to be grumpy in the middle of the afternoon. What's the matter, sis? This is your hard-earned vacation. You're supposed to be enjoying it."

Randi assured her she was, explaining about being tired from the full day she'd had. She went on to describe the quilt, which her sister couldn't wait to see. She made Jill promise not to mention it to Matt, so he'd be surprised.

"You realize, don't you, that a four-year-old won't care beans about its antique status," Jill told her. "You'd better pick up some terrific plastic neon junk gizmos, as well, kiddo, if you know what's good for you.''

Randi chuckled. ''Okay, okay. But I bet you and David've already loaded Matt down with plenty. Duly emblazoned with cartoon logos from mouse country.''

''Better believe it. In every color, from hot fuchsia to psychedelic yellow.''

Randi laughed again, her tiredness forgotten. Jill often did that for her, and the reverse was also true. They were a terrific team. *We may not be able to boast any famous granddads, but in the sister/aunt department, we do okay.*

''I don't suppose you've had time to come up with anything on the, uh, research front?'' Jill's change of topic was uttered casually, but Randi heard an eagerness behind it.

''You don't suppose right,'' she quipped, ''but tune in tomorrow, same time, same station. Maybe I'll have something for you.'' She went on to explain about her eight-o'clock date, then wanted to kick herself for calling it a date.

''Saturday night at eight, huh?'' murmured her sister. ''Sounds interesting. Better wear that slinky new—''

''Forget it, sis. The object here is to find out what he wants, not keep him hanging around for, uh, whatever.''

''Hmm,'' Jill murmured cryptically, then changed the subject again. ''How's the weather up there?''

''Great for the beach. Hot, not a cloud in sight.''

''Hah! You don't know hot until you've been in Florida in July. But listen, Randi. David was watching the weather channel, and—''

She broke off, saying, ''Hold on, sis. It's the guys. They're back from their pig-out at the ice-cream parlor. Here, Matt, say hello to your mom.''

''Hi, Mom!'' Matt's voice bubbled with energy. ''Wait'll ya hear what *we* been doin'!''

Randi grinned as she listened to her son's excited description of the gooeyest ice-cream sundae ever invented.

He sounded like he was having a ball. He went on to describe his morning, which included an encounter with Goofy and then Mickey himself.

"He sure is big for a mouse, Mom. So's Goofy, but he's a dog. I wish *we* had a dog, even if it couldn't be big as Goofy. He's 'most as tall as Travis."

Wincing, Randi manage an enthusiastic "Wow!"

"Yeah, wait'll you see! We got pitchers 'n' everything."

"Pictures, huh?" said Randi, storing away his words about a dog and thinking of Ulysses. She said nothing to Matt about Travis's pup of course, but promised herself to give it more thought. "Shots of you with Goofy and Mickey?"

"Yeah, an' lots of stuff. Boy, this place is great! We saw Princess Jasmin 'n' Aladdin 'n' 'Ventureland 'n'...."

Listening to her son's breathless recounting of Disney World sights, Randi wished she was with him. Still, she told herself as they said goodbye, it was important that Matt could enjoy himself apart from her, wasn't it?

So why did their conversation leave her feeling so bereft? she wondered as she stretched out on the bed. With the phone call behind her, tiredness washed over her again. The last thing she remembered thinking as she drifted off was that maybe she ought to set her alarm, but she'd just close her eyes for a minute first...

TRAVIS FROWNED when he knocked on Randi's door for the third time and no one answered. Dammit, where was she? And why weren't there any lights on in the place? It was a little after eight and nearly dark. Had she forgotten?

The frown became a scowl. Forgotten, or had she decided to stand him up?

But her car was still in the drive. Besides, he didn't see Randi Terhune as the type to cry off without a note or phone call. Too much the proper lady.

He frowned as he considered this. Proper ladies were

hardly his type. They reminded him of his mother, and he'd never been drawn to women who did. Family values were simply not part of the criteria he considered when pursuing romantic interests.

Not that "romantic" was the right word, exactly. "Romantic" implied things like love and commitment, which might work for some guys, though he had his doubts.

An image of his friend Rafe O'Hara with his bride, Francesca, flashed in his mind. Okay, maybe romantic love happened. Maybe it even worked once in a blue moon for a rare few. But for him? No thanks. Give him a casual liaison with a woman who'd been around, any day. A mature woman who knew the score and didn't expect hearts and flowers by the third kiss. Or, God forbid, a ring on her finger.

Glancing at the packages under his arm, he scowled. So why was he standing here in front of her door, holding...

Muttering something no proper lady would approve of, he shifted the packages in his arm and banged on the door. Loud enough to wake the dead, but he didn't care. If she didn't answer this time, something was wrong, and he was just in the mood to—

"Travis, 'zat you?" came a groggy voice from inside.

Finally. "Who else?" he asked testily. "Unless you've made two dates for tonight. Randi, what's wrong? I've been knockin' since—"

The door swung open. "Oh, I'm really sorry," Randi said. "I just meant to—"

"Hey, are you okay?" Travis gave her face and wrinkled robe a quick perusal. She didn't really look sick, which had been his first thought. Her face had a rosy flush which he could see by the hall light she'd thrown on. And the rest of her was...something else.

She looked kittenish and sexy, with her golden hair tangled softly around her face and tumbling over her shoulders that way. Yeah, and good enough to gobble up whole.

"''Fraid I took a nap," she said sheepishly. "I meant to set the alarm, but..." She gave an awkward shrug, then stifled a yawn.

"No harm done, sugar," he said softly. He couldn't resist reaching out and tucking a long strand of hair behind her ear. Unable to help himself, he let his fingers linger there, savoring the textures of her.

Which might have been a mistake. The silky feel of her hair sliding through his fingers, not to mention the petal-soft skin of her neck, sent an unexpected message to his groin. The way she looked, the elusive scent of her, all muzzy and warm from sleep...God almighty! She was doing things to his body that no proper lady would welcome. Not at this point, at any rate. Later...well, he'd wait and see.

At his touch, Randi felt something curl and unwind deep inside. Never entirely alert when she first awakened, she responded with the unthinking reaction of someone still half-asleep. She didn't examine what she was doing, just swayed toward the source of that delicious pleasure.

Tucking her head to one side like a cat wanting to be stroked, she leaned into Travis's warmth. Until she felt those strong yet gentle fingers graze her cheek. Until he cupped it and she found herself turning her mouth into his palm and pressing her lips against his flesh.

Travis's breath caught in his throat. She was soft and warm and all things female. Arousingly female. Dammit, he was getting hard again, but arousing female or no, he knew this wasn't the time to do something about it.

"Lord, kitten," he murmured, his voice low and husky as he let the packages he'd been holding slide to the floor. He raised the hand this freed, threading his fingers through her hair. He was more aware than ever of its silken texture, of the heady scent and feel of her. "You're just about the softest thing this side of heaven."

"Mmm," Randi murmured dreamily, curling into his embrace.

He released an unsteady breath as his arms closed around her. She was slender and willowy, yet there was no mistaking her female curves, the full breasts that pressed against his chest, with only thin layers of cloth between. The narrow waist that flared into womanly hips just where his hand held her to him, itching to move lower. To cup and caress.

Yet the way she snuggled against him, all sleepy and warm, sent a warning message to his brain. A message that had him gritting his teeth against the arousal straining his jeans. She was clearly not awake yet. If she had been, she'd never have welcomed what her body had to be sensing about *his* body.

Only a bastard would take advantage of a woman who wasn't fully cognizant of such things, and a bastard he wasn't. He'd been raised to respect women. A gentleman simply didn't take advantage, no matter how his body tried to make him forget the standards he'd been raised by.

"Listen, darlin'," he said, taking a deep breath and gently disengaging and setting her away from him. "Why don't you go pull on some sweats or somethin', okay? Nothin' fancy, now. We're just goin' to the beach."

"Um...the beach?"

"Yup," he said, flicking the tip of her nose with his finger. "I got a permit to build a fire and brought some wieners to roast. And I sure hope you like champagne."

"Champagne?" She was fully awake now. "Did you say champagne?"

"Piper Heidsieck," he said with a grin, "but that was because the Philistines around here didn't have any Louis Roederer."

"Piper Heidsieck," she murmured, recalling that the last time she'd had anything so extravagant she and Jill had been toasting Matt's baptism. "You've brought Piper Heid-sieck for a wiener roast?"

"And marshmallows for toastin'." He indicated the packages resting at his feet. "Now, scoot." He turned her by the shoulders toward her bedroom, resisting an urge to deliver a playful pat to her shapely bottom.

"The ice in that bucket I left outside," he added, dragging his gaze away and clearing his throat, "won't last forever, and champagne's no good unless it's chilled."

"CARE FOR ANOTHER, sugar?" Travis pulled a long twig from the fire and blew out the flame on a plump marshmallow that was charred to perfection.

"I really shouldn't," Randi said, taking a sip from one of the champagne flutes he'd brought. *Crystal flutes for a wiener roast on the beach! Honestly, is there anything the man doesn't think of?* "There's something terribly decadent about eating toasted marshmallows with champagne."

He chuckled. "That's the general idea, darlin'. You are, after all, on vacation." Pleasantly full after a few roasted wieners, they were sitting cross-legged on the blanket, facing each other before the fire. He didn't have far to reach as he held out his burnt offering and grinned at her. "Go on, live a little."

"Well," she murmured, reaching for the marshmallow and wishing for the thousandth time she was more immune to that grin, "maybe just one more before— Ouch!"

"Damn!" He dropped the twig and caught her hand. "Did you burn yourself?"

"N-not really," she stammered as he lifted her hand to his mouth. She felt a ripple of pleasure as he blew on the fingers that bore telltale smudges of charcoal. And when he licked them with his lips and tongue, a delicate shudder ran through her.

"You sure, kitten?" he murmured, cradling her hand in

his and pressing a kiss to the sensitized pads of her fingers and then to the center of her palm.

"N-no. I mean, yes." She released a quavering breath as he met her eyes and those perfectly chiseled lips curved into a slow grin.

"'S' matter, honey woman?" His thumb made lazy circles on the sensitive skin of her palm. "Can't decide?"

"H-honey...?" She couldn't finish. God, what was happening to her? A single glass of champagne shouldn't be affecting her this way. She was light-headed, and a heaviness had invaded her lower torso—and her breasts, which felt achy and swollen.

"Mm," he murmured, still holding her hand. His thumb moved over her knuckles, massaging them with a slowness that was altogether deliberate, and as sensual as his voice.

"Remember those moments in the ER when I first saw you?" he asked softly, his gaze caressing her face.

She shook her head in numb bemusement, and he smiled. "I do. I couldn't help thinkin' 'bout how you looked—all tawny 'n' golden, y'know? Just like honey, darlin'. Wild honey. All deep 'n' golden, gently warmed by the sun 'n' sweeter'n heaven itself."

Closing her eyes, she slowly drew in a breath, then released it in a sigh. They had the moonlit beach to themselves. An occasional pop and crackle of the fire punctuated the sound of the surf. It was otherwise quiet and still. Except inside her, where her heart beat like a trip-hammer.

Travis saw the pulse against the fragile skin at the side of her neck. He recalled how that skin had felt back at the cottage. He had an overpowering urge to taste it.

Not yet, a voice in his head cautioned. *You've got to take it slow and easy with this woman.*

He smiled to himself, anticipating how he'd do just that. "You never got your sugar treat, darlin'," he said. Reaching for the discarded twig and removing the aborted marshmallow, he replaced it with a fresh one.

"Wh-what?" Randi couldn't think clearly as she focused on the deep indentations bracketing his mouth. Only vaguely was she aware he was toasting something in the fire.

"But this time, honey," he murmured, his gaze on her mouth as he removed the perfectly charred morsel from the twig, "we're not riskin' your lovely hands."

Blowing on the melted marshmallow suspended between his fingers, he leaned forward and raised it to her mouth. "Open for me, kitten," he commanded gently, meeting her eyes. "C'mon, now."

God, his eyes...his voice. Had there ever been anything in her experience as compelling? Obedient as a child, Randi did as he said. The sweet warm taste filled her mouth, a perfect counterpoint to the chilled tartness lingering on her tongue from the champagne.

"Good?" he asked, his gaze dropping to her lips, where the pink tip of her tongue licked a hint of sticky residue. *Sweet Lord in heaven, does she have any idea what she's doing to me?*

He decided to find out.

Leaning forward, he lowered his head, angled his mouth against hers and captured her lips, just as the tip of her tongue darted into view again. Tongue met tongue.

He sucked in his breath as he felt her tremble. Yet he wasn't sure if her reaction was from passion or from fear. Exhaling slowly, he backed away on the blanket, stretching out long legs encased in skin-hugging jeans. He noted she watched him warily. *Fear, then. Damn.*

He didn't know why a mature woman who'd borne a child and had a successful career in nursing should be so skittish in male-female situations. She was like a newborn foal, and he had to do whatever was necessary to gentle her. Time for figuring out why later.

"C'mere, darlin'," he whispered, holding out his hand.

She glanced at the hand, then back at his face, uncertainty in her eyes.

Seeing her hesitate, he softened the request with a smile. "You've been sittin' in that position for over an hour. You can't be any more comfortable than I was."

Before she could argue, he leaned over and lifted her toward him as if she weighed nothing. Randi found herself sitting with her back braced against his chest, her legs outstretched. She swallowed thickly; her hips were sandwiched between long muscular thighs.

"Relax," he murmured somewhere over her left ear. She felt her heart hammering frantically against her chest. He was too close, too large. Above all, *too male.*

And yet she couldn't move. His nearness was doing impossible things to her senses, even while her mind urged her to pull away.

Travis's hands came up to rest gently on her shoulders. "Easy does it now, honey," he whispered, his voice a low, soothing caress.

Slowly he began to massage the taut muscles supporting her neck. Feeling her tension ease, he murmured approvingly against her hair, "That's it, darlin', relax. Nothin's gonna happen that you don't want, hear? Easy, now…"

It was as much the reassurance in his voice as his words that soon had her leaning bonelessly against the solidity of his chest. Looking dreamily out at a night sky filled with stars, she wondered why she hadn't noticed them before. Or the velvet feel of warm ocean air on her skin. Or the moonlight glinting on the water, fragmenting into a thousand splinters of light as the waves advanced and retreated.

It was as if, with the easing of tension, all her senses had begun to sharpen and expand. Her perception of things around her had never been this keen. She felt suddenly more alive, more aware in every pore.

And not the least of what she perceived was the heady masculine presence in close proximity to hers. Travis's hands had progressed to her arms. He was running his palms gently down their length, then up again, where the process started anew.

His hands were large, yet incredibly gentle, for all their size. With her heightened awareness, she could feel the texture of them in contrast with her skin. A man's hands, callused at the heels, as if he used them for a particular labor. Karate? she wondered, but the thought faded away. She shut her eyes and sighed, surrendering to the sweet lassitude invading her body.

"That's it, darlin'," he murmured, pressing a soft kiss to the crown of her head. "Nothin' to worry 'bout. Nothin' at all."

He eased his hands to her waist and gently encircled her with his arms. "Warm enough?" he asked in the lazy drawl she'd forever associate with warm summer nights and a sky full of stars.

"Mm-hmm," she managed.

"Good," he breathed against her ear, and then proceeded to nuzzle it. "Unlike champagne, darlin'," he added, his voice a bare whisper against her hair, "honey's no good when it's chilled."

She shivered as his velvet tongue circled her ear, then dipped into its center. And when his teeth sank ever so gently into the lobe, her breath broke.

"You're beautiful, Miranda Terhune," he murmured, "and I can't seem to get my fill of lookin' at you…or touchin' you…" Slowly, almost imperceptibly, his hands moved to her breasts, cupped them gently.

"Tell me if you want me to stop," he whispered as a ragged breath tore from her throat.

Restlessly her head moved from side to side. What was happening to her? She'd meant to say stop, hadn't she? But the feel of those hands cupping her breasts, as if testing their weight, Lord, she wanted it to go on forever!

She heard him murmur something low and inaudible in

that sultry drawl. She felt his thumbs graze her nipples. Nipples that were pouting against the soft cotton of the sweatshirt she'd donned—without a bra, because of the sunburn.

Dear God! A jolt of undiluted pleasure shot from the peaks he teased to the crevice between her thighs. She gasped.

He heard her gasp and immediately stilled his hands. But a low ragged moan from deep in her throat let him know it hadn't been fear, and he released the breath he'd been holding. "Want me to stop?" His warm breath caressed her ear.

When she only stirred restlessly against him, he smiled knowingly and let his thumbs resume their work. *She's no ice queen now,* he thought as his teasing brought her nipples to taut prominent buds. *So responsive! Good thing she doesn't want me to stop. Any second now, and I won't be able to.*

He used his fingers now to gently twist those outthrust peaks, worrying them into aching points of unbearable pleasure. She began to twist and moan beneath his hands, and he wondered if she felt the pressure of his arousal at the base of her spine. He wanted her. Wanted her in a way he'd never wanted a woman.

Yet she was clearly a novice at all this. He felt it in her, heard it in the surprised little whimpers she gave whenever he changed his caresses and taught her a new way to receive pleasure at his hands. The mystery behind this intrigued him, but he didn't stop to puzzle it out now. He was so hard it was painful, and the urge crowding out his thoughts was to seek the only remedy he knew.

Slowly, carefully, murmuring reassurances in her ear as he nuzzled it, he slipped one of his hands lower. Smoothing it over the waistband of her sweats, he massaged her flat belly with slow indolent strokes. His other hand continued teasing her nipples, and she hardly seemed aware of anything new.

Moving very slowly, Travis slid his hand back toward her waistband. Using just the tips of his fingers, he lifted the elastic and sought the warm flesh beneath.

"Randi?" he whispered. "You okay?"

She felt the sensual haze swirl and eddy around her. She was on a moonlit beach, and Travis was doing impossible things to her body. Intimate things...

She grew suddenly very still, and Travis stopped his questing hand, resting it on her bare navel. But it was getting hard to stop and start this way. She wasn't wearing a scrap of underwear beneath the sweats, and the realization brought sweat to his brow.

"Randi?" he tried again. "Talk to me."

All at once, the sensual haze was gone. The moonlit beach was gone. She was huddled in her bedroom and she was sobbing. She held her old teddy bear, clinging to it desperately as her tears dampened the worn fur. But Teddy couldn't save her. No one could. And the footsteps were coming nearer...nearer. *"No-o-o!"*

Travis froze as she screamed and tore herself from his arms. "Randi, what the—"

"Don't!" she shrieked, tears flooding her eyes as she scrambled wildly, stumbling. *Never again. Never!* Somehow she picked herself up and staggered to her feet, the male figure before her, a hazy blur through her tears. *"Don't touch me."*

Travis watched in confused shock as she backed away from him. That was terror he saw in her eyes! "Randi, what's the matter?" he asked, reaching out to soothe her.

"I said, don't touch me!" Pivoting, she lunged away, sobbing uncontrollably. Then she ran from him, and it was as if she ran for her life.

Dumbfounded, he stared at the slender figure tearing up

the beach. She looked, he thought, as if all the devils of hell were pursuing her.

His mind fastened suddenly on an image of a small boy with hair the color of his own. Stifling a curse, he concentrated on the woman with hell in her eyes. What would put that kind of terror in a woman when a man had been making slow, careful love to her? Did it have anything to do with that counseling she and her sister had undergone?

Again an image of his son filled his mind, and he felt a prick of fear. Had Matt ever seen those devils? He'd read about kids who were raised by unstable parents...but Matt seemed so *normal*. Still...

His eyes narrowed and he set his jaw grimly. "Whatever your devils are, Randi Terhune," he growled into the darkness, "I'm makin' it my business to know what they are. Count on it."

CHAPTER THIRTEEN

RANDI HAD NIGHTMARES that night. Genuine dyed-in-the-wool nightmares. In the morning her bedclothes were tangled in a twisted jumble and half on the floor; her hair and nightgown were soaked with sweat. She'd awakened with her fists clenching on the sheets and her heart slamming against her chest.

Oddly enough, she couldn't remember the content of the nightmares; and her memory of what had happened on the beach was rather vague. She remembered the bonfire with Travis, the wieners and marshmallows, the champagne. But that was all. The rest faded into a blur she didn't care to examine or try to recall. She only knew that somehow she'd left, gotten herself to the cottage and then into bed.

But she did know she had no desire to continue seeing Travis McLean. Research or not, she wanted to drop the whole idea, and Jill would just have to understand. As for McLean's designs on Matt...

"I'll deal with that later if I have to," she muttered as she hurried into the shower. "If I avoid him, maybe he'll get the idea. Then I won't need to deal with him at all."

But to avoid him, she had to be where he couldn't find her. His habit of showing up unannounced made it imperative that she not be here if he did. At first she considered leaving the cottage early. But to do that, she'd need to explain her reasons to Jill and David, who'd planned to return with Matt to the cottage. But how could she explain to them what she hardly understood herself?

A plan began to form as she dressed; it solidified as she gulped down a couple of cups of strong coffee. If she needed further proof of having had her sleep disturbed by nightmares, her body's lethargy confirmed it; she felt like a zombie.

Her plan involved not answering the phone in case Travis tried to call. Of course, she'd first need to make a quick call to Jill in Orlando, inventing some excursion that would be keeping her away from the phone for several days; she didn't want Jill and David to worry. Then she'd spend every waking hour out of the cottage—sightseeing, antiquing, whatever. As long as it kept her away from the cottage and beach. Away from the places where Travis would look for her.

With all this firmly in mind, she was pulling out of the drive by nine that morning. The phone had rung as she was leaving the cottage, but she didn't answer it, despite the fact that it could have been Jill. Unfortunately no one had answered when she called Jill and David's suite, and she'd had to leave her message with the hotel desk. But perhaps that was for the best; her sister was a shrewd judge of her moods, so speaking to her directly might have alerted her; then she'd have had awkward questions to answer.

Meanwhile, she had an itinerary worked out, and she'd stick to it. Travis wouldn't find her. He might even think she'd left for good. She'd drawn the shades and locked up as if she had.

Her only moment of uncertainty came when she was speeding down the highway. When disturbing images of a warm male body and drugging kisses intruded. Muttering a curse, she thrust them aside.

TRAVIS SLAMMED DOWN the receiver with a frustrated growl. Beside him on the bed, Ulysses raised his head and whined, as if to ask what was wrong.

"Sorry, fella." Travis reached out and stroked the pup's

shaggy head reassuringly. "It's not your fault she doesn't answer."

He'd been phoning Randi's cottage since before nine. It was now past noon. In the interim he'd even driven over there, only to find no one home. Moreover, the cottage had looked deserted—shades drawn, no swimsuit hung out to dry, no Jeep in the drive.

He'd even searched the beach; but though he combed it for a good mile in both directions, there'd been no sign of her. Dammit, it looked as if she'd gone home. Yet he knew she had more than a week of vacation left. Had last night spooked her so badly she'd cut her time here short?

It was possible, he supposed, given her state of near hysteria last night. Remembering the terror in her eyes had him swearing softly and eyeing his suitcase; there was a company shrink in Langley; maybe he could finagle some answers out of the guy. Answers as to what could make a woman act that way, given the circumstances.

The circumstances. The thought brought a sardonic twist to his mouth. The plain fact was that a woman had gone ballistic while he was in the process of making love to her. Not exactly what a man had in mind after a romantic picnic under the stars.

He glanced again at the suitcase standing beside the dresser, then shook his head. Langley would have to wait; Ulysses had an appointment with the vet tomorrow, and it made sense to have his leg checked by the vet who first saw him.

Travis leaned back on the bed, his face a resolute mask. It wasn't just the shrink he'd consult in Langley. The data base held the name of the counselor the Terhune girls had seen, even if the nature of their sessions was too privileged a piece of information to show up. But if the counselor was still in business, the guy would probably have a file on them.

He might be way off base, but Randi's fit of hysteria on

the beach had Travis deeply worried; it couldn't be normal, and she *had* been in counseling for quite a bit of time. What if it left her functioning normally most of the time, but subject to irrational behavior under certain circumstances? Dammit, there was Matt to think of!

He smiled grimly. It wouldn't be the first time he'd broken into someone's private files for information that couldn't be had any other way. Jason Cord would never sanction it of course, but Jason didn't need to know. Jason, he thought, his fear making his imagination mushroom, didn't have a son being raised by a woman who just might be wacko and maybe, just maybe, unfit to be a mother.

JILL GLANCED at the sleeping figure of her nephew in the back seat of the Volvo and frowned. It wasn't like Matt to fall asleep in the middle of the day. Always a lively child, he'd given up morning naps before he was a year old and had quit needing naps altogether before he turned three.

"David," she said, turning to her fiancé, "did Matt seem unusually subdued to you at breakfast?"

David shrugged. "Maybe a little. Why?"

She explained about the naps.

He smiled. "He's probably worn-out, honey. God knows, I am. I don't think I've ever walked so much in my life. Not even in the army."

He glanced at her, giving her cheek a gentle stroke before returning his eyes to the road. "How about you, lady? Aren't you just a mite tired, too? C'mon now, 'fess up."

"Who, me?" Jill looked indignant. "I can't imagine what makes you say that. Just because my feet feel like they've been bent into pretzels? And the thought of waiting in one more line has me ready to spit? Or, hey, I know! It's because I look like the wicked witch of the west just as she began to melt into a little puddle, right?"

"Huh, some wicked witch. If they all looked like you, the fairy tales would be in trouble. Wicked witches are supposed to be ugly, y'know. And they sure aren't supposed to have long sexy legs!'' He glanced at them and whistled.

She chuckled, batting her lashes at him and raising the hem of her miniskirt higher.

''Woman,'' he groaned, ''behave yourself. We have an innocent child in this car!''

She chuckled again and blew him a kiss. She was thoroughly at home with her sexuality and loved these playful little exchanges with David. She was also aware it was something she never could have achieved without the help of Dr. Carol Martin. Or David.

He was the only lover she'd ever had, all she'd ever want, and she thanked God for him every day of her life. It sometimes seemed a miracle that she'd found this sensitive caring man to love. To love her as she grew stronger and recovered from her childhood trauma of sexual abuse.

She sighed. If only Randi could experience the same miracle. But her sister needed to come to terms with her own abuse first, and she feared Randi wasn't open to doing that.

In the back seat, Matt mumbled incoherently in his sleep. She caught a ''Travis'' among the garbled sounds.

David caught it, too. ''Uh-oh, sounds like the half-pint's still engrossed with Mister You-know-who. Ol' Randi's not gonna be too happy about that.''

''Not unless she found out something promising about the man's intentions, which I rather doubt,'' Jill said. ''You see, what *I* might regard as promising isn't likely to be viewed as such by my sister.''

''Come again?''

''Well, maybe I'm just being a foolish romantic, but...''

''There nothing foolish about being a romantic, love.''

She smiled at him, reaching over to touch his hand. ''I fully agree, darling. From our perspective, there isn't, but Randi's another kettle of fish. And yet... Oh, David, I know it sounds crazy, but wouldn't it be neat if Randi and this Travis could somehow…''

"Now, that *does* begin to sound…well, not foolish, but certainly unrealistic, sweetheart. You know your sister's got a big wall around her where men are concerned. And we both know that wall's not likely to come down unless she goes back into counseling.''

Jill had taken David into her confidence with regard to what she knew about Randi's own trauma. He was to be her husband, after all, and she wanted no secrets between them.

She knew the confidence was safe; David would never say anything to anyone about it.

She sighed. "You're right of course, but that doesn't keep me from hoping for a miracle.''

"I know, love, but the only miracle Randi seems to want right now is for McLean to disappear from her life—and from Matt's.''

She nodded. "Yet from the sound of things, that's not likely to happen.'' She glanced at the car phone. "Drat, I wish she weren't away on those walking tours, so we could call her.''

"Yeah,'' he agreed, "and not just about McLean. I'd feel better if we could be sure she's heard the weather forecast.''

Again Jill nodded. A tropical storm had been building in the Caribbean during the past few days. They'd left early because of it. Its winds had built to more than seventy-five miles an hour, making it a full-fledged hurricane. They'd tried to reach Randi to alert her but hadn't been able to reach her. A hurricane threatening the mainland could jeopardize more than Florida. The entire Eastern Seaboard was a possible target; there was no telling how fast Hurricane Alphonse would move or which path it would take.

Frowning, Jill turned on the radio and searched for a weather report.

RANDI ENTERED the cottage with a tired sigh, setting down her packages and flicking on lights. It was still an hour till sunset, but the day had turned dark under a leaden overcast sky. That presaged a storm, if she was any judge, and she hoped it would blow over by morning. She didn't fancy all these shopping expeditions in bad weather.

She set a kettle on the stove for tea and then slumped onto a kitchen chair. There were few things more depressing than rain on a beach vacation.

While waiting for the water to boil, she massaged the tired muscles at the back of her neck. Between sightseeing and shopping, she'd worn herself out. Still, a satisfied smile hovered on her lips.

To help kill time, she'd gone back to the antiques shop where she'd seen the mermaid weathervane. To her surprise, the proprietor had been running a one-day sale. Ten percent off everything, and on the weathervane, that amounted to a few hundred dollars. Still, that didn't make it cheap.

Yet she'd been tempted, and she'd asked about the piece, learning its provenance, or authenticated history, from the proprietor. Mr. Connelly was an elderly man with a kind smile, and they'd enjoyed a lengthy conversation about their love of old things. Randi had openly admired the weathervane, but explained about her limited budget, even when it came to buying a wedding gift for her only sibling. To her amazement, Mr. Connelly had offered to take another ten percent off.

The mermaid was currently resting in the hallway, along with some plastic gismos for Matt, and she wasn't a bit sorry. She'd cut down on some personal luxuries in the coming year, that was all, and stretch her budget to cover it.

The kettle whistled, and she rose to make her tea, just as headlights appeared in the drive.

"Uh-oh," she murmured, praying it wasn't Travis as she

moved to the window and peered out. The Volvo? What were they doing back this early? There were still four days to go. She felt a stir of uneasiness as she ran to greet them.

Her sister gave her a huge hug as David hauled Matt, barely awake, out of his car seat. ''Mommy?'' the four-year-old mumbled sleepily.

Randi glanced at Jill, and her uneasiness grew. Matt hadn't called her anything but ''Mom'' for ages. ''Jill, what's wrong? Why are you back so early?''

''We'll explain in a minute, but Matt's just been awfully tired this trip,'' Jill said. ''I guess Disney World finally wore him out.''

Randi took her son from David and drew him into her arms for a fierce hug. ''Lord, I missed you,'' she murmured into his tousled hair. She drew back a bit to examine him. ''How's my guy? Are you hungry?''

''Uh-uh,'' Matt said around a huge yawn, ''but I'm awful sleepy.'' He leaned his head on her shoulder and closed his eyes.

Frowning, Randi put a hand on his forehead, but he didn't feel especially warm. She glanced at Jill, who looked as if she were about to say something, but David spoke first.

''Randi, we can't stay long, and we think you and Matt should leave tonight.''

''Tonight?'' Randi had been carrying Matt to his room, and she turned to look questioningly at David. ''But why?''

''It's the hurricane,'' said Jill. ''It's only nearing Florida now, but—''

''Hurricane?''

''Where have you been?'' David asked. ''It's on all the newscasts. Hurricane Alphonse. They're saying it could be a bad one.''

Randi felt foolish. In her efforts to avoid Travis, she'd been out and about for days, and not once had she gone near a TV—the cottage didn't come with one—or turned on a radio. While in the Jeep, she'd operated only her CD player when she had a yen for music, and when she'd returned each night, she'd gone straight to bed. "I hadn't heard," she murmured awkwardly.

"Well, no harm done," David said, "as long as you get yourself and Matt out of here tonight. Alphonse may not come anywhere near the Eastern Shore, but I don't like the idea of you guys being here, even if the possibility's remote. Better to play it safe."

She nodded, glancing at her slumbering son. "I'll just put Matt down in his room while I pack. Will you guys at least stay for some tea or something?"

Jill and David looked at each other and nodded. "Tea sounds great," Jill said as her fiancé headed for the kitchen.

"Didn't I see a radio in here somewhere?" he called as Randi laid Matt on the bed and covered him with a blanket.

"It's next to the microwave," she called back, then checked Matt's forehead once more for fever. It wasn't like him to fall asleep this early. But then again, he'd been riding in a car for hours and he'd had a busy week.

When his brow still seemed cool to the touch, she shrugged. He could sleep in the Cherokee easily, which was just as well. He didn't need to endure another long car ride awake.

The three adults drank mugs of tea while David tried to get a weather report, but the ancient radio gave out nothing but static. Jill and David washed up in the kitchen while Randi finished packing, and a short while later, the engaged couple were on their way out the door.

"See you soon," Jill called as they waved goodbye. "And drive carefully!"

Randi chuckled as she waved them off. Jill, the mother hen. As she closed the door, she stole a glance at the sky and frowned. There were no stars visible, what with the overcast. A stiff breeze was blowing from the ocean. Still, there wasn't any rain yet.

She moved thoughtfully toward Matt's bedroom. She was bone-tired from all the shopping and sightseeing, and driving for several hours tonight seemed like more than she could handle. Not that she'd said anything to David and her sister about it. They'd only have worried, and she was a big girl, after all, capable of making adult decisions.

Tiptoeing to the bed where Matt slept, she gazed down at him. Asleep, he looked so very young and vulnerable, she reflected, and a lump formed in her throat. He *was* young and vulnerable of course; but he was growing up so fast. When she'd taken him from David's arms, she'd been astounded at how heavy he was. Next year at this time she probably wouldn't be able to carry him at all.

Lord, where had the time gone? It seemed like only yesterday she was bringing him home from the hospital. A tiny bundle in a soft blanket, smelling of baby powder and that special scent that belonged only to infants.

Surprised at the wetness on her cheek, she brushed it away and bent to place a kiss on her son's brow. "Matt?" she said loudly enough for him to hear without difficulty. "Matt, can you wake up?"

He stirred in his sleep, but didn't awaken.

"Matt, it's Mom. Can you wake up just for a minute, honey?"

But he slept on, and Randi found herself fighting a yawn. The combination brought her to a decision. Matt was obviously exhausted. And so was she. It didn't make sense to drive for half the night in such a state, and they'd both feel better in the morning after a night's sleep. Besides, it didn't look as if Alphonse was anywhere near the Eastern Shore yet, if it ever arrived at all.

Stifling another yawn, she headed for the other bedroom. She'd set her alarm for an early hour and drive home then. Jill and David need never know. Meanwhile, she'd be rested for the long drive. Safer. Much safer.

CHAPTER FOURTEEN

"MOMMY..."

Randi raised her head groggily from the pillow. She had a hazy awareness of something beating against the windows. Rain. Was that what had awakened her or something else? A summer storm was apparently buffeting the cottage. Maybe the wind—

"Mommy..." the cry came again.

Matt! She came instantly awake, scrambling out of the covers and stumbling toward her son's room. Dear God, it was Matt, and he sounded terrible!

"Sweetheart, I'm here," she crooned, dropping to her knees beside Matt's bed and turning on the bedside lamp. "Tell me what's..."

She sucked in a breath as she felt the heat radiating from Matt's small body. Her hand went immediately to his brow, though she didn't need to touch him to know he had a fever. When she did, she let out a choked cry of alarm. *He was burning up!*

"Mommy..." It came out as a whimper now, though she could see he wasn't awake.

"Matt, honey, Mommy's here." Her mind raced as she thought what to do. She was an experienced nurse, accustomed to dealing with things far more serious than a fever. Yet a fever was merely a symptom, the body's signal that it was fighting an infection.

But this was *Matt*. He'd always been a vigorous healthy child. She'd never had to nurse him through anything more daunting than a cold. He'd never even experienced those slightly elevated temperatures following childhood inoculations.

And this was no slightly elevated temperature. God in heaven, it felt like it was well over a hundred.

The thought galvanized her, and she ran to her room where her baggage lay. She always carried a digital thermometer, as well as aspirin for herself and acetaminophen for Matt. She'd take his temp, then dose him with the latter to bring down the fever.

Switching on lights as she ran, she became more aware of her surroundings. Rain lashed the windows in torrents, and the wind had a high-pitched keening sound. The word *hurricane* flashed in her brain, and she fought against a rush of panic. She had to keep calm.

Minutes later she held the thermometer with a hand that shook and felt a ripple of fear along her spine: 104.6!

Matt tossed restlessly on the bed, alternately seeking relief from the heat by trying to throw off the covers and huddling beneath them, succumbing to fits of shivers. Her hands still none too steady, Randi reached for the bottle of liquid acetaminophen, thankful she hadn't brought chewable tablets, which might be hard to get into him.

"Matt, darling," she urged, holding him steady by one of his narrow shoulders as he tried to twist away, "here's something to make you feel better."

Inserting the dropper in the corner of his mouth, she squeezed the bulb at the end and watched anxiously as he swallowed the liquid. Compounding her concern was that he gave no indication he recognized her, only mumbling incoherently from time to time and whimpering her name. He was delirious.

A deafening crack resounded from outside, and she gave a startled cry. A glance at the window revealed nothing but darkness beyond the rain-lashed panes. She thought of the Cherokee in the drive, then of darkness and shrieking winds and torrential rain. With a grim shake of her head, she discarded the notion of driving to a doctor or hospital.

At that moment the lights flickered and went out. She gasped, barely relaxing when they came back on a moment later. Dear God, what would she do if the electricity failed? The heating system was also electric; loss of light and heat would cripple her ability to do anything.

Yet she was limited in what she could do, anyway. She was a trained nurse, yes, but without proper medical supplies or facilities. Again the lights flickered, and she fought to contain a rising panic while she thought what to do.

Turning abruptly, she ran for the kitchen, *hurricane* reverberating in her mind. The number of the local hospital was listed on a card the owners had taped beside the phone on the wall. It was time to call for an ambulance.

Moments later Randi felt fear clawing at her throat and she swallowed a sob. The phone was dead.

The image of her Cherokee, with its four-wheel drive, came to her rescue. The mere thought of driving in this weather frightened her, but she'd do it. For Matt, she'd do whatever it took.

As if needing sight of the Jeep's reassuring presence to steady her nerves, she ran to the front door. Throwing on the floodlight, which was aimed over the drive, she unlocked the door and pulled it open a crack—

And yelped, as the wind nearly tore it from her grasp. Pitting her weight against the door to keep it steady, she peered into the howling night. Wind-driven rain pummeled her face and soaked her nightgown. She shoved a skein of wet hair away from her eyes, trying to see.

Dear Lord, no!

The entire hood of the Jeep was caved in. That was the crack of noise she'd heard. It had been smashed by the weight of the flagpole, which the wind had snapped like a matchstick and hurled onto a vehicle parked yards away. She was entirely cut off. Helpless.

TRAVIS SPOKE SOOTHINGLY to Ulysses as he maneuvered his car through the teeming rain. He'd intended leaving hours before, but the unspoken needs of his landlady had changed his plans. The handyman Mrs. Muncie relied on to help with heavy work at the bed-and-breakfast had suffered a back injury, and she'd had no one to help her prepare for the hurricane. Travis had spent hours boarding up windows and generally securing the building. He'd then insisted on driving the elderly widow to her sister's house, which lay on higher ground.

Now, as he squinted through the windshield that his wipers barely cleared enough to glimpse through, he swore softly. Mrs. Muncie's sister and brother-in-law had urged him to stay at their place, at least for the night. He should have listened to them.

Alphonse had bypassed most of Florida and headed out to sea; then it had veered unpredictably westward until it hit land, where it straightened and charged up the coast. The eye of the hurricane, according to the last report before he'd made his decision to chance driving home, was still some sixty miles to the south. How was he to know that was close enough to cause these hellish winds and pounding rain?

But something—call it an inner sense he couldn't put a name to—had urged him to go. And now that same undefined feeling was taking him past the bed-and-breakfast and on up the road. To the cottage where Randi and Matt stayed. Why, he couldn't begin to say, but—

"Damn!" Travis exclaimed, slowing the car. Carefully tapping the brakes to avoid skidding, he stared incredulously through the rain. There were lights on in the cottage!

Was it Randi or had she left? Maybe it was the owner, stopping by to batten down for the storm. But if it was Randi, why the hell was she still there? Furious that she could be so incautious, he turned the rental car toward the cottage.

"Sweet Jesus..." He swallowed a lump of fear as his headlights picked out the wreckage of the Cherokee under the broken flagpole. Had she been inside when...

He didn't allow himself to complete the thought and brought the car to a halt. Speaking a few reassuring words to Ulysses, he cut the engine. Wasn't that sister of hers supposed to bring Matt back to the cottage when they returned from Orlando? What if...

He wouldn't allow himself to complete that thought, either.

He told himself the lights in the cottage meant Randi, and maybe his son, were inside. Shoving his arms into the slicker Mrs. Muncie had insisted he take, he urged Ulysses to stay. Gusts of wind threatened to tear the car door off its hinges as he emerged from the vehicle. He ran to the Jeep, bracing himself for what might be inside. *Nothing, thank God.*

Racing to the door, he hammered on it with his fist. "Randi, open up! It's Travis!" He gave the doorknob a twist and was amazed to find it unlocked.

"Randi!" he shouted. "It's Travis and I'm comin' in, so—" He froze after barely managing to wrestle the door shut behind him. Randi had stepped into the hallway. She wore a nightgown that was dripping wet, and her long hair was plastered to her head and shoulders. She came toward him, and his heart leapt to his throat when he saw the ravaged look on her face.

"Travis," she said in a voice not her own, a naked pleading in her eyes. "It's Matt. *Help me.*"

Flinging the slicker aside, he closed the distance between them, his hands settling gently on her shoulders. "Easy, sweetheart. Tell me..."

With a sob, she broke away and whirled toward the bedrooms. He ran after her, trying to make sense out of her stammered account of what was wrong. He grasped the words "burning up" and "flagpole," but little else.

Then they were in the room, and he understood all too clearly as he saw his son. Matt was tossing on the bed, shouting and flailing at the twist of blankets covering his small body. He was obviously delirious.

"Randi, listen to me," Travis said, taking her by the shoulders and giving her a shake as she babbled something and lapsed into violent sobs. He shook her again, harder.

She gasped, then seemed to get hold of herself, meeting his eyes. "Okay," she replied through bloodless lips. "I'm...okay."

"Good girl," he said, grabbing a rumpled sheet that lay on the floor. "Now, go to the bathroom and wet this with cool water," he ordered briskly. "Hurry."

He was already turning toward the bed as she obeyed. As he approached, his jaw tightened. Matt's small body had begun to jerk spasmodically. Convulsions! Rare in a child as old as four, but not unheard of.

Quickly he lifted the child's upper body from the mattress, wincing at the heat emanating from the small frame. Tilting Matt's head back to assure he had a clear passage for air to pass, he wondered where Randi was with the wet sheet. His free hand went to the buttons on Matt's thin summer pajamas, deftly undoing them, despite the tremors that shook the boy. Meanwhile, his eyes watched the sweep of the second hand on his watch. The phrase *brain damage* hovered at the edge of his consciousness as he counted out the seconds. If the convulsions lasted much longer...

Randi ran in with the sheet and nearly lost it again when she saw Matt's convulsions.

The sheet was torn from her grasp. Without a word, Travis began applying sections of it to the child's fevered flesh, already stripped of the pajamas.

Randi bit her lip, dimly aware of the taste of blood as she watched. Matt shuddered and jerked as Travis worked, applying cool compresses to lower a dangerously high fever. She should have thought of that. Yet she'd panicked

and become useless, unable to think. But Travis, thank God,
hadn't. Nothing in the man's demeanor suggested the kind
of inner turmoil she felt. He was all calm efficiency and
controlled purpose.

Only Travis knew what his control cost him; inside he
was a mass of roiling emotions. This was his son, and he
knew then that he loved the kid more than his life. Losing
his control would help no one, and he struggled to retain
the calm necessary to the physician he'd once trained to
be.

And he prayed. Prayed the wet sheet would lower Matt's
temp and end the convulsions. If it didn't...

He throttled yet another thought before it could form.

RANDI SAT SILENTLY beside her son's hospital bed, her eyes
never leaving his pale face. *He's going to be all right,* she
told herself for the umpteenth time since their arrival. *He's
going to be all right.*

Vaguely she was aware of howling wind and rain beating
against the panes of the room's double windows. Just as
she was vague about the details of the endless car ride that
had brought them here. She recalled little beyond that hot
little body in her arms as they drove through the night and
the storm. Hot, yes, but mercifully free of convulsions.
Convulsions that had made brain damage a harrowing possibility.

She also recalled, from that interminable ride in the car,
the gut-wrenching fear that Matt could die before they
reached this place of help and safety. Now she remembered
one more thing.

Travis.

Without stopping to piece out the details, she had an
unfailing sense of Travis McLean as a rock-solid presence
during the entire ordeal. His arrival at the cottage alone had
seemed a godsend; even now she wanted to weep with

relief at the miracle of it. Just seeing him there, strong, confident, capable.

At the very moment she'd begun to lose hope, he'd given her the strength to hang on and do what needed to be done. To pull herself together. Shame burned her cheeks as she remembered how she'd lost control. An experienced ER nurse!

So it had been Travis who'd made the difference in the end, not she. Travis, who'd saved Matt. She'd only done what he told her. She'd never have acted without his help.

She thought of the confidence he'd inspired. Dear heaven, he'd have made a wonderful doctor! She thought about his years of medical training and wanted to scream at the waste. Surely the world needed competent physicians more than it needed spies.

Matt stirred restlessly in his sleep, pulling at the IV tube that dripped an antibiotic into his arm. A urinary infection, they'd said. As for the convulsions, yes, they were rare in a child this old, but it happened; even adults occasionally had them.

Matt moaned softly in his sleep; frowning, she reached to feel his brow, then released a pent-up breath. Still feverish, but nothing like before. *He's going to be all right.* She repeated the words like a mantra. *He's going to be all right....*

"MR. MC LEAN?"

Travis's head jerked up from the magazine he'd been staring at without seeing. An attractive brunette who looked vaguely familiar entered the waiting room; she was followed by a lean man with sandy brown hair.

"Jill Terhune," the woman said, extending her hand as he rose to meet her. "Thank you for calling us," she added, gesturing to the man beside her. "My fiancé, David Brooks."

The men shook hands, taking each other's measure while

Jill stood aside and surreptitiously assessed Matt's father. Her first thought was that this was what her nephew would look like in thirty years. But there was so much more.

Movie-star handsome and radiating maleness like a huge neon sign, McLean was the sexiest piece of testosterone-laden flesh she'd ever laid eyes on. Even minus her fears about Matt, it was no wonder Randi wanted to keep him at a distance. A man like this was way out of Randi's league. If, she amended, her sister even had a league where men were concerned. But she'd have been alert to the dangerous male animal implicit in every inch of the man.

Then he turned, giving Jill a tired smile, and she found herself quickly reassessing. There was an undeniable sense of decency, of basic human kindness, in the tired lines of his face. Yes, and sensitivity lurking in the blue eyes that crinkled at the corners when he smiled. Intelligent eyes, she realized at once.

"Y'all got here pretty quickly," Travis said. "No trouble with the roads, I reckon?" He'd managed to get the phone number from Randi before they arrived at the hospital, and he'd called Jill at once. "Have you seen Randi yet? Or Matt?"

"No," Jill said, "but we spoke to the pediatrician on duty, and he seems to think Matt's out of danger, thank God."

Travis nodded. "A urinary infection, which spiked a high night fever." He smiled softly at both of them. "Don't y'all worry now. We got him here in time."

"We're about to go on up to the room," David said, "but we wanted to see you first and thank you."

"No thanks necessary. Matt's my...my flesh and blood, and even if he wasn't, I'd have done what I could to help. You'd have done the same."

"I'd have tried," David said with a wry smile, "but I hardly have your expertise. I understand you have a medical background."

"Uh...yeah." Travis glanced away from David's curious gaze.

A nurse entered the waiting room, crisp in her white uniform. "Miss Terhune?"

Jill turned, nodded.

"Doctor says you can go up now."

Jill and David both moved, and the nurse added, "Sorry, but the rules say only two visitors at a time. And his mother's already there. Been at the bedside the whole time, you know."

"You go on, sweetheart," David said, putting a gentle hand on Jill's shoulder. "I can—"

"Uh, David?" Travis's voice turned both Jill and David toward him. "I was wonderin'," he said, "if I might have a few words with your fiancée—" he looked questioningly at Jill "—if it's all right with you, that is?"

Jill nodded. She'd been hoping to talk to McLean. "You go up first, honey," she said to David. "I don't mind. Just tell Randi I'll be along shortly, okay?"

David hesitated a moment, searching her face. Apparently satisfied with what he saw, he nodded and followed the nurse.

"Mr. McLean—" Jill began the moment the door shut behind them.

"It's Travis," he told her. "We all share too much to be formal with each other. Uh, it's Jill, right?"

She smiled a nod at him. "But look, Travis, despite what you told David, we all owe you a deep debt of gratitude. No," she added when he shook his head and began to wave this away. "It's clear, even from the little you told us, that if you hadn't helped..."

She choked back a sob, and Travis handed her his handkerchief, waiting patiently while she regained control.

"Well," she said at length, "I wanted you to know we're grateful, that's all. Matt's your flesh and blood, but he's ours, too, and we love him to blazes."

"Yeah," he said softly, a tender smile on his face, "me, too."

She raised teary eyes to meet his gaze. "What you did was done for your son, but it gave us the miracle of *two* lives that might've been lost, Travis. I...I don't think Randi could've survived. You see, Matt's her whole world. She'd never be the same if anything happened to him."

He nodded solemnly.

"I don't know how we can ever repay you," she went on. "Still, there must be *something*."

He started to wave her words away again, then stopped. He eyed her steadily for several seconds before he spoke. "Okay, Jill," he said, and the blue eyes were grim as they met hers. "There is somethin' you can do."

"Name it."

"You can tell me why your sister's afraid of men."

CHAPTER FIFTEEN

JILL DIGESTED Travis's words in stunned silence. This was the last thing she'd expected. Her mind raced as she tried to form a reply.

Her first instinct was to tell him it was none of his business. The truth, because it wasn't anyone's business but Randi's. And Randi was loath to discuss it with anyone, even her own sister. Jill would be betraying a confidence, the magnitude of which even Randi couldn't see—or face.

Yet that was just the problem. Randi needed to unlock the door to her past, needed to face it. Because if she didn't, Jill was certain she'd never find the happiness she herself had found by confronting her past and going beyond it.

Could Travis McLean be the key to unlocking that door? His question said he was aware of a problem, which was a wonder in itself; Randi had never let a man get close enough to sense even that much. Had the bond they shared through Matt broken down some of her sister's carefully erected barriers? Or was it more basic than that? Was there something in the man himself that inspired trust, inspired Randi to let him inside, if only a little?

Taking a deep breath, Jill decided to do some careful probing. "Tell me something, Travis. Why is it important for you to know this? I mean, I assume it's important or you wouldn't ask. You didn't want any other compensation for what you've done."

"Smart lady," he said, a flash of approval in his eyes.

"Huh," she said with a grin, "no one ever accused my folks of raising dummies."

He smiled, then his face sobered. "It's important for two reasons. The first is Matt. Never doubt this, Jill. It was only weeks ago I learned I had a son. But I love the kid more than anything in the world. What happens to him, his welfare, is major with me. So I can't help worryin' if his mother's...problem won't leak over onto him."

She nodded thoughtfully. "I understand, but I don't think you need to be concerned. Matt's a happy normal child. Surely you've seen that. Randi's got good instincts. They've translated into excellent parenting skills. Thanks mostly, I think, to our folks, who were wonderful parents." She paused. "I'm not a bit worried, Travis, so I don't think you need be, either. After all, I ought to know. I'm closer to Randi and Matt than anyone. Now, what's your other reason?"

He was silent for a moment, digesting what she'd said. Matt did seem normal and happy, and Jill certainly didn't appear concerned. Still...

Deciding to keep his mind—and options—open with regard to Matt, he pondered how best to answer her question. To phrase something he'd only begun to try to fathom himself.

"My other reason," he said slowly, feeling his way carefully through uncharted waters, "has to do with Randi. Of course, I don't know your sister all that well..." He thought of that day in the parking lot, when Randi had told him she refused to discuss her reasons for having a child by the means she'd chosen. "Though not for lack of tryin'," he added wryly.

"Still, there's somethin'—" he plowed a hand through his hair and heaved a sigh "—hell, I'm not even sure why, but...there's somethin' about your sister, Jill. And I'm not just talkin' 'bout her bein' Matt's mother here. It's more than that. There's somethin' 'bout Randi that makes me give a damn 'bout what happens to her, y'know?''

Again Jill nodded. She believed that. Travis had begun to care for Randi, perhaps more than he knew. Or was willing to admit even to himself.

She ran her gaze over his face, its lines of fatigue a testament to a long sleepless night filled with stress. To what he'd endured as he raced through a hurricane to reach this place, knowing Matt's life hung in the balance. To the hours he'd kept vigil, awaiting word of his son's condition.

Travis McLean, she decided, was a good decent man who cared deeply about the child he'd fathered. And who, perhaps, cared more than a little about that child's mother. And maybe, just maybe, he'd prove to be something more. Maybe Randi's chance for a normal life, for genuine happiness, was finally within the realm of possibility.

Praying she wasn't being fanciful or, worse, making a grave mistake, she placed a hand lightly on his arm. ''C'mon, sit with me. I think there's a story you ought to hear.'' She gestured to a set of chairs.

''Once,'' she began when they were seated, ''there were two little girls…''

And so, not without difficulty, she told him. Not all of the story, but the part she felt free to reveal. A story of two frightened young girls, newly orphaned, then stalked by the stepfather into whose care they'd been innocently left. The story of how that responsibility was monstrously abused. Of how this left the older girl a victim of sexual abuse, the younger, badly frightened and forever wary of men.

More than this official version of the tale, she didn't reveal; it wasn't hers to tell. But she clearly implied that, through the trauma of having been stalked and of having witnessed her older sister's plight, the younger child was just as much a victim, and just as badly hurt.

''In some ways, Travis,'' she concluded, fighting tears as she switched at last to the first person, ''my sister suffered more than I did. She…she's only two years younger, b-but when you're a kid, two years can make a big difference. Randi, oh, God, Randi was the b-baby, and I'd always kind of looked out for her—with Mom and Dad's backup. But with our parents gone, and me…me…'' She swallowed, unable to finish.

"With your folks gone and you a helpless victim," Travis said grimly as he handed her his handkerchief, "she felt the rug had been ripped out from under her. You both suddenly had no one to turn to. No one to protect you. It must've been hell."

Jill blew her nose and nodded, watching him carefully for his reaction. He sat across from her, leaning forward, feet widespread, elbows on his knees. A casual enough pose. Until she noted the hands he held clasped in front of him. They were white at the knuckles.

At length he raised his head, and she saw his eyes. She flinched at the look in them, even knowing it wasn't directed at her.

"I knew somethin' was wrong," he said tightly, trying to contain a red haze of rage that fogged his brain. Rage that made him want to bring back the piece of human slime who'd done this thing. For the unmitigated satisfaction of killing the bastard, slowly, oh, so very slowly, and without pity. *Get a grip, McLean. It all happened a long time ago, and your anger won't help Randi or Jill. Or Matt, either.*

"I just didn't have any idea what it could be," he went on. "I—I've never had any experience with this sort of thing."

"Most decent people haven't," she said quietly, "or think they haven't."

He shot her a quizzical glance.

"The sexual abuse of children," she said wearily, "is more common in our society than most of us think. The victims, sadly, are the least likely to talk. And sometimes, even when they do, they're not believed. If our stepfather hadn't been killed in that car accident, I might never've come forward. Who'd believe me? I used to think. It would be his word against mine.

"You see, he'd threatened me about that, about my telling anyone," she said tautly. "He said no one would take a kid's word over an adult's. Especially when that adult was an upstanding pillar of the community, which was the disguise he wore, by the way. Went to church every Sunday, attended PTA meetings, volunteered to drive our local senior citizens around. Yeah, a real model citizen."

Travis was still trying to eradicate the visions her story had conjured up in his mind. Having the bastard painted with detailed strokes didn't help.

"But you did get someone to believe you," he said. "And you eventually got counselin'?"

"Yes, thank God." She told him about the school guidance counselor and then about Dr. Martin. "Two wonderful compassionate women, Travis. Not to mention the support we had from our dear aunt Tess. We were very lucky."

He gave a brief nod, met her eyes. "But I don't get it, Jill. I mean, *you* seem to've come outta this thing okay. That is, I'm assumin' so, since you're gettin' married. David seems a decent guy. A blind man could tell y'all love each other."

"You've got *that* right," she said with a grin, then quickly sobered. "I told you we were lucky in the support we had in the aftermath of what happened. But what I didn't mention was, perhaps, where we were luckiest of all."

"And that was...?"

"In the same thing that gave Randi her good parenting skills. The positive relationship we had with our parents, particularly, our father—our biological father. Dr. Martin certainly felt it paved the way for my healthy relationship with David. Though it did take long hours of counseling to erase the effects of...of the other."

Travis dipped his head and nodded, thoughtful. Finally he raised it and met her gaze. "But what about Randi? Why hasn't she…"

"Why hasn't she come out of this thing okay?"

This time his nod was grim.

She paused, debating how to explain without betraying the ultimate confidence, the one even Randi couldn't acknowledge. "Because," she said at length, "when Dr. Martin pronounced me ready and able to get on with my life, to put the trauma behind me, Randi assumed she was equally okay. She left counseling when I did, despite Carol's urgings that she remain. Said if I was okay, she was okay, and that was that. She never went back."

Travis smothered a curse. "But that's like two people who begin takin' swimmin' lessons together, with the slower learner quittin' and declarin' himself a swimmer just because the other is. Hell, people don't progress at the same rate."

She sighed. "Try telling that to a certain blonde we both know."

He stifled an obscenity. "Of all the stubborn short-sighted—"

"Miss Terhune?" The nurse approached. "Your fiancé asked me to tell you it's your turn now. Your sister would like to see you."

"Yes, of course," said Jill, rising. "Please tell them I'm on my way up."

The woman turned and left. Travis rose to walk Jill to the door, stopping her there with a hand on the shoulder. "Thanks, Jill, for tellin' me. I know that it wasn't easy for you. Specially considerin' how…well, how slightly you know me."

She gave him a wry smile. "Just don't make me regret it. Outside of counseling, I've trusted no one else but David with this confidence."

"I won't abuse that trust," he said, meeting her gaze with a sincerity she couldn't doubt.

"No, I don't think you will," she returned slowly. "Besides, you're Matt's father, and I do know this—you love him."

"Thanks for that," he replied with a crooked smile. "Oh, speakin' of confidences, you won't tell Randi I know, okay?"

She pondered this for a moment. "Not if you don't want me to."

He nodded. He didn't know where he was going from here—he had a lot to think about—but Randi was skittish enough without feeling vulnerable to him on that score. And he did know he wanted to be a part of Matt's life; he couldn't risk it.

Brightening, he gave Jill a playful punch on the arm. "Hey, lady, you're okay in my book."

She grinned. "Same to you, fella."

Then he sobered. "Jill, before you go, I want you to know one more thing."

"Shoot."

He reached into a pocket and withdrew a card. "My unlisted phone number, as well as the number where I can be reached at work," he told her. "If Matt ever needs me, I'm a phone call away. Promise you won't hesitate to make that call if it's needed?"

She took the card. "I promise," she said solemnly, and the two shook hands. Then she was gone, leaving Travis alone with all he'd learned.

Alone, and more shaken than he'd let on.

RANDI LOOKED OUT the window of David's Volvo, gazing absently at the uprooted trees and other debris they passed. A lot of damage had been left in Alphonse's wake. Beside her in his car seat, Matt made Donald Duck noises as he played with a couple of brightly colored Disney figures. He sounded normal, right as rain, and he was. Completely recovered, and they were taking him home.

So why was she feeling out of sorts? She and Matt had come through the worst kind of nightmare together. They'd survived it. Of course, if it hadn't been for Trav—

Her mind tripped on the name, prompting a scowl. That was it, of course. Travis, damn him. Why had he left the hospital so abruptly? Without seeing her, without even saying goodbye.

She couldn't understand it. As soon as Matt was out of danger, she'd inquired about Travis. She'd learned from Jill and David that he'd stayed in the waiting room all night, until he'd been assured Matt was okay. And then, the next thing she knew, he was gone.

Gone. Just like that. Lord, she hadn't even had a chance to thank him, although she knew Jill and David had. But that wasn't the point. *He saved Matt's life,* she thought, gazing with another surge of relief at her son. *And possibly mine, or at least my sanity.*

Travis had been like an anchor through that long horrible night. She'd wanted to see him, *talk* to him! The fact that he'd left so abruptly…

Face it, Terhune. It hurts.

Okay, she'd face it. It hurt. Especially after she'd learned he'd come by to check on Matt before he left. She'd been sleeping, finally giving in to her exhaustion and stretching out on that cot they'd put in Matt's room. Had his behavior been deliberate? Had he wanted to say goodbye to his son but not to her?

"Travis was here, Mom!" Matt had announced the next morning. "I was kinda sleepy, but I saw him. He said to get well real soon, 'n' then he told me about his new puppy. His name's 'Lysses, 'n' Travis said he had to go 'cause he had to feed 'Lysses. Wow, a puppy!"

They were the first words her son had spoken on awaking, and she'd wanted to laugh and cry at the same time.

A long speech like that! He was definitely on the mend. And she *had* laughed when his next words were "I'm hungry!"

Well, in pediatrics, she thought, *we always used to say kids are made of rubber. They bounce back. From illness, even from disappointment.*

Returning her gaze to the window, Randi wondered why the same wasn't true of adults.

"MCLEAN? MCLEAN! Dammit, what in hell's the matter with you?" Jason Cord's voice on the intercom sounded exasperated, even for him. "I've been trying to get your attention for a full minute!" It was an exaggeration, but Jason wasn't noted for his patience.

Travis frowned, dragging his eyes away from the page that had just appeared, via the Internet, on his computer screen. "Uh, sorry, Jace. Just got distracted there."

It was the truth. The information he'd been seeking all morning had popped up and caught his eye. Could he help it if it was in the middle of a routine conversation with his boss? This was important!

"Well, shoot, ol' buddy—" Cord's voice dripped sarcasm as he replied in a grossly exaggerated Southern accent "—whah didn't y'all say so? Ah mean, fah be it from me tuh stand in the way of an impawt'nt distraction!"

"Look, I said I was sorry, man. I—"

"Never mind! Now, would it be too much to ask you to bring those new budget figures to the meeting this afternoon? Maybe you haven't realized it, buddy, but this Congress is in a cost-cutting mood. So just in case you've missed the point, if we don't supply them with cost-effective figures, all our butts'll be in a sling!"

The intercom went dead and Travis heaved a sigh. He was well aware of the mood of the Congress. It reflected the mood of the entire country. In the wake of a few scandals, the public and its elected officials weren't kindly disposed toward the CIA these days. The current director of the Agency had made one thing clear at the outset of his tenure: unless they justified the effectiveness of every avenue of operations, their careers were all on the line. Hell, the future of the Agency itself was on the line.

Fortunately Travis had his facts and figures in order, having worked on them months before and finalized them in the two days since he'd returned from leave. He buzzed his secretary for an update on the final typing of the report, was assured it would be ready for the meeting and returned his gaze to the computer monitor.

Half an hour later, he sat back in his chair, folding his hands across his middle as he contemplated what he'd read. He'd dug through reams of material for it, since the company shrink hadn't been willing to discuss anything that wasn't directly related to company business. Well, screw the shrink. It had taken more time, but he now had the answers he'd sought.

According to the latest available information, gleaned from such periodicals as *Psychology Today* and the *Journal of the American Psychiatric Association,* Jill's counselor had probably been right: the ability of a person to form a normal healthy relationship with a member of the opposite sex depended heavily on the family history. Especially the person's relationship with the parent of the opposite sex.

When that history was tainted by parental sexual abuse, most professionals doubted it was possible for the person to succeed in a normal male-female relationship. But when the violation came from someone else, some felt the future wasn't such a closed door; if the patient was a woman, a warm, loving father was thought to be able to mitigate the trauma. Depending on how severe it was, and providing the patient had professional help. Like the help Jill Terhune had been lucky enough to come by.

The help her sister had abandoned.

But *why?* Travis shut down the terminal and swung out of his chair. Shoving his hands in his pockets, he began to pace.

He was still trying to deal with the disturbing facts of Jill's story. Why had it had shaken him so badly? News of the sexual abuse of kids wasn't entirely alien to him; the media were full of it. Famous people were coming forth every day to reveal the ugly truths they'd once have kept hidden. Ordinary people, too.

But their stories were part of the public domain. He'd read or heard about them—horrified, yes, but safely insulated by distance. They'd happened to *other* people. People he knew of, perhaps, but none that he actually *knew*.

The Terhunes' history was different. Never before had the tragic fact of childhood sexual abuse hit so close to home. He *knew* these women; one of them was the mother of his child.

Randi. He couldn't get her out of his mind.

He'd had two largely sleepless nights to prove it. He'd lain awake in bed, seized by memories of their brief time together. Images came and went...

Randi, standing on the beach, fiercely protective of her son—their son—ready to do battle with anything or anyone that threatened him. The sound of her laughter as they romped with that son in the surf. The look of compassion in her eyes as she stroked the head of a hurt and abandoned puppy. The earnest concern on her face when she inquired about a medical career that had been ditched.

Most of all, he couldn't erase the sweet warmth of her in his arms. It was different from what any other woman had ever made him feel, the sense of *rightness* to it, which he couldn't escape no matter how hard he tried.

And then, finally—the image he came back to again and again—that awful fear in her eyes when he'd tried to make love to her.

Abruptly ceasing his pacing, he reached for his Rolodex and flipped it to his sister's name and number. Grabbing the phone, he punched out the digits, praying Sarah was in. He'd attend Cord's blasted meeting, but then head straight for Georgetown. He needed to talk to someone he could trust. Someone he loved. Who loved him, knew him. And it wouldn't hurt, he suspected, that that someone was a woman.

CHAPTER SIXTEEN

"NOW, LET ME SEE if I've got this straight," Sarah said. Seated across from Travis in a booth at the coffee shop where they'd gone before, she leaned forward, keeping her voice low. "You recently learned you'd fathered a child? Who's now four years old?"

"I know I've shocked you, Sarah, but..." Travis shook his head and sighed.

She used both hands to sweep her straight chin-length hair away from her face, then flattened her palms on the table and met his eyes. "I suspect you wouldn't be tellin' me this unless there's more to the story. What's goin' on, Trav?"

Travis searched her face. "What would you say, Sarah girl," he said carefully, "if I told you I've spent time with my son durin' the past few weeks? That I've gotten to know him...love him?"

"Holy Hannah! But how? I thought the confidentiality in these clinics was—"

"It is," he interrupted, "but I reckon you could say fate stepped in 'n'... Yeah, it was fate, all right. And fate has a way of payin' confidentiality no mind, Sarah, no mind at all."

He told her then of the accidental encounter with his past. Of meeting his biological offspring's mother in the ER at Johns Hopkins. Of his shock on seeing his childhood double, right on the heels of recalling where he'd seen the mother years before. And then realizing what Randi Terhune had probably done to conceive her child. He told Sarah, too, of the time spent with Matt and Randi on the Eastern Shore, the immediate sense of bonding with his son, all of it.

Sarah sat, wide-eyed, her mouth forming a silent O as he finished with a recounting of the night of the storm, his long tense vigil at the hospital.

"So that's about it, Sarah. The kid came through it okay, thank God." He shrugged. "And, well, here I am."

She nodded slowly, needing time to digest it all. "My God, Travis," she murmured at length, "what a story. What a crazy incredible story!"

"Isn't it?" he said wryly. "I sometimes can't half believe it myself."

"What's he like, Trav? Your son. Matt, I mean. Lord, I'm an aunt! I can scarcely *believe* it."

He grinned at her. "He's beautiful. Full of energy, y'know? And incredibly curious and bright. Man, the questions he asks! And, Sarah, you should see him smile. A smile so sweet, it'll break your heart."

"Or steal it," she said in a voice full of wonder. She was blown away by what she saw in her brother. By the glow that surrounded him as he spoke of his son. By the love and pride that rang in his words, the light and pure joy in his eyes. "Any fool can see he's stolen yours," she added with a soft smile.

He gave her a level look. "I told you I came to love him, Sarah. But it didn't take much. Easiest thing I've ever done, lovin' that kid."

She nodded, and they sat in silence for a minute, both pensive. "Travis," she said at length, "tell me more about the mother. So far, all I know is that she seems to've raised a healthy happy child. Uh, not that that's a small thing, mind, but...forgive me, Trav, but what kind of woman avails herself of a sperm bank to, well, deliberately become a single mother?"

A woman terrified of men, he thought but didn't say. He forced a casual shrug. "A very independent-minded woman, I'd guess, though she hasn't done it entirely alone." He explained about Jill and David.

"Apart from that," he went on, "she's a competent professional." He spoke of Randi's nursing career and how she arranged her hours to accommodate her parenting. He mentioned nothing of her panic the night of the crisis; many doctors refrained from treating their own family members for emotional reasons. Hers had been a parent's very natural and human response.

He also didn't mention his own reaction that night, thought he remembered well how he'd been infused with a sense of purpose. And how, in the aftermath of Matt's recovery, he'd been filled with the deepest satisfaction imaginable; he'd never known anything like it. Of course, the implications of that gave him a lot to think about. But he'd take his time with it, examine it carefully, before giving voice to an idea that had been forming in his mind since that night.

"In short," he finished, "I'd say Randi Terhune has her life pretty well thought out and organized. She's no lightweight, Sarah. She's a careful person, with her feet planted squarely on the ground."

Sarah sensed a certain reluctance in Travis's description of this Randi. What was that about? Her eyes held a glint of mischief as she urged with a wily grin, "Tell me more."

"More?" Travis played dumb. It was a game they'd engaged in since childhood; intensely curious, Sarah had a way of worming out the tiniest details of a story, whether you wanted to reveal them or not. And in this she showed no mercy. Still, he always stalled a bit before he gave in. "Now, Pumpkin, what more could there be? I've told you all there is. Honest."

"Uh-huh," she replied, enjoying the game. "Okay, listen up. So far, I know this Randi's a good mother and a skilled competent nurse. Okay, fine. But what else? You know, the little things that make a person unique? Look, I'll make it easy for you. Start with what she looks like.''

He chuckled. ''That's easy. She's gorgeous. A pure knockout—but not in the way that sounds. I mean, nothin' overpowerin' or blatant. She comes off as a little, uh, cool, y'know? Sort of in the Grace Kelly mold. Tall and leggy, long honey blond hair like spun silk, eyes that make you think of...well, wild honey, all shot with sunlight, y'know? And the way she moves! If you looked up 'graceful' in the dictionary, it oughtta have Randi Terhune's picture next to it.''

''I see,'' Sarah muttered, more intrigued than ever. ''And what about—''

''Oh, I forgot to mention her nose.''

''Her nose?''

His mouth curved in a reminiscent smile. ''Damnedest thing I ever saw. One minute you're lookin' at this beautiful face, with a perfect fine-boned nose—and then she laughs. Next thing you know, it's all crinkled up, and you notice there's a sprinklin' of freckles 'cross the bridge.''

''Ah,'' Sarah said thoughtfully, but he wasn't through yet.

''The guys on the staff at Hopkins refer to her as an ice queen, but she's got all kinds of surprises buried under that cool exterior.'' His mind held an image of Randi near tears when she learned of Ulysses' mistreatment. ''She's compassionate, for one thing. Compassionate, yeah, 'n' warm 'n' intelligent 'n'—'' he chuckled ''—she can be downright fierce when it comes to protectin' Matt. Yeah, she's full of surprises. Fact is, I've never known a woman like her.''

He cocked an eyebrow at his sister. ''Well?'' His voice held amused tolerance. ''Will that do, you little ferret?''

She studied him carefully for a moment. Not only had he given her more than she'd wished in his sketch of this woman, he'd done it with precious little coaxing. There was definitely something brewing under the surface here. Impatient with their game, she came straight to the point.

"Travis," she asked, looking him dead in the eye, "are you in love with her?"

Taken aback by her bluntness, he lifted a brow before letting his face settle in a frown. In love? What did that mean, anyway? The stuff they showed on TV and in the movies? That nonsense poets wrote about? Hell, it was all an illusion. The trouble with movie plots and romantic poems was they only showed the first part. The idyllic time when emotions were fresh and new, and reality hadn't kicked in yet.

But what about what happened after the glow wore off? What about the countless marriages that started off sweet, then ended in bitterness and divorce? Or worse, marriages like his parents', where love was a pretense? A sham that caged two people together for life, both of them trapped and miserable? Where were the script writers and poets when reality hit, huh?

His mouth twisted in a rueful smile. "Sorry to disillusion you, little sister, but the only love I believe in's the family kind—if you're lucky, that is. You know, the kinda thing I feel for my son, the bond between you 'n' me 'n' Troy. All the rest's somethin' for poets 'n' fools. It doesn't last. Or it was never real in the first place."

She gave him a disgusted look. "When did you become such a cynic, Trav?" She held up her hand as he started to reply. "Never mind, I don't want to know. But I do want an explanation. Why've you gone to such—dare I call them poetic?—lengths in describin' this Randi? Eyes the color of wild honey, huh?"

She saw him flush beneath his tan and leaned forward, meeting his gaze with intense interest. "Travis, no man describes a woman the way you did without... well, without feelin' *somethin'!*"

He was clearly irritated. "I told you—she's gorgeous,

and gorgeous women have a way of... Hell, Sarah, I may be an old man by your reckonin', but I'm not dead yet.''

She was shaking her head. "Sorry, big brother, but it won't wash. You've got some special feelin' for this woman. You've connected with her, and you know it!''

He shrugged. "Sure, I feel somethin' for her. Is that so surprisin'? She's the mother of my son. Through Matt, we share a bond, a bond I couldn't ignore even if I wanted to. That's the connection. The *only* connection.''

She gave him what he'd always called her "superior woman's smile,'' even when she was a kid, and he heaved a disgusted sigh. Truth was, she was usually right when she smiled that way. But that would mean— Hell, no! Scowling, he abruptly changed the subject. "How're things on the home front these days?''

"Oh, you know—everyone's at Sunnyfields, doin' the usual,'' she replied. Mother's tennis game's better than ever. She and Susie Whittaker won the women's doubles at the club. Daddy, of course, has been away a lot. He just spent a week in Miami at some conference, and, matter of fact, he left just ahead of that hurricane you got caught in.

"And Troy's been seen with Betsy Chalmers—Debutante of the Year in 'ninety-two?—but I don't think it's serious. When he's home in the summer, he mainly dates to please Mother, and—''

"I can't stand it!'' Travis growled. "When's Troy gonna get some backbone, Sarah? His professional life's been dictated by the old man, and his social life's tailored to suit Mother. When's he gonna live his life for himself?''

"Don't be too hard on him, Travis. You know Troy's always been...well, different from you 'n' me. He's not cut out to be a rebel. But he's a good person, Trav, gentle 'n' kind, and there isn't a soul who doesn't like and trust him. And I know you love him, so—''

"'Course, I love him! That's just the point. I love him

too much to see him dolin' out his life in bits 'n' pieces to please others. It half kills me to see it!''

She threw him a look of sympathy. ''But the way things are, Trav, you're not really around to see it, are you?''

''What's that s'posed to mean?''

She shook her head wearily. ''This terrible division in the family. It's so almighty awful. You 'n' Daddy each pretendin' the other doesn't exist, the rest of us caught up in it. I wish to God there were some way to fix it.''

''Tell that to the old man,'' he said in disgust.

It was the sort of response she'd expected. Their father might have been the main cause of the rift, but Travis hadn't helped. Stubborn and proud, he staunchly defended his position, continuing to vilify their father without making a move toward reconciliation himself. Okay, so Daddy was autocratic and difficult; but his older son was hardly a Boy Scout. As long as Travis maintained his attitude, nothing would change.

Still, she had to give it a shot. ''Y'know, Trav, I believe Daddy's a deeply unhappy man.''

He greeted this with a snort, which she ignored. ''He's his own worst enemy, Trav. He doesn't see how his attitudes toward parentin', to his family, created all this strife.''

When Travis didn't comment, she placed her hand gently over his, which rested, clenched in a fist, on the table. ''Yet I do believe he loves us, Trav, all of us, you included. I think he's always loved us—in his mistaken way, of course.''

''Of course,'' he echoed mockingly.

She ignored this, too. ''He misses you, Trav, and I think he deeply regrets the breach. No, don't shake your head. It's true. It's just that he's foolishly put all the blame on you—just as you've done with him. And even if you're right, what good does it do? With each of you blamin' the other, neither of you'll make a move to heal things. As a result, we all suffer, don't you see?''

He'd heard all the arguments before, though largely from their mother. But this time he caught a new note in the litany. He glanced sharply at her. "You all suffer. You tryin' to tell me somethin', Sarah?"

She grimaced. "Oh, Trav, I'm so sorry! Daddy's furious and more unreasonable than ever. He's blamin' *you* for my decision to abandon medicine!"

DRIVING AWAY from the meeting with Sarah, Travis was more disturbed by her last piece of news than he'd let on. She was right, he realized. The breach between him and his father had filtered down to hurt the innocents in the family—his mother, Sarah, likely Troy, as well. They all suffered from it.

His hands tightened on the wheel. But it wasn't the traffic that had him tense. It was guilt. It wouldn't leave him alone. For the first time since the rift, he began to wonder if he shouldn't do something to try to mend it. But what?

Go to the old man and eat crow? But even if he did, what good would it do? His father's lack of forgiveness was tied irrevocably to his son's abandonment of the hallowed family career, and—

His breath caught as something jelled in his mind. Was it possible? Had the thing he'd been pondering since the night of the crisis with Matt given him a *double* window of opportunity? Not just the idea he'd been wrestling with, but a chance to mend fences he'd never considered mendable?

Of course, given his father's unbending attitude, the latter was really a long shot, but it was something to keep in mind. The other, though...

He changed lanes, eyes on the road but his mind fixed on the night he'd handled the crisis with his son. Again he savored that keen sense of purpose he'd felt, despite his fear. Then he recalled the confidence he'd had that he could do something to help. And finally he remembered the humble satisfaction that came with the news that Matt would be okay.

It had been on his mind constantly. So much so he was now doing what once would have been unthinkable. Imagine! *He was considering returning to medicine.*

Not surgery, of course, heart or otherwise; that still held all the pitfalls that had driven him away before: a demanding schedule, with long unpredictable hours at the hospital, impossible pressures that kept a man away from his family. And of course, an unyielding father's insistence that his son follow in his sanctified footsteps.

But what about pediatrics? He'd always loved kids. What could be more fulfilling than devoting a life to helping them? And pediatrics was a different game from surgery. Not that pediatricians didn't work hard, but the hours didn't have to be as crazy. He knew. Leon Rosenfeld, his roommate in med school, was now one of the foremost pediatricians in the D.C. area. He and Leon had kept in touch; in fact, were still close friends.

Pulling over to the side of the road, Travis picked up his car phone and punched out a number.

CHAPTER SEVENTEEN

"THANKS, LEON." Smiling, Travis clapped a hand on the shoulder of his old college roommate. "I 'preciate your makin' time for me this mornin'."

Leon, founding partner of a thriving practice he shared with three other pediatricians, snorted. "Time, schmime! Is that any way to talk to an old friend? It was terrific seeing you again, Travis. Only next time, don't make it so long till you show your face, huh? A person could grow old already!"

Travis ran his eyes over Leon and grinned. Standing five-two, weighing perhaps 110 pounds soaking wet and sporting a shock of unruly red hair and freckles, Leon still looked like a kid. He was one of those people who never seemed to age. This had been a trial to him at Harvard, where he'd received a lot of good-natured kidding about it. The only thing, he used to wisecrack, that spared him total disgrace was his class rank. He'd been number one.

"You? Grow old?" Travis said. "When's the last time you got carded, Leon?"

"Last year, at my son's bar mitzvah, but don't tell anybody. And speaking of bar mitzvahs, his brother's making his in October, and Sherry says she's putting you at the top of the guest list."

"Tell her I'm honored."

"Hah! You better make this one, pal. My wife doesn't understand baseball. With Sherry, it's two strikes and you're out!"

Travis gave a rueful chuckle. He'd been out of the country on assignment during their older boy's spiritual coming-of-age, and he'd deeply regretted having to miss it. "Tell Sherry to keep her socks on," he said as Leon walked him to the door of his office. "I'm not in the field much these days. It's becomin' more 'n' more of a desk job all the time. If the invitation arrives early enough, I should have no problem makin' time for your shindig."

Leon slapped his forehead with his palm. "A shindig, he calls it! May the rabbi never find out!"

They both laughed, but when Leon paused at the door, his face sobered. "A desk job, huh? Doesn't sound like much fun. Maybe you oughtta give our talk some careful thought."

Travis nodded, smiling at the sounds coming from the "well child" waiting room down the hall: high-pitched voices punctuated with laughter, a toddler's exuberant shout. "Yeah, ol' buddy," he said, his face dead serious as they shook hands, "I intend to do just that."

BEHIND THE WHEEL of his Alpha Romeo, Travis made good on his intention. The talk with Leon had clarified much of what had been on his mind.

He smiled to himself as he maneuvered the car into the stream of traffic. A sense of rightness had settled in the region of his gut. It could work. As a pediatrician, he knew he'd work hard, but he could still have a life, time for a family.

Leon was a family man. He adored his wife and four children, and spending time with them was a priority. Yet he also enjoyed a successful fulfilling career in pediatrics.

"The trick," he'd told Travis, "is to set up a practice with partners. With partners—all selected for compatibility and competence of course—you share the workload. And the hours. Sure, we each work some evenings, but not *every* evening. And we're each on call only one weekend a month. Also, remember, my partners' names are Vitelli, Whitson and Chen. Since we have different ethnic backgrounds, spending holidays with our families is seldom a problem. I tell you, Travis, it's the only way.''

The only way. It made sense. Why hadn't he thought of it before? Or had he been too caught up in defying the old man to think clearly? Had an immature need to rebel blinded him to viable alternatives?

But then, nothing about the practice of medicine had called to him in those days. Certainly nothing like the strong pull he'd felt following the crisis with Matt.

A strong pull, all right. Just like the other thing he kept coming back to in his mind. Another pull he found himself unable to ignore. Randi.

What was it about her? Okay, the lady was beautiful, but so what? He'd known scores of beautiful women in his time, a number of them intimately. Yet not one had remained on his mind after they parted company. Fact was, he'd be hard put to recall most of their names.

But his memories of Randi Terhune just wouldn't quit. Yesterday he'd run into a ballet dancer he'd once dated, and all he'd been able to think about was how Randi's walk was even more fluid and graceful. This morning he'd awakened with an image of her face in his mind, her incomparably lovely face and that special way her eyes slanted and caught the light when she laughed. And last night he'd gone to sleep thinking about the way she felt in his arms. Hell, he grew hard thinking about it, and he hadn't even slept with her!

Maybe that was it. Maybe it was just the challenge she presented. The challenge of a sexually frightened woman, and he the one man who could set her free....

He gave himself a shake. No way. He'd never been one of those males who were obsessed with the challenge of the chase. Who were concerned with scoring, for God's sake. The very notion made him sick.

And when he considered Randi's history and her very real and understandable fears, when he recalled the terror in her eyes when she'd run from him, all he could think of was how desperately wrong that was. How she deserved better. God, how it haunted him! *She* haunted him.

Maybe it was time he did something about it.

"CAN I GET YOU something from the kitchen, sis? Jill peered at Randi from the doorway of their family room. "That brie's finally ripe, and I picked up some great gourmet crackers this morning."

Randi glanced up from the book on her lap and smiled weakly. "No thanks, love. I'm really not hungry."

But you hardly ate any supper, Jill wanted to say, yet held her tongue. Randi had lost weight—pounds she couldn't afford, since she'd always been on the slender side. Her appetite had been off for some time, and none of Jill's coaxing had had any effect. She also seemed listless, and there were smudges under her eyes; she hadn't been sleeping well. Something was troubling her, and Jill wished to heaven she knew what it was.

But she had her suspicions.

Randi had been this way since returning from the Eastern Shore. At first Jill had thought it was a mild case of post-traumatic shock. Fallout from the ordeal with Matt. Now she wasn't so sure.

Her first clue had come shortly after they'd returned. Randi would hurry to grab the phone whenever it rang, only to look disappointed to learn who was on the line. Then, after four or five such calls, she'd questioned Jill—in a nonchalant manner Jill suspected was feigned—about Travis; she'd wanted to know if he'd mentioned any future plans.

Omitting any mention of that confidential discussion she'd had with McLean, Jill had merely told her what he'd said regarding Matt: that if Matt ever needed him, he was only a phone call away. She'd shown Randi his card, which was now stuck to their refrigerator door with a magnet, along with their emergency numbers.

But Randi's subsequent behavior had been telling; whenever Jill saw her pass the refrigerator, Randi's gaze would move to Travis's card, then she'd sigh forlornly and walk away.

Damn the man! A couple of weeks had passed since they'd returned home. But had he contacted them? He had not. And Randi was upset because of it. Hurting, even, judging by the look in her eyes whenever Matt mentioned the man, which he still did, though not as frequently as before.

Well, Randi wasn't the only one who was upset. Jill, too, wondered about his withdrawal. Worse, she wondered if she'd made a mistake revealing those intimate details of their background to him.

Had the ugly facts of her and Randi's past so disturbed him he couldn't handle the situation? Is that why he'd backed off? If so, she'd greatly misjudged his character. Yet she'd have sworn...

Too late for second-guessing now. She ran troubled eyes over her sister. Randi wasn't reading the book she held, but simply staring off into space.

Muttering an oath under her breath, Jill stalked into the kitchen. Stopping by the refrigerator, she glared at his business card. *McLean, I promise you,* she fumed silently, *if you ever do call or show your handsome puss around here, you're gonna answer to me!*

Little did Jill know, her chance to make good on that promise would come the next day. She was working alone in her home office, coordinating paint with fabric swatches for a client, when the doorbell rang. With Randi at work and Matt playing with Robbie next door, she was forced to answer it herself.

"Okay, okay, I'm coming!" she grumbled as the bell

rang a second time. Figuring it was a delivery man with some samples she was expecting, she was unprepared for the ecstatic yelp that was unmistakably Matt's as she opened the front door. "What on earth...?"

The query died in her throat. An explosion of male laughter competed with Matt's giggles as Travis McLean tossed his jubilant son in the air. When he caught him and wrapped him in a bear hug seconds later, Matt shrieked with delight.

"You came!" the four-year-old crowed as he hugged the man he resembled. "I knowed you would! I just knowed it!"

"Did, did you?" Travis asked with a chuckle. "Well, that just shows how smart you are!" He was still holding the boy tightly against his chest, showing no inclination to set him down. In fact, Jill thought as she took in her nephew's happy face, the pair of them looked as if they'd never let each other go.

A spate of canine barking drew their attention to the blue Alpha Romeo parked at the curb. Robbie Spencer stood beside it, grinning up at the open window where a shaggy pup had both paws hooked over the edge and was announcing his presence to the neighborhood.

"A puppy!" Matt exclaimed as Travis set him on his feet. "Is...is that 'Lysses?"

"Sure is, Tiger," Travis told him as Matt caught his hand and pulled him toward the car. "You 'n' your friend wanna meet 'im?"

"Wow—yeah! Hey, Robbie! This is my friend Travis I told you 'bout, 'n' that's 'Lysses. Travis says we can..."

Both irritated and fascinated, Jill watched as Travis McLean stepped comfortably into the role of father to the son he barely knew. Or perhaps "hero" was a better term, judging by the adoration on Matt's face. In a matter of minutes, man, dog and two jubilant youngsters were cavorting on the lawn amid shrieks of boyish laughter.

I may as well be invisible, she groused to herself, *for all the attention they've paid me.* Yet her eyes remained glued on the scene. Or more specifically, on her nephew.

She hadn't seen Matt this happy in ages. He shared his romp with the dog, giving Robbie equal time, as he'd been taught; yet it was clear that between Matt and the shaggy pup, it was love at first sight.

Travis took a Frisbee from the back of the Alpha. He spent a few moments showing the boys how to throw it, but Ulysses needed no demonstration. He lunged and caught it easily, no matter who threw it. Yet every time he retrieved the plastic disc, it was Matt he chose to surrender it to.

"There's somethin' magical that happens when you put a boy 'n' a dog together, isn't there?"

Intent on her nephew's amazingly deft Frisbee arm, Jill hadn't seen Travis approach. Her gaze swung to his. "Not as magical as a certain party's appearing out of thin air after weeks of unexplained silence!" she snapped.

"Uh-oh," he said, taking in her tightly drawn lips. "Looks like we'd better have a talk." He glanced at the Frisbee game, still in full swing. "Uh, is there a backyard where it might be safe for them to—"

"Be my guest," she interrupted coldly, gesturing at the gate to the fenced backyard.

When Matt and Robbie were safely ensconced there with Ulysses, she led Travis into the house. "Okay, McLean," she said as they entered the kitchen, "talk. And it better be good."

RUNNING HER FINGERS through hair she'd freed of her nurse's cap, Randi grabbed her purse and headed for the elevator. It had been a long grueling day in the ER: six cases of elderly people with heat stroke, one of them fatal; a teenager who'd likely never walk again after diving into a shallow pond, cracking several vertebrae and injuring his spinal cord. Plus the more usual injuries. Everything from an accidental poisoning of a toddler from a carelessly left can of drain cleaner to an assortment of broken limbs.

Then there was the woman they'd brought in, half-dead from a beating at the hands of her live-in boyfriend. And the poor thing insisting she'd merely fallen down the stairs! But her neighbors had told the police a different story. Randi and her crew had done their best to patch her up, but the fear in the woman's eyes wouldn't leave Randi alone; this was something their skills couldn't heal. Well, the woman was in the hands of Social Services now; maybe they had some answers.

The elevator let her off at the ground floor. She waved tiredly to a knot of coworkers gathered in the hallway, then headed for the door to the parking lot. The Cherokee was being serviced, so Jill was picking her up. It was only seven o'clock, yet all Randi wanted was to go home and fall into bed.

And pray that this night would be free of the nightmare that had been haunting her for weeks.

She shivered, despite the blast of hot humid air that hit as she left the air-conditioned building. It was always the same—the footsteps in the hallway drawing nearer, the sound of the door to Jill's room creaking open... All of it too horribly familiar.

Only, something was wrong in the dream as it appeared lately. Something that made it different from the nightmares of her adolescence. Now it was *her* door that was pushed ominously ajar. Wrong. Wrong, wrong, wrong! That wasn't the way it had been, and—

"Hi, Mom!" Matt's voice pulled her back to blessed reality. Shaking off the confused and frightening remnants of her thoughts, she looked around. Where was Jill's car?

"Over here!" Matt called again, and she followed his voice to a blue Alpha Romeo parked at the curb. And stopped dead in her tracks.

Travis. Sitting at the wheel of the car, wearing a confident grin. And Matt, belted into his familiar car seat behind him. Her son's grin was the spitting image of his father's, and she felt a tug of something sweet and at the same time painful. She was dangerously close to tears and didn't know why.

"Surprise! It's Travis 'n' 'Lysses!" Matt exclaimed as a shaggy form rose from the seat beside him and licked his face. "C'mon, Mom. We gots to get you home 'fore my bedtime, y'know. Aunt Jill made Travis promise."

Randi mustered a wobbly smile as she made her feet move in their direction. Travis. She'd thought him gone for good. Yet why this hadn't brought the welcome feeling of relief it once might have was a question she couldn't answer.

Travis jumped out and came around to open the door for her. At the same time, he ran his eyes over her slender frame. He barely kept from frowning as she turned toward him. Beautiful as ever, he thought, but too thin, and looking tired, too. What had she been doing to herself?

"Your coach awaits, milady," he said, erasing the frown and offering his hand with a warm welcoming smile.

A smile that turned her insides to jelly, just as it always had. She tried to gather her thoughts. Why was he finally here?

She thrust the question aside. He was here, and that was what counted. Because whenever she'd been able to push the nightmares away, it had been Travis who'd haunted her dreams. Travis, with his heady male beauty and negligent charm. But even more important, his bedrock confidence and unsuspected strengths.

Qualities that somehow made her feel protected and safe, she realized as she took in his handsome profile. Just seeing him in the flesh, dear God, the reality was even better than her dreams. She just couldn't believe how much she'd missed him.

Travis tucked her into the Alpha's bucket seat and rounded the car in time to see her smile in a way that erased the tiredness from her face. And sent a jolt to his gut. He was astonished to realize how fiercely he'd missed her. How on earth had it happened?

But it had, and the time for questioning was over. He suspected he could love this woman. Maybe he'd begun to already. Well, the notion could take its place beside the other about-faces now firmly planted in his mind: he was going back to medicine, and he was going to attempt the long overdue mending of a certain breach.

He'd told Jill about his decision to return to medicine because he needed to convince that fiercely protective mother hen that he'd not abandoned Matt and Randi. That he'd had a lot to think about since the Eastern Shore. Of course, she'd still berated him up one side and down the other for not calling "to let us know you're alive." But in the end, he'd won her over.

Well, sort of. She'd warned him he'd have to "make it right with Randi" before she'd forgive him. "Matt may be a pushover for you, McLean," she'd said, "but my sister's not a child."

No, she wasn't a child, he thought as he eased the Alpha out of the parking lot. But she was caged in by a child's nightmarish fears. He needed to unlock that cage.

It was the final thing he'd put to Jill before he got her to agree to let him take Matt and pick Randi up from work. "I want the chance to—gently, mind—break down your sister's fears," he'd told her, "and I've got an idea on how to go about it, but I'll need your help."

"Oh, yeah?" she'd challenged. "And just what do you know about such things, McLean? You may have been to med school, and you may even succeed in becoming a pediatrician, but you're hardly a practicing shrink."

In the end, though, she'd agreed to think about his plan.

If he succeeded in making things right with Randi first, of course.

Randi. While she asked Matt about his day, he stole a glance at her. Well, she hadn't told him to get lost. Maybe she was more forgiving than her sister. Maybe. He needed to talk with her before the evening was through. But if the way she'd looked at him when she first saw him was any clue, he'd already made some headway. And if he succeeded tonight, then everything was up to Jill. Because if she agreed to his plan... *God, please let it work!*

CHAPTER EIGHTEEN

"I CAN'T BELIEVE how much that pup's grown," Randi said. She stood with Travis on the back porch, watching Matt romp with Ulysses in the yard. It was getting dark and well past Matt's bedtime, but so what? She couldn't deny his plea to spend time with Travis and Ulysses after supper.

"Pups have a way of doin' that," Travis said quietly. He and Randi still hadn't talked, yet he was unwilling to disturb this tranquil domestic interlude.

A nearly orange moon had risen over the treetops; he was mesmerized by the way it bathed her delicate features in its mellow light. Night sounds had settled around them: the chirp of crickets, muted music from a neighbor's house, the chink of silver as Jill loaded the dishwasher after insisting they join Matt and leave her to clean up the supper they'd shared.

"'Course," he added as they watched Matt make Ulysses obey the commands to sit, stay and come he'd been taught, "it sure would be a shame if that pup's full-grown before Matt sees him again." He glanced at her. "Half the joy is watchin' 'em grow 'n' develop."

Randi saw the corners of his lips struggle to contain a grin, and she suspected it wasn't just puppies he was talking about. She released a small sigh. They'd indulged in nothing but small talk since leaving the hospital, and she couldn't help wondering what else was on his mind. Why had he turned up so suddenly after weeks of silence? What did he want? She was dying to know, yet couldn't bring herself to ask.

When Travis hadn't called or come around, she'd been certain it was because she'd driven him away; something had happened between them on that last night they'd spent alone together. She couldn't recall the details, but she knew that somehow she'd reacted badly. It was the only thing she could think of to explain his abrupt disappearance after saying goodbye to Matt at the hospital.

That disappearance had hurt. So had the empty days that followed, and...

Empty? Simply because there was no Travis? Am I really thinking such a thing?

But it was true. She'd missed him like the devil. Ached with some unfathomable yearning every time she'd heard Matt mention his name. Every time she'd seen that damned card on the refrigerator. Like it or not, Travis McLean had somehow worked his way not only into her son's heart, but into her own.

How had it happened? More to the point, why did she want him around after all her determination to get rid of him? Of course, after the events of that awful night, Travis had suddenly been transformed in her eyes; she could no longer see him as a threat. How could she when he'd saved them? Proved himself beyond question as a man you could rely on. Trust. Even...care for.

Uneasy with the thought, she reeled it in. If she cared for him, it was because he'd proved himself a friend. A good friend, but that was all. And now, grateful to have him back in their lives, she was loath to say or do anything that might send him away again. *Keep it light, Terhune, and let him make the first move.*

"You wouldn't be hinting at something more permanent between Matt and that dog, would you?" she asked archly.

"Well," Travis drawled, "I did manage to teach Ulysses some manners, and he *is* housebroken now..."

"I see," she said, just managing to hold back a smile. "So you were thinking...?"

"So I was wonderin', Miz Terhune, if you've given consideration to a certain proposal I made. The one that prompted me to do all that dog-trainin'?" The grin emerged, full-blown and as engaging as ever.

Lord, the man could charm the birds out of the trees with that grin, and she was certain he knew it. Still, she needn't make it easy for him. "I have," was all she said.

"And?" he prompted, trying not to sound impatient.

"Well," she said, purposely drawing out the word, "I still haven't spoken to Jill about it, you see, and—"

"I have," he cut in. "Your sister said it was fine with her, but the decision was yours." The grin was ear to ear now, and Randi burst out laughing.

"You win, McLean!" She threw up her hands. But when Travis suddenly caught them and gave them a quick squeeze, she felt her heart trip in her chest.

"Wrong," he said, releasing her hands and flicking her nose playfully with his finger. His eyes found hers, and he smiled to take the edge off his contradiction. "It's Matt who wins, Randi."

"Wins what?" Matt demanded breathlessly. They turned, surprised to see him standing beside them, a tail-wagging Ulysses at his heels. "What do I win, Travis, huh? C'mon, tell me...puh-leez?"

Joy and laughter and the love of two parents to share it—to share a life with you, if I can manage it, Travis promised silently.

"Uh, I'll let your mom tell you, Tiger," he said, glancing at Randi. "And then, since you've been real good, how'd you like a piggyback ride up to bed?"

"NOW THERE'S A PICTURE," Travis murmured as he and Randi stood gazing down at their son half an hour later. Matt was sound asleep, as was Ulysses, curled into a furry mound at his new master's feet. Watching the angelic smile on Matt's face, Travis felt his throat constrict. "I swear, I don't think I've ever seen anythin' more beautiful."

Randi heard the emotion in his voice and made no protest when he captured her hand and held it gently at his side. It was time to face the truth; she no longer had a single reservation about Travis's presence in Matt's life. *He really loves him,* she reflected silently, *loves him and belongs with him.*

"I know," she managed, despite the emotion that threatened to overwhelm her. When had things changed? Again her mind went back to the cottage, to that hellish night. The terrifying drive to the hospital. To the long days when she longed to hear his voice again, and her son never forgot his "friend Travis." Was that all there was to it? She didn't know; she only knew that Travis McLean and Matt belonged together, and she was a part of it. And gladder of this than she ever would have imagined.

"Whatcha thinkin', lady?" Travis's voice, soft in the quiet room, stole across her thoughts.

"That I'm glad you're here," she murmured, "even if it took me a while to…to accept such a thing."

Using his free hand to tilt up her chin, he met her gaze. Relieved to see not a shadow of doubt there, he smiled. "It doesn't matter—only that you do now."

Slowly he lowered his head and brushed her lips with his. "Thanks, Randi."

"For what? For being sensible enough to admit the truth?" she said, savoring the touch of his lips, wishing the kiss had been longer.

"A lot more than that," he replied. "Certainly, for allowin' me to be part of this." He smiled and gestured to the bed. "But mostly, for trustin' me with your…with our son."

"You've more than earned that trust," she whispered. Her pulse accelerated as he raised her hand and pressed a kiss to the knuckles. "I—I'd trust you with Matt's life." She gave a small breathless laugh. "In fact, I already have."

He was still holding her hand as their gazes met and locked. For several long seconds the silence stretched between them. It was as if the air in the room was charged, pregnant with unnamed emotions each was aware of, yet uncertain how to voice.

"C'mon." He gave her hand a warm squeeze. "Walk me out to my car."

She nodded and allowed him to lead her downstairs. They said good-night to Jill, who was off to bed, having an early fitting for her wedding gown in the city. And if Jill noticed her sister's hand engulfed in Travis's as they went outside, she said nothing of it. Her lips, however, curved in a satisfied smile as she climbed the stairs.

Travis paused with Randi before the door of the Alpha; he had yet to release her hand, which he seemed intent on studying as he massaged her knuckles with his thumb.

"You're awfully quiet," he said at last, raising his head to meet her eyes. "I was sort of...well, expectin' a barrage of questions." At her bemused look he added, "You know—about why I haven't called or come around all these weeks."

"Oh. That." She shrugged. "I figured you had your reasons." *Like the way I drove you off that night on the beach. Because I did—I know I did, even if I can't remember why.*

But you do remember said that voice in her head, startling her with the sudden insight. *Even if the details are cloudy, you know. It was because you were afraid!*

He gave her a wry smile. "You're either a lot more forgivin' than your sister, or you're not tellin' me everythin'."

"My sister? What did..."

"She blistered my ears for not showin' my face till now, I can tell you," he said with a chuckle.

She looked horrified. "Jill? But—"

"Shh." He stilled her lips with his thumb. "Fact is, she had every right to do it." He shook his head ruefully. "I should've called, if only to see how Matt was doin'. 'Course, I knew when I left the hospital that he was gonna be all right, but..."

He gave a helpless shrug. "I'm not excusin' my behavior. It's just that I had some heavy thinkin' to do, Randi. Real heavy, and I needed some time alone to do it."

She dropped her gaze. *About what's wrong with me? About why I— Oh, God, what if he asks? What if...*

"Thinking?" she repeated, throttling the thought.

"Yeah, 'bout my life. If that doesn't sound too grandiose or melodramatic," he added wryly.

Relief washed over her like gentle rain. It hadn't been about anything *she'd* done, then. It hadn't been about her at all!

"Randi," he said, watching her face carefully, "I've decided to go back into medicine. With the intention of becomin' a pediatrician."

"What?" If he'd told her he planned to sprout wings and fly, she couldn't have been more astounded. "How, I mean, when...uh, that is..." She gave up, floored by his announcement. Not to mention the certainty in his eyes and the wide smile on his face.

"I know," he said, laughing at her dumbfounded look. "I'm as amazed as you, to tell the truth. But I'm also dead sure. As sure I've been of anythin' in my life."

He went on to tell her then of the things he'd felt the night he'd tended Matt. Of the soul-searching he'd done in its aftermath. And finally of the discussion with Leon, which had solidified his decision.

She listened solemnly. It was an enormous step he was taking, yet she felt in her bones it was the right one. He'd been so obviously in his element that night. She'd worked with many doctors in her time, yet never had she observed one more attuned to the challenge required of him.

True, it had been his own son he'd tended, but that might have made it even more difficult for him—look what had happened to *her!* Besides, she couldn't envision Travis doing less for some stranger's child. He would make a fine physician, she just knew it. And she was touched, actually humbled, that he'd share with her the process involved in his momentous decision.

"So," he said finally, almost tentatively, when he'd finished, "what do you think?"

"I think," she said, smiling into his eyes, "that it's...wonderful." With the last word she gave a gurgle of laughter and flung her arms around him. "Oh, Travis, I'm so glad for you. You'll make a terrific pediatrician. The best!"

He felt something ease and slip into place as his arms went around her. He hadn't realized how important it was to him that she approve. It only served to drive home the other thing that had been nibbling at the edges of his mind. *She* was important to him. She and Matt, and the life he hungered to share with them.

"I don't know 'bout bein' the best," he said, keeping his arms about her, but drawing back to look into her eyes, "but I sure plan to *give* it my best. Thanks, though, for the vote of confidence, Randi."

She nodded, suddenly unable to speak. She'd launched herself against him without thinking, caught up in her exuberance. Now she could hardly breathe for thinking about the way she felt in his arms. The way he was looking at her as his eyes roamed her face, settling finally on her mouth. The way it would feel if he kissed her. As she'd longed for it, all those many weeks when she feared she'd never see him again.

Travis saw her tongue slide over her lips. It told him what he wondered if she knew herself: that she wanted his mouth on hers. He had all he could do to school himself to resist the hunger he felt. *She's an innocent, McLean,* he cautioned as his head slowly lowered, *a badly frightened innocent who can't begin to know the joy that's possible between a man and a woman. It's up to you to show her the way. But slowly, man, slowly...*

Randi felt his warm breath fan her face, and she sighed into his mouth before he captured hers in a gentle taking. His lips were warm and pliant as they moved leisurely over hers. Gliding, tasting, they lulled and teased at the same time. Until, without knowing how it happened, she felt her own part, inviting him to explore the interior of her mouth.

Another jolt of desire hit him with this innocent invitation. Beneath those childhood fears was an unconsciously responsive and deeply sensual woman. No wonder he'd never guessed there was anything wrong when he tried to make love to her that night.

Moving his hands to cup her face, he slid his fingers into her hair, deepening the kiss—but slowly, as if he had all the time in the world. He could feel her pulse fluttering against the palms of his hands as he let his tongue trace the silken contours of her lips. His own heart began to hammer when he felt the tip of her tongue graze his. *Oh, Randi, darlin', you make it damned hard for a man to take it slow!*

Yet that was what he did. Savoring the taste of her, gently questing, tenderly probing, he let his tongue explore. But ever so slowly, moving with a lazy rhythm that soothed and excited at the same time. Until at last he heard her moan low in her throat and felt her arms slide up and loop about his neck to pull him closer. *That's it, darlin'. Tell me what you want. You're in charge. You, and nobody else.*

Randi wasn't certain what was happening to her. After those first few moments of anticipation, she'd felt almost dreamy, content with the simple pleasure of his mouth on hers. But something had changed. She found herself impatient, unwilling to be drawn along at this snail's pace, however pleasurable. She itched for more!

Without another thought, she stood on tiptoe and wound her arms about his neck, pressing her body fully against his. Unaware of the moan that came from her throat, she touched the tip of her tongue to his. And felt the blood singing in her veins as their tongues danced and mated.

Travis heard a roaring in his ears as she communicated her hunger. Stunned by the force of it, he let his hands slide over her shoulders, dropped them to her waist. Locking his arms about her, he pulled her hard against him. Their mouths crossed and crisscrossed, seeking closer union. My God, he wondered, where had this come from? One moment she was shyly accepting his careful kisses, and next thing he knew—

Whoa, McLean! With the self-chastening command, he pulled his mouth from hers, doing his utmost to control his ragged breathing. He planted a kiss on her brow, then cradled her carefully in his arms, making sure their bodies didn't touch below, betraying his arousal. *Damned fool, you nearly lost it. Remember who this is!*

"Travis?" she said against his chest in a bewildered voice. "What...what's wrong?"

"Shh, darlin'," he whispered into her hair. "Nothin's wrong."

"Then why..."

A chuckle vibrated within his chest. "Because you're too temptin' by far, sweetheart, 'n'...let's just say it's gettin' late 'n' I need to be goin', okay?"

He pulled away and raised her chin with his knuckles, smiling into her upturned face. "Call you tomorrow?"

Giddy from what had happened, Randi could barely nod as she drank in his features, loving the play of moonlight on his face.

"Night, sugar," he murmured. "Sleep well." A brush of his lips over hers, and before she knew it, he was gone.

"Night," Randi whispered belatedly into the darkness. She touched her fingers to her lips, still tasting him there.

Amazed, she realized she hadn't wanted the kiss to end. Yet she wondered, as she turned to the house, why, for all its aching sweetness, the thought should provoke a tiny frisson of fear.

TRAVIS SLOWED and turned the Alpha between the massive stone pillars that marked the entrance to Sunnyfields, his family's Virginia estate. Cruising past the huge oaks lining the drive, he tried to ignore the knot that had formed in his stomach. Tried, but couldn't. It was the same feeling he'd had as a kid whenever a confrontation with his father loomed. He was a man, many years out from under his father's roof, yet the meeting he anticipated had the capacity to reduce him to a bundle of childish dread.

Borrowing a trick he'd learned while under pressure in the field for the Agency, he took a deep breath and released it slowly. Then another, repeating the process until he felt the knot begin to unwind. Good. His father was a master at sensing others' weaknesses and using them to control them; Travis needed to be the one in control if he was to make this reconciliation work.

If the old man didn't have him thrown off the place before he even got the chance.

"TRAVIS! OH, MY GOD, are you really *here?*" Judith McLean's eyes shone with tears as she ran them over her firstborn. "I—I'm not dreamin', am I?"

"We're both wide awake, Mother." Travis bent to embrace her. "Lo, the prodigal son returns!" he added with a chuckle, then lifted her off the floor and whirled her around as she began to laugh and weep at the same time.

"I can't believe it, I can't believe it!" she kept repeating as Higgins, the longtime family butler, looked on with suspiciously bright eyes.

"Higgins," Judith managed as Travis set her back on

the foyer's marble floor, "run and fetch Sarah. Hurry! She won't believe this, either."

"Sarah's here?" Travis asked as the servant left.

"For the weekend, yes." His mother ran her gaze avidly over his tall frame. "You're...you're well, son? Your shoulder, it's..."

"Good as new," he assured her.

"Well, all right, if you're sure..."

"I'm sure. See?" He swung his arm in a wide circle, to demonstrate, and gave her a wink.

She nodded and gestured him toward the spacious living room. He noted her hand was trembling and felt a moment of deep regret. How much grief had his actions caused her over the years of his rebellion? How much pain?

Curling an arm about her shoulders, he drew her to a halt just inside the living-room doors. "I love you, Mother," he said quietly. "And though you haven't asked, I'll tell you right off. Yes, I'm here to make peace with him—if it's at all possible. It's time we were a family again."

He meant it, Travis thought as they waited for Sarah. It *was* time. High time. He *wanted* this family. He wasn't here simply because he found it convenient after deciding to return to medicine; the decision simply gave him a window of opportunity to heal the breach. A window he'd lacked before. He'd regretted the breach for a long time, to be honest. Now, if only he could get the old man to listen...

"DADDY'S CAR'S just comin' up the drive," Sarah said to her mother and Travis as she peered out the living-room window. She looked at her brother. "How d'you want to handle this? Should Mother and I make ourselves scarce?"

In the hour they'd talked since his arrival, Travis had informed them of his decision to return to medicine. Both had been astounded, then delighted at the news. Although he didn't plan on becoming a heart surgeon, his mother felt it would nevertheless pave the way for a reconciliation with his father.

Travis wasn't so sure. Marring their reunion was their awareness of Trent McLean's fury about Sarah's switch to law; their father, apparently, still blamed it on Travis's influence.

"I think y'all had better leave me to face him alone," he told the women. "Just have Higgins let him know I'm here and uh, keep your fingers crossed."

While his mother offered a shaky smile and turned to leave, Sarah ran up and gave him a quick kiss on the cheek. "We'll do more than that, love," she told him. "We'll pray—so hard, you'll think there were a hundred trumpets soundin' and the judgment day in sight!"

Which it might just be, Travis told himself gloomily as he watched them leave the room. He was by no means sanguine about the encounter with his father. The old man hadn't yielded an inch in the past when Travis had tried to reason with him; why should he now? Still, it was something he had to try.

He was tired of living outside, like a pariah. With the discovery that he had a son had come the realization that family was important to him—this family, as well as the one he longed to nurture under his own roof. And like it or not, Trent McLean was a part of it. He was Matt's grandfather, damn it, and—

"Who in the hell d'you think you are, bargin' in here like this?" The icy voice had Travis turning to face the door.

Trent McLean III. With one of those odd flashes of memory, Travis recalled the only reason he himself wasn't named Trent McLean IV was that there'd been an infant who'd died, who'd been christened with that name first.

"I wasn't aware I'd done any bargin'," he replied with deliberate mildness. He gestured toward a silver tea service Higgins had brought and from which his mother had poured. "Considerin' the hospitality I've enjoyed from my mother in the hour I've been back," he added, one hand thrust casually in his pants pocket as he leaned against the mantel over the fireplace, "I'd say I've been received most graciously...*sir.*"

Trent's eyes flashed a warning as he moved into the room. The inflection in Travis's "sir" hadn't escaped him. When his children were young, he'd demanded they address him as "sir," but he had no doubt Travis was mocking him with it now. "Don't play games with me, boy!" he thundered.

Travis wanted to kick himself. He hadn't intended the tiny insult; it had just slipped out. *Can't erase years' worth of bitterness overnight, I reckon.*

He took a moment to appraise his father as Trent went to the bar hidden behind a sliding mahogany panel and fixed himself a drink. The old man had aged. Not that he wasn't still an impressive figure. The expensive cut of his hand-tailored suit outlined the tall physique that Travis had inherited and that Trent kept trim through regular dates on the tennis and raquetball courts. But there was a stoop to his shoulders that hadn't been there before. The lines on his face, which once had been slight, merely lending it a suave maturity, were now deep grooves. And there was far more gray to his hair than blond.

Finally, as his father took a sip of the neat bourbon he'd poured and faced him, Travis noticed his eyes. This was where he seemed to have aged most of all. They were...bleak. Travis gave himself a shake. Bleak? The mighty Trent McLean? What in hell could possibly have—

"Don't look at me that way!" the older man snapped. "I don't usually have a drink in the middle of the afternoon," he added defensively, "and you damn well know it!"

Do I? Do I really know anything about you after five

long years? Even way before that. You spent so little time
with us I doubt we ever really got to know you at all.

Trent was shaking his head. "I don't know why I should
be tellin' you but, fact is, I lost someone on the table today." He took a big swallow of the whiskey. "Someone I
know—*knew* well, a friend, and I'm still not sure how it
happened. It *shouldn't* have happened, dammit!"

"Who?" Travis couldn't help asking.

Trent downed the rest of the bourbon with a grimace,
shook his head and let his eyes flick over Travis before
looking away. "Wally Reston," he said.

"Reston? My God, I just saw him a few—"

"I know. He told me 'bout it when he called to ask if
I'd perform this operation personally, as a special favor to
an old friend." Trent poured himself a second drink. "Said
he knew it was just a simple bypass, but that he'd still feel
better if I was the one did it. Said he trusted me... Oh,
God! A simple bypass, and he died. *Under my scalpel.*"

A bitter laugh issued from him before he downed the
bourbon. "The poor bastard trusted me, and I let him die."

Travis didn't know what to say. He'd never seen the old
man like this. Then it struck him. Trent McLean, for all his
aura of infallibility, was as susceptible to guilt and failure
as any other mortal. For the first time in his life, he was
seeing his father as human.

"I'm sorry," he said, carefully feeling his way along
unfamiliar emotions. "Truly sorry. I know the two of you
went back a long way. I also know, if there was anyone
could've pulled him through, it was you."

Trent glanced at him sharply. "Y'do, do you?" There
was a sneer on his face, a challenge in his voice. "What
would *you* know about it?"

It took every ounce of control Travis possessed not to
respond in kind. "I never questioned your competence as
a surgeon, sir." The final word was issued without mockery

this time. "You're one of the best—world-class. I simply didn't want to be forced—"

"For no reason but sheer spite, what you *wanted* was to wallow in the mud of your infantile rebellion. Wallow! And rub my nose in it at the same time!"

Travis's control finally snapped. "Wrong! And if you'd ever listened to a word I said, you'd know that. But you never did listen, did you? Not to me, not to Troy or Sarah, not—"

"Sarah! Don't you dare talk to me 'bout Sarah, you connivin' ungrateful viper! You put her up to this insane thing she's done. You engineered this…this betrayal."

"Wrong again! I had no idea—"

Trent slammed down his glass and whirled on him. "D'you deny your sister's followin' in your disgraceful footsteps? Indulgin' in a childish rebellion? A childish rebellion, Travis, *just like yours!*"

"No," Travis said quietly, regaining some control. "It *was* a childish rebellion—mine, that is. Sarah's is another matter, but I swear to you, I had no hand in her decision, and I hope to God her motives were different."

For the first time in Travis's memory, his father seemed totally taken aback. He stood frozen, a disbelieving look on his face as he faced his son.

"Am I to believe," he said at last, his jaw working as he seemed to search for words, "that you've come here to admit you were wrong in what you did to me five years ago?"

Travis heaved a disgusted sigh and struggled to control himself. Trust the old man to see it all as a personal affront.

"No," he corrected. "What I'm hopin' you'll understand is, I'm admittin' that what I did—to myself primarily—was done for the wrong reasons."

"I see," Trent said tightly. "And what would you say were the right reasons?"

"The right reasons were the same ones I hope are motivatin' Sarah now—the pursuit of a different path for its own sake. Not from bein' hell-bent on defyin' *you*.''

"So you admit you did it to defy me!"

Travis smiled wearily. "That's what I just said, didn't I?"

His father's smile was gloating. "Well, well, well. Can it be we're makin' some progress here? After all these years—"

"After all these years," Travis said rounding on him angrily, "you still don't get it, do you, Father?" He strode forward, closing the distance between them, until their faces were inches apart. "Well, let me see if I can spell it out for you." He clenched his hands into fists at his sides.

"I don't have to listen to this—" the older man began, but Travis cut him off.

"You *don't*, but you *will*. When I'm done, you can have me thrown out, for all I care, but just this once, you're gonna listen!"

It all came pouring out. The painful memories of a boy yearning for the father who was never there. The attempts to please, only to find them ignored when they failed to align with the father's vision. The anger and frustration that simmered over the years, finally erupting in a boil that tore at the heart and fabric of a family. A dysfunctional family, because it was under the controlling thumb of a father who didn't give a damn about anything but his own selfish ends.

"And the worst of it is," Travis finished bitterly, "I'm as guilty as you are." Tears were streaming down his face, but he didn't notice. "In my need to spite you, I derailed myself from the more sensible course I might've taken. And I'm heartily sorry for it, Father. So damned sorry."

"Wh-What?" Trent's voice, sounding alien and thick with emotion, echoed in the sudden quiet. Swiping at his eyes with his sleeve, Travis peered at the older man with shocked awareness. His father's cheeks were wet.

"What—" Trent blinked to clear his eyes "—what did you say?"

Not quite believing the pain and remorse he saw in his eyes, Travis prayed for the right words. "Father, I came here today to try to heal things between us. I'm not very good at this, but...but I want you to know, I'm sorry for all the pain I've caused you." He paused for a breath. "You've gotta believe that what I did at the time I did because I felt it was right. I thought I was bein' true to myself. Now I know otherwise. I did it mainly to thwart you, more than anythin', 'n' for that, I'm sorrier than I can say. Can...can you accept that? Can you forgive it?"

"My God," the older McLean whispered brokenly. And then he began to sob.

CHAPTER NINETEEN

"SIT DOWN, SON." Struggling to collect himself, Trent awkwardly gestured Travis into a chair across from him.

Son. He hasn't called me that in decades. Stunned, Travis lowered himself into the chair. He felt a compassion he hadn't thought possible as he watched his father grope for words.

He was at a loss for words himself. He knew how difficult this must be. His father, for all his faults, had always been a proud man; breaking down as he had, especially in front of his estranged son, had to have cost him plenty.

"I left the hospital today," Trent said, staring at his tightly clasped hands, his voice raw and uneven, "as badly shaken as I've ever been in my life. It was as if...as if, in losin' Wally, I'd reached some sort of...personal watershed. A crisis of monumental proportions."

He raised his head, meeting Travis's eyes. "When I stumbled out of that operatin' room today, Travis, I could feel the weight of my own mortality on my back.

"Y'see, I'd already begun to question myself about...well, about many things. As a man gets older..." He shrugged, gave a self-effacing smile. "'Course, you wouldn't know 'bout that yet, son."

Wouldn't I? I've done some heavy questioning of my own with the passing of time.

"At any rate," Trent went on, "it was in this godawful vunerable mood that I came home to Sunnyfields. And then, to find *you* here! Well, I reckon it's much easier to mask such feelin's with anger than admit to 'em.'' He gave Travis a rueful smile. "And anger was par for the course, anyway, where you're concerned.''

Travis nodded, managing a wry smile.

"Well, as I said, I'd already begun to question myself, doubt myself. And then came your bitter diatribe. No, son, let me finish. This has to be said.

"Y'see, your accusations—your *rightful* accusations— drove home, as nothin' else could, those doubts I was havin'. Doubts about the values I've embraced to the detriment of things I should've placed first in my life, but didn't. Things...I lost, because I'd thrown them away.'' His gaze reached deep as it held Travis's. "Like a son. Like a family.''

Travis felt light-headed. Was this really his father speaking?

"The last thing Wally Reston said to me before they put him under—'' Trent's voice trembled with emotion "—was that he prayed I'd have my son back again. That, when all's said 'n done, a man's children are his only immortality. And that family is a gift too precious to sacrifice on the altar of pride and...and ambition.''

Travis swallowed thickly, a look of contrition on his face. "And I wrote the man off as a meddlin' busybody. I hope I never pass such unfair judgment on anyone again.''

His father smiled at him. "Seems poor Wally's given us each a gift, then, a lesson, and we've both been enriched by it.''

"A lesson?'' Travis asked as he saw that his father was still smiling. A warm smile, open and kind. Taking it in slowly, he was aware he was seeing his father as he'd never seen him before. As perhaps no one had ever seen him.

"Travis...'' Trent became choked up, had to begin again. "Son, I've wasted so many years. I...I love you, and...and I only hope it's not too late to ask you to forgive me. God, I've been such a fool!''

Watching him bury his face in his hands and sob, Travis felt his own eyes fill again. "Maybe you're not the only one," he said gruffly. He swiftly knelt beside his father's chair and pulled him into his arms. "And it's not too late. I...I've come home and, dammit, I love you, too!"

HER FIFTY LAPS completed, Sarah lay stretched out on a large monogrammed towel beside the Sunnyfields pool. Water trickled from her short wet hair; a light breeze fanned the drops beading her sun-bronzed skin, raising gooseflesh. She scarcely noticed. Lost in thought, the youngest McLean tried to absorb the enormity of what had happened this day.

To say she'd been shaken by what she witnessed a few hours earlier was an understatement. Anxious about Travis's meeting with their father and noting the worry in her mother's eyes as the two women awaited its outcome, she'd tiptoed to the living-room doors and peeked inside. Never could she have imagined that scene!

The sound of Trent McLean's sobs had been jarring enough; not once in her lifetime had she seen her father cry. But the sight of Travis clutching Daddy in his arms, his face wrenched with emotion, had nearly torn her apart. And filled her with unbearable joy.

Her memory of what happened afterward, was jumbled. She recalled running to the den to fetch her mother. And the look on Mother's face while she tearfully babbled what she'd seen. The two of them deciding to give the men time to compose themselves, though dying to know what had happened. And finally that moment when father and son, arms about each other—*arms about each other!*—came to the den to announce a miracle.

Sarah shook her head, still hardly able to take it all in. Daddy was a changed man. That alone was hard to digest, though his story about his dead friend made sense. But even more incredible was what Travis had explained: that his reconciliation with Daddy had come without a word being mentioned about his decision to return to medicine!

Instead, Travis had saved that piece of news until the two of them joined the women. And then Daddy had *protested,* of all things! Travis didn't need to do that, he'd said. It was all Travis could do to convince him he'd reached the decision quite apart from his desire to reconcile with his father.

"Better put some gunk on those shoulders, Pumpkin." Travis's voice broke into Sarah's thoughts. "That ol' sun's hotter 'n Hades."

"Where are you off to?" Shielding her eyes with her hand, she peered up at him, noting the car keys dangling from his fingers. "What's up?"

"Oh, this 'n' that," he said enigmatically.

"Travis McLean, don't you dare be mysterious with me!"

He grinned at her. "Well, among other things, I just got permission to borrow the *Sarah Anne* for a few days."

Sarah pushed herself to her knees. "From Daddy?" The *Sarah Anne* was the family's yacht—all 130 feet of her— and Trent McLean's pride and joy; he never let *anyone* sail on it unless he was aboard.

"Uh-huh." He was still grinning.

"But he never..."

"Did this time. Uh, after I explained to him 'n' Mother that I needed it to do some fancy courtin', that is." He winked at her.

"Courtin'? D'you mean you're seriously pursuin' that woman who's..."

"The mother of my son, yeah." Travis gestured toward the house, just visible beyond the tennis courts. "Told 'em 'bout that, too."

"Omigosh! What'd they say?"

"Mother can't wait to meet Randi 'n' Matt." He shook his head and chuckled. "She also said I'd better put a weddin' ring on the lady's finger right quick. Then she changed her mind 'n' said to make it an engagement ring. Said she wants to play mother of the groom at a big formal weddin'.''

Sarah grinned at him. She'd left for her swim while their parents had been deep in a private conversation. Her mother had never looked so relaxed. Nor her father, for that matter. "And Daddy?" she asked. "What'd he say?"

"Said to marry the woman if I love 'er, then studied me a second 'n' said, 'Never mind, any fool can see you do.' And *then* he asked when he could meet his grandson! Said he has a golf swing he wants to show 'im, 'n' lots of other things, too. 'Grandfather-to-grandson things,' he called 'em.''

Sarah felt a sudden rush of tears. She blinked them back and met her brother's gaze. "He means it, doesn't he, Trav? He's really truly changed.''

Not trusting his voice, Travis nodded. So much had happened so fast his system was threatening to go into overload. His father had even offered to speak to Aunt Louise about sponsoring Troy at Stanford, if Troy really wanted to go into research, as Travis suggested. And when he'd left them, his parents were planning to go to Europe for a second honeymoon.

He shook his head in wonder. He'd never believed in miracles, yet he knew he'd seen one today. Now all he needed was a little faith, and maybe he'd be graced with another.

Randi. Could he dare hope to free her from her past? What he hadn't told Sarah was that he'd just made a phone call to Jill Terhune, and the results had been encouraging. She was making no promises, but Jill said she'd think about what he had in mind. She said she had some good feelings about recent developments between him and Randi. And Matt, of course.

Matt. God, but he loved that kid! Matt was a miracle all

by himself. But Randi worried him more than he liked to admit. Was it possible to get past her fear? Get her to care for him, as he'd begun to care for her? Huh, might as well quit mincing words. *As he'd begun to love her.*

He smiled, remembering her face after he'd kissed her last night. Maybe he did have a chance. He'd never believed in romantic love, either, and look at him now. Hell, maybe the age of miracles had arrived.

"RECONCILED! TRAVIS, that's wonderful news!" Randi and he were walking in the park near her home. Up ahead, Matt tossed a Frisbee for Ulysses, laughing each time the dog caught it. It was nearing dusk, and with Travis's impromptu visit, the little imp had again won a postponement of his bed time. "How did it happen? Tell me."

Travis chuckled. "Lord, if you don't remind me of Matt when you get excited!"

"Well, of course I do. I mean, we're related, aren't we?" She felt herself blush, glad it was growing dark, so maybe he wouldn't notice. She was remembering the countless times she'd thought the same about him—that he reminded her of Matt. And how at first this had unnerved her, made her uncomfortable. And how it no longer did. How, instead, each little quirk, each similarity, filled her with an undeniable warmth, a curious sense of peace and...joy!

"Aren't sons and their mothers supposed to share a few genes?" she demanded, hoping to cover the silly grin that had started to spread across her face with these thoughts.

"Yes, ma'am," Travis said, smiling down at her. "I believe y'all are." Without pausing, he captured her hand as they walked, savoring the feel of her slender fingers, pleased when they curled within his clasp.

A tender warmth stole through her with this contact, and Randi exhaled slowly, barely avoiding a sigh. She felt so *good* when he held her hand this way—as he had last night. Lord, she'd had the sweetest dreams about those moments they'd shared—the way he'd looked at her as they stood over their sleeping son, the way he'd kept her hand in his, his touch gentle, the way he'd kissed her....

He made her feel warm and protected...and cherished. Travis, whose very presence had once made her want to grab her son and run. How had they come this far? How had she come to... She swallowed thickly. Could it be...? Were her feelings running *that* way? Deep enough to be called...

Unwilling to complete the thought—at least for now, with Travis beside her and perhaps able to sense something—she quickly drew their conversation back on course. "Uh, we were talking about you and your family, remember?" She still couldn't get over his news.

He recounted his visit to Sunnyfields, omitting the most private moments with his father, but explaining about Wally Reston. Reston, whose funeral he'd be attending tomorrow. That this would postpone his plans for the *Sarah Anne* was something he also omitted. Of course, Jill hadn't yet given her sanction, but—

"Hey, Travis, didya see that?" Matt came running up with a Frisbee-bearing Ulysses at his heels. "I throwed it reeal far—" he gestured toward the distance, where a man with a small boy waved as they strolled away "—an' that kid's dad helped Lysses find it. It was in the bushes, but Tommy—that's the kid—says his dad's a real good Frisbee finder. But I tol' him 'bout you 'n' how you're a good finder, too." He looked at Randi. "Right, Mom?"

Breathless with this recital, he glanced at Travis, then back at Randi. "Mom?"

"What, sweetheart?"

"Could Travis be my daddy?"

Randi swallowed, hard, an ocean of conflicting thoughts whirling through her brain—that Travis *was* his father, that her son's poignantly innocent question only served to drive home her doubts about what she'd done, that Matt's longing for a father who'd be a part of his life, like this Tommy's dad, was tearing at her very soul...

And that this was the most awkward moment of her life. God, she wished the ground would open up and swallow her, so she needn't respond!

Noting her discomfort, Travis swallowed past the sudden constriction of his throat and stepped in. He smiled at his son, determined to make it seem as if Matt's question was nothing out of the ordinary. In her distress, Randi had released his hand, and he used it to ruffle Matt's hair. "Tell us what you'd do first thing, Tiger, if somebody waved a magic wand—"

"Like a fairy godmother?"

"Yep, like a fairy godmother...or maybe a fairy god*father*..."

Matt giggled.

"And after she or he waved it, let's say I'd be your dad..." Struggling to keep his voice light, Travis hoisted Matt to his shoulder, retrieved Randi's hand and headed back the way they'd come. "What would you do with me, huh?"

Matt looked thoughtful as he pondered this. "I'd 'vite you to camp out—in a real tent!" he said, sliding a glance at his mother.

"Hmm," said Travis, "sounds neat. What else?"

"Well, we could play ball 'n' stuff, 'n' you could help me 'n' 'Lysses find Frisbees."

"But don't we do some of those things now?"

"Yeah," Matt said, "but if you were my dad, you'd be around to do 'em *all* the time."

His father nodded, wanting to look at Randi for her reaction, but sensing she wouldn't appreciate this right now.

"An' y'know what else?" Matt added brightly. "Every night, when you 'n' Mom tuck me into bed—like last night?—I'd tell you how much I love you. I'd tell God how much I love you, too, 'n' 'member you in my prayers!"

Travis couldn't speak. By sheer force of will, he kept walking, aware of how Randi's fingers clenched within his grasp. Finally, unable to help himself, he glanced at her face.

Like his own, it was wet with tears.

"BUT, MO-OM, Robbie's camped out lotsa times at his cousins', 'n' he's a four-year-old, too."

Randi heard the tears threatening Matt's voice and felt like an ogre. She couldn't help recalling his words to Travis a couple of nights before, wondering if he'd been hinting at this at the time.

Hinting that with a dad, he wouldn't need to plead, since the dad would probably join in the all-male camp-out.

Oh, Lord, don't think about that. You've lost enough sleep over the things he said the other night, as it is! Just deal with what's going on now, Terhune!

But her stomach clenched at the thought of Matt on an overnight camp-out with Robbie Spencer and Robbie's ten-year-old twin cousins. What if something happened? Like another urinary infection. The boys would only be in the cousin's backyard, true, but how would the other children recognize an emergency if it happened? They were just kids!

"Matt, sweetheart," she began tentatively, searching for a way to say no without upsetting him, "I know you've got your heart set on this, but—"

"But!" he cried. "When you say 'but,' you always mean no!" Face screwed into a contortion heralding tears, he turned toward his aunt, who was mixing a batch of brownies at the kitchen counter. "Aunt Jill, make her unner-stan'!"

As Jill turned to face them, Randi shot her a look that said, *Make* him *understand*.

Jill sighed. Randi was becoming overprotective. The signs had been increasing over the past year; and since

Matt's recent crisis and hospitalization, his mother's tendency toward excessive fear and restraint of the child's emerging independence had mushroomed. Something had to be done.

"Matt," she said softly, "why don't you take Ulysses for a romp in the yard while your mom and I talk?"

His lower lip thrust out, Matt cast a doubtful eye over the two women. His aunt smiled at him, and he glanced at his mother and managed to pull in his lip. "All right," he mumbled. "C'mon, 'Lysses—" he signaled the pup "—we gots to let these wimmens have a talk."

"YOU COULD'VE SUPPORTED me," Randi accused when she and Jill were alone. She gestured in the direction of the backyard. "That little stinker's sharp as a tack, and like most bright children, he's not above playing off the adults in his life against each other."

Jill shoved the brownies in the oven, turned to her and sighed. "I know, love, but hear me out, okay?" She smiled to take the edge off what she was about to say, and Randi gave a reluctant nod.

"Randi, I know you worry about Matt and only want to protect him from harm, but isn't it possible you could be, uh, overdoing it a bit?"

"Overdoing it?" Randi looked hurt. "What if something should happen with Matt, and the other boys don't realize it? What if they can't see he's in trouble?"

"But the parents will be only yards away."

Randi speared her with a look that said she wasn't budging an inch.

"Okay," Jill said, "if you're not comfortable with the setup as it stands, what if we send along our cellular phone and teach Matt and the boys how to use it? Better yet, we could give 'em a call every so often. Maybe we'd be waking them up all night, but kids fall back to sleep with no trouble. But if something was wrong, we could alert the parents. They'd be there in moments.''

Randi was silent as she digested this. Trust Jill to come up with a creative solution; it went hand in hand with her other artistic talents, she supposed. But Randi's apprehension didn't ease, though she was hard put to say why. ''I don't know, Jill,'' she began evasively. ''I mean, Matt's just a baby. He's—''

''He's not a baby. He's four and a half years old. But he could resent being *treated* like a baby if you don't lighten up a bit.''

''Lighten up!'' Randi was stung. Yet, try as she might, she couldn't ignore the ring of truth in Jill's words. Matt *had* sounded resentful. That had stung, too.

''Look, sweetheart,'' Jill said gently, putting an arm about her shoulders, ''no one knows better than I how loving and caring a parent you've been. No kid could've had a better mom. All I'm saying now is, you might wanna take a fresh look at the situation. Your little boy's growing up. He needs some freedom to try his wings.''

She's right, Randi thought, *so why does it hurt? Why can't I relax about this?*

Though Randi was silent, Jill could tell she'd given her pause. ''Tell you what,'' she said. ''Why don't you think about it awhile? The camp-out's not till the weekend. No one's demanding you make a decision right now.''

Randi cocked her head toward the backyard and managed a grin. ''Oh, no? Did you see the look young Master Terhune tossed us as he left?''

Jill chuckled, relieved to see her sister's sense of humor peeking through. ''Just you leave Master Terhune to ol' Jill the pill, kid. By the time—''

''Mom! Aunt Jill!'' Matt's voice cut across the yard. ''It's Travis! Travis is here!''

''Oh, no!'' Randi cast an eye over the paint-stained jeans and T-shirt she frequently wore around the house. Her hand went to her hair, caught in an askew ponytail that was still damp from the shower she took after jogging. "Lord, I'm a mess! Why *does* that man insist on showing up unannounced?"

Jill flushed. She'd known Travis was coming and why. But Randi wasn't supposed to know about it, for fear she'd resist what he had in mind—what *they* had in mind, now that he'd talked her into it. And in this, she still had some uncertainty; she prayed she wasn't making a mistake. "Uh, why don't you run up and change while I keep him entertained, sis?"

Randi needed no urging. Flashing her a look of gratitude, she exploded out of her chair and flew upstairs.

"BEST BROWNIES I ever tasted," Travis declared as he sat at the kitchen table with all three Terhunes.

Matt chimed in with "Me, too!" then glanced at his mother. "Uh, 'cept for Mom's," he added loyally. "Her 'n' Aunt Jill make the bestest brownies in the whole world. They're lots better 'n Robbie's mom's. She puts *nuts* in 'em. Yuck!"

"Say, Tiger—" Travis glanced at the wall clock and then at Jill "—if it's okay with Mom and Aunt Jill, why don't you take one over to Robbie right now? He might like 'em, too."

"But for heaven's sake, don't say anything about the nuts!" Randi warned, prompting a giggle from Matt.

"Matter of fact," Jill added with a glance at the clock as she sectioned off four brownies, "you can take some for all the Spencers."

"Okay," Matt said cheerfully, "but that baby can't eat any." He made a face. "She gots no teeth."

Chuckling, Jill covered the plateful with plastic wrap and handed it to Matt.

"Robbie won't care 'bout the nuts, though," he called

over his shoulder from the back door. "He eats *anything* chawk-lit!"

"Okay, you two," Randi said when Matt had disappeared out the door, "what's going on? I saw you glancing at the clock, and you couldn't wait to hustle Matt out of here. C'mon, what's up?"

"She's quick," Travis said to Jill. "I'll say that for her."

"Sharp as scissors, my sister," Jill agreed with a nod. "Maybe she missed her calling. Does the CIA hire women?"

"Very funny," Randi grumbled, "but it doesn't take a rocket scientist to figure out there's something in the works between you two. Now, out with it."

"Tsk, tsk." Travis shook his head. "Bossy, too. Maybe you'd better tell her, Jill."

"Tell me what?" Randi demanded.

"And impatient!" Jill said with a laugh. But when Randi threatened to hurl a brownie at her, she held up her hands in surrender. "Okay, okay!"

Randi lowered the brownie to her plate and Jill told her, "You know Travis has reconciled with his family, right? Well, one of the percs of being a full-fledged, dues-paid-up member of the McLean clan is the use of—get this, sis—the family yacht!"

Randi's eyes went wide, but Travis ran a hand over his jaw and groaned. *Yacht.* He never called the damned thing a yacht.

"And," Jill went on, "he'd like your permission to take Matt out for a cruise."

"Oh," Randi said. Just Matt? Why not Matt and her? Why not all three of them? Were women routinely excluded for some reason? "All by himself?" she asked, trying to keep from sounding hurt—and worried.

"Well, no," Travis said. "I mean, I'll be sailing with him, and there's the captain and crew, of course."

"It'll only be for a few hours," Jill put in, seeing the

reluctance on her sister's face. "We'd wait for them at this little restaurant at the yacht basin Travis told me about."

Randi shook her head. "I don't know, Travis..." she began, then caught the arch look on Jill's face. A look that said, *There you go again!*

"It'll be perfectly safe," he assured her. "But, tell you what—why don't I take you out there today? I can show you how safe it'll be."

"What, right now?"

"For somethin' like this, darlin'—" his gaze was strangely full of promise, sending tendrils of that old nameless longing to her nerve endings, "—yeah, now's the time."

CHAPTER TWENTY

AS TRAVIS GAVE HER a tour of the *Sarah Anne,* Randi was awestruck. The sheer size of the yacht, not to mention its grand appointments, boggled the mind. It hit her now just how wealthy Travis, or his family at least, was. The furnishings alone had to cost multiples of what she made in a year.

"Hope you brought an appetite, darlin'." Travis's lazy drawl invaded her unsettling thoughts. "Unless my nose is lyin', Etienne's cookin' up a storm in the galley."

The tantalizing aroma of something delicious drifted up from below. Randi sniffed appreciatively as he led her toward a set of stairs, carpeted in a plush turquoise wool.

"Etienne?" she asked, suddenly aware of the warmth of Travis's hand on her arm. She was aware of his "darlin'," as well, though she'd long since told herself this was nothing more than a casual endearment, perhaps something he threw at many women. But in recent days she wasn't so sure; memories of the quiet intimate moments they'd shared with Matt, not to mention the kisses they'd exchanged, said there was far more than the casual between them. And if that were true—

"French chef extraordinaire." Travis's reply cut off these disturbing musings. "The sucker just lives to cook!" he added with the smile that made her feel giddy and nearly stumble over her own feet.

"Watch it, darlin'," he warned, running his eyes down

the slim length of her white slacks to her rubber-soled shoes. "The carpet's not always footwear friendly."

His arm curved around her back as he helped her down the stairs; it was sure and strong, in no way overly familiar, yet she'd seen the gleam of appreciation in his eyes when he looked at her. His attentions left her oddly uncertain, breathless even, and she wondered why she couldn't relax with him. This was Travis, a man she knew and trusted, not some stranger. With an effort to appear calm, she glanced about.

The yacht's interior was done in turquoise and terra-cotta, with varying shades in between. The cooler hues ranged from the carpet's rich blue-green to the soft aqua of the silk wall covering; warm earth tones in the upholstered furniture gave way to paler apricots and peaches in various accessories, and tasteful objets d'art graced tables and walls. Everything spoke of luxury and sophistication, with an emphasis on comfort, and was a far cry from anything in her experience.

And if the yacht's interior wasn't imposing enough, she was still all too aware of Travis's closeness. Of the mere inches that separated them as he guided her past a grand piano to a cozy lounge with floor-to-ceiling windows affording a view of the bay. Here, two deep comfortable-looking velvet chairs faced a low table of heavy hammered brass; it bore a tray of delicious-looking hot hors d'oevres. A silver ice bucket held a foil-capped bottle; two fluted glasses rested beside it.

"Let me guess," she said. "Champagne?"

He shot her a lopsided grin and winked. "Louis Roederer at last!"

"With or without marshmallows?" she quipped, still trying to ignore the effect he was having on her. But that was like trying to ignore a tidal wave, and the results were just as devastating. Tall, tanned and masculine to the last pore, his golden perfection radiated strength and quiet confidence. As he seated her, she caught the clean male scent of him; it mingled with the hint of salt air and sunshine that clung to his hair and clothes.

Taking a deep breath, she released it slowly, trying to dispel the teasing assault to her senses. Yet despite all this, she found herself regretting the loss of his warmth when he moved to his chair. *What's wrong with me? Do I want the nearness or don't I? Make up your mind, Terhune!*

"No marshmallows at the moment, darlin', but if you want some—"

"Oh, no...no, that's all right. Um, what were you saying about the chef?" She fiddled nervously with the ends of the knot that tied the tails of her navy silk blouse at her waist.

"Oh, Etienne." Travis reached for the champagne. "He's a former Michelin four-star chef, and a permanent fixture aboard. My father won't say, but rumor has it he bribed him away from Onassis some years back." He grinned. "We'll be samplin' his specialty for dinner."

"Dinner?" She checked her watch; it was only four in the afternoon. "But I'm just here for a quick tour to—"

"To see if it's safe for Matt to sail on the *Sarah Anne,* I know. But you can't make that decision while she's in port," he added smoothly. "Any decent tour's gotta include a little run across the bay." He wasn't about to add that Etienne's dinner was scheduled to be served around midnight, and by then, they'd be far out to sea. Randi didn't know it, but she was about to be courted. Yes, courted. An old-fashioned term, maybe, but he meant it, which was what had convinced Jill to agree to what he had in mind; he wanted to marry this woman, to build a life with her—and their son.

"Oh. I see." She felt warmed and foolish at the same time. She recalled her disappointment back at the house, that he'd asked Matt and not her; yet it seemed she'd been invited to sail, after all. And these hors d'ouvres were just a beginning. Imagine—dinner by a four-star chef. She flashed Travis a bright smile. "How long a run?"

God, that smile! How in hell can they dub her an ice queen with a smile like that? A man could die happy, drinking it in. "Uh, how long? Oh, a couple of hours or so," he said vaguely as he gently popped the champagne cork.

He told himself the white lie was necessary; his object was to help her past her fears, past the reasons she came across as an ice queen, and to do that, he needed a few days, at least. Besides, by the time she realized what was up, he'd have her too relaxed to care. He hoped so, anyway. If he didn't, she'd likely never trust him again.

WHEN THEY'D CONSUMED enough champagne and hors d'ouvres to make Randi wonder how she'd ever make room for Etienne's dinner, Travis introduced her to Captain Baker. Baker, who joined them in the lounge, was a soft-spoken man of about fifty, with silver hair and a close-cropped beard to match. In his crisp navy jacket and white slacks, he looked like someone straight out of an ad in a yachting magazine.

For Randi's benefit, the captain described the standard for maritime safety regulations. He also explained how the *Sarah Anne* met and exceeded the standard in every respect.

"Does that ease your mind, darlin'?" Travis asked after Baker excused himself to see about getting them under way.

"Oh…um, yes," she answered tentatively. She'd had no idea of the extent of such regulations, and she certainly felt relaxed about the impending cruise. On the other hand, why was he insisting on taking Matt our separately? She'd feel a lot more at ease if she could go along when they…

Your little boy's growing up, love. Jill's words slipped into her thoughts, and Randi put a lid on her misgivings. Matt would be with Travis, and she trusted Travis, didn't she? Of course she did.

As if on cue, with the captain's departure, a sound system began to pipe in soft orchestral music. It was languid and dreamy, drenched in long mellow chords carried by the strings.

Travis smiled lazily and reached for her hand. "May I have this dance, ma'am?" Without waiting for a reply, he caught her hand and led her to a polished wooden floor tucked discreetly behind the piano.

As he took her in his arms and began to move to the soft romantic music, she felt light-headed. Maybe she should have passed on the champagne. Yet she suspected it wasn't the champagne but Travis's nearness that was intoxicating, stealing along her senses like curling wisps of smoke.

Since he was more than a head taller, she found herself breathing in the scent of him rising from his open-throated shirt: a faint hint of spice from the soap he'd used, maybe a trace of cologne, and the essence of clean healthy male.

"Penny for your thoughts, darlin'." Throaty and low, his voice drifted somewhere over her ear. She had a fleeting thought that he was holding her just right: comfortably, and not too close, guiding her over the mirror-smooth floor with just the slightest pressure of his hand at her back.

"Mmm? Oh, I was just thinking what a good dancer you are." She surprised herself with this. Jill had taught her to dance when they were teenagers, and she'd enjoyed learning. Yet she'd always hated school dances. Dancing meant being held by a male partner. She invariably found herself stiff and awkward in the embrace of some adolescent boy she barely knew. After a while she began to invent excuses for not going.

Later on, when she was in college, she limited herself to fast numbers that didn't require the partners to touch. Yet even then, she'd had to force herself to participate. Just the sight of all those gyrating bodies on a dance floor made her uncomfortable. She realized with a start that Travis McLean was the first adult male who'd ever held her in his arms on a dance floor. More surprising yet, it felt...easy, as if they'd been doing it for years.

"Funny," he murmured, "I was just thinkin' the same 'bout you. Knew you'd be a good dancer, though."

She glanced up at him questioningly.

"Didn't anyone ever tell you? You're grace itself, Randi. The way you move, the way you carry yourself, it's as if you can't set a foot wrong if you try. Where'd you come by all that, hmm?"

"I—I'm not sure but, well, I guess it could come from athletics. I've always loved sports." She laughed. "When I was a little girl, Daddy used to say I was a natural athlete and wasn't I lucky. I could just plunge in and enjoy a sport, while the rest of the world had to work at it."

Travis found himself as entranced by the sound of her laugh as he was by her smile. She didn't laugh nearly enough and should do it more often. He made a mental note to work on it. "Sounds like your daddy was a real special person."

"Oh, he was!" Her eyes closed for a moment and a soft smile curved her lips. The smile widened as she looked up at him. "He was a big blond bear of a man, and the gentlest person I've ever known. And he was *funny*. He was always making us laugh with the craziest antics you could imagine. Lord, when I think of some of the things he did, I still get the giggles."

Travis smiled into her shining eyes. "Tell me," he encouraged softly.

She chuckled. "I remember a Mother's Day when I was about six or seven. Jill and I conspired with Daddy to surprise Mama with a special breakfast in bed. He woke us at an ungodly hour—it was still dark outside—and we sneaked downstairs to make flapjacks. Jill and I mixed the batter while Daddy fried sausages."

Another chuckle. "Jill and I got flour everywhere, all

over the kitchen and ourselves. But Daddy didn't scold. He just announced that we'd all be clowns. Said flour made the best clown makeup in the world.

"And before we knew it, he was helping us smear butter on our faces and dust them with flour. We found a do-it-yourself cake-frosting kit in the pantry, and we used the little tubes of colored frosting to draw clown eyes and big smiling lips. There was a powder room off the kitchen, and we closed the door before crowding around the mirror to apply our 'makeup,' so our giggles wouldn't wake Mama."

She smiled reminiscently. "Then we carried Mama's breakfast to her singing 'All the world loves a clown' at the tops of our lungs. Lord, if Mama hadn't been in bed, she'd have been on the floor she was laughing so hard."

Chuckling, Travis executed a graceful spin on the dance floor that brought her closer, but she didn't seem to notice. She was telling him about other comical things her father had done: the time he'd coaxed Jill into practicing her piano lesson by covering himself in tin foil and pretending to be a metronome; the way he didn't just read bedtime stories, but acted out all the parts.

"Our favorite was Maurice Sendak's Where the Wild Things Are," she finished. "The faces he made! And he roared the funniest loudest roars."

Travis was still chuckling. "Sounds like one hell of a guy. Wish I'd known him."

"I...I wish you had, too." She thought of the things he'd told her about his own father, and her heart ached for him, for the child he'd been. "And I wish you'd had...uh, that is..." The words trailed off awkwardly, but Travis only smiled.

"Well, I didn't," he said, looking down at her as he drew her right hand to his chest and curled his fingers around it. "Have a warm 'n' lovin' father, that is. But miracles do happen, even if they arrive a little late."

He went on to tell her more about Trent McLean's transformation. When he told her about his father's eagerness to meet Matt and teach him to swing a golf club, his voice caught and he had to look away.

But she'd seen the sheen of moisture in his eyes, and was greatly moved by the certainty that the estrangement from his father had cut more deeply than he'd let on, for Travis wasn't a man easily given to tears. That she somehow knew this, without understanding how she knew, was something she didn't stop to ponder; it simply was.

"Travis," she found herself saying in a burst of enthusiasm, "what if...well, I suppose we'll have some careful explaining to do, to prepare Matt, but perhaps we can arrange for them to meet?"

He wondered if she realized what this would mean. Careful explaining could involve telling Matt who Trent was. And if he learned who Trent was, then it followed that he'd learn... His heart began to pound. Was that what she was saying? Did he dare pursue this now?

Randi watched a frown cross his face and misinterpreted it to mean he was uncertain about his father, after all. "I mean," she hastily put in, "if your dad's really had a change of heart..."

"He has," Travis said, an image of his father in the living room at Sunnyfields that day filling his mind. He found himself suddenly blinking back tears as he looked at her. "He means it, Randi, though I sometimes need to mentally pinch myself to believe it."

She smiled into his eyes. "I'm glad. Better late than never, as they say." Searching his face, she gave her head a rueful shake. "I only wish it'd come while you were still..."

"I know," he said quietly. They'd stopped dancing; the soft music flowed around them, blending with the easy movement of the yacht through the water.

"But it means just as much to me that it's happened in time for Matt. I love that kid, Randi. I want a life that's better for my son than what I've had. I mean, isn't that what bein' a parent's all about? I know I'm no expert, but..." He shrugged.

She felt as if she could drown in the blue blue gaze that held hers. How had she ever doubted this man's sincerity? His need to be involved in the life of the child he'd fathered, no matter how that had come about. His ability to care deeply for him in a healthy way, a selfless way.

"Sometimes, Travis," she began quietly, "love creates its own expertise."

A shaky smile trembled on lips that fought to contain a sob, and to conceal the emotions threatening to tear him apart, he captured her hand and led her to a sofa beyond the piano. Dear God, she'd accepted that he loved Matt! A small miracle in itself, he thought as his pulse tripped into double time. Now to work on the bigger miracle. *Please, Lord, let me be right.*

His emotions finally under control, he stopped before the sofa, lifted her hand and raised it to his lips. Placing a kiss on her palm, he closed her fingers over it, feeling a shiver course through her as he met her gaze. "Sit with me, darlin'. It's time we talked 'bout a few things."

A look of uncertainty crossed her face. What things? she wanted to ask, but then he joined her, draping his arm along the sofa behind her back, and the words evaporated on her tongue. His nearness drove her crazy with an ambivalence she didn't understand; she both wanted it and feared it, and she still didn't know why.

"Randi," he began, choosing his words carefully, "I can't tell you how much it means to me to hear you acknowledge my love for Matt. We've come a long way, darlin', from that standoff on the beach."

She nodded, managing a small smile. "You terrified me, you know, coming on the scene that way. All I could think of was—" she swallowed, staring down at her tightly folded hands "—that you'd come to take him away from me."

"Oh, sweetheart—" he captured her chin, turning her face toward him "—not in a million years. But then, you couldn't know that, could you? Lord, darlin', I'm sorry. I should've been more sensitive. You didn't know me well enough to realize I'm not—"

"Not the sort of man to do such a thing?" she said, stilling him with her fingers on his lips. "You're right. I didn't know that about you. I didn't know you at all."

"And now?" he asked, capturing her hand and kissing the tips of her fingers before releasing it.

Trying to ignore the wild leap of her pulse, she cocked her head to the side and managed a smile. "Well, uh, now that I know you a little better..."

He grinned. "Yes?"

"I know you don't mean to...to do the things I feared back then. It isn't in you. You...care."

He nodded solemnly. He'd hoped she felt this way, sensed she did, but he wanted her to articulate her feelings. "And my presence in Matt's life now? In both your lives?" He held his breath. "Randi...where d'you see us goin' from here?"

She swallowed past the lump of trepidation his words called up and didn't answer. It was one of the things she'd been wrestling with, both awake and in her dreams. Matt's asking about Travis being his daddy had brought such things to a head; she couldn't continue to sweep them aside.

Travis chuckled softly. "I think we both know where Matt sees us goin'," he said as if reading her mind. Again he turned her toward him; his gaze was intense as he studied her face. "I'd like him to know, Randi. I think I'd trade my soul for him to know I'm his father."

"Don't say that!" she exclaimed for want of something better to say. But she was stalling and she knew it.

"Just a figure of speech, darlin'," he said. His gaze became even more intense. "But, Randi, I need for you to know how important this is to me…as I feel it's important for Matt. For all of us."

She swallowed and managed a small nod. It was out on the table now; more importantly, he was telling her the decision was hers to make. But could she do it? Make him Matt's father in name, as well as in deed? *Share her son?*

There, she'd acknowledged it. That it sounded selfish was something she also realized, and she felt herself flush. But it was true, wasn't it? She'd lived for five years now with the idea that Matt was hers and hers alone. She was a single mother—not an easy thing, by any means—but she'd done it, and she felt a certain pride in knowing she'd done it well.

But as a mother, a good mother, which was what she'd always tried to be, she had her child to think of first. And Matt wanted a daddy. He wanted Travis.

"Will…will you give me a little time to think about it?" she asked in a small voice.

He smiled warmly at her, savoring another small step of progress. "I won't press you, darlin'. But I did think it was important for you to know where I stand."

A small frown creased her brow. "Travis, how would it work, do you think? I mean, if we told him, how would we work it into our…well, our daily lives?"

I'd marry you, and we'd go from there. "C'mon," he said aloud, pulling her up from the sofa. "Dance with me some more, 'n' I'll give you my thoughts on the matter."

The music hadn't stopped, she realized; she'd simply been preoccupied with the things they were discussing. Now she felt its dreamy chords swelling around them as he took her back in his arms.

They danced as before, slowly, with just the right amount of closeness, Randi thought. She listened as Travis gave her the scenario he envisioned. He could move closer to her and Matt, so that he lived in the district where Matt would attend school; they'd operate as some couples who were separated or divorced did, but with joint custody. When this was handled right, he'd read in a study, the children moved easily between the two households, accepting the situation as normal.

That this was the last thing Travis had in mind for their future was something he didn't tell her. He simply sketched for her the possibility that was least threatening. *One step at a time,* he thought, schooling himself to be patient. *One careful step at a time.*

Randi pondered his idea, saying it sounded plausible, but she'd like to see the study he'd read. And she ignored the inner voice that asked her why she felt a stab of disappointment when he mentioned operating like a divorced couple.

Travis was only too happy to agree. She was softening to the idea. It wouldn't be too great a leap to his true scenario. But time for that later. Patience, he reminded himself, patience.

"You feelin' relaxed, darlin'?" he asked with a casual change of topic. "Enjoyin' the cruise so far?"

She was relaxed, she realized, though he was now holding her closer. But after the things they'd discussed, being in his arms was the least of her concerns. "Mm," she murmured, "and the dancing."

"Good," he whispered, and his gaze fastened on her mouth. "Now stay that way, darlin'," he breathed as he slowed his steps and pulled her even closer, "all nice 'n' easy 'n' relaxed..."

And with devastating tenderness, Travis slowly lowered his head and began to kiss her senseless.

CHAPTER TWENTY-ONE

RANDI HAD TROUBLE drawing breath as his mouth slowly descended. He captured her lips, a gentle claim that stole across her senses like no champagne ever could. The music flowed and ebbed around them, and she realized she recognized the melody. It was called the *Liebestraum*—the "dream of love." Travis's lips and tongue played unhurriedly with hers. Molding, shaping, deliciously teasing, until she was giddy with sensation and wanting more.

When his tongue skimmed the seam between her lips, they parted, and without thinking, she met it with a tentative dart of her own.

A murmur of approval vibrated in his throat, and he deepened the kiss, widening his stance against the swaying of the boat as he drew her closer yet. With utmost care he began to probe the moist heat of her mouth. He traced the sensitive crevice between her upper teeth and lip with his tongue. He captured her full lower lip lightly between his teeth, then releasing it slowly, nibbled at it almost carelessly, finally pulling it into his mouth with a gentle suction that made something careen wildly inside her.

"So lovely..." he murmured as his hands slid over her shoulders to cup her face. "Ah, lady, I love the taste of you." And he kissed her again, a long drugging kiss that had her reeling. She was tumbling heedlessly into a warm sensual place that had no name. Just that of the man whose fingers threaded through her hair as he deepened the kiss and took her there. *Travis!* her heart shouted with every wildly thudding beat. *Travis Travis Travis!*

He felt her hands go to his shoulders. He knew from the way she clung to him that it wasn't the gentle swaying of the vessel that made her unsteady, for he was having the same problem. Stifling a groan, he cautioned himself to go slowly. Randi was still inexperienced, still a novice at such things. An innocent whose kisses were only beginning to grow accomplished under his careful tutoring. But, dammit, this was hard. She went to his head like wine.

"Back to dancin', darlin'," he murmured huskily. But when they began moving to the rhythm again, their bodies were closely aligned.

Randi sensed this with only a vague dreamy awareness. She sighed as she felt his chin resting on her head, his thighs brushing against hers with each slow gliding step. Melting against him, she felt herself carried along by the swelling strains of the music. Images flowed and ebbed in her head, mingling in a subtle blend of past and present: her father's big comforting arms about her, Travis's warmth as he held close, gentle laughter that could have belonged to either man, protective male strength. Safety.

And so, when he paused and drew her more intimately into his arms, she went as if it were the most natural thing in the world. When his mouth again began its tender assault, skimming her hair, her eyes, trailing kisses along her neck and throat, she moaned with pleasure. When he captured her mouth in a heady sensual invasion that left her breathless, she leaned into him, silently begging for more.

And finally, when he swept her up into his arms and began carrying her—where, she neither knew nor cared—she closed her eyes and clung to him, curling into his warmth. Here was comfort and sharing and pleasure all rolled into one. Here she was safe.

Aching and sweet, the muted strains of the *Liebestraum* followed them as he carried her. Travis was taking her to his private stateroom. He'd debated this, wondering if it wasn't too risky. But in the lounge, anyone could walk in on them, and they needed privacy. He promised himself he'd do nothing she wasn't ready for.

A masculine haven done in deepest tones of earth and sky and sea, Travis's room had a huge canopied bed at its center. Bed hangings of sheer azure silk billowed with the gentle breeze sifting through an open window.

Randi noticed none of it. Caught in the warm cocoon of his arms, she felt something soft undulate beneath her as he placed her on the bed. "Mmm," she murmured lazily.

He smiled as he joined her on the water bed, recalling how he'd hated it and carried on about it as a teenager when his mother's fancy decorator had had it installed. Now he could only appreciate its chief advantage—helping lull this skittish woman he cared so much about into the dreamy relaxed state suited to his purpose.

At least he hoped she was lulled.

"Randi, darlin', look at me," he murmured, smoothing tendrils of honey blond hair away from her face and watching her struggle to raise her eyelids. He answered her smile with his own as she gazed languidly at him through thick tawny lashes.

"Kitten," he whispered, kissing her temple, the tip of her nose and then her mouth, lingering there to savor the taste of her. "I have a confession to make."

She couldn't imagine anything softer than the surface cradling their entwined bodies. And Travis's hand stroking her hair was so delicious, soothing. "Mmm?" She ached for the feel of his mouth on hers again.

Hoping he'd judged the moment right, he let his hand slide along her neck and over her shoulder. It stroked the silken fabric of her blouse in a slow downward glide that ended in the capture of a generously rounded breast. As if on command, her nipple sprang to life, jutting through the silk to tease the center of his palm.

He heard her moan softly, and she leaned into his caress. *Thank God,* he thought, then bent his head to nibble at her ear, catching the lobe between his teeth, nipping it lightly before using his lips to soothe the sensitized flesh.

"T-Travis..." she stammered breathlessly. He was molding both breasts now, finding their hardened peaks through the silk. She couldn't think.

"Uh-huh," he murmured encouragingly, continuing the assault on her ear and the sensitive flesh below. "Now, 'bout that confession, love..." he continued in the same soothing voice.

"Confession?" she whispered shakily. His fingers were doing mad impossible things to her throbbing flesh. She couldn't concentrate. Lord above, her whole body ached! Ached with a need that hovered somewhere between pleasure and sweet unbearable pain.

He nudged the sarong-wrapped silk aside and gently bit a nipple through the barely existent lace of her bra. "Y'see, love," he continued, feeling her shudder with swiftly building need, "we're not goin' back to port tonight."

"Not going...?" What was he talking about? Why was he even talking at all?

"This cruise—" he nudged the lace aside and drew the puckered tip of her breast into his mouth, sucking gently on it before he released it "—is a surprise...just for you, darlin'." Maybe he wasn't playing entirely fair, but that was the risk he had to take; all that happened between them now depended on getting her to trust him, and that meant not just emotionally, but physically. He suckled the worried flesh again, felt her shudder beneath him.

Randi felt a liquid warmth settle in the region below her navel. Her thighs trembled uncontrollably, and the place between was hot and throbbing. The maddening suction of his mouth seemed directly linked to the heat below. *Dear God, the pleasure!*

"Did you hear me, sweetheart?" Travis persisted. He

might be aware he'd stacked the deck in his favor, but he still wouldn't settle for a mindless response, much as he was tempted. He wanted her to know what was happening, that he'd conspired to steal her away for a few days. To court her, and win her, body, mind and heart. And for her to trust him, in spite of his little deception. Only then would he be ready to ask her for the ultimate in trust: to share a lifetime with him.

"We'll be cruisin' for a few days," he added. He raised his head to watch her face, but continued to caress her with sure knowing hands.

Randi blinked, focusing at last on his words. "Did you say a *few days?*" She stiffened under his touch.

"Uh...yeah." He eyed her shocked face with mounting trepidation. "It's all right," he said quickly. "Jill knows about it and, uh, sends her love."

Jill? She tried to keep her mind on his words, despite the anxiety spiraling through her. "Jill's back h-home with M-Matt. Th-they're expecting us to...to..."

"Not for a few days, sweetheart. We've all— *Oof!*"

"Don't you *dare* call me that!" She shoved at his chest and scrambled away, the undulating surface of the bed making her movements awkward.

"Randi, wait! It isn't—"

"You lied to me!" she cried. "Just a little cruise to set my mind at ease," she sneered as her feet found the floor. "A couple of hours, you said. But it was a lie! I trusted you. *Trusted!* And you *lied* to me!"

Travis winced. Her tone, her expression, every nuance of body language said his hope for a miracle was gone. He was a fool. He'd gambled on the impossible and he'd lost.

"I should have realized," she said bitterly. Her hands shook as she fumbled awkwardly with her blouse. "But you were making damned sure I *wouldn't* realize, weren't you?"

"Randi, I—"

"All this—" she gestured wildly at the room, the bed "—and the music, the champagne! It was calculated to seduce me, wasn't it? A big lie to get me into your bed!"

"No!" He rolled off the mattress, scrambling in his mind for the right words, knowing he could lose her forever if he failed, terrified he already had. "Randi," he pleaded, "it's not the way you think. I only—"

"Take me home," she cut in icily, not looking at him.

He swallowed a lump of anguish. What in the name of God had he done? He'd known how tenuous a thing trust could be. How fragile. And now, through a petty deception he could have easily avoided, he'd destroyed the bridge between them. A trust that had taken weeks to build. *Fool* didn't begin to describe him!

But, dammit, he cared about this woman. It couldn't end like this!

Then fight for her, said a voice inside his head. And his heart. "Randi, please don't go," he urged, following her to the door. "You've gotta know I never planned a...a seduction. It was s'posed to be a courtship, I swear!" He placed a hand on her arm to stay her. "I want to marry you."

"Take your hand off me!" She pressed her back to the door, reminding him of a frightened animal. She was staring at him, but not seeing him. Her eyes were unfocused, and she shook uncontrollably.

"I know what happens when a man t-touches you," she said. "I saw it happen to Jill. Saw the way he looked at her...at me."

"Randi, stop." Travis hovered there, uncertain what to do or say. Things had gone horribly awry, and it was all his fault. "Please, baby, don't do this."

It was as if she hadn't heard. "He forced her...hurt her!"

"Randi..." Raw emotion laced his voice as he realized what she was reliving in her mind, and he knew he needed to stop her. Her hands were clenched into fists, and her face was ashen.

And he wanted to smash something, annihilate the horrors in her memory— No, he wanted to go back in time and kill! Erase the very existence of the animal who'd done those things, put this fear into her. "Randi," he repeated in a choked plea, "please stop this."

She never heard him. "He forced her!" she cried. "Just like he forced me, don't you see? He forced both of us, and we couldn't stop him! We were just g-girls and he was so s-strong, and he m-made me...made me... *Oh, my God*..."

There was a stunned silence.

The silence grew and hung in the air like an accusing finger as their eyes met. Vaguely, in some distant part of his brain, Travis noted she was focusing again. Seconds passed as they stared at each other in dismay. In horror. And in the pregnant silence that screamed at them was a single thought: *Not just Jill, but Randi, too.*

"Oh, baby..." Travis finally got out. He reached for her, wanting to comfort and protect. Wanting to turn back the clock and undo. If only it were that simple.

"Don't!" She twisted away, her face pale with shock, and something else, he realized with a sick feeling. She was seething with anger. "Don't you *dare* touch me!" she ground out between clenched teeth. "Not ever. Not ever again!"

"Okay," he said, backing off a step, trying desperately to sound reassuring. "I know how you must be—"

"You *know*," she mocked savagely, her eyes hot and accusing. "You couldn't possibly know! But you had to force me to this, didn't you, Travis? Corner me, till I— Oh, God, why did I have to remember? But I do. I remember *everything*. God, I can't bear it!"

Travis closed his eyes, sensing her pain as if it were his own. *Not just Jill, but Randi, too.* And now she was blaming him for what she'd obviously just recalled for the first time. But somehow he had to make her understand. "Randi, I swear to you, I had no idea…"

She began to sob, and he plowed a hand through his hair, staring at her helplessly. Feeling so far out of his element he had to grope for words. What did he know about things like blocking and buried shock? Trauma, he remembered they called it. He knew how to treat physical trauma, but this? He was no shrink. He was only a man, and right now, he felt less than that.

"Randi, listen to me," he pleaded, using the one thing he could think of, hoping it would be enough. "I *care* about you, deeply, and I wouldn't hurt you for the world. I know I was wrong using the method I did to bring you here, and I'm sorrier for it than I can say. But I meant what I said when I told you I intended to court you. I want to make things right for you…help you…*be* with you. I'm talkin' 'bout marriage, Randi. I want us to be a family—you, me 'n' Matt."

"What right did you have," she snarled, rounding on him with tight-lipped fury, "to barge into my life this way? To just take over? To expect that all you had to do was take me in your arms—" she waved a hand at the rumpled bed "—seduce me into compliance and…and then assume you'd make everything right? Marry you! I wouldn't marry you if you were the father of *ten* of my children!"

She twisted toward the door and grabbed for the handle. "Now be a good little blueblooded Boy Scout," she spat, "and get this…this floating palace turned around!"

Stung by her scathing sarcasm, Travis reached for anger to cover what felt curiously like hurt. Which was ridiculous; he hadn't been that thin-skinned since he was a kid. "Okay, lady," he said tightly, "you've got it."

CHAPTER TWENTY-TWO

"AND THAT'S ALL I know, David." Jill gave a helpless shrug. "Randi came home way too early from that surprise cruise, angry and upset, and she's been really down ever since. Meanwhile, Travis has been calling and calling, but she won't even talk to him. And neither is she willing to tell me a thing." She paused, took a shuddering breath. "Something went terribly wrong on that trip, and I feel I'm partly responsible. If only I hadn't—"

"Honey, don't." David reached across the kitchen table, where he'd joined her for lunch, and clasped her hands reassuringly. He'd been out of town on a week-long business trip until the night before, and this was the first chance they'd had to discuss what had happened while he was away.

"Jill, listen to me. You only had Randi's best interests in mind, from what you've told me. I mean, the guy said he wanted to *court* her! What's wrong with helping to engineer a little time between them? Especially when Randi'd been showing all the signs of a romantic interest in the guy herself."

Jill nodded pensively. "They were holding hands, David, like lovers. And whenever she came back after being with him...well, I'd never seen her like that. She had stars in her eyes."

"You see?" He smiled. "So don't go blaming yourself for what may have happened between those two when they were alone this time. In fact, look at it this way—you might even have done Randi a big favor.''

"You mean because she's decided to resume seeing Dr. Martin." It was the one positive thing Jill clung to; two days after the aborted cruise, Randi had announced just as she was going out the door that she'd made an appointment to see Carol Martin at her office. Just like that. Then she'd left for work—without a word of explanation, without even a hint about what was going on.

"Well, you've got to admit," David said, "nothing else ever persuaded her to return to counseling."

"I know," Jill said diffidently, "but I wish it weren't under such...strained circumstances. I mean, if you'd seen her eyes when she returned that evening! They looked— Maybe I'm being silly, but I could've sworn they looked...haunted. And then, all that anger. Lord, I wish she'd talk to me about—''

"Aunt Jill! When's Mom comin' home?" Matt's voice preceded him through the back door. "Is it time yet?"

Jill quickly pulled herself together and glanced at him. "Matt Terhune, mind your manners and say hello first." She smiled to soften the chastisement. "You must've noticed Uncle David's car in the drive when you came from Robbie's.''

"Uh, yeah." Matt tossed David a sheepish grin. "Hi, Uncle David."

"Hiya, Matt." David ruffled his hair and made a show of looking him over. "You've been growing again, kid. I'd better watch it. Next thing I know, you'll be borrowing my clothes!''

Matt giggled, prompting a bark from Ulysses, who'd followed him in. 'Yeah, 'n' I'm gonna grow even bigger, I betcha. Like my friend Travis. He's real big!''

David and Jill exchanged a look that said it was all too obvious who still occupied Matt's thoughts, despite the estrangement between his parents.

Oblivious to their exchange, Matt turned back to his aunt. "*Now* can you tell me when Mom's comin'…puh-leez?"

"Any minute now, honey," she said with a glance at the clock. "What's up?"

He heaved a sigh. "You know—Mom thinks I'm too little for a two-wheeler, but I'm not! I've been practicin' on Robbie's bike. He let me try it, 'n' I can ride it, honest. I only fell once, 'n' I didn't even hurt myself—see?" He held out his palms, which were grass stained but otherwise unblemished.

"Smart of you to practice on grass," David said as the sound of a car in the drive drew Matt's attention.

"She's home!" he exclaimed, and raced out the door.

Jill sighed. "I'd have bought him a bike weeks ago, but Randi—" she gave a helpless shrug "—won't even agree to letting him have one with training wheels."

"You're still worried about her being overprotective."

"Well, isn't she?"

He shrugged. "I don't know all that much about raising kids, honey—" he gave her a tender smile "—not yet, anyway. But I do know Matt's very bright and extremely well coordinated. He seems awfully precocious, while maybe Randi's just being cautious. You know all those child-development books she's always reading. Maybe she's using the guidelines they set for the average four-year-old. I mean, my sister's kid didn't even *mention* a two-wheeler till he was in second grade."

"I suppose it's possible," Jill replied without much conviction, "but that still doesn't make things any easier with Matt. I can't help feeling the poor kid's straining at the bit, David, and Randi…" She made a helpless gesture.

"Look, sweetheart," he said, again taking her hands, "I know how much you love those two, and it's only natural for you to worry about them. But you're just weeks away from a very important wedding, love, and in case you've forgotten, you're the main attraction. Brides-to-be are supposed to be happy—'' he caught her chin and leaned across to give her a kiss, then smiled into her eyes ''—right?''

''Right,'' she murmured with a soft sigh.

''Atta girl. Now promise me you'll stop this fretting and leave your sister to Dr. Martin. If Randi's in danger of becoming an overprotective parent, I'm sure it's something she'll address.''

''Maybe...but we both know there's a larger issue that needs addressing.''

''True, but didn't you once say that Carol counsels the total person? That she doesn't just address a specific problem?''

Jill nodded, recalling how Carol had worked on her home environment. ''She was as much responsible for helping me to be better organized—to get my homework done on time, that sort of thing—as she was for helping me get past the trauma.''

''Well, there you are, then. Carol's sharp. If there's a problem with the way Randi handles Matt, she'll see it.''

''I suppose so,'' Jill said, making an effort to look cheerful, since Matt and Randi could be heard approaching.

For David's sake, she resolved to leave Randi's problems to the professional. Still, she couldn't help wondering what had happened on a certain cruise that was beginning to seem like the dumbest thing she'd ever agreed to.

''THAT'S WONDERFUL NEWS, Jill. I really 'preciate your tellin' me.''

Jill had just told Travis that Randi had gone back into counseling. He shifted his grip on his car phone and sighed. ''She won't even talk to me.''

''I know,'' she replied sympathetically. ''But she's hardly told me any more than I've just told you.''

''So she's freezin' you out, too? God, I'm sorry, Jill. I should never have dragged you into this.''

''Yeah, well, you didn't exactly twist my arm. Besides,

she hasn't frozen me out exactly. It's just that…she's been awfully quiet lately. I guess we'll just have to respect her need for privacy. Hey, a guy in your line of work should understand the need to keep secrets occasionally, right?''

He chuckled. ''Right.''

Jill detected the sadness beneath the chuckle. ''Yeah, well, just don't make me sorry I told you what Randi wouldn't and get yourself over here. Matt's been missing you, Trav,'' she added softly.

''Jill, I'm sick with missin' him—*and* his mama. Still, I'm afraid Randi wouldn't 'preciate—''

''Not to worry. Matt's been pestering her, so she's agreed to let me invite you over—'' there was a moment's hesitation ''—when she's not here, that is.''

Checking a rude response, Travis scheduled a visit with Matt for the next day.

''Good enough,'' Jill said, ''and don't forget that other thing we talked about, huh?''

He assured her he wouldn't and said goodbye, but not before thanking her again for the good news.

At least, he hoped it was good. He stared broodingly into the distance, not ready yet to pull back onto the highway and resume driving. Randi was in counseling again, thank God. He could only hope it would help her deal with the shattering revelation he'd been inadvertently made privy to on the *Sarah Anne*. As to whether it helped dismantle the wall she'd erected to shut him out…

With a growl of frustration, he muttered a choice phrase and started his engine. He really was the world's biggest fool. It was what he'd always said about people who thought they were in love, wasn't it? So far, his foray into romantic love had brought him a hell of a lot of grief and not much else. A wise man would just give it up.

''Dammit,'' he said as he pulled onto the highway, ''if it weren't for Matt…''

The words trailed into silence as an image intruded: the

agonized wounded look in Randi's eyes as she'd stumbled on the truth. As she'd unconsciously voiced the bitter reality behind all that fear. A reality that had lain buried in her subconscious mind for years.

"Ah, Randi," he whispered, "I'd give anythin' to take away your pain. To undo the unspeakable things that put that hellish look in your eyes. But I can't, and it's drivin' me..."

He sucked in his breath, then released it slowly, forcing himself to abandon this fruitless line of thinking. The truth was, *she* experienced those things. She *had* been the victim of sexual abuse as a child, and nothing he said or did could change it.

Taking another calming breath, he forced himself to concentrate on the positive. On the softness of her eyes as they'd danced, on the sound of her laughter. He swallowed thickly. To see her that way again, to hear her laugh, he'd risk everything he had, do whatever it took. And if that made him a fool, so be it.

Besides, he told himself as he headed for Sunnyfields, romantic love wasn't the only kind that exacted a toll. A frantic call from his mother, and then another from his father, had alerted him to an unexpected crisis at home. It seemed Troy was furious over something Travis had done. Troy? Furious? His brother didn't have a furious bone in his body. What in hell was going on?

"DAMMIT, TRAV, what right d'you have to meddle in my life?"

Travis gaped at the brother he faced across a stretch of living-room carpet. Troy *was* furious. Jaw belligerently outthrust, eyes glittering dangerously, his normally mild-mannered sibling was looking daggers at him. He couldn't believe it!

"Mind tellin' me what this is all about?" he asked carefully.

"You bet I'll tell you!" Troy gestured wildly out the window, where their father could be seen practicing his golf swing. "Out of the clear blue, at breakfast this mornin', the father *you* coached informed me he got in touch with Aunt Lousie at Stanford yesterday."

Frowning, Travis nodded, still uncertain where this was leading.

"He also informed me," Troy went on tightly, "that the way was all clear for me to go there and work with her. And that I had *you* to thank for it!"

"Well, hell," Travis replied, "I thought—"

"Well, you thought wrong! The fact is, I have no intention of goin' into medical research. Not with Aunt Louise or anyone else!"

"But—"

"But did you take the trouble to find that out?" Troy demanded hotly. "Hell, no. Not the great all-knowin' Travis McLean! You just come sashayin' in here and...and take over, don't you? Well, just who d'you think you are? Who gave you the right to run my life?"

Travis was floored. It had never occurred to him to check with Troy first. But he loved his brother and he'd known he was unhappy. He'd just assumed...

But this wasn't the first time he'd wrongly assumed something about a person he loved. *What right did you have to barge into my life this way...to just take over?* Randi's angry words, so similar to his brother's, came to him with unnerving clarity.

"Troy," he said, feeling his way blindly through the possibilities suggested by the jarring comparison, "I never meant to tell you how to run your life. All I wanted—"

"All you wanted was to be in charge," Troy accused as he crossed to the door. Reaching it, he turned back, his anger unabated. "Dammit, Travis, you're every bit as controllin' as the old man ever was! I'm fed up. From now on, I'll thank you to butt outta my life!"

Stunned, Travis watched him slam the door behind him. Finding his way to a chair, he slumped wearily into it, dropping his head into his hands. Bewildered and hurt—he loved Troy and had only meant the best for him—he never heard the door reopen until a soft voice intruded.

"Guess he was pretty hard on you, huh?"

He raised his head and met Sarah's sympathetic gaze. "I could hardly believe it was Troy, talkin' like that."

She sighed. "I know...but, Trav?"

"Hmm?" he replied absently, still smarting under Troy's condemning comparison of him to their father. Controlling! Is that what he was?

Sarah placed a hand gently on his arm. "Travis, Troy sounded awfully harsh, I realize, but think about it. Is that necessarily a bad thing—for him, I mean?"

Pondering this for a moment, he heaved a sigh. "You're thinkin' maybe it's a good thing, is that it? That maybe ol' Troy's been overdue for somethin' like this?"

She nodded. "From what I've seen and heard from him lately, it could be he's finally comin' into his own."

"Go on," he urged, interested despite his bruised feelings.

"Well, followin' the reconciliation between you 'n' Daddy, a lot of things've been happenin'. But I'd say Troy's behavior's been the most remarkable..."

A FEW HOURS LATER Travis climbed into the Alpha, greatly sobered by what he'd learned. Following the exchange with Sarah, he'd sought out his brother and apologized. From the heart, and Troy had known it. Then they'd had a long talk.

Though Troy didn't want to go into medical research, he'd made up his mind to make a career change. On his own. Travis had wanted to jump up and hug him, but he'd wisely held back, sobered by the new strength and maturity he saw in Troy; he didn't need or want approval from his big brother.

Troy was giving up surgery to study sports medicine. Given his love of sports, it was perfect. So perfect Travis wondered why it hadn't occurred to him, then throttled the thought; he'd sworn to butt out, and that started now. It wasn't his business to speculate on his brother's affairs. Or try to run his life.

In the end Troy had apologized for the comparison to their father at his worst. He said he realized Travis was motivated by love, whereas the old Trent McLean had been blindly selfish. Still, Travis had acted blindly, too. He hadn't seen what he was doing.

Just as he hadn't seen what he was doing with Randi? A good question. He loved the woman, and he'd have sworn he was only trying to help her. But he'd have sworn the same about Troy, and Troy had practically accused him of being a control freak, for God's sake! Was that what he was?

Heaving a sigh, he headed for Langley. The company shrink wouldn't talk to him, but maybe he could consult the Internet for some insights. He had a lot to think about.

CHAPTER TWENTY-THREE

LIPS PURSED, twisting this way and that, Matt eyed his reflection in his mother's antique pier glass. They were in her bedroom, and Matt's apparel for the wedding had just arrived from the tailor. "Boy, this getup sure is fancy," he muttered.

"Ring bearer's an important job, honey," Randi said fussing with a cuff on his tuxedo pants—no easy matter, given his squirming—"and weddings are pretty fancy affairs."

"Yeah, but I'm glad we didn't get those stupid shorts." He wrinkled his nose. "They were *too* fancy."

Suspecting Matt's definition of "fancy" ran along less-than-positive lines, his mother smiled to herself, but didn't comment. The "shorts" he spoke of were the formal short pants that were traditional garb for ring bearers. Matt had refused to wear them. And while Jill had gone along, Randi thought he looked so adorable in them she'd tried to push the issue. But not too far, thank goodness.

It was one of many checks she'd made on such behavior lately. Controlling behavior, according to what she'd learned in sessions with Carol Martin. She hadn't merely been growing overprotective, as Jill had once suggested; at a time when Matt needed to become less dependent, she'd been trying to keep control of him in lots of little, but telltale, ways.

Children who've suffered abuse often grow into controlling adults. The doctor's words echoed in her mind. *Be-*

cause they once felt so utterly helpless, they're driven to prevent this from happening again. By exerting an iron control over their lives, they hope never again to become victims. But through this behavior they make themselves victims of another sort, becoming prisoners of their own fears. And when these fears extend to their children, they can become overcontrolling parents.

"Mom, how come we don't do stuff with Travis anymore?"

Matt's words jarred her; she blinked at him, trying to focus on his question. Or, more to the point, form a reply.

Travis was a delicate subject. He was in her thoughts more than she'd admitted to anyone except for Carol, but she avoided discussing him at home. She missed him so fiercely she feared breaking into tears in front of everyone; those she shed at night, aching and alone in her bed, were bad enough.

But she'd sent Travis away, and he finally seemed to have taken her at her word; following that initial flurry of phone calls, he'd made no further effort to contact her. Ironically this hurt, since she'd avoided contact herself; but she had a lot to sort out with regard to Travis. Surrendering control for Matt was one thing; surrendering it to a man— a man who'd already demonstrated his ability to make her lose control of her body—was something else entirely. It frightened her.

Counseling was helping her to understand and deal with her fears. But then there was the guilt. The guilt she felt every time she looked at her son and remembered how happy they'd all been together—she, Matt and Travis. Every time she looked into her son's eyes and saw not just the son, but the father. Every time Matt mentioned that father and she couldn't reply—because she'd sent him away. Every time—like now. *Think fast, Terhune!*

"Oh...well, honey, uh, didn't you just see that Disney movie with him last week?"

"Yeah, it was great!" Matt's grin faded as he turned to her. "But that was just me 'n' Travis, Mom. How come we don't do stuff with *you*? Don't you like Travis anymore?"

Like him? I ache for him, but I'm afraid! Oh, God, I'm so confused! He said he cared about me, that he wanted to marry me, even, but...how can I believe him or trust him when he— Don't cry, Terhune. Don't you dare cry!

Stooping to pick up some tissue paper that had fallen from the tailor's box, she avoided Matt's eyes and summoned a reply. "Well, honey, I've been awfully busy lately, what with the wedding and...and my work at the hospital."

It sounded lame even to her. The look she glimpsed on Matt's face said he didn't buy it, either.

"Tell you what," she said briskly. "Let's get you out of these things. We don't want them to get wrinkled, and—"

"Mom..."

She looked at him, and the unfamiliar sadness in his eyes was an arrow through her heart. "What is it, darling?" she asked.

Matt's bottom lip trembled as he looked up at her out of Travis's eyes. "I really do wish Travis could be my daddy. I wish it so hard, Mom! I'm gonna tell God 'bout it tonight, but...do you think God'll listen to me, Mom? I mean, I been tryin' to be real good, but..." He swallowed a sob.

Randi nearly staggered under the pain as she moved toward him and bent to take him in her arms. *Dear Lord, help me. Help me respond without hurting him. Help me erase the sadness in his eyes.* "Matt, darling, listen to me. You *are* good, and I don't doubt for a minute that God knows it. He knows everything."

"Yeah, but will He *do* it, Mom? Will He make Travis my daddy?" Tears trembled through the plaintive query, and she felt them clogging her throat, as well.

"I...I can't answer for the Lord, son," she stammered, "but I do believe He hears our prayers. As for answering them, though...well, God does what's best for us, though we may not always agree. Sometimes we just have to wait and see what He has in mind."

It was a temporary answer at best; but how could she give him a more definitive one when she didn't know where she herself stood with Travis? Fortunately it seemed to satisfy Matt. With a sniffle, he nodded against her chest.

She gave him a squeeze, then somehow managed, in a more cheerful voice, "Hey, isn't it nearly time for 'Barney'?"

He brightened instantly, and Randi swore eternal gratitude for the smiling dinosaur, syrupy lyrics and all.

"Barney's great, isn't he, Mom?" Matt asked with a grin. As Randi helped him out of the wedding clothes, he broke into the familiar lyrics about love and a happy family.

A happy family, her inner voice taunted. If only she hadn't blown it. If only she wasn't such a coward.

A FEW DAYS LATER Randi hurried out of the elevator at work, car keys in hand. It was after two in the morning, and she was bone-tired. Yet her shift in the ER had been no more demanding than usual; she knew her exhaustion had to do with sleeping poorly, not the job.

She'd been having disturbing dreams. Or, rather, a single recurring dream. But it wasn't one of the nightmares she'd suffered before. Those, thank heaven, had disappeared once she'd begun addressing her buried memories in counseling.

But this dream was no less troubling. It began with Matt saying his prayers. Prayers that asked God fervently if Travis could be his daddy. Then the scene shifted, and Matt was there again, but he was all grown-up; he looked just like Travis, yet she knew it was Matt, because he spoke to her: "Why'd you do it, Mom?" he asked. "Why'd you hide my daddy away?"

Quelling the stab of guilt summoned by the vivid image, Randi hurried toward the employees' parking garage. The underground space was brightly lit; a scattering of cars belonging to those on the night shift threw stark shadows on its cement floor and walls as she made her way to the Jeep.

The Cherokee was parked in a far corner. As she approached, one of the shadows detached itself from the concrete. She gave a start, halting at the sound of an all-too-familiar voice.

"Randi?"

Travis. She wasn't prepared for this. Why had he come? What did he want?

"I'm sorry I startled you." Travis saw her unvoiced questions and read the dismay in her eyes. "And if you want me to leave, I will. But I'm hopin' you'll give me a few minutes, Randi. Just a few minutes...please?"

He was handsome as ever, although about his mouth and eyes she detected lines of tiredness that hadn't been there before. She watched him search her face, and his eloquent gaze shone silver in the artificial light. Her heart gave a little twist as memories swirled and imploded in her brain....

Sitting on a moonlit beach, sharing marshmallows and champagne...his boyish grin as he offered her a bouquet of wildflowers...his solid strength beside her as he drove through a storm while she held their child in her arms...his laughter, merging with hers over funny stories about her father...his gentle careful hands on her body while she— God, she had to stop this!

"Travis, it's—" she swallowed around the painful lump in her throat, began again. "It's awfully late, and..." She heaved a sigh. "All right, then. What is it?"

"A couple of things." He tried for a reassuring smile, but didn't quite succeed. "First, it's about the apology I kept tryin' to make all those times I called. I was way off base with that cruise idea, Randi, and I'm so godawful sorry. Sorrier than I can put into words, but…well, words are all I have right now.'' He shrugged helplessly.

When she didn't say anything, he went on, watching her face, trying to gauge her mood. ''And I'm sorry I dragged your sister into it. It was all my idea, and Jill only went along reluctantly. She's not to blame for—''

''Maybe you should be telling that to Jill!'' she snapped. She'd been stung to learn of Jill's participation, but had long since put it behind her; she'd figured her sister was as much a victim of Travis's machinations as she was. She knew how persuasive he could be. ''I haven't mentioned it to her myself, but if you've got a guilty conscience, you might—''

''Uh, I have actually, but I…well, I just wanted to touch base with you on that score.''

He'd been talking with Jill? She supposed it shouldn't surprise her; she was aware of the good rapport the two of them had, and she knew Jill had arranged for his visits with Matt. Still, the notion that they'd been discussing other things—discussing *her*—didn't sit well. ''Oh? And what else have you two been discussing?'' she asked testily.

Travis stifled a sigh. This wasn't going well at all. Still, he had to try, especially since Jill had given him an ultimatum regarding what he was about to say. ''Well, now that you ask, we—Jill and I, that is—think you oughtta know 'bout somethin' she, uh, once told me.''

Randi felt a premonition of dread. A lump of ice settled in her chest as she caught the look in his eyes. Was he saying…? No. Jill would never have told him any of that. She couldn't have!

''Randi, Jill confided in me. Weeks ago. She, uh, told me all about herself. Told me what happened to her when she was a kid. 'Bout the…abuse. She wanted me to know.''

There was a loud humming in her ears as she stood there, desperately trying to make sense of this. Of why Jill would impart such knowledge to Travis. And weeks ago, he'd

said. Dear God, weeks ago, he'd been a virtual stranger!
"But I d-don't understand," she stammered. "Why?
How...?"

"Because I was deeply worried, Randi, 'bout you and
Matt. I knew somethin' was wrong, somethin' that was
makin' you afraid. Of me. Of men. All kinds of crazy ideas
were goin' around in my head. And so I asked Jill about
it, and...and that's when she told me."

"She told you," Randi repeated dully. It didn't seem
possible. None of this seemed real. If Jill had shared that
with him, had he guessed the rest? When she, herself, had
stumbled on the harrowing truth about herself on the *Sarah
Anne*, had Travis already known?

He saw the turmoil on her face and rushed to explain.
"It was *her* history I heard, Randi, not yours, except in-
directly. You'd been affected, she said. Frightened by what
you'd witnessed as a kid." He gave her a look so intense
she nearly stepped back from the force of it. "And that's
all she told me, I swear it."

"But...but it was private! It was family business. Aside
from the professionals who helped, no one who's still alive
knows about it, except David, and he's as good as family.
Why would Jill tell *you*?"

Pain lanced through him. *Because I'm family, too. Because at the time she told me Jill recognized this even if
you didn't. Knew my involvement with Matt had gone far
beyond biological ties. Jill knew I loved him, dammit!*

As the silent words rang in his mind, Travis fought to
hide the pain and form a reply; he was here to try to rebuild
the shattered trust between them, not aim accusations that
would only drive her further away.

"Maybe," he began carefully, "she did it for Matt's
sake, Randi. I don't know, but she did it. It was only the
other day, when we talked on the phone, that we...we
agreed it was time to let you know."

What Jill had said actually was that she'd no longer be

bound by his insistence that Randi not know he'd been told.
"I don't know what went on between you two recently,"
she'd added, "but I've got a feeling it has to do with trust.
Trust isn't something my sister has in great supply, and I
don't want to add to that insecurity. It's time all our cards
were on the table, Travis. If you don't find a way to tell
her, I will."

Randi didn't move. Was that pain she'd glimpsed in his
eyes? She couldn't tell; she was wrestling with her own
pain. What kept going round and round in her head was
how terribly vulnerable she was to him. He knew the most
intimate things about her—the shame of her past, her fears,
the way those fears were impinging on the present in ways
she was only beginning to understand. And all the while,
in the back of her mind, she could still hear Matt's voice
in the dream—*Why'd you hide my daddy away?*

Dear God, help me! I don't know what to do!

Travis felt something in him twist and tear at the trapped
look in her eyes. Maybe it had been a mistake to come.
For all his good intentions, he always seemed to make
things worse. Maybe she'd be better off if he just let it
alone. Hadn't he learned he wasn't in charge here? Had the
exchange with Troy taught him nothing?

The uncertain silence yawned between them like a vast
sea, with the two of them on opposite shores. Finally Travis
remembered the last, but most critical, reason he'd come.
There was one thing more he had to say to her. One thing,
and then he'd leave.

"Randi, before I go, there's somethin' I need you to
know."

He paused, and she realized he was waiting for her to
acknowledge something. The importance of what he was
about to tell her? Her assurance that she'd listen? It was so
unlike him she nearly winced, unprepared for the stab of
regret she felt; of all she'd regarded as characteristic of him,
his utter self-confidence had always topped the list. *Oh,*

Travis, have I made you so uncertain? I never meant to. But I'm still so afraid, don't you see? I'm afraid!

Saying none of this, she managed a tight nod and tried to look away, but his gaze caught hers and didn't let go.

"Randi, listen to me." He took a step toward her, saw her stiffen ever so slightly and backed away with a sigh.

"First of all," he told her gravely, "I give you this promise. I won't lay a hand on you, touch you again in any way, unless you ask me to. Not ever. Do you understand?"

"I think so."

He shook his head. "Not good enough, darlin'. I need you to be sure. When I say I won't touch you, it's because I couldn't bear it if there was fear in your eyes when I did. I'm puttin' you in the driver's seat with this, Randi. You and nobody else. Now do you understand?"

Slowly nodding, she was aware of the irony in her response. He was giving her control! Even as she sought to relinquish her need to control so many other things in her life. But in the arena of what went on between a man and a woman, she knew he was right to do this; she wasn't ready to relinquish control there, not yet. Maybe never.

"Beyond that," he went on quietly, "no matter what happens, I want you to know I'll always be here for you, Randi. If you need me, that is. If you ask. Because I think I understand what it must've been like. To be vulnerable and helpless, with no one to go to when...when the need was there. No one to protect you.

"And your private history's safe with me. I'll guard it—and you—with my life. That's a promise, too. I'll do whatever it takes to protect you, Randi—even if it's from myself. I'd cut off my arm before I'd ever hurt you or let harm come to you. And if that means...never seein' you again, you've got it—though you have to know, too, that's not what I want. You're that important to me, Randi. You 'n' Matt."

With this he turned and walked away, his footsteps ech-

oing in the cavernous underground space. She watched him
go, wanting to call him back and tell him how his words
had touched her. How he'd become important to her, too.
Wanting to, but not knowing how.

SEVERAL NIGHTS LATER Jill looked up from the wedding
invitations she was addressing when she heard Randi come
in. The sound of cheerful humming echoed from the foyer,
and she grinned to herself. Randi had been to a counseling
session, and from the sound of things, it had gone well.

"Hey, sis," Randi said as she stuck her head in the door
of Jill's office, "you're working kind of late tonight."

"Oh, it's not decorator stuff. Just a few last-minute ad-
ditions to the guest list." Jill leaned back in her chair and
motioned her in. "How's it going, kid?"

Randi knew the question could be taken generally or
specifically, referring to her session. Jill never pried, leaving it up to Randi to confide in her or not.

In the beginning, in the difficult days after the trauma of
the *Sarah Anne,* Randi had told her nothing. She knew
she'd returned from those early sessions in a bad humor—
angry, upset, often near tears—and Jill had wisely left her
alone. But lately the sessions had begun to feel better. She
was making progress. By inches, it felt sometimes, with
occasional minor setbacks, but progress nonetheless.

"I'm finally getting a handle on it, Jill," she said, smiling. "Carol's so darned good at what she does—but I don't
need to tell *you* that." The smile turned to an impish grin.
"You really should've convinced me to go back to her
years ago."

"What!" Jill pretended to throw a pen at her. Randi
pretended to duck. Then they broke into laughter.

It was a watershed moment. When they'd collected themselves, Randi fell into a chair and began to talk. To share
the intimate details she hadn't been ready to share before,
not even with Jill.

She began with the truth, the key fact that had been eluding her for years: that she had suffered exactly what Jill had. Jill prudently refrained from telling her she'd always known, instead reaching out for her sister wordlessly as she came around the desk. The moment was cathartic; they wept in each other's arms.

But Randi wasn't done. It was like a dam had broken, releasing a river that had been held to a trickle for years. She told her everything. About the terrible dreams that had been pushing at her conscious mind, urging her to recall the past as it had really been; about her denial and the need to block; about her need to control and how this had been affecting her life, especially her parenting, as Jill had noticed. And then how she'd begun to do something about it.

Finally she talked about Travis. About her inability to trust him, to open herself up to him. Despite a growing attraction that, surprisingly, was physical, but also emotional, and growing stronger all the time. Despite his demonstrating he was good and kind and decent. Despite knowing he loved Matt and cared deeply for her, as well.

"I know it's the control thing again, with how I feel about him, Jill. But things are slowly changing," she added as she finished. "I can feel it. It's...like a heavy chain has been dragging at your ankles for years, but suddenly it's lighter, and you know that one day soon you'll wake up and it won't be there anymore, y'know?"

"I know," Jill said softly, blinking back tears.

"Yeah, I guess you do." They smiled at each other.

"So," Jill said after a moment, "what's next, or shouldn't I ask?"

Randi sighed. "Oh, you can ask. I just don't know if I have all the answers—or even if I ever will."

It was the first uncertainty Jill had heard. "Travis?" she asked gently.

"Travis. I didn't handle him at all well, Jill. I mean, I

accused him of such terrible things that night on the yacht. Of scheming and lying to me and—"

"You might've accused me of those things, too," Jill cut in wryly. "I mean, I was in on it."

"I know," Randi said with a rueful smile. "But I didn't have a problem with *you*."

"Uh-huh, because you don't have a problem *trusting* me."

Randi nodded. "He told me about…about how you confided in him a while back, you know. About…"

"I was wondering if you were ever gonna bring that up. Randi, are you angry with me for telling him? Upset?"

"I guess I was at first, but he explained your reasons, and you know, it's odd, but I was more upset with him than I was with you for telling him." She sighed. "Guess I didn't handle that too well, either."

"The trust thing again."

"Yes, just as it was on that darn cruise." Randi gave her head a wry shake. "You know, Jill, it's funny, but with a better understanding of my underlying fear of men, of relationships, I'm beginning to see how I used that little escapade he organized as an excuse to…to cop out. It wasn't really his so-called deceit that made me cry off. It was the *fear* at work. The buried terror that—"

"But, honey, surely you can tell him that. *Talk* to him. He's not an unreasonable man."

"Oh, Jill, if only it were that simple. But I'm still not comfortable that way around men. Around *him*. You know, speaking the way we are now—intimately. I mean, look how long it's taken me to talk to *you* about all this. And it's not only that. You see, I'm afraid I… Oh, never mind."

"What, love?" Jill felt her heart turn over at the sadness and regret she glimpsed in her sister's eyes.

Randi swallowed a sob. "I blew it, Jill. I rejected him, pure and simple. And now he's gone. I mean, what man hangs around for more of that kind of thing? I blew it, and now when I feel I might be ready to try, I haven't got the guts to reach out to him!'' *It would take a miracle.*

''Oh, sweetheart—''

''Hey, enough of all this soul-baring!'' Randi's laugh was a little too quick as she rose to give her sister a peck on the cheek. ''It's my problem, not yours. G'night, love. Don't stay up too late.''

Jill murmured in kind as the door closed. She stared absently for a long time at the wedding invitations in front of her, Randi's words drifting through her mind. *I blew it...I haven't got the guts to reach out to him...my problem, not yours.*

''Hmm,'' she mused as she pondered the crisp white envelopes on the desk. ''Hmm...''

CHAPTER TWENTY-FOUR

TRAVIS RAN HIS GAZE approvingly over Sarah's elegantly clad figure as he held the car door open for her. "You look gorgeous, Pumpkin. Reckon I'll be real busy this evenin'."

"Thanks," she replied as she got in. "Uh, busy?"

He grinned as he shut the door and came around. "Yup, fightin' off all those eager beavers you're gonna attract."

"Travis McLean, don't you dare!" It was part of a long-standing feud between them. When they'd been younger, their mother had assigned Travis and Troy the duty of protecting Sarah from overeager beaux at various functions. Both had complied, but Travis had been impossible. As a result, Sarah had frequently gone with no male company at all. "Mother-r-r," she'd wail, "he's my brother, not my keeper!"

He chuckled as he started the car, but the mirth soon faded. They were on their way to Jill and David's wedding. With Sarah as his invited guest, he was going at the specific request of the bride, who'd practically begged him to come, and to bring his sister.

"You're not only my nephew's father," she'd said when he sounded reluctant, "you're a friend. Besides, David wants you there, too. And Matt'll be ecstatic. Uh, not that I've told him you're invited—just in case something happens and you can't make it." She'd explained about their policy of not getting Matt's hopes up in advance, to avoid disappointment if things fell through. "So please don't mention it to the squirt, okay?"

He'd agreed to that readily enough, but had pressed her about Randi's feelings regarding the invitation.

"It's *my* wedding, Travis," Jill had replied. "How could she possibly argue with me about who I choose to have as guests?"

"I don't know, Jill. She might go along for your sake, but—"

"Travis," she'd interrupted, "just how much do you care about my sister? Do you want to be with her or don't you?"

"If she'd have me," he'd told her solemnly, "I'd marry her tomorrow. I love her, Jill. These past weeks've been hell."

"Then why haven't you been beating a path to her door? You don't strike me as a guy who gives up easily. You've made an effort to see Matt, but not Randi. Why?"

He decided not to mention the encounter in the hospital parking garage; nothing had been resolved there, anyhow. "I figured she needed time, Jill, to sort things out, digest what's been happenin' with us. And...maybe I needed time myself. Your sister, uh, left me with a few things to think about." *Your sister and my brother, Troy.*

In the end, he'd been persuaded to attend. Maybe because he'd been encouraged by the way Randi had looked when he left her with those final words that night in the garage; maybe she was ready to see him now. He'd also reasoned that Jill had to believe this, or she'd never have included him. Maybe Randi's counseling sessions had begun to pay off.

Maybe. And with Randi gaining some insights into her feelings, and with the insights he'd gained about himself, maybe, just maybe, they had a chance.

RANDI STOOD in the reception line, unable to believe what was happening. Pain lodged in her chest, and her throat burned. Dear God. Travis—*here!* But why? How? A new

wave of pain hit—the smile Jill just tossed him said she'd
invited him! It hurt almost as much as seeing Travis this
way—with another woman on his arm.

A stunning little brunette with huge green eyes and *debutante* written all over her. Her dress was a designer original if ever she'd seen one; she and Jill had spent too much
time studying designer gowns for the wedding for Randi
not to recognize the look. How *could* he?

Her lips tightened as she sought to contain a surge of
pain. *Damn you, Travis! You said you'd never hurt me.
That you'd protect me. Damn you to hell!*

Travis caught the anguish in Randi's eyes before her face
hardened into an angry mask. She hadn't known he'd be
here! Ol' Jill had pulled a fast one—on both of them! He
heaved a sigh. A big mistake. He should have questioned
Jill more carefully about whether Randi was in on this.
Now he was stuck playing a part he hadn't been sure he
wanted in the first place. *Poets and fools...*

The line moved Sarah and him along until he faced the
bride and groom, with the maid of honor just a few feet
away. "You're a beautiful bride," he told Jill. "Every happiness, darlin'—even if you are a sneaky devil," he added
sotto voce. He kissed her cheek, then shook David's hand
and congratulated him.

"I'd like you both to meet my guest," he added as Sarah
smiled at the happy couple. "This is Sarah, my sister."

Randi's head swung in their direction at the mention of
the woman's surname.

McLean? *God in heaven, he's...he's married!* Disbelief
warred with shock and nausea. This was a nightmare; she
was dreaming, and any second now, she'd awaken and find
everything back to normal.

But the nightmare went on. Travis and Sarah McLean
were moving toward her now, and she was expected to
paste a smile on her face and...*God, Jill, why? Why put
me through this?*

But maybe Jill didn't know...about the wife, anyway. Tears threatening, she braced herself, wondering how she could endure this. But Matt was a few feet away, and she couldn't break down in front of him. For Matt, then. For Matt, you can do this!

She stood there, dazed, as he moved toward her.

"Hello, Randi," Travis said carefully. "I'd like you to meet my sister, Sarah. Sarah, this is—"

"Travis!" Matt's voice rang out from the end of the reception line. "I didn't know you were comin'!"

Randi watched as her son broke rank and ran toward his father. Then Sarah smiled and extended a gloved hand. "I'm so happy to meet you, Randi. Although Travis has told me so much about you I almost feel I already have."

Still feeling foolish, and limp with relief, Randi managed to smile back. "You can't possibly know how happy I am, too."

"Hey, Mom, can we go get some food now? I'm starvin'!" Matt was at eye level, grinning unashamedly at her from the vantage point of his father's arms. He indicated the rest of the guests, who'd already passed through the reception line. "Everybody's done shakin' hands, y'know."

Randi chuckled, blushing as she felt Travis's gaze on her. "Almost, sweetheart," she told Matt. "There's just one more hand to shake."

She turned to Sarah and smiled. "Sarah, I'd like you to meet my son, Matthew. Matt, this is Travis's sister." *And I've never uttered gladder words!*

Travis set Matt down to shake hands with his aunt. He glanced at Randi, but she was avoiding his eyes. He swung his gaze to Jill, but the bride merely shrugged at him and grinned. The little traitor! He was on his own.

His gaze returned to Randi, and his face softened. On his own? Not if he could help it. He'd had his fill of being alone. He needed a woman to share his life. This woman.

Now all he had to do was convince her.

WITH A GRACIOUSNESS acquired from birth, Travis endured
the elegant reception that followed. He smiled and chatted
with fellow guests as toasts were proposed, as a sumptuous
banquet was consumed, as the dancing began, led by the
happy couple. Yet his eyes rarely left the maid of honor.
Randi, resplendent in a gown of bronze silk.

He'd decided to make the best of the situation. Since he
was here, he'd try to talk to her, see how things stood.
When the wedding rituals wound down, maybe he'd find a
chance.

Randi, meanwhile, was trying to find a moment to talk
to the bride alone—not easy, with all of them in the spot-
light. But she had no intention of letting Jill off the hook
where a certain surprise guest was concerned. What had
gotten into her? After their heart-to-heart that night especially, Jill should have realized how awkward this would
be for her.

And someday Jill the pill and she were going to have a
talk about just who was doing the controlling around here!
It was ironic really. Here she was, trying to work past her
own need to control, when she found herself the object of
controlling efforts by others. People she loved!

A frown knit her brow. Everyone engaged in controlling
behavior to some extent, Carol had said. Only when it became an overruling compulsion was it a problem.

"Um, something wrong, pipsqueak?"

She heaved a sigh and turned to face her sister, who'd
just finished a photo session with David and his side of the
family. "You might've warned me, Jill."

There was no need to mention what—or whom—they
were discussing. "You know you'd have gone ballistic on
me," Jill said.

"Agreed, but still…"

"You did tell me you felt you'd blown it with him,

didn't you? And that you didn't have the guts, I think you said, to reach out to him, right?''

"Well, yes, but—''

"Oh, Randi, please don't be upset with me, even if you've a perfect right to be. Don't you see? I reached out *for* you. I mean, I know it was sneaky and underhanded, but I gambled you trusted me enough not to hate me too much for—''

"Jill, the idea! I could never hate you.''

Jill grinned at her. "Well, all right, then. So, uh, how about thanking me? Playing Cupid's hard work, you know?''

Randi gave her head a shake, lapsing into a helpless chuckle. "You stinker! Okay, thanks…I think.''

"Whew! One down and one to go.''

"Huh?''

It was Jill's turn to blush. "Well, I'm afraid you weren't the only one I, uh, kept in the dark about a certain invitation.''

"Oh, no! You mean, Travis came here thinking I knew he'd been invit—''

"Um, guilty as charged.''

"Jill Terhune, how *could* you!''

"Uh, shouldn't you be callin' her Jill *Brooks* now?''

"Travis!'' Jill exclaimed as they both whirled to face him. "Just the person I wanted to see.''

"Do tell.'' With a wink for Randi, he glared at Jill, spoiling the effect with a lopsided grin. "I mean, I can't *imagine* why.''

"Now, now, no need for sarcasm,'' Jill told him breezily. "Don't you know it's bad form to make the bride squirm?''

"Huh, I could talk up some other stuff that's bad form. Since when are brides s'posed to be so sneaky?''

Jill made a face at him. It demolished any remaining tension in the air, and all three of them chuckled.

"Well, that's more like it,'' Jill declared. Without waiting for a response, she grabbed them each by the hand and headed for the French doors leading to a veranda.

"Jill, for Pete's sake!" Randi protested, but found herself fighting a giggle; Jill had a bee in her bonnet, judging from the look on her face, a look she remembered well from their childhood. "What's this all about?"

"Yeah," Travis demanded as the bride dragged them beyond range of several curious wedding guests, "what gives?"

"Okay, you two," said Jill, "listen up. There's a couple of beautifully wrapped wedding gifts sitting amid the pile that arrived back at the house—one from each of you—and I know David and I are gonna love 'em, so thank you."

"Uh, you're welcome," Travis murmured, whereas Randi merely gave her a look that asked if she'd flipped.

"Now it's my turn," Jill went on. "You see, I'd like to give the pair of *you* a gift."

Randi and Travis glanced at each other, but said nothing, eyeing Jill with considerable bemusement.

"Now, you can tell me if I'm way out of line with this," Jill said, "but it seems to me the two of you need some time together to talk in private. But you're both so darn busy circling each other, not wanting to make a move, you won't do it on your own. So I'm doing it for you."

"What do you mean?" Randi asked warily.

"I mean, if you and Travis would like to leave here, right now, and find a place to have that talk, just say so. I've only gotta make a phone call to Matt's baby-sitter, who's on standby to sit with him for the entire length of our honeymoon, if necessary, so his mom's free to do this."

Mentally crossing her fingers, Jill heaved a sigh and sent them each a look that pleaded for agreement with the idea. "Now, am I all wet, or will you accept this gift?"

Travis wanted to agree at once, but he glanced at Randi and hesitated, concerned about her; the last thing they needed was for her to feel squeezed, pushed into doing something she wasn't ready for. He hid a sardonic smile; there was a time, he mused wryly, when he would have pushed without a second's hesitation. He was learning.

"Huh," Randi groused, "put that way, sister mine, it's an offer we can't refuse." But she was smiling as she said it. Smiling, because there suddenly wasn't a doubt in her mind that they should do this. It felt as though something inside her had broken free. The old Randi—heck, the Randi of even a week ago—would have hedged or refused outright; she'd have been afraid—of herself, of Travis, of being alone with him. Of wanting to talk to him, but not knowing how.

But the woman who stood here now was remembering a moment when she'd wanted to reach out and couldn't— *You're that important to me, Randi. You 'n' Matt.* Remembering and knowing, thanks to the sister who loved her, that she'd been given the rarest of gifts: another chance.

CHAPTER TWENTY-FIVE

TRAVIS TOOTED the horn, and Randi waved to Matt as Travis backed the Alpha out of her driveway. There was no mistaking the grin on Matt's face, Randi thought, as he stood on the stoop and waved back. She wondered which was more responsible for it, his delight that she was back in Travis's company, or the company Matt himself was keeping tonight.

Sandwiched between Mrs. Casey, his favorite sitter, and pretty Sarah McLean, Matt looked like the cat who'd stolen the cream. He and Travis's sister had gotten on like a house on fire at the reception. When Matt learned he'd be home with the sitter this evening, he'd asked if he could invite Sarah. It seemed his "good buddy," as he called her, just loved a certain magenta dinosaur, and he wanted to show her a "Barney" episode Randi had taped for him. After checking by phone with Mrs. Casey, Randi had been persuaded to agree to the invitation; Sarah had been delighted to accept.

"Your sister's awfully good with children," she said as Travis fiddled with the car radio. As if by unspoken mutual consent, this sort of safe neutral comment had characterized their conversation since they'd accepted Jill's gift. But deep inside, where her emotions stood teetering on a precipice, Randi felt a keen-edged tension; she was as nervous and uncertain as she was hopeful. But she beat it back. Time enough for the heavy stuff when they reached their destination.

"It's hard to believe," she went on, thankful her voice

held none of this anxiety, "how Matt's taken to her. It's as if they've known each other for years."

She had to admit she'd taken to Sarah herself, though perhaps that shouldn't surprise her; bright, pert and energetic, the youngest McLean reminded her of Travis in everything but looks. Reminded her of Matt, too.

"Oh, Sarah's crazy 'bout kids." Travis adjusted the radio's volume, and soft classical music sifted into the car. "Matter of fact, all of us McLean brats are. Sarah's done loads of baby-sittin', 'n' I spent five terrific summers as a camp counselor in a program for inner-city kids. Meantime, brother Troy's been runnin' tennis clinics for sprouts at the Y far back as I can remember." He shrugged. "None of it payed much, but we sure loved the work."

"You mean you all worked at these things for *pay?*"

"Don't sound so surprised. The clan may be well-heeled, but that cut no ice with my mother where her kids were concerned. She firmly believed in teachin' us the value of a dollar. But more importantly, of work itself. We never received an allowance, but there were always opportunities to earn a buck, even when we were little guys."

He chuckled. "Once, when I was Matt's age, I was paid a penny for every weed I pulled from the garden. 'Course, I had to learn to distinguish 'em from Mother's prize dahlias, as I recall. Mr. Tibbs was real fussy 'bout that."

"Mr. Tibbs?"

"Uh, the gardener?"

"Oh, of course. Silly me."

He darted a glance at her. "Is there a problem there, Randi? I mean, with my family's, uh, life-style?" That was all he needed, he thought with an inner groan. Her being uncomfortable with his background, on top of all the other uneasiness he caused her. Lord, wasn't it time for some of the breaks to go his way?

"Um, not a problem exactly," she hedged, "but I do recall being a bit...overwhelmed when I first saw your yacht."

He cut her another glance. "Okay, maybe I'm bein' a mite dense here but, Randi, if you're uncomfortable with it, why'd you select the *Sarah Anne* for this, uh, talk to-night?"

He'd been mystified when he asked where she wanted to go to indulge in Jill's insightful offer and she'd chosen the yacht; it had to hold unpleasant associations for her. Still, bent on accommodating her, he'd agreed without comment; as he'd already told her, she was in the driver's seat. He was done controlling in the name of love.

"Randi?" he prompted when she didn't answer.

But Randi suddenly couldn't speak; in truth, she found it hard to breathe. A surge of emotion tumbled over the precipice and gripped her without mercy. His question had strayed beyond neutral territory, but it wasn't what held her frozen; no, this was something she couldn't anticipate, something beyond her control. And therefore devastating.

The *Liebestraum* playing on the radio, soared sweetly. Without warning, the lilting chords wrapped themselves around her, returning her to that summer night at sea, when a dream might have come true, but didn't. Her pulse leapt as time melted away, and memory conjured magic, the magic that had claimed her mind and body when she'd heard the piece last.

And suddenly, with all that aching sweetness in her ears, calling up memory and stealing into the heart of her—oh, yes, the heart!—suddenly she knew. She loved this man who sat beside her, unaware. Travis. She *loved* him.

Stunned, she closed her eyes, familiarizing herself with this certainty borne on the wings of a song. With the truth that had been chasing her through all the endless days and nights without him. She loved him!

"Randi?" Travis's voice was soft yet taut with concern. He remembered the *Liebestraum* all too well. Remembered every sweet response of the woman in his arms that night. Remembered, too, the bitter disappointment that followed. "Darlin', are you all right?"

Randi gave herself a shake and groped for a response as emotion thundered through her. God, she couldn't give in to it now! Perhaps later, when she could think clearly. It was all too new, too raw.

"Why the *Sarah Anne?*" she said at last. There. Her voice even sounded normal. Now, how to explain.

She'd chosen that setting for a reason. Despite the magic summoned by the *Liebestraum,* the yacht itself represented all that had gone wrong that night. All that had crippled the dream that hadn't come true. Couldn't come true, not when nightmares barred the way.

But she'd come a long way since then; thanks to the counseling, she was a lot stronger. She wanted, needed, to face the scene of the disaster that had turned her life inside out and killed a dream she hadn't even known she held in her heart. She loved this man. That, in itself, made facing it necessary, but it was more than that. She was done being a coward.

"I've heard," she replied, glancing at him as the last strains of the *Liebestraum* faded and died, "that when you fall off a horse—" she took a steadying breath and released it "—you should climb right back on and ride."

She saw him swallow, as if to digest this, his tanned throat working above the collar of the shirt he'd opened and stripped of its tie. For a long time he didn't respond, didn't look at her, just kept his eyes on the road and drove. She held her breath as the muted tones of the radio announcer and the engine's purr underscored the silence that stretched between them.

His answer, when it came, was thick with emotion. "Don't ever let anyone tell you," he said, and she saw him swallow again, "that you lack courage, Randi Terhune. Lady, you've got it in spades!"

ALERTED BY TRAVIS'S phone call before they left, Captain Baker welcomed them aboard with the quiet courtesy Randi recalled from before. There were a few shy smiles of recognition from members of the crew, as well, and before she knew it, she and Travis were settled in the lounge where they'd once nibbled hors d'ouvres and drunk champagne.

After speaking a few words to the steward, who nodded deferentially and disappeared, Travis smiled at her. "You looked elegant in that bridesmaid's gown, but it's best you took the time to change." Warm appreciation filled the eyes he ran over her, and he shook his head. "Damned if you don't still look elegant. You're the only woman I know who can inspire that comment wearin' jeans 'n' a T-shirt."

Blushing, Randi whispered a thank-you and stared at the hands she held folded in her lap. All too aware of her new-found feelings, she was a taut bundle of nerves, but she wouldn't let this defeat her. She wouldn't!

She made herself raise her eyes, though her glance barely lit on the beloved face before skittering away. "I...liked you in that suit tonight," she managed, hating the schoolgirl callowness of her reply.

She knew they had to talk, but now that they were here, the enormity of her emotional discovery threatened to make it impossible. Talk? She could barely *think*. "Um, I mean," she added awkwardly, "I never saw you in a suit and tie before, and...well, you looked very, uh, smart."

"Why, thank you, ma'am." Would she ever be at ease with him when they were alone like this? Travis wondered. They needed to talk, but he wouldn't crowd her. He'd resolved to give her space—the space she needed to grow comfortable with him. To trust him, however long it took. He wasn't going to rush her, though he wanted desperately to reach out to her. No, the impetus had to come from her.

"Here you go." He handed her a glass from a tray the steward left before disappearing as unobtrusively as he'd come. "Etienne's a whiz with fresh-made lemonade."

"What, no champagne?" she quipped, trying for insouciance, fearing she sounded querulous, instead.

His gaze was solemn and direct as he faced her across the hammered brass table where they'd once sipped the bubbly. "I want no fuzzy thoughts between us this trip, Randi. What needs sayin's much too important."

Yet he saw that she was taut as a drum, that he needed to put her at ease. "But all in good time." He rose and took the barely touched lemonade from her hand, set it aside. "C'mon, darlin', there's a heavenful of stars need watchin' up top."

"All right," she said, rising. The smile he sent had her blood pulsing madly through her veins. The air topside would be welcome; she needed a clear head.

But as he led her up on deck, something felt wrong, and she tried to think what it was. He escorted her, but...but without touching her, she realized with a stab of disappointment. Without taking her arm or her hand, as he had in the past.

Yet Travis was a toucher; she had only to recall the countless times she'd seen him ruffle Matt's hair or grab him for a hug, not to mention the myriad ways *she'd* felt the touch of those gentle hands.

But he hadn't touched her at all this day. Not to lead her to his car, nor to help her in or out of it, not even to dance, though the celebration had been in full swing by the time they left. What was wrong?

IF THERE WERE ANY HANDS on deck, Randi didn't see them; there were just the two of them under an inky sky that blazed with the promised stars. For a long time neither spoke, and at first she despaired, wondering if they even could; perhaps there was just too much that stood between them.

But after a while, as they strolled the pristine deck, the silence grew more comfortable. Moonlight etched a path across the sea, from the horizon to the smoothly gliding vessel. Up close, it pearled the things it touched, encasing them in an incandescence so lovely it made her sigh.

Hearing her, Travis stopped, leaned against the railing and found her gaze. "So, gutsy lady, how's the horse?"

"The horse? I don't…" With a gurgle of laughter, she deciphered his meaning. "Oh, the horse!"

Smiling, she moved to lean against the railing, also. Beside him, but not touching him, since this seemed to be how he wanted it. That this troubled her was something she pushed to the back of her mind; perhaps it held no significance at all, and she was just imagining problems that didn't exist. Those she was sure of were challenge enough, and now was the time.

"Well," she said, "I've climbed back on the silly nag. Now all I've gotta do is ride."

His quick reassuring grin gave her courage; she took a deep breath and plunged in. "Travis, I owe you a deep apology, two of them, in fact. No, don't shake your head. It's true, and I need to tell you about it…please?"

"Go on," he said quietly, reading the need in her face.

"Travis, on a beach last summer, you…you began to make love to me," she said in a voice so low he had to strain to hear it. "You were the first man who ever did. You didn't know that of course, yet you were utterly gentle and considerate of me."

She took a deep breath, expelled it in a quavering rush of air. "And I ran screaming from your arms. You didn't deserve that, Travis. And I'm so heartily sorry for it. So sorry, I could— No, please, let me finish.

"That was the first time, and bad enough. The second time was much worse. It happened here on the *Sarah Anne*, of course, and you deserved my behavior then even less because you tried to tell me that you…that you cared. Yet all I did was spew venom at you. And, Travis, I'm so deeply sorry about that night. Sorrier than I can put into words, although I'm going to try."

Travis heard the anguish in her voice, saw tears glisten in her eyes, and he wanted to hold her, tell her to stop. She owed him no apologies. She'd had it right that night; he'd brought it on himself, with his damnable penchant for trying to control other people's lives.

He wanted to hold her. Tell her what he'd learned about himself and beg her forgiveness for being so blind and stupid. Wanted to, but couldn't, not until she—

"But telling you I'm sorry isn't enough." Randi's voice shook as it cut across his thoughts, yet gathered strength as she went on. "You see, there are reasons I rejected your...intimate touch. The same reasons, pretty much, why I once refused to explain choosing to conceive Matt as I did."

There was a tremor in her voice, but she made herself go on. "Travis, when I was barely twelve years old, I was...touched—used—in unspeakably intimate ways by a grown man. An adult. My dead mother's second husband—my stepfather."

Beside her, Travis's body tensed; she could feel it. But he didn't move to touch her, and when she continued, her voice was laced with pain.

"A man we'd been told to respect, even if we couldn't love him, because he was now in Daddy's place." She gave a small mirthless laugh. "In his place? Dear God, he was as much like Daddy as a gargoyle to an archangel! Oh, he was handsome enough, big and muscular. Yes, I remember very well how strong he was. He'd hold me down, you see, and—"

"Randi—"

"No, I need to tell it!" She turned her head toward him, and moonlight glistened on the tracks of her tears; he longed to soothe them away; seeing her face, he didn't dare.

"There was nothing I could do or say to stop him, though I tried. Dear God, I tried! I fought him, but he was so much bigger, and I was such a skinny little kid. When that failed, I pleaded. And then I begged."

She took a shuddering breath. "But the begging only seemed to make him more eager and...and rougher. So after a while I stopped begging. I stopped doing anything at all.''

Her voice became a monotone as she described what she meant. "It was as if I left my body and floated free up to the ceiling, and it was someone else lying down there on the bed. Someone else lying under him, while he panted and sweated and groaned. That wasn't me whimpering and powerless down there, oh, no! It wasn't happening to me at all.''

She paused, staring off into the moon-washed dark. ''And that's how I endured it. Week after week, month after ugly month. Until that blessed day, half a year later, when he was dead. When he was killed in a car accident, and for Jill and me…''

She paused again, considering whether she had the right to tell him her sister's history, then recalled he already knew.

"It's all right," Travis said in a voice shaking with emotion. "You don't need to go on." He'd heard the basics from Jill, but until now, until Randi's description of what it had been like, he'd had no idea of the raw pain words could evoke. He tried to imagine himself as such a child, helpless, utterly powerless. Subject to the demands of someone bigger and stronger. And he wanted to howl like a mad dog baying at the moon. Like a beast, using claw and fang in impotent rage, to say what language couldn't.

"He was dead," Randi repeated dully, "so for Jill and me, the nightmare was over." She gave a short bitter laugh. "Well, it wasn't really over, because I had nightmares about it for years. I just didn't remember what they were about when I woke up."

She managed a tremulous smile as she looked over at him, into his beloved face. "But on the night we…you began to make love to me, something triggered a recollection and broke through the block I'd erected to keep the truth at bay.

"In those few terrifying seconds, I relived it all. I recalled everything, every hellish moment, just as it...as it really happened. I knew the truth then—all of it—and I couldn't bear it.

"So I hurled my pain at you, Travis. I blamed you, when you were blameless. You weren't the enemy, but I made you—"

"Forget about me. You were wounded." He swallowed thickly, feeling her anguish. "God, if only you hadn't stopped seeing..." He glanced away, running a hand through his hair, then heaved a sigh and looked at her. "I know who Carol Martin is, Randi, and that you've begun seein' her again, but only recently."

"Jill?"

He nodded. "She's one strong together lady, your sister. And she says Martin's help was critical. That it enabled her to go past the abuse, usin' the sense of herself as a survivor—to empower her, I believe she said."

"I know. I should've done the same years ago, but...well, I didn't."

He winced at the regret in her voice. "I'm not judgin' you, Randi," he said quietly.

"Oh, and you're not pitying me, either?" There was misery in her eyes.

"No, I'm not," he countered sharply. "Compassion isn't pity, so disabuse yourself of that notion. Look," he added in a gentler tone, "I'd do anythin' to take away what happened, Randi, but that's not possible. I reckon the best I can hope for's to try to help in any way I can, *if* I can. But *only if you want me to,* understand? Only if you ask it of me."

"But that's not why I've told you this!" she cried. "I told you because I *owed* it to you, don't you understand? I owed you an apology, and with it, an explanation. Especially after what we both heard me say in your stateroom that night. Travis, you deserved some answers, that's all. You're not responsible for me. *I'm* responsible for me."

"Yes," he said emphatically, "you are. And that's why,

if anybody owes somethin', it's me. You were right in what you accused me of that night, Randi. I *was* tryin' to take over and not just in settin' up that cruise.''

His voice softened. ''I apologized for that in the garage that night, you'll recall, but it doesn't begin to cover what I'd been doin'. Now I'm apologizin' for the bigger sin. The habit of a lifetime that pushed you so hard you freaked out. It's no thanks to me you didn't go off the deep end altogether.''

''What habit of a lifetime?'' she asked, puzzled.

He told her of the exchange with Troy and what he'd learned from it. Of all it drove home to him, following, as it did, the things she'd thrown at him that night. He told her, too, of the hours of self-examination and a promise he'd made to himself: that this habit of confusing control with caring would come to an end.

''I may not always succeed in avoidin' the impulse to control those I care about,'' he finished with a wry half smile. ''But I'm workin' on it, Randi. I'm tryin'.''

''My God,'' she murmured, more to herself than to him, ''we've both been wrestling with the same devil.''

''Devil?'' he echoed, aching to hold her, wondering if she realized just how much.

''I've begun to call it the C-word,'' she said, smiling wryly up at him. ''C for controlling. It's been my nemesis, too, you see.''

Before he could ask, she told him about her own frantic efforts to control every aspect of her life she could. About the little ways this manifested itself, her attempts to keep Matt from trying his wings, even her secret wish not to share him. How it sprang from the abuse, which had made her feel helpless. How it was her way of making her world feel safe.

The words tumbled freely. It occurred to her they were finally having their talk, and it was easy.

''I lived with fear for so many years, Travis, that *it* controlled *me*. I'd do anything not to feel that vulnerable again.

So I avoided those I couldn't control, those who might hurt me, even if the possibility was only in my mind. I avoided men, Travis. I avoided *you*—or tried to.''

He heaved a sigh. ''And I came on like a runaway train. God, Randi, can you ever forgive me? I was so involved with pursuin' the dream of a relationship with Matt, I made myself blind to the signals you gave out. And then, when I realized I was fallin' in love with you, I just bulldozed right past— Randi, what's wrong?''

She choked on a sob, torn between laughter and tears. ''Travis McLean, I've been standing here trying to work up the courage to tell you I love you, not knowing if I dared! Not knowing if I could surrender my...fear of making myself that vulnerable to you.''

She went past the dumbfounded look on his face; now that she'd begun, her words gathered speed like a downhill racer. ''Not knowing how much, or in what way *you* cared, Travis. So what do you do? You tell me the most crucial words a woman can ever hear from the man she loves— and wrap them up in a throwaway line. 'Oh, by the way, Randi, I just happen to be falling in love with you.' ''

He gaped at her. ''Dammit, woman, I told you I cared. And I recall quite clearly sayin' I wanted to marry you.''

''Cared! What does *that* mean? Or even your offer of marriage? For all I knew, it was all about Matt, not me. You had no problem saying you loved Matt. But I never once heard you say anything about loving *me!*''

''Lord, woman, I...'' But she was right, he realized. He'd avoided all mention of love—to her. Talked around it, but never said it.

''Randi, darlin','' he said finally, ''you're lookin' at one helluva prize fool.'' He gave a rueful smile. ''I don't think I ever told you this, but anyone who's known me long has heard me say I don't believe in love, that romantic love doesn't exist. Or if it does, it's for poets and fools.''

''And now?'' she whispered, tears brimming as she

ached to be held, wondering why, even now, he wasn't reaching out for her.

"Now I know I was doin' some big-time avoidin' myself. Like yours, it was caused by fear. The fear of bein' vulnerable, because that's what love asks. That you bare yourself, risk yourself for the other...for the beloved."

He gave her a tender smile. "But until now, until you, I was afraid to do that. I'd seen my parents do it for years and concluded they never loved each other at all, though what I'm seein' these days has had me rethinkin' that assumption."

The smile became sardonic. "No wonder I went into the field for the CIA. It was a perfect cover. A place where I could hide while pretendin' to be brave. I mean, physical danger's small potatoes compared to what I *really* feared."

With a sad smile, he reached out as if to touch her cheek, then stopped, dropping his hand. "And that fear, my fear of vulnerability, was at the root of my reluctance. I was afraid to love a woman, Randi."

She nodded, her eyes reflecting the sadness in his.

"I think," he said after a moment, "that we've both been wounded children, darlin', just wounded in different ways. I'm only sorry, so damned sorry, it took me this long to realize it."

Tenderly he ran his eyes over her face, met her gaze. "I love you. I wish to God I'd been able to tell you sooner."

"Travis, I—"

"I beg your pardon, Mr. McLean." The steward suddenly appeared, carrying a cellular phone. "Phone call for the lady, sir. You said that if any came..."

"Yes, of course. Thank you, John." Travis quickly handed the phone to Randi.

Alarm written all over her, she grabbed it as the steward left them alone. "Hello?"

"Randi, it's Sarah."

"Sarah!" She felt Travis freeze beside her. "Is something wrong? Is Matt okay?"

"Yes, don't worry. He's fine," Sarah assured her quickly, "and sleeping in his bed as we speak, with a great big Barney-smile on his face. But there's been a minor glitch, Randi. You recall I was supposed to be driven home by someone named Steve?"

Mouthing the words, "Matt's okay," to Travis, Randi felt relief wash over her. "Your friend at law school, yes," she told Sarah.

"Well, Steve's car won't start, and on top of that, Mrs. Casey just admitted she has a crashing headache. So I told her I'd check with you to see if it's all right if I stay with Matt so she can go home. I'll put her on if you like."

Randi had a momentary flicker of concern; Sarah had never minded Matt before, and what if...

She gave her head a shake, recognizing the C-word in one of its sneaky attempts to suck her in. "No, Sarah, that's all right. Tell Mrs. Casey I hope she feels better. And thanks. We'll be there as soon as we can."

"No problem," Sarah said, "and stay as long as you like. Matt showed me his Barney sleeping bag. If I get tired, I'll bed down on the floor in his room, so I can hear him if he needs anything."

Randi thanked her again and hung up, then explained the situation to Travis.

"We'll head right back," he said, already moving to the stairs.

He fought to keep his regret from showing; the need to finish this was throbbing in his gut, and he ached from the thwarted hunger to take her in his arms. But she hadn't given him the signal he'd been waiting for, and now it was too late; he knew how she worried about Matt. Maybe later, he thought ruefully.

"Travis?"

He turned, caught by the plaintive note in her voice.

"Travis, Sarah sounds as if she's got everything under control..."

He waited, seeing she was trying to tell him something, half-afraid to hope.

"So there's, uh, not really any reason to rush." She took a hesitant step toward him, then stopped.

"Go on," he whispered, feeling his heart begin to pound at the look in her eyes.

"Well," Randi said, swallowing hard, "it's just that we confessed we loved each other a little while ago, and..." She hesitated.

"Don't stop there," he urged, his love for her shining in his eyes.

She made a small diffident gesture with her hands. "Travis, aren't...aren't you going to hold me?"

"Are you asking me to, Randi?" The blood pounded in his veins.

"Asking you?"

"Don't you remember, love?" he said softly. "The night we spoke in the garage, I made you a promise."

She nodded slowly. "That you'd protect me," she began, trying to recall his exact words, "even...even if it meant protecting me from yourself."

"That's right," he said, "but there was more."

She stared at him in bewilderment for an endless moment, and then her jaw dropped. "You swore not to touch me—*unless I asked.*"

Nodding, he made no move. Yet his eyes blazed with a tenderness so fierce, it nearly staggered her.

"Travis," she said, blinking back tears, finally aware of what it must have cost him to wait for her, "I'm asking."

"Gutsy lady," he said huskily, moving toward her. And heard her laugh through her tears as he pulled her into his arms.

CHAPTER TWENTY-SIX

"WAKE UP, SLEEPYHEAD," Travis murmured as he nuzzled Randi's ear. "Time to rise 'n' do our best to shine."

"Mmph," she mumbled, snuggling into his warmth like the tawny kitten she reminded him of this morning.

He smiled indulgently and drew her closer, relenting for the moment, though he'd have to rouse her soon; they'd be reaching port in an hour, and she'd probably enjoy breakfast and maybe a shower before they docked.

The smile grew. It was his fault she was still sleeping so soundly, but he couldn't regret it. He'd made love to her several times during the night, the last time, just a couple of hours ago, as dawn was breaking. It was as if he couldn't get enough of her. Or she, him, he mused as the smile became a grin.

She stirred and he pressed a kiss to her brow. Lord, he loved this woman, adored her, cherished her. The sheer force of these feelings he'd once shunned astounded him, filling him with a humility and gratitude he knew he'd carry in his heart all his days. Without question, she'd become central to his life. She and Matt.

Thoughts of their son had him eyeing the clock. Sarah and Matt would be meeting them at the yacht basin in just an hour, driven by the boyfriend, who'd had his car repaired. A call to Sarah had ascertained she'd be able to mind Matt overnight, but she and Steve had to be back for classes at Georgetown this afternoon, so...

"Randi, darlin', wake up," he urged softly.

"Mmm?" A smile curved her lips, and Travis couldn't resist capturing them with a gentle kiss. He loved holding her this way, when she was all soft and muzzy from sleep. He kissed her again.

Randi was aware of his mouth before she opened her eyes. *Travis,* she thought drowsily as pleasure welled inside her, teasing her slowly awake. *Travis, I love you.*

Her lips parted under his. Like the petals of a flower opening to the sun, he thought, deepening the kiss.

Randi sighed into his mouth. She felt the pleasure grow, creep sweetly along her nerve endings, intensify.

"Lord, kitten," he breathed as her arms slid enticingly around his neck, "if you keep this up, we'll miss breakfast, and there won't be time to shower or..."

The tip of her tongue lightly probed the corner of his mouth, an erotic touch she'd learned from him, and he groaned. "Sweetheart, we're dockin' in an hour..."

She tugged playfully at his lower lip with her teeth—another thing he'd taught her.

"Randi," he said, his voice thickening as he felt her move sensually against his bare chest, "we'll be late if we don't..."

Reckon we'll be a little late. It was his last coherent thought as he took her mouth with his.

"HI, MOM! HI, TRAVIS!" Matt shouted from the rear window of a gray sedan before the car even stopped. "We're here!"

Sarah grinned and waved as Steve cut the engine. She got out and came around to get her nephew, who was ensconced in his car seat, which they'd removed from Randi's car and installed in Steve's for the trip.

But before Sarah could reach her nephew, Randi and Travis were already there. "Hiya, Tiger!" Travis flung the door wide.

"Hi, darling!" Randi bent to kiss her son as his father helped him out of the seat.

Matt endured hugs from both, but it was clear his interest was drawn elsewhere. "Wow!" he exclaimed as he took in the *Sarah Anne*'s gleaming hull. "Is that Sarah's boat?"

Sarah looked abashed as Travis and Randi's gazes swung to her. "Uh, all I did was explain how she was named after me—honest! I tried to tell him she's Daddy's, but..." She shrugged. "You know how kids get an idea in their heads sometimes and..." She shrugged again.

Randi laughed while Matt tugged at Travis's arm, obviously bent on dragging him to the yacht for a closer look. "I do," she said, "but I suspect this is your first acquaintance with the phenomenon in such a, uh, single-minded form."

"Don't be too sure of that," Sarah said with a laugh. "Remember, I grew up with Travis."

"So you've noticed the similarities, too, huh?" Randi murmured as she fondly watched father and son inspecting the boat.

"Yes," Sarah replied. "But I won't hold that against the child. In fact, nothing can change my opinion of that little dynamo. What a great kid!"

"Thanks for minding him, Sarah."

"A pleasure, and, uh—" she glanced at Travis who stood before the yacht with Matt perched on his shoulder, Matt chattering away a mile a minute "—how'd things go, if you don't mind me bein' little-sister nosy?"

Randi flushed. "Well, we... Sarah, I'd like it very much if you were a bridesmaid at our wedding. Do you think you might?"

"With bells on!" Sarah cried, giving her a hug. "Oh, Randi, I'm so glad!"

"Travis?" Matt queried, eyeing the display as his father walked him toward the women. "Why's Mom sad 'bout Sarah huggin' her?"

"I don't think she's sad, son." Travis's throat closed. *Son.* Soon, he'd be using the word in a more literal way—after he and Randi made sure their son understood exactly how it had that literal meaning.

"People—" he swallowed thickly "—people sometimes cry when they're happy, Matt."

Sarah introduced Steve, a tall soft-spoken man who looked at Sarah with adoring eyes. Travis invited them for coffee aboard the yacht; Sarah thanked him, but declined, because she and Steve were running behind schedule and had to hurry if they wanted to make their classes on time. There was an exchange of hugs and promises of seeing one another soon.

As they drove off, Matt gave the couple a last wave, then glanced at Randi and Travis. "Steve's okay, even if he doesn't talk much," he said consideringly, then his whole face brightened. "But I like my good buddy, Sarah, the bestest. She's neat!"

"She sure is, Tiger," Travis agreed, "and so's her, uh, boat. Would you like to sail on it?"

Matt's eyes widened. "Oh, wow! Can I, Mom? Can I?"

Chuckling, Travis hoisted him to his shoulders and put his arm around Randi before she could respond. "It was your mom's idea, Tiger. And there's even somethin' better we're all gonna do." He winked at Randi.

Matt slanted questioning eyes at his mother.

"How'd you like to sail on the *Sarah Anne* with us and then sleep there tonight?" she asked with a grin.

"Really?" Matt said, and when she nodded, he broke into a cheer.

"Whoa there, Tiger!" Travis cautioned as the child's enthusiasm threatened to unseat him. He swung him to the ground and the two adults took him by the hand as they approached the boarding ramp.

"Before we sail, though, son," Travis added, "we're all gonna have a little talk, okay?"

"Okay," Matt said cheerfully. "'Bout what?"

"The three of us," his father explained as he met Randi's shining eyes over their son's tousled curls, "are gonna have a talk—about daddies."

And miracles, Randi added silently, swallowing past the lump in her throat as they climbed aboard. *Miracles...and answered prayers.*

HARLEQUIN SUPERROMANCE®

A trilogy by three of your favorite authors.

Peg Sutherland
Ellen James
Marisa Carroll

A golden wedding *usually* means a family celebration.

But the Hardaway sisters drifted apart years ago. And each has her own reason for wanting no part of a family reunion. As plans for the party proceed, tensions mount, and it begins to look as if their parents' marriage might fall apart before the big event. Can the daughters put aside old hurts and betrayals...for the sake of the family?

Follow the fortunes of AMY, LISA and MEGAN in these three dramatic love stories.

April 1997—AMY by Peg Sutherland
May 1997—LISA by Ellen James
June 1997—MEGAN by Marisa Carroll

Available wherever Harlequin books are sold.

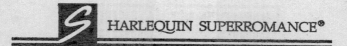

HARLEQUIN SUPERROMANCE®

THE OTHER AMANDA
by
Lynn Leslie
Superromance #735

Who Is She?

Amanda Braithwaite has been found nearly beaten to
death in a park. At least, everyone *calls* her Amanda—
her aunt, her uncle, her grandmother, her doctors. But
Amanda remembers nothing, remembers no one. Except
Dr. Jonathan Taylor. He saved her life, and he knows
more about her than he'll reveal....

Does she really *want* to know the truth, or is the past too
painful to remember?

Look for *The Other Amanda* in April
wherever Harlequin books are sold.

Look us up on-line at: http://www.romance.net

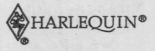

LOVE *or* MONEY?
Why not Love *and* Money!
After all, millionaires
need love, too!

How to Marry a MILLIONAIRE

**Suzanne Forster,
Muriel Jensen
and
Judith Arnold**
bring you three original stories
about finding that one-in-a million man!

Harlequin also brings you
a million-dollar sweepstakes—enter
for your chance to win a fortune!

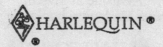

HARLEQUIN ®

Heartbreak RANCH

Four generations of independent women...
Four heartwarming, romantic stories of the West...
Four incredible authors...

Fern Michaels
Jill Marie Landis
Dorsey Kelley
Chelley Kitzmiller

Saddle up with Heartbreak Ranch, an outstanding
Western collection that will take you on a whirlwind
trip through four generations and the exciting,
romantic adventures of four strong women who
have inherited the ranch from Bella Duprey,
famed Barbary Coast madam.

Available in March,
wherever Harlequin books are sold.

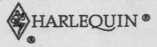

HARLEQUIN ®

HTBK